Ex Libris

Lowell R. Kantzer

. . . IN THE

HIGHLANDS

SINCE TIME

IMMEMORIAL

...In the Highlands Since Time Immemorial

JOANNA OSTROW

Alfred A. Knopf New York 1970

TO HOPE

AND DAVID

WATERS,

AND

TO ROBIN

Is e Calum an righ

                Callum is the king.

Tha mac an righ a' ruarchd

                The king's son is digging.

         (Scots Gaelic)

Used
in the
Highlands
Since Time
Immemorial

$\mathcal{M}$ary talked to herself at one time, in both languages. "Mhairi. Are you there, then, Mary. Are you busy. Are you pleased."

"No. *Chan an eil neach sam bith an so.* No. I am not very pleased."

"What is it that is on you, then?"

"Everybody is emigrating, and we pretend that they are not. Also, Callum is taking me to stay at Croichan, and I want to live where I am."

Mary had not said that aloud, but Shonach the cow, the long-horned, long-haired, orange cow, came to the kitchen door as if she had heard something, and stood. Mary was baking scones, going back and forth between the kitchen table and the fire. Shonach stood, seriously waiting. Matted hair hung over the cow's face and gave her a Viking look, eyeless and berserk, but she was tame enough; if Mary said the right things to her, she would let herself be milked in the open, on the Hill. She was a useful cow. After a while, Shonach began to swing her head from side to side, and her horn spread was so wide that, with her face looking in at the open door, one tip knocked the kitchen windowpane. Still Mary had no time for her. At last the cow groaned—a sound so deep that the pendulum clock on the mantelpiece stopped for a second and pinged in response.

"*Bi samhach,*" said Mary sharply, to both of them. She took a new scone, split it, buttered it, put on the jam, and brought it steaming through the door to Shonach, who opened her slimy mouth and lapped it in. Mary went back to work, wiping her hand on her cardigan. The cow's own milk was in the scone, after all. Shonach went away.

Mary did the baking now that her mother was dead, and she was prepared to go on doing so for the rest of her life. That was not bothering her. Every other day, she made oatcakes, pancakes, and scones. When she had been a little girl, they had not used any store bread, but now the baker's van came up twice a week and she bought one or two plain-wrapped loaves as well. Still, her own baking was important, and she measured it carefully: so many for Callum, her husband—he was big; a few for herself; an extra few to go with the tea she would give to the shepherd, or the gillie, or the van men, or the postman. The postie did not often come. But that day she had to double the amount, and bake twice.

Four people would be with them in the afternoon, and she knew exactly what it would be like because it had happened before, with other sisters, brothers, cousins. They would knock and come in at the front door, not through the kitchen. That was meaningful, and meaning would gather about every little thing they did all afternoon. They would go into the Room and have tea, looking at the formal fire. They would start to talk at random, about the weather or the sheep, without looking at each other or saying one word about their purpose. Then something would take hold of them, some last protesting kink in their spirits, and the kink would work itself out—not in sorrow, which would have made sense, but in malice. They would choose a victim, usually someone who was not there, and grind him up with small gossip. The best insults would be the softest ones. After that, they would stand up and go out through the front door; they would not say *slan leat, beannachd leat*, goodbye of any kind; and Mary would never see any of them again.

"When people die," said Mary, "we go on and on about it. A death is the most interesting thing we have."

Her mother had died in the windowless room off the kitchen and had been laid out in the formal Room across the hall. There had never been such a long party with them before, and Mary had done most of the work. The activity had excited her and made her think. She could bake, and milk, and straighten the Room without noticing, so she spent a lot of work time thinking. Why, for example, was death a long party, while this emigration—and what was it, after all, but just a family going to live in another place—was a catastrophe that made people go quiet and look the other way? When Mary did not understand something, she was still young enough to fume and talk to herself about it. She was alive in both languages. Gaelic was the best for muttering and subtlety. Knowing Gaelic, she did not need to be educated.

Mary rolled the dough with a floury bottle, swung the griddle down over the peats—the fire was cooler now, burning blue—and when the new bread was baked lifted it off, piece by piece, and stacked it around her, flicking it out like a gambler dealing cards: the only cards she would ever play, being Free Church. The deck came up triangular scones, gray oatcakes, fawn-colored, dry pancakes. The peat fire made Mary sweat, and her skirt stuck to her ankles. Outside, there was no wind. The pine trees in the steading sagged around like old brooms. Wasps came in the door, droning and singing, crawling toward the syrup. She whacked them dead with the ladle. It was a thick, gray day. Mary was not at peace in summer; it didn't suit that country, or herself. In summer everything was feverish, overworked, straining to grow in the short, white nights. Summer was an intrusion—"*sgimeilearachd*" was her word, which is contemptuous. Winter was the proper state of things. This was, at least, September.

And it was the last time she would do the baking in

that dim, low kitchen. Tomorrow, the croft-changing would begin. They had bought a bed and Callum had made a table for the new house, but everything else in the whole steading was waiting to be moved: "The two work garrons," she said. "The black bull. Shonach.

"The hens. The stirks. The five black cows.

"The Cheviot ewes—thirty of them. They are not my affair. And the Border Leicester tup. Nor is he. Fochan and Callum will see to the sheep." Fochan was the shepherd.

"I will drive the beasts up on the Monday. Callum will see to the plough. The harrow. The harness. The cart. What am I going to do about the milk bowls and the churn? And everything else, my God."

They were going to leave Cnoc-na-Coille, where Mary and her family had always lived. As the oldest child, Mary owned the crofting rights to Cnoc-na-Coille, to use or rent or sell back to the Laird. She had decided to let the house to a neighbor's daughter and have Callum continue to farm the land. They were going to live at Croichan, the last and furthest hill croft above that valley, which was called Strath-Ard. Callum's family kept the rights to Croichan, but the steading had been abandoned for fifty years. Now he insisted on going there.

Mary was afraid of that place. She had seen it as a square of foundation rubble, windswept out of line, and an empty cow byre and barn. The byre roof had been still thatched in the old way then, with heather sods—prickly, reaching divots that made the building look like a live animal, humping across the empty space. That was Croichan, wind and space: so much wind and space that the brain lost all support and thoughts peeled away like gray gelatine leaves. Above Croichan to the west was the Keeper's Cottage. Maggie Harrower, the gamekeeper's wife, kept hens and an Ayrshire cow and grew a few rows of potatoes, but they did not try to farm. Above the cottage was the moor, *sliabh monadh*, the Hill, where it was not possible to live.

Mary was afraid of Croichan, but she did not fight back, because she was even more frightened of Callum. She did not know him and she was not sure yet why she had married him. It had happened too quickly for her to be sure. In 1918, unlike many of the young men from Strath-Ard, Callum had come back alive from France, and before the excitement had died down, he had married Mary, per-suaded the Laird to let him reclaim Croichan, and built a new house on the old stones. He was a craftsman; he could mix mortar, lay bricks, slate a roof, and do anything with wood—but slowly, as if he were thinking about something else.

While he was building the new house, he started to fix up the byre, too. Slowly, ponderously, he tore down the black, furry thatch of the old roof, swearing in Gaelic and English, burying himself in spiders and rot. The joists were still sound, but there was no man left in Strath-Ard who knew how to build a heather thatch. So Callum decided to put on a tin roof, but he had trouble with it. He was up on the walls holding down the corrugated sheet and trying to nail it in place when the wind caught the flat metal and scooped it up on end, knocking Callum backward into the byre. Then the wind took the roof away and walked it across the road, over the fences and down the hill, in no hurry, corner over corner in the sun. The tin went flashing corrugated gleams like water, very pretty. It got lost in thick woods in the river valley.

Mary thought Callum would go mad with rage, but he did not even waste time swearing. He went to find the roof and dragged it patiently out of the trees and across the boggy open ground. Slowly, but not angrily, he tied it onto the turnip sledge and went behind the sledge, guiding it, while the two work ponies hauled it up the wet and tangled hillside back to the steading. Then he set it in place again, weighting it with rocks, and nailed it down hard. It was what he did next that frightened Mary. He let all his other work go while he sat underneath the roof all day, inside the byre, with his eyes closed; the sun slid in bars across the cobbled floor, and he sat listening to the tin rattle and struggle in the wind.

Today, that last day at Cnoc-na-Coille, he was up at Croichan finishing the well while Mary prepared the Room for tea. First, she set the chairs in a formal square against the walls. Nothing would be said, but it was understood that there had to be courtesies. People had been emigrating for so long that the good manners had all gone quiet; but there was a shape to the silence. If they still made up songs, which they did not, there might have been singing. Once there had been. Now singing was too obvious and would have embarrassed them. It was no outlet anymore. The awful shivering half notes, the olive-green and blue sounds, had all gone inside, and were making trouble there.

Mary lit the fire. The walls and floor around her smelled damp, but that was proper for a Room; it proved that it was a real parlor, seldom used. First, she lit birch twigs, then small wood, then put on a few peats in a standing triangle. The flue was stone cold and feathers of smoke came curling out at her. Perhaps there were jackdaws living in the chimney again. When the fire was going—soggy, but snapping and burning a little—she left it alone and got four small tea tables from the corner and put them squarely between the chairs. Then she took four starched white tablecloths and spread them out on the tables. They would use the good cups, and the saucers as well.

She heard Callum come in and go upstairs to the loft bedroom to put on his other clothes, and at the same time, the wind changed and kicked into the house, a sudden gale blowing from the west. The fireplace smoke belled heavily into the Room and then changed direction, too, and went tunneling up the chimney with the new draught. Callum was so vague, and so fair, and so big all over that he seemed to jar loose bits of weather as he walked around. He would slam the door, and rain would come showering down. If he went west to cut peats on the hill, grouse and hares and even ptarmigan would explode out of cover, and he would smile. They would never jump and run so for anybody else. Mary was getting used to it.

Late in the afternoon, past milking time, the MacRae family walked up the road from their croft, Balmacarra, through the woods to Cnoc-na-Coille. These lower crofts were in clearings between woodlots; only Croichan was above the tree line. The sun came in low, dusty lines of light through the tree trunks, and the wind was a hard blue slant from the west. The women's skirts and scarves blew out behind them, hard as wood in the gale. There was one old woman, Mrs. MacRae, and her two sons, Kenny and Duncan MacRae. There was Jessie, Duncan's wife, who was Mary's younger sister. Jessie was five years younger, and softer than Mary in every way. There were Jessie's two little boys, who were wild and did not want to learn English, and flickered like rabbits in and out of the bracken by the roadside. All these people were going to Canada together. They did not really know who to blame for sending them there.

Mary watched them through the back bedroom window, which had a bench set below it, especially for watching. When they knocked on the front door, she pretended that she had been busy in the kitchen. She was supposed to watch and she was supposed to pretend. To change the rules would have upset everybody. They greeted each other quietly in the hall, and the MacRaes went into the Room while Mary made jam pieces for the boys in the kitchen. They were not allowed into the Room. She split the new scones, buttered them, put on the jam, and handed them through the door to the little boys. Like Shonach, they went away.

Then she took the teapot into the Room. They were all sitting, at first, as the chairs were placed: upright, knees together, apart from each other.

They would speak in Gaelic, through the afternoon. Old Mrs. MacRae began, saying. "It was warm, earlier, the day. It was very close."

Mary said, "It was."

Jessie said, "It is a fine gale now, however. It is refreshing."

Mary said, "It is."

Callum walked in wearing his uniform with the Cameron Highlander kilt, and of course they could not let that get by. Kenny MacRae began it, saying, "Och, see the kiltie. See See Himself. What an awful toff he is, dressed like that. Indeed, I would not know how to speak to him."

Callum blushed. He was fair enough to do that. He had a high forehead, and the skin on top, which was covered by a cap outdoors, was not even weathered and went blazing purple. "Shut your mouth," he said. "It is my Army dress. I have not got any other. Shall I go and put on the trousers I was digging the well in, the day?"

Everyone sat sipping tea and looking at the Room's flowery best wallpaper, while the wind outside pushed and swung about the house. They decided without saying it: Not him, not Callum; find somebody else.

Kenny MacRae said, "Surely not. The well, then. Speak about that. Surely there must have been a well at Croichan already."

"There was," said Callum. "But it was only a spring, west, between two rocks. Mine will be an improvement."

"Without it, I would be carrying all the water fifty yards uphill," said Mary. Callum looked mildly at her. The well was an improvement to his croft, not to her housekeeping. She knew that.

"How will it be getting on, then," said Duncan MacRae, who was more serious.

"I dug seventeen feet down," said Callum, still in Gaelic. "That will be far enough. Then I started to work on the masonry. I had Hector Ross to help me, to stand on the planks, set across the well, you see, and he was to lower the bricks down to me in a sling. But devil a foot would he put on those planks. He would pretend to do so, while I was watching him, and then he would take a wee steppie backward and heave the bricks over the edge. Before we finished, he was throwing the bricks down upon the top of me."

There was a soft laugh around the Room, and soft comments—"Och, no," "And would he do that, then." Callum had given them a victim. Hector Ross was a fat and timid crofter who lived in the village. They called him *townie*. They leaned forward in their chairs, drew them in toward the fire. Peat smoke spiraled up from the grate, burning their eyes with its coal tobacco smell.

Jessie MacRae giggled and said, "And will you tell us now, Callum, has the furrow become straight yet," and again there was that murmuring laugh, as if the Room itself were laughing. They all knew about that. One day at the beginning of the war, before he had gone away, Callum had offered to plough one of the Cnoc-na-Coille fields for Mary's mother. Horses were scarce then, and he had borrowed Hector Ross's old white mare for the day. But the horse turned out to be exactly like Hector, fat and timid. It had gone mad at the harrow jingling behind it, and Callum had kicked it in a zigzag around the field all day, screaming *whore* and *bastard* at it in English. Callum won in the end, so the joke was on Hector and the horse; Strath-Ard had collected it and kept it for times of need.

Old Mrs. MacRae developed the theme, and the talk began to carry the rhythm of church—the sung-out line and murmuring response of their Free Church service. "And were you seeing Hector's brother Jimmie Ross when he came back from Edinburgh."

"No, we did not. How was it, then."

"He had come," said Mrs. MacRae with elongated irony, "to visit his *Ancestral Croft Home.*" The last in English. They found English bitterly funny, because it was destroying them. "He came down the road, so, wagging his bottom (he is not so fat as Hector), on past me, quite the toff. He had a grand big pair of shoes on him, brogans with the flap and the wee tassels, and did he not have his *clan* kilt with his wee white knees sticking out, and a wee knifie put into his stocking."

"Surely he would be cutting himself with that."

" '*Ah, Mrs. MacRae, good day.*' 'How are you the day, Jimmie.' '*I'm taking the air.*' In English, that grand. '*I can't resist the magnificent view.*' But it is Himself that is magnificent, is it not so."

"It is." They were in ecstasy, and the Room quietly laughed. Mary took the teapot to the kitchen fire for fresh water. It would not do to have the kettle boiling in the Room. She knew that they would wait for her. The talk made her uneasy, would make her discuss it afterward with herself, but she was part of it, too. Jessie followed her out of the Room and went outside through the kitchen door. Mary thought she would be seeing to the children, making sure they were not guddling the dairy or teasing the bull. A bucket was clanging and rolling in the wind, across the yard, chasing the hens. Some shirts that Mary had pegged out on the line were cracking like ship's sails. Jessie did not come back, and when Mary got tired of waiting she took the teapot into the Room.

There the air was thick with what was not said. They had waited, in their gentle silence. Mary poured fresh tea, and as the leafy steam rose up Kenny MacRae got them going again.

"I was there to see Jimmie as well."

"And will you tell us what you were seeing."

"I will tell you. Jimmie had a wee bookie under his arm. 'What is it that you are reading then, Jimmie.' '*Folklore.*' "

The English drone was devastating, but the more they liked it the quieter they got, until, when Callum finished it with "Jimmie, Himself, has seen the Water-Horse in the Knockmuie duckpond," nobody laughed out loud at all. It was inside. After that, there was not much left of Jimmie Ross. Hector had been used up before Jimmie. Outside, a pine branch began to swing in the wind and tap against the window, they way Shonach had knocked her horn on the kitchen windowpane for Mary. There was tension in the Room.

"Where is your sister?" said Duncan MacRae to Mary.

"Away out," said Mary.

"I know where she is," said Mrs. MacRae. "We are not to wait for her."

Callum went to the sideboard and brought out a small bottle of whiskey. Even Mary and Mrs. MacRae got some, which made it serious. *"Slàinte,"* they all said, not in chorus but in a sardonic and ragged agreement. Then they did not know what to say. After a long silence, Kenny MacRae thought of Croichan.

"Will you not show us around the new house, then, Callum. I have not seen it since the roof went up."

"I will, if you like," said Callum, but he was thinking about something else. "Croichan," he said, "I mind that name has got 'cross' in it somehow. There was a Museum Man up saying that there was a stone cross standing somewhere west, and I looked to find it, but I never did."

"And if you found it," said Mrs. MacRae, "would you be keeping it? Or would you be giving it away to the *folklore* man?"

"Och, I would bury the thing," said Callum with distaste. "I would sink the whole thing in a bog."

Mary thought that was blasphemy. She did not like it at all.

The MacRaes and Mary and Callum put on coats and scarves and buttoned up well against the wind. They went out through the front door—the occasion would be formal until the very end. The whole forest was roaring and swaying around the croft. The sky was still light, but the gale was so strong that the hens had given up and gone to roost. There was no sign of Jessie or the children.

"They have gone west the road to get brambles," said Mrs. MacRae. "We will catch up with them."

They went down the Cnoc-na-Coille drive and onto the unpaved road leading up the glen. As they went by the pasture, the two work garrons stopped grazing and followed them along the fence. The garrons were short as ponies but square as draft horses; one was yellow dun and the other grey dun, and both had wild-horse stripes down their backs. With their chin whiskers and heavy heads, they looked like cave paintings, swamp ponies. The wind ruffled their fur and tore at their long whipping tails and manes. They did not look dangerous, like Shonach the cow, but if they got loose on the hill they would never come back.

Leaving the horses behind, Mary and Callum and the MacRaes went on, uphill and west, toward Croichan. Soon they passed the tree line. In the open air, the wind was less savage, as if it had more room to move, and made less noise. They could smell the heather in bloom farther west. It was rich, like rotten honey. Here, instead of swaying trees, they were surrounded by little blowing plants: mosses and brown turf, tiny white flowers, blueberry bushes in a reddish-green mat along the road. The hedges were tangled with juniper scrub, birch, and willow, and the biggest trees were the rowans, their red berries marking a perspective down the hillside. In the sheltered hollows there were patches of bright green grass and enormous orange toadstools, domed and spotted with white.

"I wonder, did the children see those," said Mrs. Mac-Rae.

To the left were high banks overgrown with gorse and bracken; to the right was the Croichan field, sloping down through second growth to thick woods in the river valley. Callum's tin roof had gone down into those woods. Most important, across the river was the long, cold, rising line of the hill Beinn a' Bha'ach Ard, purple just now with flowering heather, spotted with sheep like white cocoons.

At last they found Jessie and the children, around a bend, picking blackberries. All three of them had purple sticky hands. "I wish I had brought my basket with me," said Jessie. "The brambles are grand up here."

"There has been that touch of frost, to bring them on," said Mary.

"I have been wanting to make bramble jelly," said Jessie.

"Och, I haven't the patience for that," said Mary. "The pips, and the straining."

Jessie looked sideways at the children and giggled. "But it was not really the brambles I was after, at all," she said, and the boys looked sideways at her and grinned and giggled, and not one of them would tell Mary where they had been. As a rule, Mary would have been angry—she could be sharp with women and children and animals, though she didn't dare get angry with men. But now they were at Croichan, and for her it was another day before marriage. It was the last time she was going to be able to stand back and look at the place. From tomorrow they—she and Croichan—would be one thing.

The new house was built on the bank above the road. There was a green iron gate across the drive, joining the sagging wire fences.

"That is a new gate, surely," said Duncan MacRae letting it swing heavily back behind them.

"It is," said Callum. "I put five bedsteads in it. There was every kind of useful thing lying about when I first came up here."

They stood drawn together in the yard. Croichan did not please them at first—it smelled of mortar and paint and fresh wood, and a croft was not supposed to smell of anything new. Mary, apart from them, still shared their one mind, and she knew how desperately they began to imagine the proper smells of peat smoke and cow dung and the soft, furry smell of hens.

Mrs. MacRae said, "I mind the old woman coming up here to get tree roots. That will have been your grandmother, Mary. She was a great one for spinning and dyeing, and she was always after this plant or that to color the wool. Apple tree roots made a fine color, but I would not be knowing what color it was. There was an apple tree at Croichan then."

There was no apple tree at Croichan now. There was one crooked larch tree, bent into a puzzle shape away from the wind. Long ago, an orderly woodpile had been started against the tree; a few long bark slabs were still leaning upright against it. There was the splitting block and even a rusty bow saw lying nearby. But the woodpile had grown into a dump full of rotten logs, tin cans, broken carts, ploughs, gates, bedsprings, and strange fallen-down trash of all kinds.

"The tinkers will have been camping here during the war," said Callum. "Let them try to come back now."

Kenny MacRae laughed. He went off with Callum to look at the new tool shed, and the others just stood, trying to make something of the place. They had to. The steading yard was a muddy square. The house—square, too, and modern, with roughcast walls and a slate roof—was on one side, the byre and barn were on another, the dairy and a few sheds on the third, and the larch tree on the last. Behind the tree was a drystone wall separating the yard from the grazing and arable land. There were no animals yet, but Mary and the others saw animals. They made themselves see a three-way vision of Croichan poised between use, abandonment, and use again—it was literally alive to them as past, present, and future. They had to. They had a language that was unbreakably tied to the churns and peat-stacks and scraggy details of the croft, and unless the croft was real their words and themselves would not be real anymore, either. Visions were the only way out. They found them very easy.

They could see the rubble and chunks of lime and new bricks in the yard, but at the same time they were perfectly aware of hens there and not there, of a dung cart with its shafts tipped up, smoking with use by the midden. Maybe Duncan went so far as to see unknown motorcars and machines, because he was a faintly practical man. But Mary, who was not practical, saw fully what was going to happen to them all in the end.

She suddenly understood that her language was fading, and all of them were fading, and in the future—if they managed to hold out that long—anyone who did not speak Gaelic would find them very dim indeed. They were not meant for English, though God knows it had been forced on them long enough; Gaelic had put them in a different color world. She also knew why she had married Callum, who scared her, who did not love her or even notice her very much. It was not to have children—she had lost one baby already. It was just that they were two people who would not transplant. Someday they were going to be the only ones left.

Jessie was laughing at her. "Is she not seeing?" And the children were pointing and yelling. "*Seall, seall, à Mhairi.*" Mary looked. She saw a string of funny shapes across the doorway of the new house. A ginger-colored barn cat had been clawing and batting up at whatever it was; now he couldn't stand the people so close anymore and ran sneaking away. He had been after a string of white oatmeal sausages hung from the lintel.

"Och, no," said Mary, forgetting and laughing.

"Take it down," said Duncan, but the children screamed, "No! No!" and Mary said, "Let it be," and ducked under the mealy puddings and went inside. In the new kitchen the table had been set with two places, but instead of plates and forks each place had a water bucket and a big, tin skimming ladle. Jessie has even stolen the Cnoc-na-Coille butter churn and put it down as a centerpiece, and she had filled it with insults—a big bunch of yellow flowers they called Stinking Willie, a poison weed, a farmer's shame.

"Now, Mhairi," said Mrs. MacRae. "Is that not a grand way to start housekeeping."

"Away, it is not," said Mary, still laughing. "What is it but cheek. The tinkers. Indeed."

Kenny MacRae and Callum ducked in under the sausages, Callum looking sour about it.

"Will you let me come in, then," said Jessie behind them.

"Come in, little sister, *a graidh*," said Mary.

When they were all inside—except for the children, who went tearing off south to the burn—Kenny MacRae brought out his own pocket flask to toast the new house. But there were no cups or glasses there yet, so they filled up one of the cream ladles and passed it from mouth to mouth. That sort of thing, like the singing, was too obvious, too stagy, for them now. It embarrassed them all.

"We are like the Lairds, passing the *cuach*," said Kenny nervously. "Are we not."

Callum said, "We are not."

They managed to exchange politenesses:

"*An la chi's naich fhaic.*"

"*Siod ort, sad ort, 's na faiceam cion ort.*"

And then they were all very tired. But Duncan MacRae had that rare thing, a box camera, and he wanted to show off and use it. "Let us have a photograph, then," he said.

"It is too dark," said Callum, who did not trust cameras.

"Och, well, let us have one anyway."

The sky outside was yellow in the west and dark blue

around Croichan; the hillside had become infinite. Callum cut down the mealy puddings, in case the photograph came out after all. Then all lined up in the doorway, so tired that they seemed to flicker in the wind. After the shutter clicked, Mary, looking down the line, realized that she did not know what those people looked like. If she were to meet them in a crowd somewhere else—unless they said something in Gaelic—she would not even know them. *Mo Dhia, Mo Dhia*, she thought, I am terrified of the future. Once they were gone, she would not be able to see them in her mind. Now they were going. One by one, they began to leave Croichan.

But one more thing happened to Mary that day. Jessie turned back and came to her on the doorstep and tried to give her a folded bit of paper and another photograph.

"It is odd that she should be mentioning the old woman and her colors," said Jessie. "Here. I thought this would be better with you."

"Why would that be so?" said Mary. She knew what it was, and she didn't want it.

"It will be of no use to me," said Jessie, surprised. "It is yourself that is staying here, and not me."

Their grandmother had left them a few things: two squares of coarse handwoven wool, her handwritten list of plants and dyes, and her photograph.

"Och, don't be stupid," said Mary. "Have I ever spun wool, and will I? I wouldn't know the first thing to do with the raw wool off a sheep's back, and no more would you. Would either of us be fiddling with the wheel, and the loom, and all those dyes, and the home solution? Do you remember the home solution? The *cailleach* would save all the urine and keep it ripening by the fire in case she would not have enough alum to use. Do we not keep our bits of blanket as special things, that we could never make ourselves?"

She felt that Jessie was trying to push the entire responsibility for the past onto her, and in this last moment she was frantic to avoid it.

"Yes, well, I used my blanket for the ironing last week," said Jessie. "It does well as a pad underneath. It takes up the heat." She giggled. "Och, I was forgetting about the urine."

They looked at the photograph. It was very old, brown, and cloudy at the edges. It must have been made by a traveling photographer when they were too little to remember. It showed their grandmother, old even then, sitting by the doorway at Cnoc-na-Coille, with her fists crossed in her lap. Jessie and Mary had inherited her big shovel-like hands. She was wearing black, and a white frilled headdress, and a covering shawl. Her face was lumpy, malicious, and resolved.

"It is a face like a *cloutie-dumpling*," said Jessie, putting the Lowland words awkwardly into English. "*A bheil cuimhn' agad oirre?*"

"Yes," said Mary, "I do remember her. I thought well of her."

Then Jessie pushed the paper at her so that she had to take it, and turned and hurried off after the others. Mary stood there by herself. She looked at the photograph again. Things were most real after they were gone, thought Mary. So that was Herself. She had a face—we all have faces, shapes, like she did. Why did I never notice them before? It's too late now.

The list was wrinkled and creamy, ready to separate at the folds. The words were mostly in English, because only scholars, or eccentrics, or ministers could spell in Gaelic, and her grandmother had been a crofter wife who had not gone beyond the Strath-Ard school. In school, of course, they had been made to speak English—Mary, too. The few Gaelic words in the list were spelled as they were spoken, and the scientific phrases were probably all wrong. But

Mary saw that the quality of the past was there: the crofting life had once been associated with learning, with grace. The handwriting was a slanted, delicate web. Mary hung on to the fluttering paper in the wind, and resigned herself to keeping it. In the near dark, she read the list she would never deserve or use:

NATIVE DYES

"Prepared and used in the Highlands since time immemorial"

Heather with alum	brown
Crottle lichen (*Parmelia saxatilis*)	yellowish brown
Crottle Corozir (*Lecanora tartarea*)	scarlet or Crimson
Common yellow wall Lichen (*Parmelia parientina*)	brown
Rock lichen (*Ramalina scopulorum*)	red
White crottle (*Lecanora pallescens*)	red
Limestone Lichen (*Urcedaria calcarea*)	scarlet
Dark Crottle (*Parmelia ceratoph*)	brown
Whin Bark (furze or gorse)	green
Dulse, a Seaweed (duilisg) "the leaf of the water"	brown
Soot (of Peat)	dirty yellow
Evonymus (Spindle tree or Burning Bush)	purple
Apple Tree, Ash, Buckthorn, Poplar and Elm	yellow
Broom (common)	lovely green

Roid or Bog Myrtle	yellow
Carmeal (braoom Fraoich)	violet
Tormentil	
(also used for Tanning)	red
Bracken Root	yellow
Sundew	
(*Drosera rotundifolia*)	purple
Root of	
Common Dock	finest black

All My Sheep

The Johnstons' second child, a boy this time, was born on September 2, 1968, at the Royal Infirmary, Edinburgh. The birth was not announced in the Inverness *Courier*, though Simon Johnston considered himself a native of Strath-Ard, a crofting community twenty miles away.

"But I've written to Mary," said Simon. "She'll talk about it. I'm absolutely positive that she will."

He hoped that she would, Jenny Johnston was sure that she would not. Meanwhile, they went on with life in Edinburgh. They named the baby Alasdair. Jenny would have preferred the Lowland spelling, *Alistair*; to give him a Gaelic name implied a background his parents did not exactly have. But she never argued with Simon about Highland matters.

They were looking forward to a quiet winter, a grey Edinburgh winter with the smell of coal smoke and brewery malt in the streets, and the smell of hyacinths flowering at home. Simon grew bulbs in pots every year. He spent money, which was scarce, on white *Innocence* and pink-to-red *Jan Bos*. He also spent patience. He needed a cool head to get through his life, but he spent days' worth of patience, keeping the bulbs in the dark till their roots were formed, bringing the yellow sprouts into rooms and arranging the pots on windowsills, staking the plants and waiting for them to bloom. Jenny did not know where he had picked up such a domestic, middle-class habit. His life so far had not been domestic or middle-class at all. The need to grow things might have come from his crofting childhood; but the patience, the prettiness, she did not understand. He was not the kind of man you would expect to see being gentle to a flower called *Innocence*.

It should have been a peaceful winter. They needed peace, and the resigned, shut-down feeling that comes with the short, dark days. They had rented a flat in a scruffy little street near Tollcross, ten minutes from the University, so that Simon could walk home for lunch between classes. After five years' night school and odd jobs, ending with three weeks as a dangerous baggage cart driver at Turnhouse Airport, he had passed his A-Level exams and bulled his way into a university grant and a place in the Honors English Degree course—out of sheer bloody-mindedness, Jenny thought, for he had no idea what he would do with a B.A. if he got it. He was not the academic type.

"And don't say wipe your arse with it," she said.

He smiled. "Don't panic. Flaunt it, was the word I was going to use."

"Wipe your arse is more like you," she said.

The flat had lots of damp cupboards, and a coal fire with fat armchairs in the kitchen, Edinburgh style, and a sooty walled garden at the back. The rent was only twenty-five pounds a month. It was in a tenement, with a rubber factory across the canal and rooming houses next door. Students, nurse-trainees from the Royal Infirmary and what the University Housing Office blandly called "Commonwealth Immigrants" lived on that street. Almost every week some lost African or Canadian or Indian rang their bell and asked if they had rooms to rent. Simon either swore at them or forced them in and smoked pot with them, depending on his mood and his supply. But the flat was all right. They scrubbed the caked grease off the kitchen ceiling and the brown stains, probably blood, off the linoleum, and Jenny made new curtains in orange, pink, and red. They bought new books for Shona Jane, the four-year-old: *The Tomten*,

Pigling Bland, Ant and Bee. The University term started. It looked like peace at last, after such a long time; at last, a quiet kind of life. Then, suddenly, they got bad news.

It wasn't the baby. They soon got used to him, routine settling down over his demands, gingerly, like a hen getting down on eggs. It wasn't the English Studies either. Simon had his first tutorial, at which he said absolutely nothing—"I sat and looked inscrutable instead," he explained. "I think I was trying to scare them"—but he felt more at ease as a student than he had as a post office sorting clerk or a baggage cart driver or as temporary crewman on a herring trawler. The trouble started two days after the tutorial. They got a letter postmarked *Inverness.*

Mary Macdonald wrote two or three times a year from the croft, Croichan, so until they read it they did not worry about this particular letter. Mary had a nervous, country-schoolhouse handwriting. Callum did not write at all. He was not expected to.

"Surely he can write," said Simon, opening the letter at breakfast. "He went to the Strath-Ard school, like I did. He terrorized the place. That's why I had to terrorize the place, too; I had to keep up the tradition. But I never saw him write, or even read, not all the time I was living at home. Mary filled in the Ministry of Agriculture forms—'the ag-and-fish,' we called it—and she read the prayers, too, of course."

"Perhaps he was too busy with terrorism to learn, and remained illiterate. Like you, dearie." He smiled at her across the table. She had the sucking baby in the crook of one arm and with her free hand, she was helping Shona with her cornflakes and trying to butter her own toast. Simon expected her to butter his toast for him, too, and pour and stir his tea.

He read the letter. She watched him and wondered how

he could say *home* so easily. She was glad he could, though
she did not always believe him. In her own case, she would
not have been so trusting. Home, for her, was the village
Windygates on the coast of Fife, where her father kept an
ironmonger's shop, where her whole family still lived and
refused to see her. The neighbors there called her Jay, pronounced Jye in the East-coast way, or would call her Jay if
she ever went back to the village, which she did not. However, that was where she came from. She looked it, too. She
was plain Scots, with a sharp, fair face and dark, straight
hair; in a few years, she would start to get thin and scraggy
and lose an upper eyetooth and then, she knew, she would
be almost a caricature of a Lowlands village wifie. She was
commonplace. Simon was more complicated.

He came from Glasgow, the child of a Belfast whore
and somebody else, never known, probably African. He had
been a pretty baby, and his mother had loved him and kept
him till he was six. He and Jenny often fought about that.
She said his mother had been brave. He said she had
spoiled his chances for a decent life.

"There's a certain kind of middle-class Christian," he
would say. "You know. They adopt black babies. It's become fashionable. Or maybe they want to alienate their in-
laws. Or start rows over who inherits the money. But they
don't foster them, none of that working-class crap. They
adopt them. Right off the bat, when they're brand new. And
half black is even better than all black, because then the
in-laws never really know what the little bastard is going to
look like when it grows up."

"You're offensive," said Jenny. "You're not being fair."

"No, I'm not fair," said Simon. "Look you, I could have
been adopted right away. I could have been brought up to
be a citizen. With a social conscience."

"You're not being fair to Mary."

"She got me too late. She doesn't count."

"Then it's not fair to your mother," said Jenny. "She did keep you. What if you left me and I just gave Shona away?"

"Ha, life's a bugger, isn't it," he said.

Once she thought of a good answer and she said, "But it wasn't fashionable twenty-odd years ago. The middle-class wouldn't have touched you with a ten-foot-pole then."

To her delight, she won that round. It was so obviously true that it kept him quiet for a while. But it remained a good fighting point between them, whenever they felt nervous. His mother had found things too confusing, in the end, and he had been taken into a Children's Home, where he had been noticeably violent even for that place. When he was eight years old he had been sent to live as a foster child with Callum and Mary Macdonald on their croft, Croichan, near Inverness. He had lived with them nine years.

Jenny knew that Simon was noticeable, and not only for violence. He had straight, dead-black hair and skin that was a stagy, fake-looking, clear brown, as if it had been dyed. He looked almost impossible—like an inexperienced actor trying to make up as an Indian, and not getting it right—but he was no white-featured black man. There was enough African about his face to make sense. He looked stubborn and strong. The children had his features and his outrageous, made-up look. Jenny often amused herself by seeing the world in pictures, with titles, and when they all went out together, to the zoo or the park, she labeled them *Miscegenation: or, Enoch Powell's Nightmare*.

Now she sat there, that winter morning, watching him while he read Mary's letter. The lines of writing showed through the paper. It was shorter than usual, but he seemed to be reading it twice. She managed to pour him tea with milk, stirred it, wiped Shona's face with a bib and then used the bib to wipe up the spilled cornflakes and milk, and helped the little girl down from her chair. Shona was talking. She was always talking, and Jenny had to admit she did not always listen. The baby was asleep at her breast, his mouth gone loose—about time, too. The crackling, smoky, coal fire, which she had swept and set ready the night before, and an electric heater, kept them warm.

"Oh, dear," said Simon, so quietly that he frightened her. She knew it was serious. If he had said "bloody hell" she would have gone on drinking her tea. He told her. Callum Macdonald was in hospital. He had been feeling ill for more than a year, but had not taken notice. Last week he had been rushed to hospital at Inverness. He had diabetes; thrombosis had developed. He was not expected to live.

Simon did not say "poor Mary," or "poor Callum." He said, "Whatever happens, there is that way of life over. Finished. It will never—it can't possibly—be the same again."

"Is that the worst of it?" she said, surprised. He gave her a strange look and didn't answer. New angles of himself were always turning up for her to understand.

After breakfast he added, "We can't let Mary spend the winter at Croichan by herself."

Croichan was a place of peaceful clear air, but Jenny did not like it. She dreaded any connection with it, and she did not know why. She had gone there twice with Simon, once when they were first married and once when Shona was in a carrycot, both times in high summer, and they had gone fishing in the blue dusk of midnight, and Simon had caught a trout.

He had tried to introduce her to Callum, but Callum had been too shy or too strange, and ignored her. His long, fair face had gone pink and he had shaken hands with her, looking somewhere else. He was oddly immobile for a farmer. She remembered him not working, not cleaning the byre or cutting oats or fixing fences, but standing still by the cow stalls or the tractor shed, or sitting by the fire, throwing shadows that seemed too active and complicated to be his. The fire shadows, moving around the room, seemed to have a purpose; and Callum, to a stranger, looked aimless and heavy as a stone.

Before Callum fell ill, Simon and Mary had written to each other two or three times a year, and she always sent them a Black Bun for Hogmanay, New Year's Eve. Her letters were misspelled and full of labels and references that looked childish to Jenny until she realized that they were "in" jokes, shorthand for experiences that Simon remembered and she could not possibly understand. Once she found him laughing at *do you mind on the Junket Wifie, she was here Saturday last.*

"What does she mean?" asked Jenny.

"I can't explain," he said. "It would take forever." He didn't let her read his letters in return; he sealed them up and posted them himself.

Now that Mary was alone at Croichan, she turned to Simon and wrote every few days, so they knew what was happening. She cycled to the bus stop twice a week and went to Inverness to visit Callum. Morag Cnoc-Muidhe drove her in sometimes. Willie-John Kilduich did the milking if she was late getting back—he was glad to come. Callum was very ill. Gangrene developed in both feet. The only way to save his life would be to amputate both legs. He agreed to the operation.

"He would," said Simon. "*Och, they'll be no use to me, have them off.*"

"Just like that."

"Aye, that is Himself." Simon's voice went Highland, with the Gaelic accent, as it did, unconsciously, whenever he thought about Croichan. "It will be hard on Mary now, seeing to the croft all alone. There is not even a dog for company any more. I wonder how long she will be able to keep going like that."

"If her way of life is really over—but you said it, dearie —she'll have to leave Croichan. She'd be eligible for a council flat in Inverness. Remember, they were building that group of ten semis, for the forestry workers. Down by the Post Office."

"Leave, hell," he said in his own voice. "She can't leave. She couldn't possibly leave. No; I'll write and tell her to sell the bull and a few of the sheep, for her own sake. She'll agree and say yes, yes, surely, Simon; and she won't do it, and that will be that."

They had to wait two weeks for the next letter. Each day Simon said, "He's not dead, then. If he was dead, Mary would tell us. She's perfect about death. It's the only thing she really pays attention to."

When the letter did come, it surprised them. Callum, in spite of his age and illness, was still alive. In fact, he was "getting on fine" and was going to be sent, soon, to a rehabilitation center north of Glasgow, to be fitted with artificial legs.

"He won't learn to use them," said Simon. "I know. He won't take them seriously. He'll wear them, but he won't learn to walk on them. He'll think they're a kind of decoration. It wrings me to think of it. Do you know those sadistic cartoon films, where you see some poor sod of an animal all screwed into a roll like a wet shirt, wrung up tight, with a couple of hands flapping out at the end. That is me—that— uptight, when I think of it."

Another part of Simon that Jenny did not understand

yet, and perhaps did not want to understand, was his feeling for Callum. Callum did not often come onto the surface of their life.

"You'd better go visit him, then," she said, wondering what he would say. "It's only an hour to Glasgow."

"Oh, my God, no."

"But how long will he be there?" Jenny's family was good about visiting the sick, sending grapes and get-well cards; they enjoyed that. They were frightened and embarrassed by death, though, and Jenny had never been to a funeral.

"Who knows? It's all mystery. Mary says that he's going away. She also says that the horse has died, she doesn't know why; and that she saw Duncan Cameron—Dunkie—from Ardgour last week, and that Dunkie's cousin Alec died in his sleep last June; and that, again, is that."

Jenny smiled. They were going to be safe after all. Croichan had touched them for a minute, and they had been threatened in some way; but now it had drawn back again, and they were safe. She relaxed. It was a Saturday morning, and the kitchen was full of the warm smell of clothes drying, of tea with milk, of bacon and eggs.

She picked up her knitting. It was to be a thick gold sweater for Shona. She had fed the baby, bathed him, given him a clean nappy, undervest, plastic pants, stretch suit, sheet and blankets, and now he was asleep. Shona was at the kitchen table, talking, and drawing with some felt pens that Simon had brought home. The colors made a brilliant grid of red, purple, and blue in the peaceful room. There was the chatter and yell of the Radio I Saturday Morning Pop Club in the background, and even that was peaceful. The flat was beginning to feel like safety around her. She knew it was going to keep them warm and dry, and trusted it not to burn down in the night. The fire coals in the grate were baking hot, like blue velvet cushions. If she could only stay here, and keep quiet, and bring up the babies in this warm place.

But Simon had a very Highland way of sneaking in desperate decisions over casual cups of tea, and now he said, "We must go up there for a while, and help Mary, at least until Callum gets back. I'll take a leave of absence from the University. I could get some of the course reading done at Croichan. I could keep the croft going for Callum —improve it, perhaps—"

He drank his tea. They didn't speak. They often fought, electrically, for fun and for real, and Simon had taught her all the obscenities and insults he knew so that she would be up to a good standard. But a fight would not help now. If she did not come with him, he would go by himself.

"Come with me, my mouse," he said. "We will eat heather sandwiches and dance around in the sun, or something."

She put her knitting down on the table, and her face in her hands. "You have it wrong; it's *you have come at the best of all the year, we will have herb pudding and sit in the sun.*"

"We could make love under a certain bridge that I know. Nobody goes there and it's all ferns and willows, super except for the flies. They buzz on your sticky places."

"How will you read at Croichan," she said, almost shouting through her hands. "They haven't any lights and it's winter now and it gets bloody well dark at midday."

The baby began to cry in the bedroom, a good excuse for her to get out. She went to him and changed his nappy, sobbing now herself, counting on his yells for cover. There was a thin line of milky vomit down his cheek, puddling in the folds of his neck, so she decided that he was empty and it would do to feed him again. She yanked open her cardigan, had a vicious few seconds with the nursing-bra hooks, kicked on the electric fire switch, and sat down on the bed with the baby. At first, she just cried. But as the baby's yells sank into snuffs and gurgles, she had to be more quiet.

She saw their future, which had never been steady, begin to shift even more uncertainly, with cracks.

She had been trained as a nursery school teacher and had spent her student years working in the Edinburgh mother-and-baby homes and children's shelters and day care centers. When Shona Jane was fourteen months old, Jenny had gone back to work in the day nursery, taking the toddler with her. So she knew what that part of Simon's childhood had been like. She wasn't afraid of him, or sorry for him, or excited by him—as women usually were— because he had been more or less a foundling; she had her own reasons for love and lust. But she knew about children's homes. She did not know about Croichan.

She tried to remember the Croichan horse, dead now. It had been a bay mare that wandered around the bogs and willow woods of the Muir, Callum's lower field, with a tattered mane and hooves overgrown and turned up like Turkish slippers. There was a car, too, half-buried in the midden by the barn. Nobody knew when it had come to Croichan, or who had brought it there. It did not matter. Mary could not drive, of course, and Callum would not touch a car. He used the horse to bring in the turnips and left the secondhand tractor rusting in the shed. Now Callum had no legs, and the horse was dead. Simon had lived at Croichan for nine years. What had happened to him there?

She stared at the orange electric fire that scorched her knees and smelled of burning dust. The warm, sucking baby was no help. What does he want? she thought. Are we going to pour our own good lives away into that place?

It came to her: Simon is making a retreat—running out. He doesn't know it. He thinks he's going there to help Mary; but if he loses his nerve, we may never come back.

Simon wrote to Mary. Four days later, Mary replied with a letter and a Black Bun. The Bun was her specialty, a cloggy cake made of treacle, currants, peel, fruit, and black pepper, baked in a flour-and-water crust. She usually sent it in December, so that it could be cut and offered to first-footers on New Year's Eve. She must have been restless, alone, and baked it early for something to do. The letter said,

> My dear Simon,
>
> Thanks for your letter. Hope you are well, and did the children have the Measels, it is in Inverness. We have been having it stormy off and on every week, it is a very Wild autumn. I am glad Callum will be away soon, when the roads get icy it will be hard to get into Inverness. The Laird's mother died last Tuesday and will be Buried on Saturday. We had old Mr. Mackay here last night, do you mind on him, the bodach 'ha radan old Aunt Maggie used to call him, he is not keeping very well but he says he will come up every day to feed the Sheep and see to the Bull. Still his Feet are very bad.
>
> I would like Fine for you to come up with the Family, it is not so bad all on my Own, I get plenty of folks ceilidh but it gets lonely in the night, when will you be coming. Morag's mother-in-law was

buried yesterday, Willie-John was here and said they had the celebration afterwards, Willie-John saw them all in Inverness in good form.

No more news hope you enjoy the Black Bun.

Best wishes and Love to all
Mary

"We must keep the flat," said Jenny. "We must have a hole waiting when we want to come back."

"Can we afford it?" said Simon.

"Sublet it, and don't tell the landlord," she said. "Whoever takes it can be your cousin. Everybody does that."

"Very well," he said, agreeing too easily.

They got ready to go. Jenny tried to shut off, one by one, each response the flat had begun to bring out in her. It was not warm. It was not safe. The kitchen fire did not shine white-hot, the color of cream. They did not have a pet cannabis plant, a spindly tropical thing, gasping for sunlight on the kitchen windowsill. How could they ask a tenant to keep it warm and watered? They would have to pretend it was an African Violet. And the winter bulbs. Croichan had power, if he could leave the narcissus and hyacinths and *iris reticulata*, his favorite—the tiny purple and blue-black flowers, like Persian miniatures, with their short life and fresh, sour smell—to go there.

Simon typed out an index card: GARDEN FLAT TO SUBLET IMMEDIATELY FOR INDEFINITE PERIOD, £30 MONTHLY. He pinned the card up in the Student Union on Monday morning, and spent the rest of the morning arranging a leave of absence. He claimed a "family emergency," and the leave was granted.

After lunch, he took their car to the garage to be serviced and winterized, "for mountain driving conditions," he said, with pride. The car was a rusty black Ford van. The front doors slid shut, and there were no side windows in the back section because windows would have meant paying a purchase tax that they could not afford.

Then he and Jenny put both babies in the pram and went to Boots the Chemist at Tollcross, where they bought economy-sized disposable nappy rolls and a whole case of baby cereal and another case of tinned baby dinners.

"In case we are still at Croichan when Alasdair goes on solids," said Jenny, and Simon agreed.

They went home, with the loaded pram, through the dirty gray streets of South Edinburgh, and when they came to their front gate, someone was waiting in the yard. He was sitting in the dustbin, which had been emptied that morning and which Simon had forgotten to carry through to the back. He was a tall young man, brown-haired and bony. He had a neglected, scruffy look about him, thought Jenny, as if he needed a wife, or a good clothesbrush. She scraped the pram around and through the narrow front gate. The pram was a battered, dirty, old one without springs, more suitable for coals or old whiskey bottles than for babies, and Jenny was fond of it. A gray wind smelling of beer malt and rubber waste came around the corner from the factory. It went up the young man's trouser legs and lifted Jenny's skirt and Simon's scarf ends and belled up inside Shona's hood, making her look like a fathead, while they all stared at each other.

"All right then, we live here," said Simon. "Get off the dustbin."

"Is this the place? said the man. "The garden flat for rent?"

"Sublet," said Simon.

"Rent, sublet, who cares, is it taken yet?"

"I only put the card up this morning," said Simon. He

could turn himself on brilliantly for women, but he often
went sullen with strange men, and Jenny saw she would
have to manage the subletting herself.

"It's all right," she said. "Won't you come in? You're the
first."

"Get off the dustbin," said Simon. He got off and Simon
them heaved the bin up into his arms and shouldered ahead of
them into the house. Jenny left the pram and the baby in
the hall, hoping he would sleep. She did not even move the
Boots parcels.

"Thank God," said the young man. "I'm desperate."

"Edinburgh is a dreadful place to find lodgings in," she
said, taking Shona's coat off, putting on a Scottish landlady
act, rather prim. Tight lips amused and suited her. "Come
this way, please. Two bedrooms, you see, and a living-
kitchen at the end of the hall. Here's the bath and W.C."

"Grotty," he said. "No shower? Never mind. It said
there was a garden?"

She took him to the kitchen. Simon was sitting at the
table, making lists. The back windows looked out on the
garden: a gray rectangle receding in perspective, gray
lawn, grimy path, black flowerbed where the last tenant
had tried to grow potatoes. Simon would have planted out
the winter's bulbs in spring and so built up a flower garden
year after year. He would have planted a border, too.
There was a sycamore tree, and then a factory wall, at the
end.

"OK," said the young man. "I'll take it, if you don't
mind. My landlady threw me out this morning."

Simon took another look at him. "Good on you. What
for?"

"What indeed. I'd better tell you my name, I guess.
Michael Berger. I'm at the School of Scottish Studies.
Graduate work."

Simon wrote Michael's name down, shuffled his lists together and sat back. Whenever Simon was not sure of himself he made lists: things to buy, to take, to pack, to read, and then he lost what he had written, or couldn't read it.

"My landlady said I was undesirable," said Michael. "An 'undesirable tenant.' "

"Well, so am I," said Simon. "Undesirable. Would you like some coffee?"

"Thanks," said Michael. "Look at that, a coal fire. Great. They'll like that. You know, this morning I was offered a bed in a shared kitchen in a stinking greasy flat in the New Town. It was in a Georgian house, so they wanted four pounds a week for it."

"Shocking," said Jenny, still playing the Scottish landlady. She got out the Nescafé and put a pan of milk on the cooker to heat. She was glad that Simon was going to be friendly. Shona came in.

"Mummay, Ah want tae paint," she said. Michael stared at her. Jenny put the poster paints, a cup of water, a piece of paper, and a child's fat paintbrush down on the table. Then Shona saw the coffee mugs and said, "Um wantin ma elevenses, too."

Michael stared again. Simon said, "The New Town is a fashionable slum. This is an unfashionable slum, in other words, cheap. Chinamen and blacks live here—you call them Them, you'd better learn—and blind men and meths drinkers, and there are gobs of TB spit everywhere you put your foot. If Jenny puts the baby in the back yard to sleep, she has to wipe the sulphur soot off when he comes back in again."

Michael did not notice their mild challenge; he sat down at the table and said eagerly, "I find that Edinburgh is a great city for poverty. There's a real strata of the traditional poor. Do you know what I mean? The culture of poverty. You go up the High Street and my God, some of those children—"

Simon smiled. "What's your subject?"

"Cultural anthropology. Yours?"

"English."

They laughed at each other. Shona said, in the piercing, piccolo voice that Simon called "transmitting for bats," "Mummay, Um wantin ma *juice.*"

"Excuse me," said Michael, "but what in God's name is that child saying?"

"She is speaking Edinburgh," said Jenny.

"There's your culture of poverty," said Simon. "The voice of your traditional poor. She spent two years in a day-care center while Jenny was working, and she picked up the Edinburgh street accent."

"Snob," said Jenny to Simon. "What kind of accent did you have when you were four?"

"I had the voice of the Glasgow traditional poor, and that's worse. What do I sound like now, I wonder. It's a good thing we can't hear ourselves."

"You both just sound sort of Scottish to me," said Michael.

"You're at the School of Scottish Studies," said Jenny. "I'm sure they've got every possible kind of regional dialect on tape, and some imaginary ones, too, no doubt. Surely you've heard something like Shona before."

"Well, I haven't been there very long," said Michael, embarrassed. "Anyhow, that's not exactly my subject."

"What is, then?" said Simon.

"The Highlands, as a matter of fact," said Michael. "I want to do something on a folklore theme—superstition in the Scottish Highlands, something like that; bringing in the Celtic roots, of course."

Simon looked blank. Jenny realized that he was caught in an emotional short-circuit and wasn't sure whether to make fun of Michael, or bully him, or discuss the High-

lands with him, or maybe even hit him. Hoping he would
not hit him, she poured out some Welfare Orange Juice
syrup into a plastic mug and diluted it for Shona, got out
sugar and a spoon for the coffee, and unwrapped Mary's
Black Bun for the first cut. She liked this Michael. He had
an odd look of purity about him, a sort of absent-minded
innocence. Why couldn't he do graduate work on the Highlands if he wanted to?

"Why did you have to get out of your digs, then?" she
said, spooning in the Nescafé.

Michael leaned back and scratched his head as if things
had been too much for him lately. "Oh, hell, I have these
dogs," he said.

"But you sound like an American, or a Canadian or
something," said Jenny. "How can you have dogs? Isn't
there quarantine?"

"I brought one of them through quarantine. It took six
months and cost me sixty pounds, plus the air freight; and
let me tell you, the airlines charge by the cubic inch. Then
I got the other one here. They gave her to me—she's a bit
of a problem. She's not sane. Well, she's crazy, in fact."

"Och, is it only that, then," said Simon. "Undesirable
pets."

"We keep children," said Jenny, sugaring and stirring
all three mugs of coffee. "I hope you like milky coffee with
sugar. Could your dogs possibly be worse than that?"

She pointed and they watched Shona, who had covered
the paper with rich, wet paint, and had smeared all the
colors together into a liver brown and a dull brown-blue.
Now she was painting with the dregs of her orange juice.
She laid both palms flat on the painted paper and made
circles. There was paint in her hair. She took her pair of
round-end scissors and started clipping the picture into

little pieces. The sodden paper chips fell like dirty snow into the paint pools and the orange-juice pools on the floor. Shona was singing.

Michael thought about it seriously. "Well," he said, "the dogs aren't so creative, but they do have more damage potential. Mm, definitely more damage potential. But they're pretty civilized, as long as you keep them warm and comfortable, and give them everything they want."

"I see," said Jenny.

"Right," said Simon, "We'll have a practical demonstration. Bring these things in. If they shit on the floor, you're out."

"They won't do that," said Michael. "They've had a walk today. I left them in the car, around the corner. Just a minute."

He put down his coffee and went out. "Don't wake the baby," Jenny called after him. He left the door ajar, and a sooty wind came into the house, bringing the rotten-urine smell of the rubber factory with it. Jenny thought how strange it was that even a sickening factory smell could mean safety to her. She put the kettle on again. Simon went wearily back to his lists.

"Don't be disappointed," said Jenny. "Not everybody is an activist, dearie, you know."

"Shall we take the carrycot and the pram?" he said.

"I shouldn't think so; the pram body lifts out. It will do for both."

They could not see the front door but they heard it open, and then shut. Michael was talking quietly to something. They heard claws clicking on the floor tiles. It sounded like many claws. Jenny knew, she knew, that it was no more than two large pet dogs. At the same time she knew, with the dreamsight that sees around corners and through furniture, that something unearthly was coming

into the flat, something that did not belong there, or anywhere.

"Shona," she said. "You stay here."

"Has he got them, then," said Simon. "Right. Let's have
a look at them."

Michael was still in the hall, saying, "Come along,
Phoebe. Clever girl. Come along, Rosiqa. It's all right.
Come along, Rosiqa. Clever girl. That's right. *Clever* girl."
His voice had the cheerful professional drone of a wild-
animal tamer, or a psychiatric-ward nurse. Jenny and
Simon looked at each other.

Shona jumped down, spilling paint, and ran towards the
hall door.

"Shona, you stay here," said Jenny. Simon grabbed her
as she went by and slung her, mud-paint-juice, into his
lap.

"Ah want tae see," she said.

"Be quiet."

"Daddy, let me see." She struggled and he gave her a
piece of his Black Bun. She took it and sat quietly.

There was no more claw-clicking on the tiles. Michael
came back alone.

"Not yet," he said. "They won't come yet. These sight-
hounds like to orient themselves before they go into strange
company. But look, do me a favor; when they show themselves, ignore them. Make believe you don't see them,
whatever they do."

"But the baby," said Jenny.

Michael looked surprised. "They're not dangerous," he
said.

Jenny picked up her knitting. "Very well."

They drank their coffee. Shona made a design on
Simon's sleeve with currants from the Bun, and picked
them off and ate them, and they heard the dogs, like deer,

take one clicking step at a time, through the trees, closer, out of the dark. A fawn-colored face, with a long nose and lemur eyes, looked into the room.

"Don't look at her," said Michael, musically.

Shona yelled, "Mummay, look at that," and the eyes withdrew. Simon fed her more Bun. The eyes advanced. Jenny, looking sideways, saw another; a long white face with black eyes, the body shading off into the dark hall. On the stove, the kettle boiled and whistled. Both faces whiffed out of sight.

"They won't come at all now," said Michael. He got up and went after them. There was a lot of fast confused claw-clicking and he came back, carrying a dog. He put it down before the fire. It was long and tall, the color of new pine, and seemed to be mostly legs and eyes and shivering bones. "That one is Phoebe," said Michael. "Want to hold her, one of you, so she doesn't get away, and I'll catch Rosiqa."

"Aw, the wee dug," said Shona. "Ah want tae hold it."

"Not just now, dearie," said Jenny, and took the leash herself, feeling vibration at the other end. The dog sat on the hearthrug and drew itself up tight, shivering. It looked something like an Afghan hound, but instead of an Afghan's grotesque mop of hair it had a discreet, moon-colored fringe along its legs and tail—a long tail, and longer legs. Its eyes were set in its long face like amber stones, big, clear, and brown. It sat upright, looking somewhere else.

Michael came back carrying the other dog. It was the same shape but grizzled grey, with a silvery face and eyes like black-burned holes. When it saw strangers, it tried to struggle but Michael swung it around under one arm, reached down and took Phoebe with the other arm, lifted them both, backed down into an armchair and pulled them both into the chair with him. The dogs must have weighed fifty pounds each, and Michael was thin, but Jenny understood. She weighed one hundred five pounds herself and she was quite able to lift Shona, the baby, the pram, and her shopping basket onto the Number 9 bus in one load. She did it easily because of what would happen if she did not. So Michael sat deep in the chair and the dogs perched on him, one to each side. It was a big chair, but the dogs' legs stuck out like elegant, slightly affected hands. They sat three in a row, overlapped, bird-brains.

"Christ bloody sake," said Simon.

Hearing his strange voice, the hounds sat upright and looked at him, suspicious, with the effect of raised eyebrows. Their long tails curved under their bellies and out between their long front legs, and they stared at Simon, their necks elongating to stare, pinheads on top. To sit up and stare better, each one braced a paw against Michael's thigh for balance; and they looked so angular and unearthly, like heraldic beasts, that Simon laughed out loud, a thing he did not often do.

"Don't laugh," said Michael. "They hate it."

"Oh, merciful father," said Simon. "Oh, my black soul."

Jenny got up to spoon in the fresh coffee. The dogs slowly relaxed, curving down against Michael. "Can you drink coffee with them sitting on you like that?" she said, but she knew he could. She could drink anything, boiling hot or full of ice cubes, with Shona or the baby on her lap; she might drip it on herself, but not on them. Michael took his mug in the hand that curved around Rosiqa, and his Bun in the hand that curved around Phoebe, and he ate and drank over their smooth heads and around their feathery ears, which were pressed against his chin, and sometimes got into his mouth with the cup.

"Are you related?" said Simon, calming down. "And what do they do?"

"That's not funny," said Michael. "And they run. They're greyhounds—salukis; so they run."

"After things?" said Simon.

"If possible. Otherwise they just run."

"You said one of them was crazy," said Simon. "Which would that be?"

"Rosiqa," said Michael. The gray one looked at him. Her white V-shaped face looked as if it had been bleached by grief. "She's a young dog, though," he said. "She was born crazy. I think she may grow out of it, if she survives." He offered a piece of Bun to one saluki, then to the other. Each in turn touched it with the tip of its nose, and looked somewhere else. "They say, am I trying to poison them," he explained.

"Who do they think they are?" said Simon furiously. "And what's the matter with the fucking Bun?"

"They don't think," said Michael. "They are. Try not to laugh again, they're beginning to feel at ease."

"I think you're stone mad," said Simon. "I think you were born crazy." But Jenny could see he was enjoying himself.

"Where did you find them?" she asked.

"I read about them somewhere," said Michael. "When I was eight years old: *saluki, the desert dog,* and from then on, I wanted one. I never saw one—I mean, who sees salukis in Boswell, Pennsylvania? I went to college in California and saw some at a dog show there, and that's how I got Phoebe. They hunt jackrabbits with them in California. Now they make my whole way of life. I often wonder how I knew so well, when you think of all the things you can buy for money—books, dogs, horses, machinery of all kinds, clothes, records, you know—how I knew that salukis were the only things I should attach myself to. It sounds narrow, but it's not at all. Once they were useful animals— they were the meat-getter of the ancient world, did you know that? But now they're not worth two cents except to look at. And the way they work on your imagination. They're a kind of passport. It's hard to explain until you know them better."

"You're a mystic," said Simon. "A dog hippie."

"No, no," said Michael. "I'm no hippie."

The salukis were beginning to unbend, as if the steam from the coffee was thawing them out. Phoebe yawned, a yarroo noise that made Shona laugh; but Jenny saw the open crocodile mouth and fang rows before the jaws shut again with a snap. Rosiqa, the grey one, struggled again, and this time, Michael let her go. She slid off his lap and stood broadside to the fire, looking somewhere else but almost touching Simon's knee.

"She's all right now," said Michael. "She'd like you to stroke her."

"How can you tell? ESP?"

"We are telepathic," said Michael seriously, "but only for emergencies. Like when they get lost, or if somebody is bothering them in the parked car. But her eyes are soft now, and she's leaning. Look at her. Salukis don't slobber all over you. They lean."

Simon noticed that Rosiqa was, subtly, leaning against his knee, so he ran his hand along her back. Jenny leaned down and her hand followed his. She found that it was a most extraordinary sensual experience. First she felt bones: shoulder blades, then vertebrae, like a knobby necklace, then two upstanding hipbones under silky hair. Then it got wilder: their hands went down her sides, over the satin, bony ribs and up underneath to the tucked-up curve of her loins and between her flat hind legs. The skin inside her thighs was bare and warm over hard muscle, hard as wood, and the fur on the undercurve of her chest was smooth and delightful to touch. Jenny saw Simon go hot with embarrassment and surprise.

"She's—sexy," he said, choked up.

"She's an object of beauty, and she's sexy," said Michael. "In an abstract way."

"Abstract, my arse," said Simon. "She's given me a hard-on. I bet you screw them. I bet that's your mystic thing."

Even that did not shake Michael too much. "No," he said, "you miss the point, completely; I don't keep them for sex, I mean, I have a girl friend—I'd marry her, but I have to convert her to salukis first—I mean, I may be a little effeminate, but you miss the point."

Jenny giggled. She reached out and stroked Phoebe's head. "I see," she said.

"I wish you did screw them," said Simon. "I understand sex, any kind. It would put you within my reach. Do you have the Gaelic?" he asked, in a sudden Highland accent.

Even Michael noticed the voice change this time and looked surprised. "No, not a word. It would be better if I did, but lots of fieldworkers do my kind of thing without it. Do you?"

"A few phrases," said Simon. "Culloch and cailleach and 'ha fliuch and a toast or two. I was thinking of learning it properly some day."

He had never said that before.

They spent a few minutes on business, arranging the sublet. Simon gave Michael the address at Croichan, for the rent checks, and told him that he was to call himself their cousin from America; but he did not explain why they were going to the North, and Michael did not ask. Then the salukis got restless and scratched at the front door and woke the baby, and Michael took them away.

The Johnstons left Edinburgh on the fourth of November. Michael moved in the night before, as he and the dogs had no place to sleep. He came in with two suitcases and a sleeping bag and a pile of comforts for the dogs: beds, bowls, tins of dog food and five big, curly, black-and-white sheepskin rugs. He unfolded the sheepskins in front of the fire and spread out his sleeping bag on top of them.

"We'll sleep here," he said. "I'll keep the fire going so you can get up to a warm house tomorrow morning."

"But I've set up the camp bed in the children's room," said Jenny.

"I'd like this better," said Michael. "This is what I do, listen: I lie on the sheepskins and the dogs curl up at each end of me. When it gets cold and dark I think I'm in the desert, lonely, like that. Sometimes the dogs come and stretch out alongside of me. We look at each other and then we all look at the fire. There are hyenas outside in the darkness: you know. It's great."

"God," said Simon. "It must be."

"I see," said Jenny, and went to put the camp bed away.

So they settled down for their last night in Edinburgh. Simon tried to pack the car ready for the morning, but whatever the babies needed they needed all the time. He would have to get the pram, the pot, the baby chair, and baby cream, and juice, and nappies, and cups, and toys, and food, and soap all into the car somehow after breakfast. At nine-thirty he put on pajamas—like lists, a sign of insecurity—and got into bed, cold and alone. In the kitchen, Jenny sat in one of the armchairs giving the baby his ten o'clock feed. The fire puffed up in smoke and crackled down as the kindling wood collapsed, lighting the coals. The ceiling light was out. Michael lay on his back on the sleeping bag, with his hands clasped on his middle, looking at the desert stars, or listening to the hyenas, or thinking about something else that Jenny could not understand at all. The salukis lay folded intricately, like Origami shapes. Sunk peacefully down into the sheepskins they looked no bigger than spaniels. Jenny had just built up the fire for the night, so the firelight was cold, not warm yet, pale and spooky. The coals flickered with yellow sulphur flames. Jenny sat, feeling weak and tired, rejecting the comfort of the room. The doorbell rang.

It was an old-fashioned bell, bouncing up and down on a spring. Suddenly the kitchen was full of big hounds with big eyes. They did not bark. Their flat, black shadows passed and repassed in the firelight as they danced around, stiff-legged, with deep wuffs and growls and a lot of claw-clicking on the linoleum floor.

"I'll go," said Michael. The dogs followed him into the hall. Outside, in the black front yard, were three children. One was wearing sheets, another a Woolworth's skeleton suit, and the last had on a dirty dressing gown.

"A penny fer the guy, mister," they said together.

The salukis saw them and reached out their long necks and bayed, hair stiffened up in a thin ridge along their bony backs. They had deep thundering voices, and the effect in the small kitchen and hallway was of one sustained, yelling roar. The baby startled, hiccupped over his milk, and began to scream. Simon, in the bedroom, said "Bugger," and curled up on the other side, trying not to hear.

"What?" said Michael.

"A penny fer the guy," said one child. "We're guysin. Yer supposed tae gie us somethin."

Michael said, "Quiet, Rosiqa, for God's sake," and grabbed for the gray dog, who yelped and leaped out of reach, and bayed again.

"D'ye want us tae sing fer you?" said the one in the dressing gown.

"Give them sixpence," called Jenny, "and send them away."

"You mean, like trick-or-treat," said Michael. "Yes, sure, want to come in?"

"Uh-uh," said the biggest one. "Ma wee sister's skeered a th' dug."

"What?" said Michael.

"They're afraid of the dogs," screamed Jenny. The salukis barked. The baby was sick but Jenny was experienced and caught the milky projection neatly in the corner of her lap cloth. Michael got angry and chased both hounds into the nearest room, which was the bedroom, and shut the door. They stopped barking and stared with horror at Simon.

"Now," said Michael. Desperate, the guysers began to sing "Yellow Submarine."

"No, that's no good," said Michael. He went to the hall coat closet and got his pocket notebook and pencil. "Sing something else," he said.

Jenny guessed that he wanted something ethnic, and she called from the kitchen, "Tell them to sing 'Three Craws.' "

"Do you know 'Three Craws'?" said Michael. The guysers knew it and sang it, and Michael took the words down in phonics. Then he gave them sixpence each and they went away. He invited the salukis out of the bedroom and they left Simon safe under the covers and went back to the kitchen, half-turning toward the door now and then, and stretching their necks and saying grrrr as they went.

"I should think they already have 'Three Craws' at the School of Scottish Studies," said Jenny. She sat the baby upright and patted his back until he gave a little hoot and was sick again, not much this time.

"That's all right, it's not my field anyway," said Michael.

He lay down by the fire again and Jenny changed the baby's nappy and carried him away, leaving Michael and the dogs to spend the night in the desert.

The fourth of November was pale and cold. The BBC Scottish Home Service said that "wintry showers" were expected in the North, and then Simon packed the radio and took it to the car. The house, to Jenny, was a dry, dead crust. Simon carried the folding crib and the big, shapeless baby equipment into the car and Shona followed him in and out, talking and carrying toys. Jenny packed carsick medicine, Activity Plastic Toys, wet washcloth, toilet paper, spoons, juice, and a thermos flask of tea, into a shopping basket, to keep under the front seat. She watched the children's things go out the door. She watched the children's things go out the door again. She found it almost impossible to stop watching.

"You look sleepy," said Michael. "I've made some coffee in my American percolator. Come have some."

"I'd rather tea," said Jenny. "But I poured the last of ours into the flask."

She sat down at the messy, abandoned breakfast table.

"I'll do the dishes," he said. "You just go. I'm a tidy bachelor."

He was to use their plates and cooking pots while they were away. Or keep them when they didn't come back. She wondered why he had not asked about their trip. It wasn't tact; she was sure he had no tact; like Simon, he probably went by his own rules and would not even be aware of a delicate situation, much less try to deal with it. They sat drinking coffee. Shona and Simon went in and out. The kitchen got colder and began to look strange.

"I would just as soon stay in Edinburgh," she said. As she expected, he did not exactly understand.

"Funny," he said. "I like traveling with the dogs. To go

to a dog show, or coursing, or even on a Sunday drive to
find a good exploring place. It takes almost as much
equipment and expertise as children, but I like it. It's satisfying. I can't explain why."

"Because walking a dog is fun, and you don't have to do
it. You choose it. That's why," she said.

"You've never seen a saluki being sick in the car," he
said. "And didn't you choose to have children? I mean, I
don't want to get personal, but you can, now, I mean these
days, can't you?"

"Of course," she said, "but it's different. The dogs
are frills, for you. Children are different. They take your
life."

"The dogs are not frills to me; I never thought of them
like that," he said.

Simon came in. "The car is packed. Bring out the baby,
will you? When you're peeing your pants about icy roads
and dangerous driving tonight, remember who was sitting
here drinking coffee at nine thirty this morning."

"We were talking about your mortal responsibility," said
Michael.

"Mortal arsehole," said Simon.

"I'm leaving the Black Bun here for you," said Jenny. "I
hope you enjoy it."

"Don't forget to water the plants," said Simon. "Whenever they get dry, give them a good soaking. And don't
open the kitchen window. That thing in front of it is tropical."

At last, they got away. They stopped and bought a roast
chicken at the MacFisheries shop, for their lunch, and then
they drove out of Edinburgh in the milky winter sunrise.
The sun was almost straight behind them in the southeast
as they drove across the Forth Bridge, and the light flickered ahead of them along the suspension cables. Below

them the water was a white sunny blue. It was early in the year for snow, but they could see white tops on the hills to the North: they were going toward them. The back of the car was packed tight with squalor and children and bad smells. The trip took eight hours instead of the usual five, and they were lucky to get there at all.

They took the A9 to Perth, and after that the road began to climb and change. At first there were open, grassy, birch woods, with a few oaks and beech trees, and the banks of blue-green rhododendron in between. Then the massive pine forests moved up against the road on both sides, and behind that first, bullying stand of pines was another wall, flowing downward like a plaited, black beard of trees, into the gorge. They went through a hill pass and the car skidded on black ice around an S-bend, and Shona laughed. The hills above the pass were domed and sliced, abrupt, and white with snow. The road twisted so that the same odd-shaped hill came at them from all directions, and they lost all sense of the map. The whole scene was black on white; they were sealed in the car, with the windows shut, so there was no sound. The baby cried. Jenny lifted him into the front seat and fed him as they drove. The twisting, black-and-white road, with the repeating, illogical hills, had a surrealist quality, like some dream of punishment. She called it *Winter Penance.*

Past Blair Atholl, the trees shut off suddenly. The last bits of willow scrub thinned away and the hills opened out around them, with a sense of letting go, of great space and absolute North. They drove on for a little while, stunned by the blank, brown country. The moor was dun-colored, cut by black peaty streams, snow-spotted in the distance; the great slopes and terraces rolled off into enormous space, turning, dizzy, and dead still: *nothing*, said over and over and over again. Soon Simon couldn't stand it any more and pulled off into the road shoulder. The car scraped against frozen heather.

"Tea," he said. "Tea, give me something, for God's sake."

"We might as well have lunch," said Jenny. She unpacked the roast chicken, with its sweet, sane smell, and the thermos flask of tea. The baby slept quietly. When the car was still, the terrible, mindless turning of the moor stopped, too. The landscape was bearable: a bank of ice and dead heather, a patch of rushes by the car, a rubble of stones and black peat where a culvert went under the road. There was a Blackface sheep lying a few yards away, staring at them with its yellow goat eyes. It had its feet tucked under like a cat, and it lay chewing, very calm; its straight fleece spread out on the heather, sank into it, grew out of it. It was a ewe, with a red tup mark on its back, showing that it had been bred.

" 'I live here,' " said Simon.

"Devil eyes," said Jenny.

"The old bitch knows something we don't know," said Simon.

"She knows that if the shepherd doesn't catch her soon she'll get snowed up, and the helicopters will have to come and drop food to her, and she'll get her picture in the *Scottish Daily Express*. She knows what that snow fencing is there for."

"It takes me a while to get used to this part of the road," said Simon.

"It's soul-destroying," said Jenny. "Thank heavens for Mac-Chicken. Put the bones in this plastic bag."

After they ate, they wiped Shona's face and hands and they all got out of the car for a moment. A hoodie crow bent its back and flapped heavily off the snow fencing as the car door shut.

"The bugger's waiting for her lamb," said Simon. "He'll

wait all winter. He's got nothing else to do. He'll just sit around."

The air was thin, and cold, and frightening, and they quickly got back into the car again. The smell of roast chicken faded away. They drove for hours, and Shona stopped talking and was quite still. She held her doll and watched the moor walk backward past them. Even Simon did not seem to drive: the road was taking him. It was taking Jenny where she was afraid to go. The Cairngorms rose like a gray wall on the right, and there were icy, white peaks in the distance. There was a quick flash of Scottish-Scandinavian chic as they passed through Aviemore, where the ski chalets and hotels were ready but not open yet. It was late afternoon. The road began to curve down towards Carrbridge, and the weather hit them there.

A solid whack of snow, blown on a gale, hit the road and the mountain slope like a fistful thrown hard. At the same time, as if on purpose, the early night shut down. It was as quick as that. The car began to bump and skid, and though Simon turned on the headlights and the windshield wipers, all they could see was dark blue and falling snow. In ten minutes, the wind had blown drifts across the road, and the tires were spinning.

"Are the gumboots within reach?" said Simon.

"No," said Jenny.

"Family of four tries to walk to shelter from stranded car, forgets Wellie-boots due to negligence of wife, found frozen. This is a very sad case, said the Procurator Fiscal."

"Surely not the Procurator Fiscal," said Jenny.

"Oh, Christ, I don't know, it's always some official in the papers who says it's a very sad case. Don't you remember the time Jimmie McHendricks and I got drunk at the barbecue and wrecked the changing-chalets on Aberlady Beach? Who said it was a very sad case then?"

Jenny couldn't answer. The car skidded around a bend

and into the shelter of a woodlot. There the road was only powdered with snow, and they went on. But at Carrbridge the snow had been falling steadily, though the village was lower than the moor, and the road was blocked in a wallowing confusion of drifts, headlights, shadows, and glare reflected in the curving scoops of snowplows. They had to wait. The baby woke up and cried, and Jenny fed him and changed his nappy. Shona said she was cold, and cried. Simon took her into the men's room of a petrol station, to play with the warm-water taps and swing on the towel roll, while Jenny sat in the car. She felt empty, inert; if someone had asked her a question, any question, she would not have been able to answer.

After a long, blank wait, the snowplow came past, grinding and scraping along in the dark. They left Carrbridge in a convoy of lorries and snowplows and crept the last twenty miles to Inverness, across the summit of the Monadliath, the second mountain range. Their low van was fogged up with diesel fumes and splattered with mud and slush, and Simon was blinded by headlights following and coming on, edging in close; but the worst part was the utter blackness and whistling snow outside as they went over the pass. The moor had been bad by daylight. At night they could not see the turning empty spaces, but they could feel them. The *nothing* became a physical response inside them, and the night drive became a trip over the edge, the mind's edge, the mind's limit.

Shona started to complain and kick at the baby, and Jenny lifted her to the front seat, onto her lap. She tried to sing to the little girl, but her mind felt so split and strained that all she could think of was "Three Craws." She sang that. Then because Shona was still twisting and whining, she sang another; but it was "The Craw Killed the Pussy-O," in a deep, minor key with a funeral beat.

"What are you moaning for?" said Simon. "Why are you going on about crows?"

"I can't help it," she said, thinking of the hoodie-crow, watching the pregnant ewe, waiting for the lamb.

> *Poor pussy's wi! the devil-O,*
> *Poor pussy's wi! the devil-O,*
> *And every mouse in Johnny's house*
> *Says, Gi' that craw a medal-O.*

Shona made her sing it three times, and then, satisfied, crawled over into the back of the van and went to sleep. At last they got to Inverness. As if the attack of midwinter had been a bad joke, they looked past the city signpost and saw the streets beyond, blue-black, clear and wet. The sign said "*Ceud Mile Falte*: Welcome to Inverness."

"Raucous laughter," said Simon. "All right, laugh, you bastards, we got here, didn't we."

"We are not quite there yet," said Jenny.

The car stank of nappies and sour milk. The shops in the city were still open, lit up and bright.

"I ought to stop for a few things," said Jenny. "It would be a nice change, to get out of the car. Stop carefully so they don't wake."

Simon steered to the curb, and braked as if they carried explosives, and pulled up the hand brake exquisitely. The children snorted and slept. Jenny and Simon got out of the van into the cold dark, feeling flat and shuffled, like cards. The drive had detached them from one world and they were not quite arranged in the other yet. Inverness was anonymous: wet sidewalks, bright shops. They went to a chemist's, and when the doorbell tinkled, it seemed to Jenny the first sound she had heard since Edinburgh. The droning of spaces and *nothing* had filled up her head and muffled her ears all day. The shop was hot and fragrant, with a rosy, soapy smell.

"How lovely," said Jenny. "After the car full of babies, it's a healing smell, isn't it."

"I know; a grocery is good, usually," said Simon, "but after a drive like that you don't want to smell cheese. You need perfume."

"You need disinfectant," said Jenny. "Look, the crowds are moving away from us."

The shop was almost empty, except for an old man buying syrup of figs, and an old woman waiting her turn, who did not notice them. They stood behind the woman, near the counter. She was wearing a frumpy "best" coat and hat, the kind of genteel tweeds that Mary Macdonald would wear, too, in town. She had on thick sheepskin boots, caked with mud, and her rough, battered hands were bare. Simon noticed what she was doing, and touched Jenny, and they moved up alongside her to see better.

She was staring, hard-eyed, at a pair of false eyelashes in the display case. She had forgotten where she was. She stared bitterly and breathed heavily and worked her mouth, and shook her head; and the eyelashes looked back, bland and silky. The exchange was so intense that the old woman ignored the shop assistant and Jenny, after politely waiting, took her turn.

"Two boxes of Farex, please, and a large black-currant juice," said Jenny, and around the rustle and ding of purchase she saw Simon getting more and more delighted with the show. At last she said, in broad Highland, to Jenny,

"Look you, would you not be wanting a pair of these."

The old woman—Mary Macdonald would call her a "crofter wifie"—stood very still. Jenny had begun to worry about the children, sleeping alone in the car, but she knew that Simon would not give it up now; so she put on a broad East Fife accent and said.

"Away. The dirty things. An' me a married Mum wi' weans a ma ain."

"But there is the green stuff to put on as well," he said, "above, and there is the wee stick pencil for the lines. It would make you look like a film star, surely. That is a revolting dialect you use," he added.

"Aberdeen is worse," she said.

The crofter wifie would not take the bait. She stood quietly, not speaking to the shop assistant, who was waiting for her, not speaking to Jenny and Simon, but quiet, thoughtful, as if she were listening to somebody else. At last she said,

"The powder for dentures, please, Jimmie; one box."

The shop assistant was a middle-aged man. As she paid him and took her parcel she exchanged a look with him, back and forth, crooked, gentle, poisonous, and amused. It was enough.

Out on the street Jenny said, "You lost."

"I was not trying to win," he said.

"Well, I'm not false eyelashes," said Jenny, "but I'm not a crofter wifie either, yet. It's a comfort."

"I'd like to be both," said Simon, "and remain uncommitted. I suppose that's too much to ask. Look, they're still asleep."

"Was she Free Church, do you think? A Wee Free? To be so savage about the eyelashes?"

"Och, aye, we all are, unless we are Catholic."

"What about Church of Scotland?"

"The middle class are that," he said. "The toffs. The enemy."

They drove on again, leaving Inverness. Expertise in driving through Inverness was important to Simon: the closer they got to Croichan, the more he had to prove he knew his way around. So instead of following the road signs or the AA map, he turned off the High Street and left the city by a secret, perhaps unnecessary, pattern of un-marked back roads. They came out by the city dump, somewhere on the edge of the Firth of Ard, and found the coast road leading West. The road went along the sheltered waterside. The Firth was ink-blue and flat, paler inland. On the right, across the water, the forest peninsula of the Black Isle joined the mainland; it was too dark to see much, but they could feel the presence, the mountain mass, of Suther-land.

After a while, Simon turned off the highway and up another secret criss-cross of climbing back roads. Shona woke up. They were getting closer, and she felt it. They went at first through larch and pine woods. A white hare floated into the headlights, balanced calmly in front of the car for a minute, then found an exit in the glaring wall and floated out again.

"Do you remember," said Simon. "The first time we drove up to Croichan, you and I, a hare did that, and we killed it. Do you remember?"

"Yes," said Jenny. "And you wouldn't let it lie. You had to get out and pick it up and take it to Croichan. You wanted to give it to Callum."

"Och, well," he said, "a bit of fresh meat is always welcome. And a hare was interesting then; there were not so many around as there are now."

"And do you remember about the hedgehog," she said. Simon smiled. "Oh, dear."

"What?" said Shona.

Jenny tried to keep the tension, almost fear, out of her voice. "Daddy knows an embarrassing story about a hedge-hog."

"Tell me, Daddy," said Shona.

"After we killed the hare, we went driving along in the dark, like this. Suddenly we saw a hedgehog in the middle of the road. He was alive, but he never moved. Mummy said his family was on that side of the road, and I said it was on this side. There were stone dikes along the road— look, we're passing the place now—so he would have to stay wherever we put him."

Jenny remembered the black woods meeting overhead, like the ridgepole of a tent, and the headlights making a corona of light around that tiny, stupid shape, that jagged hump of utter passivity, in Simon's hand; she remembered what a fever that had both been in about it.

"At last I went to *that* side," said Simon, "and I dropped him over the wall, feeling pleased with myself. We waited. We expected to hear him go rustle, thump, right down into the leaves on the other side. But we didn't hear anything. There was a long silence. A long, long, long silence. In the end, we heard *splash*. We were on a bridge. We had dropped him into the river."

They had their own silence, in the moving car.

Shona said, "Go on, Daddy."

"That was the end," said Simon.

"It had been on my conscience all this time," said Jenny.

"Aye," he said. "And on mine."

The paved roads became dirt roads, always climbing. As they drove higher they began to be aware, from the vibration inside the car, that a strong wind was blowing now, bending the tops of the trees. They passed a phone booth. It was on a black wooded corner where two roads met, and it was lit up, glowing red, translucent, like a shell. It wasn't doing anything, in the middle of the forest. There was a boy standing by the phone booth. He wasn't inside it or doing anything to it. His coat was torn and his hair was long, not fashionably long. He stared at their lights going past. His hands were wet and glowing red, too, in the cold.

"For God's sake, what's he doing standing there at night like a fool?" said Jenny.

"He is a fool, perhaps," said Simon. "Or a tinker—they often camp below the bank there in winter. Or one of Morag's boys. There is not much difference."

His accent was pure Highland now, with the longest possible *a*, turning *that* into *thot*, and the Gaelic, rather Scandinavian inflection. It was a graceful way of speaking, but it scared Jenny. It was another angle of himself that she did not understand, that she found permanently strange.

"Morag's are illegitimate," he said, "and Morag herself, and Morag's mother and grandmother back to the original bastard; but they were born here, not from Glasgow like the rest of us. All the crofts took orphans. They had to; they had no children of their own to help with the work. Anyhow they were all mental, Glasgow and Morag's alike. I was the only one in the school with wits. It made me think too much of myself. I was the leader." He smiled. "And I was very tough. You wouldn't catch anyone calling me darky."

"If everyone else was half-witted, Callum would have been proud to get you, no doubt. You were the prize package."

"Och, no, darling, he wouldn't notice it at all. Up here, a thing like that does not make any difference. But it worked both ways. He wouldn't say, '*what am I doing raising someone else's half-caste bastard,*' either."

Still driving up and up, they started to pass clearings and cottages. He was excited now and names began to boil out of him. "That croft is Morag's, Cnoc-muidhe, look: old Mr. Mackay will be staying in that shed by the house.

Here's Cnoc-na-coille—look; Mary owns it; Callum's old Aunt Maggie used to live in it, before she died. Empty now. Did you see, the front window has been broken in. Balmacarra—that has always been empty. Cruive, empty. The Laird keeps straw in it now, Mary was telling me, but I remember families at Cruive. The boys and I set a whin bush alight with paraffin once and burned off all the spring grazing. Kilduich—Willie-John lives there. His wife died the year I left home. There's the path through the woods—look, it's almost overgrown; it took us ten minutes to get down to school and an hour to climb back. In winter, we could slide."

Now they could hear trees humming in the wind, and when they came out above the treeline at Croichan, the wind beat at the car suddenly and almost turned it into the ditch. They could see the edge of the steading roof against the sky, but there was no light. Callum and Mary had no electricity and only one lamp, and they always sat on in the dark as long as possible, and then lit the one lamp in the kitchen, facing the hill.

Simon drove the car lurching up the steep bank, through the gate, into the yard. He stopped the engine and switched off the lights. For a moment, Jenny was aware only of dark, and quiet, and the thumping of the wind against the car—a distant noise, as if the car were a box way underground—and a total disconnection from whatever she had done or thought about before.

Jenny began to see dull yellow lights in the kitchen windows and a tail-end of light in the yard, sleeking over pools of mud and chopped-up hoofprints. She saw Mary open the scullery door and come out to meet them, the wet wind flapping around her. Simon opened the car door. The roof light went on and there was Shona, pale and sleepy, resenting the dim light, and the baby, disturbed, twisting his head from side to side, getting ready to cry. Jenny took Shona and Simon took the carrycot and they carried the children to the house in the dark, with Mary hurrying in front. There was a reek of wood smoke and cowdung. They heard the baa of one sheep, far up on the hill to the west. The small sound hooked at them, and the wind took it away again.

They went through the back door into the scullery. That was a leanto room off the main kitchen, about eight feet square, dim and gray, with a sink and a pump on one wall and a bottled-gas stove on the other. At the back was a narrow passage to the larder and bathroom. There was no smell of wood smoke inside the house. The scullery smelled of gas, and cold, and dishwater; and there was no light except the soft shine coming through the kitchen door. But they met there.

Simon bent across the carrycot and kissed Mary with a flare of love that made the old woman giggle and turn pink, and made Jenny want to cry. Mary and Jenny shook hands, and Shona picked her nose, trying to pretend that Mary was not there. Mary's hand was bigger than Jenny's, bigger than Simon's, dry, and very cold. Everything was cold: things and living things, all surfaces were cold, there was nothing warm to touch.

They went into the kitchen. "Did you think we were late coming?" said Simon. "There was snow at Carrbridge."

"There has not been any with us," said Mary. "But I was seeing white on the Beinn this afternoon."

The paraffin lamp was on the kitchen table, hissing and throwing white glare and black shadows around the room. It was a big, square room with a wooden ceiling and a big, square table in the middle. There were two windows on the outside wall and doors on the other three sides. The window curtains were drawn. There was an old man sitting in a straight chair between the windows, sitting in a drawn-tight, tactful position, as if he and Mary agreed that he was not worth keeping warm.

Mary was wearing three cardigans and had a woollen scarf around her neck and a woollen scarf over her ears. The old man had a thick, blue peacoat on. The room was dead cold. There was a small, wavering fire in the grate; it kept the kettle simmering but gave no heat. Jenny and Simon went to the fireside chairs, shivering. Simon put the carrycot down on the hearthmat, and Jenny took Shona on her lap. Shona sucked her thumb.

Mary and the old man had been drinking tea, and Mary started making tea again. She set out cups—no saucers—on the oilcloth tabletop, and a plate of scones, fawn-colored pancakes, and dry, gray oatcakes. There was a dish of butter and a Woolworth's glass dish of raspberry jam. The old man had his cup in his hand when they came in, but now he put it quickly behind the curtain, on the windowsill, well hidden, and sat tight and shy as a rabbit, looking at the wall.

"Simon, here is Mr. Mackay," said Mary, putting fresh boiling water on the old tea leaves in the pot. "Do you mind on him, you'll no' have seen him since the day Willie-John snared the pheasants on the Kilduich stacks."

Simon, who probably did not remember that day years and years ago, pretended that he did. "How are you keeping, then, Mr. Mackay."

The old man nodded. He began to say, "Aye. Aye. Aye," in a loud, resigned, droning voice, as if he were answering, not for his own health, which was failing, but for the hard seasons, and the loss of the past, and the pleasure of death, coming soon. Started, he did not know how to shut himself off, and kept on droning and nodding, "Aye. Aye," while Mary took a scone, split it, buttered it, put on the jam, gave it to Simon, did it all again and gave it to Jenny, forgot about Shona, poured two cups of tea with milk and no sugar and gave them that, too. The tea was full of leaves and so bitter that Jenny's throat shut down around it and she could hardly swallow. It was boiling hot and stronger than coffee. The hot tea made the room even colder by contrast. Shona moaned and shivered so Jenny let her sip at the tea, and gave her half the scone.

Jenny thought that the worst thing about Mr. Mackay was his eyes. They had aged past color, as if they had been dipped in egg white, and the lower lids hung down, making a white U beneath the pupils. He looked like a zombie, or an old hound; he might have been a watercolor sketch, a caricature of senile decay. The flesh of his face was blue and loose, as if the bones were not well connected inside. He stopped droning and, feeling more secure, tried to find his tea behind the curtain; but he couldn't reach it at the first try and took fright and got up, groaning, and limped to the scullery door.

"Good evening. To you all," he said, and went out.

"Good evening, Mr. Mackay," Mary said and then remarked over her tea, "Mr. Mackay will be doing the *heavy* work until Callum gets back."

"Och, yourself will be getting fat, Mary, with nothing to do," said Simon.

"No, Simon, Mr. Mackay is *use*. He can feed the sheep and turn out the bull."

"But you have to do the milking, and the hens."

"Och, well, I always do that. And Cheekie is dry the now. You'll be wanting hotties for the childrens' beds. What will they eat?" She looked worried, as if she had suddenly remembered that children did eat.

"The scone will be fine for Shona tonight," said Jenny. Shona was sucking the butter, the jam and the chunks of scone off the ends of her separate fingers. "I have some things to keep them going, and the baby only takes milk now, anyway."

"But there's no' much milk this time of year. Could he drink the Carnation?"

Simon smiled. "Jenny is the cow, in his case."

Mary went pink again. She blushed easily. She went and got two hot water bottles from a hook behind the scullery door. One by one, she filled them from the sooty kettle simmering on the grate, punched them till they released their puffs of steam, and sealed them up. There was the smell of hot rubber, another deception in the cold room. She handled the hot water bottles in that absent-minded, perfect way; she had done them over and over, the automatic hands' job, for how many years? Jenny did not know what she was thinking about.

Alasdair had gone back to sleep but was beginning to stir again. Jenny sat and cuddled Shona, feeling the tension between herself and the hungry baby, while Simon went in and out with their suitcases, a folding crib for Shona because Mary had no spare bed at all, the blankets and books and toys, taking them through to the Room. Whenever they came to Croichan, they slept on the bed-settee in the Room, across the hallway from the kitchen. Jenny got Shona's nightclothes out of the suitcase, holding the little girl with one arm and sorting through the layers of packed clothes with the other hand, thinking about Michael balancing the salukis on his lap. The fireplace was divided into four parts: the grate, a baking oven directly above, and two warming-ovens to the left. Jenny put Shona's pajamas, wool socks, and thick wool sweater into the bottom warming-oven, pushing aside the kindling and a box of salt that was drying there. Each time Simon opened the front door, the wind sucked the warmer air out of the kitchen and the fire reached weakly up around the kettle. Sparks caught in the chimney soot, glowed and burned out.

"The fire is at the back of the chimney," said Mary. "Callum would say that it was going to snow."

At last, Simon got the Room arranged and came back to the fireside. In Edinburgh, he liked bathing Shona and reading to her, but in front of Mary he became a Highland man and would hold his children, perhaps, but not take care of them in any way. He took the baby in his lap. Alasdair was getting violent now, wringing his fists and screwing his mouth sideways, hoping to suck. Jenny dressed Shona quickly, put the limp child on her lap, hugging her for the pale warmth that came out of the pajamas, and read soothing to her in this strange, cold room:

> The farm is deep in the middle of the forest.
>
> Once upon a time someone came here, built a homestead and farmed the land. No-one knows who. The stars are shining in the sky tonight, the snow lies white all around, the frost is cruel. On such a night people creep into their small houses, wrap themselves up, and bank the fire on the hearth.
>
> Here is a lonely old farm where everyone is sleeping.
>
> All but one—

Shona went suck-suck-suck loudly on her thumb, and went to sleep. Jenny carried her to the Room and wrapped her up in bed, hoping that the hot water bottle would not split. Then she took the baby and changed him quickly on her knees by the fire, while he screamed and Mary sat, embarrassed and shaken by such noise in the silent house. The yelling baby drove Mary into a further level of her own silence; she obliterated the noise, she tuned out, like someone changing stations on the radio. She sat quietly, ignoring the disturbance, polite, gentle, arrogant, looking somewhere else.

The disposable nappy would not burn in the dying fire. Jenny held it out with two fingers. "What am I to do with it?" she said.

"Och, put it in a bag," said Simon, displeased. Mary tuned out. Jenny, smiling to herself, sealed it in a polythene bag. Then she took a flashlight from the sideboard, took the carrycot in one hand, dragging and bumping it against her leg, got the baby and the light, somehow, in the other arm, and went through to nurse him in the Room. It would not do to open her sweater in front of Mary.

She fed him sitting on the open bed-settee, while her breath smoked and the flashlight beam shrank and hardened in the cold. The beam cut out a diagonal slant of lace parlor curtains and best gold-flowered wallpaper. She could smell fresh wallpaper paste. Had the Room been done up for them? There had not been time. What for, then, if it was never used?

There had been a lacy, best room at Windgates, but the television had been there, and her mother had often invited people to tea. Simon had told her that the Croichan Room was used for Hogmanay, and for weddings, and for funerals. The last funeral had been Callum's Aunt Maggie, who had gone from Cnoc-na-Coille to a Home, but had come back, at the end, to Croichan.

"There were special white socks for the laying-out," Simon had said. "I remember Mary taking them out of a drawer."

The last wedding had been—whose? Callum and Mary,

perhaps? She did not know. She and Simon had been married in Edinburgh. Jenny knew, suddenly, as if the Room had said it, that there would be no more weddings here.

At the edge of the light beam, cut diagonally half-light, half-black, were four framed photographs. She could not see them plainly. Lifting the baby in the crook of her arm, she carried him, still sucking, to the wall, and turned the flashlight full on the pictures. The yellow light fell in moving rings, as if it was water, and she was looking at each photograph from the circling rim of a well. Two were of weddings. The wedding people were dressed in country-Edwardian clothes and they all looked alike. They were one family. The women all had long, broad hands: Jenny remembered Mary's broad, cold hands in the scullery that evening. Which one was Mary? One of them might have been Mary. One of the men was wearing a kilt.

Another picture was too brown and cloudy. The flashlight made the surface rise and seem to float, the way dust motes swim in a light beam. Some figure in it was wearing a white hat. That was all Jenny could see. The last photograph must have been taken at night. She saw a family lined up on a doorstep. There were children, looking the wrong way, and another man in a kilt; the same man perhaps. All of them were faceless, without identity. Mary's past, her family past, was strangely foggy, as if it had escaped or deliberately confused the camera. And there was not one photograph of Simon.

The air in the Room was thick with absolute cold.

She wrapped the baby in a shawl, put on his knitted cap and rolled him in five blankets with the hottie inside, hoping he would make his own heat in the carrycot, like a little cub. After the Room, the kitchen seemed hot and full of life. Simon and Mary had been drinking more tea.

"Alasdair got milk sherbet," she said. Mary did not understand, and gave her a cup of tea. Simon looked sour. Jenny wondered what opaque, unimaginable gossip he and Mary had been busy with.

Mary said, "Shona has the same name as you, twice."

To Jenny, this was the perfect *non sequitur* to end that day of dislocation and cold dreams. She was exhausted. "Surely not."

"Och, aye; in the Gaelic," pronounced *Gahlic*. "Shona would be Jane, and there is Jane already, after, so she would be Jane Jane. If she were Shonach, she would be Jenny Jane. Then you would be Jenny together."

"But I'm Janet."

"Och, well, that is Shonach, too."

"What about Jennifer?"

"That," said Mary, "is English."

Jenny gave up and drank the bitter tea. Both Gaelic and Mary were too complicated, out of reach. At first she had seen Mary as no more than a poor hard-working crofter wifie, with a bent back and gray curls, and had been touched and embarrassed by the size of her hands and feet. But now Jenny suspected that Mary, like Gaelic, was full of diminutives and malice; Mary and her language, on their own ground, in one body, even. *Gaelic at Bay*. She saw a picture, a small rat, perhaps, backed into a corner, timid and smoky at the edges, but amused as well, and with wicked little teeth.

Simon was angry, because he had insisted on Shona's name, and he tried to bully Mary. "Mr. Mackay will be more trouble than help to you," he said.

But Mary answered in her usual impenetrable way. "Och, aye, but he'd no' go away, now that he is here. He is a joke, you see, Simon. The bodach 'ha radan, Aunt Maggie used to call him. Aunt Maggie was awful wicked to him; they were enemies. She said he was poisoning her well with the dead rats. Once she set a trap for him." Mary giggled. "The cailleach, she did that. And she caught him, too. It was a gin trap; it must have been sore on his poor footie. And she went down the road saying, 'I have a rat in my trap, I will cut off its ears.' But in the Gaelic, you see. 'Ha radan, ha radan.' You have heard that story, Simon."

"Aye, I have," he said.

"It is better in the Gaelic," she said.

If Simon had heard it in the Gaelic, thought Jenny, he had not understood it; but Mary did not seem to realize that, and he did not mention it.

"She was awful wicked, Aunt Maggie," said Mary, and then added, thoughtfully, "Callum was no' afraid of her, not all that much."

Soon after that Mary took the flashlight and went outside for a few minutes. When she came back and started filling hotties, for herself and them, Simon got up.

"Come along, love," he said to Jenny.

"What for?" she said.

He put his coat on and got hers too. "We can do without the light," he said. "Come along. Boots on, too."

She followed him out into the dark. The steading yard was dark blue and black, and the wet wind beat at them, bringing sprays and bursts of rain. Her boots went down into cold mud that she could not see. He took her hand. Even the wind seemed to be dark blue and black, and hollow; it came out of empty space, where there was nothing except a few vague sounds of bleating sheep. He led her behind him and they both struggled through the mud.

"My God, Simon," she called. "Where are we going?"

"To pee," he said, pulling her.

They went past the black byre and tractor shed to the furthest corner of the long, low building, at the edge of the road bank. In daylight, that corner overlooked the road and all of Strath-Ard. Even at night, it was exposed to every shattering wind. In the dark, it was like the Monadliath— exposed, past reality, past the edge of the mind. Simon turned to the corner and began, placidly, to urinate down the wall. There was the gentle bawk-bawk of dreaming hens in the henhouse inside.

"This is the place," he said. "Away you go."

"What are you doing?" she asked, meaning why.

"Peeing," he said. "Feel."

"I mean, no, not here," she said.

"This is the place," he said. "This has always been the place. Hurry up, I'm finished, do you want me to freeze my balls off?"

"Well, zip up," she said automatically. Then, "There's a toilet inside. We've always used it before. Why here? Why now?" She wanted to cry, childishly, in this childish situation.

"The inside one is for show," said Simon. "For visitors. For the toffs. Every time you flush it you empty the water tank, and then you have to pump the bugger full again. That takes an hour, and the pump leaks, and the well is bad to begin with; if you pump the well dry there will be no water at all. Away you go, love, we live here now."

So Jenny squatted down against the corner wall and put her face in her lap. At least there would be some imaginary enclosure. Even in the woods, one picked a hollow between trees, or behind the stems of a broom bush. Simon stood looking into the dark, pleased because he knew the rules and she did not. It was funny, and it was not funny. She had a strongly physical feeling of despair, as if something inside her had swung heavily to a stop, involving her will.

"Are we allowed to have paper?" she said weakly.

"Och, aye, but bring it back with you and put it with the nappies," he said.

"Where do you go in the daytime?" She got up, feeling wet.

"In the byre drain. And you always crap in the byre drain, night or day. Then it will go out with the cow muck, you see."

"Must the children?"

He thought about it as they staggered back to the house. They could see the kitchen window, a steady rectangle, lit, curtained. The rest of the house flowed, in the wind, as if it were under water; as if a black river were running past it. "Och, I think it would be all right in the house, for them. You'd no' have to flush, for Shona."

The house inside was cold, but still. The stove gas smelled of rotten onions. Mary gave them the flashlight and two hotties, and they said goodnight and went into the Room. The children were asleep. They got their long woolen underwear out of the suitcase, and stripped, and frantically tried to get into the wool clothes, feeling mist and frost on their bare bodies.

"This is the last time I'm going to be found naked this winter," said Simon. "Tomorrow you can sew me into these in the good old-fashioned way. None of this pajama crap, and nudity is out."

"In that case, I'll sew up the fly, too, dearie," she said. "You're not coming near me if you don't change your drawers for six months."

They got into bed and clutched each other in the cold, trying to keep their bare feet away from the hotties, which had gone cold and felt like cold bladders between the sheets.

"I just want to go to sleep," he said.

"I know," she said. "So do I."

"I didn't think I would. I thought I'd be so happy to-night. But now I can't be bothered. If I took it out now, it would freeze and snap off, anyway."

She hugged his shoulders from behind, and put her face against his back, but she could not get close to him.

"Have we bedsocks?" he said.

"I'll knit some, when I get Shona's jumper done," she said. "Dearie, would you explain about the old man? What was Mary telling us about him? Whatever it was that was better in the Gaelic."

"What, were you lost with all that?" said Simon, proud to translate. "Aye, he used to be the ratcatcher in Strath-Ard, when he was well. But his feet were always very bad. I think perhaps it was something that happened to him in the First War. He had a secret way of killing the rats, and he would chase the children away with a stick if we followed him about. He would go into the byre at night, bare-handed, without a terrier, even; I think he had a lure of some kind in his pocket. He would say something about a 'tantalizer.' That was his word. In the morning there would be a grand pile of dead rats, and Mary would give him a Piece, a scone and jam, for his breakfast, and some tea, and he would go away. And do you know, darling? He has always been old. He has always looked exactly the way you saw him now.

"I remember," he said, getting sleepy. "There was a cow that got a Piecie at the scullery door each morning, too. Whitey was her name; she was part Ayrshire. And Callum had a dog that would bring the cows in on its own.

"Radan means rat. Bodach means old man. Callum used to call him the bodachan, the little old man; Callum is so big, you see, but it means more than size, it is a bit of an insult, too. The diminutive is insulting sometimes. Darling, let me sleep. I want to get work done in the morning. The pump is leaking again in the scullery, were you seeing, and no one has put antifreeze in the tractor, surely, and there will be the threshing to do or the beasts will run short of fodder, and God knows what else has been left rusting and lying about—"

He went to sleep, quickly, maddeningly, as usual. Whatever his troubles were, he did not stay awake with them. She had no troubles, she thought, only his; and tediums, and crying children, but she was always the one to lie awake. She had seen the pump dripping into the hen food bucket under the sink. So: the well was bad and often ran dry. She had known that before, but had not thought the toilet was involved. Why had Callum built Croichan on the one waterless ridge in all that country of moor and bog?

"Why?" she had asked Mary once, on their first visit, when they were washing dishes in one pint of coppery water and detergent scum.

"Och, for the view," said Mary. "It is a grand view." The scullery window overlooked the valley of the Ard River, and the cloudy, shifting mass of Beinn a' Bha-Ach Ard.

"But He's no' doing the washing up," said Mary, and did not answer the next question; and Jenny, after a while, realized that she did not know if Mary had been sardonic or serious about the view, whether He had been the hill, Callum, or both, or neither. In fact, there had not been the slightest communication between them at all. Later, Simon explained that there had always been a steading at Croichan, that Callum had built a new house on the old site, that there had been a good well in the lower field, but that Callum, wanting to make improvements, had sunk another, closer, but had stopped digging many feet too soon.

On that first visit, Jenny had not understood why Mary

had left all that unsaid. She still did not understand but she was beginning to see the pattern. Most of Croichan existed somewhere else—on a level of instinct or habit, on webs of communication above, below, inside, different, anyhow, from the outward affairs of ordinary people. She did not know why, but she could feel the nerves of the place go tight with fear if she asked too bluntly why, for instance, Mary fed the hens twice a day, or if Callum had ever been to Edinburgh. It was as if Callum and Mary, and the fields and steading, too, and Simon, when he was with them, all went around asleep; dreaming, inarticulate, shifty, and yet reaching each other completely. But Jenny herself was forced to keep awake. She called it *what was not said*.

Now she began to fall into her own sleep, but inside a circle of odd thoughts. If she needed the toilet in the night, or if Shona woke up calling, as she often did, "Mummay, Um *needin*," how would she find her way through the bitter dark house, and though the muddy yard, out to the edge of the hill? And what would it be like in the daytime, in the byre, squatting at the caked, muddy heels of the black bull and the cows? Jenny was not at ease with cows.

The last thing she remembered was the smell of the sheets. They were damp, but clean. In summer Mary would wash sheets in the burn, and spread them on the whin bushes to bleach and dry. But in the winter? How did you wash anything at Croichan in the winter?

Some time later, the baby began to cry in the deep black of the Room. Jenny woke, felt her breasts prickling with milk and guessed it must be near six in the morning. All she could see was a slit of stars where the curtain was drawn back; all she could hear was the wind thudding regularly, like a pendulum, against the house. She slid out of bed into the bitter cold. If she ignored the baby her breasts would leak anyway and soak the pillowcase, and Simon would wake, milky and outraged. At one time, she had tried to disturb his blankets as much as possible when getting up to feed the babies, and had rather liked drenching him with milk; but even that malice had left her by now.

She felt for the carrycot in the dark, lifted the baby and hurried back to bed with him, shivering. His mouth found her breast by instinct in the dark. His nose was like the icy end of a metal rod, but his wrapped-up body was warm. They lay in curves, Simon, Jenny, Alasdair, hugging each other like warm cats. Jenny's bones began to feel soft and comfortable at the ends. Simon often said, "I wish I were three cats, all at the same time. Three in one. They understand love. They lie heaped up, body and soul." She couldn't sleep for fear of smothering the baby, but, half-awake, she began to dream.

She thought about Mr. Mackay. When he was in the byre at night, long ago, how had he called the rats to come and be killed? And how had he killed them? The baby's cold hand touched her ribs in the dark, and she shuddered. Had they touched him like that, with cold noses?

She tried to work out the Gaelic words: *bodach 'ha radan*, the old rat man, the old-man-who-is-a-rat; Gaelic could be ambiguous, insulting. The baby's hand touched her again, unpleasantly. Mr. Mackay's hand was so old, so blue, that the bones and nails seemed unstable, ready to separate. Then, with her closed eyes, she saw the baby's hand, but it was grown old, too. His fingers, fresh and waxy now, were going to age, were going to become unstable and ugly, like the bodach 'ha radan's. Her own child was going to get old and, like that old man, die. She could not do anything to stop it. That scared her; she found it pitiful, and cried a little in her sleep. She had not thought about it before.

As she was a logical person, her thoughts followed in sequence, so after that came: and when this baby's hand is dead of old age and buried, where will mine be? For the first time she looked straight, with imagination, at a vision of her own death; and her dream dissolved in a horror that was purely physical, and she woke sobbing and saying out loud, *It is a death watch, a death watch*: though whose death, exactly, she was witnessing—even hers had passed, now—what death she was waiting for, she could not say.

Simon half-woke and stroked her. The baby was asleep, wrapped in his own innocent stupidity. He had been there, sucking, but he had not seen what she saw. The light began to come through the window, cold and odd. The noise of the cockerel and the hens in the steading yard had a muffled, far-away sound, like rusty doors opening.

"Mary will be starting a fire," said Simon. "I heard her outside a while ago with the milk pails. Did you have bad dreams? I felt you jump. I had horrible dreams. The curl-up-and-die kind."

"I don't want to hear about them," she said.

"They were worse than yours. I'm shattered. I couldn't tell anybody."

"That means you intend to," she said. "Don't tell me."

"I couldn't possibly," he said. "I dreamed about Callum. He was sitting up on a bed in that small room off the kitchen there. He was in a pleasant mood, and he was smiling. He took the blankets off the stumps of his legs and made me look at them."

"Will you shut up," she said.

"He made me touch them. I didn't want to. I don't remember what they felt like, but they were pleasant to look at. They were light brown, with rings, like sawed-off trees."

She didn't say anything.

"Then I had a wet dream. Then I woke up."

They saw why the morning light was so cold and
crooked, like blue neon. A gray striped cat jumped up on
the windowsill outside the Room, twitching all over and
shaking his paws. He was an old barn cat, with only three
legs, and he was half-covered with snow.

Simon got up and put Shona in bed with Jenny, who already had Alasdair on the other side. Shona sucked her
thumb. Her cheeks were icy cold but her feet, in the wool
socks, were warm. Jenny lay on her back, watching the
smoky drift of Simon's breath as he went around the Room,
getting dressed. He took off his underwear bottoms and
dug for his second pair in the suitcase.

"What shall I do with the mucky ones?" he said.

"I don't know," she said, rejecting the day to come. "I'll
have to do a wash sometime. We can't wear the same
clothes all winter."

"I'll roll them into a ball, and hide them in a corner of
the suitcase," he said. "It can be our Secret Horror."

"We could make up a parcel of dirty clothes, and send
them to Michael," she said. "There's that laundromat on
the corner of Gilmore Place."

"We might do that," he said, "but I don't think we can
afford the postage."

"You'd better not do this sort of thing very often," she
said.

"I'll have to fuck you every night, then," he said. "And
sleep with my cock in a bottle. Bring Shona to the fire, and
dress her there."

"There is no fire," she said.

"Look you, Mary will be going out again to the hens,
and while she is away I'll bring in a bit of extra coal and
build the fire up for you."

"Perhaps we could pay for the extra coal with Michael's rent checks," she said.

"Och, darling, it won't be poverty; the bunker is full."

Jenny went wide awake with surprise. "But why, then?"

He sat down on the edge of the bed; his weight made her feel, not comforted, but trapped. "They will be getting by, all right, with the subsidies, and Callum has been getting his pension since 1964. It is the way of life, you see. It would upset Mary, if she saw us trying to change her. It is acceptable, if we do it behind her back. Stay in bed for a while."

He went out of the Room, and soon she heard the clang of the coal bucket, and the crunching as he threw more coal on the kitchen fire.

At breakfast, the kitchen was so cold that the spoons stuck to their fingers, and the lukewarm half pint of milk Mary brought in from the cow steamed as if were boiling hot. Mary shook the few lumps of cream out of the jug into Simon's bowl and put her own share of skim milk into a cup. She dipped her salty porridge, spoon by spoon, into that. Jenny and Shona poured their skim milk over the porridge and ate it out of the bowl, and Jenny let Shona have hers with sugar, for energy and heat. The porridge was not made with oatmeal but with "CROFTER Ready-to-Cook Rolled Oats, Quick and Easy," out of a box.

The baby slept in his carrycot, in the corner by the fire. While they were eating, the extra coal caught and crackled brightly, and the wooden ceiling flickered yellow and red. They could almost feel the heat in the middle of the room. Mary put the kettle down to boil for tea. After she poured the tea, she raked out the fire and let it die. She opened the scullery door and the outside door, rolled up the hearthrug and the floor mats and went to shake them outside. The wet, snowy wind came into the house.

Simon stood up, lifting his chair behind him, backed across the room with the cup in one hand and the chair held behind him in the other, and thumped the chair down again by the dying fire. He sat luxuriously down himself and Mary, coming in with the mats, laughed.

"Aye," she said. "That was Callum's trick."

"And then he would put one boot on, and sit and sit a wee whilie longer, and he would say, 'I'll be getting to work now,' and let you do the sweeping all around him; and then you'd build up the fire again for the baking, and he'd no' get the other boot on past eleven."

"The lazy tinker," said Mary, sweeping dust out the door as the white cold flowed in.

"But I'll be getting to work now," said Simon. "I was thinking perhaps I could bring some wood in for you first. The children are not so active," he said tactfully. "They will be needing that wee bittie extra warmth."

"Och, aye," said Mary, thinking about something else, or nothing at all.

"What is it that needs doing, then," he said. "Has the thrashing been done? Have the beasts got enough to be going on with?"

"Och, aye, Simon," she said. "Willie-John was here at the weekend and he did a grand wee stack. But the tatties are still in the ground. I was thinking they would be rotting and we would lose the whole crop. The old man's no' fit to stand in the cold, with his feet that bad."

"Where is he?" said Simon.

"Och, around and about," said Mary. "Sometimes he's no' up here until dinner."

"It's a wet snow," said Simon. "The ground is soft enough underneath. We could both be at the lifting and afterwards I could come along and collect them with the tractor and clamp them in the field. Where are the tatties this year?"

"Up West, by the Keeper's Cottage."

"Very well."

"Could I get the dinner ready?" said Jenny.

"Och, well," said Mary. Jenny tried to tune in, and thought she understood: *it was not said* that she could get the dinner, if she did it decisively and did not mention it again.

Shona was clinging and whimpering with cold, and Jenny saw that her main job would be to provide a permanent lap for the children, to keep them out of Mary's way while she obeyed the imperative, meaningless demands of the day, and out of Simon's way while he propped up the visible remains of Croichan and of himself and of the whole Scots Gaelic culture as well, if he pleased. Mary built up the fire again and prepared to bake. The days were going to pass, always, exactly like that.

Jenny took Shona to the bathroom, where they brushed their teeth, sharing one cup. There was a blue-green pear of copper deposit under the cold tap in the sink, but the tub had never been used, and was netted across with spider webs. Shona used the toilet, said, "It's got a handle, not a chain; look, Mummay, I can flush it myself," and sent ten gallons of water gurgling down out of the tank.

So they went to the scullery to pump the tank full. The scullery sink was coppery too, an Egyptian, sensual blue-green that did not go with the cold and smell of dishwater and rotten onions and, now, potatoes: Mary had put the hens' bucket on with potato peels to boil. There would be copper salts in the tea as well. Jenny saw a picture of Mary in cross section. Her insides were jointed and piped like plumbing. The pumping was in cross section, too, and was furred and corroded with bright blue-green from drinking tea at Croichan how many—forty, fifty?—years. The label, in Victorian letters, read, *Wonders of Medicine*.

The pump was set in next to the sink. It had an upright

wooden handle that had to be pulled and pushed through the half circle. Shona took hold below Jenny's hands and they worked the handle back and forth: thunk thunk, thunk thunk, and the rhythm absorbed them. The depth of the valley drifted past the small window above the sink, and Beinn a'Bha-ach Ard, gray and white, drifted past at the other side of the valley, and suddenly the black bull and the cows drifted past the window frame, because Simon had just let them out of the byre. The snow had stopped, and the clouds were beginning to break up in the wind, showing blue. It took them half an hour to pump the tank full. Then a thin line of water came out of the runoff tap, and they were able to stop.

The baby woke, and she changed and cleaned and fed him. Then she took Shona and her knitting to a fireside chair. The grate was black and cold, and a thin waver of smoke went up the chimney past them. Shona sat on her lap, inside her knitting arms, and together they watched the snowlight on the varnished wood ceiling, and looked at the swing of the pendulum on the mantelpiece clock. It went "tick, tock. Tick," like a man stamping slowly across the room.

They looked at the fireplace calendar, which was working-class genteel, with a picture of three Scottish Terrier puppies; but it was open at July 1966. Then Jenny saw a set of cork tablemats in a holder on the mantelpiece, and took them down to see the pictures. Each mat showed a Regency street scene.

The first mat said, *Violets, Won't You Buy Some?* A pretty beggarwoman, with rosy children, approached a lord and lady. They refused her.

The second mat said, *Strawberries, Ripe and Red.* The beggarwoman's bodice was very low, and the fashionable lady had a plumed hat on. They refused her again.

The third mat said, *Gingerbread, Nice and Hot.* This time the beggarwoman's eldest son had a crutch and a bandaged leg. The lord and lady had pale faces; they turned away in disgust.

The fourth mat offered them *The Latest Ballad.* The beggarwoman had bare feet. The lord took out a lace handkerchief. They refused the ballad.

The last mat tried *Apples Ripe,* but the lord and lady looked angry, fed up, ready to call the police. Shona was fascinated, and made Jenny read the mats to her three times over. Then she took them down and got from Jenny's lap and spread them out on the floor, and began to play some strange, singing game of suffering and rejection on her own.

Jenny went to make the dinner. The larder was a shelved cupboard room off the scullery passage, with a screened open window overlooking the valley and Beinn a'Bha-ach Ard. It smelled of Oxo cubes and cold oilcloth. She did not find much there: a breadbin, the dairy pans and jugs, Carnation Milk tins, sugar, flour, salt; a row of packet soups and freeze-dried vegetables. There was barley, and pudding rice, and currants, and Crofter Quick-Oats. She saw neck of mutton in a white enameled basin, turnips and carrots and potatoes in a basket on the floor and she knew there was a shabby kitchen garden in front of the house, which would surely have leeks and kale. She would make broth, and boiled potatoes, and rice pudding. Cooking was a gesture. It would prove she was still alive against the cold.

She got the soup pot going on top of the stove, and the pudding in the oven, and then went into the Room, to look out of the west window. Simon and Mary were working far up on the hill to the west. They were forking and breaking out the drills; bending, picking the potatoes by hand out of the frozen ground; stacking them on burlap squares alongside. Then Simon drove the tractor to each stack and he and Mary lifted the square, tipping the potatoes gently onto the trailer. The field was ridged black and white with snow. The sky was gray again. The whole scene had a sunken, muddy look, the grazing slopes half-melted, half-green, but a dull green, as if the sun withdrawing to the south had taken all the colors with it. The cattle wandered around, their hooves sinking into the mud and snow. After a long time, Simon and Mary climbed onto the tractor and came down through the fields and the muddy gate into the steading yard for dinner. The black bull followed them down.

Just as they got to the house, the snow came down again in a whipping white sheet. The bodach 'ha radan appeared at the scullery door wearing shoulderpads of snow, and stamped the snow off his boots, slowly, hurting his bad feet. He limped into the kitchen still wearing his overcoat, and a pair of fingerless wool gloves, and cap with earflaps; but the flaps were off-center, and missed his ears. Simon and Mary washed the mud off their hands with cold water, at the kitchen sink, Jenny put the broth and vegetables and meat into soup plates and carried them to the kitchen, and put the potatoes into a separate serving bowl. They all sat down at the table.

Mary bent her head and said a long grace ending with *for Christ's sake, amen.* They ate the soup first and then put the potatoes into the same plates and ate them, dry, with salt. Mary and the old man forked up their potatoes and peeled them neatly with their knives. Simon was out of practice and took off thick, clumsy peelings. Jenny could not do it at all and peeled hers and Shona's with her fingernails.

"Is it drifting, then, Mr. Mackay," said Simon.

That reached the old man and he answered, with effort, "Aye. Aye. But the sheep are no' buried. I found them behind the stacks." His hand shook with the excitement of speaking, and he licked a potato crumb off his knuckles.

"I'll be getting those tatties in the ground this afternoon," said Simon. "I'll bring up a load of straw and dig a good clamp by the field. Do you want me to bring down a bag or two for the cooking, Mary?"

"Och, no, I'm no' liking the Kerr's Pinks, Simon. I have three rows of Golden Wonders in the garden. They'll do the now."

The bodach 'ha radan spoke again. "I was meaning to tell you, Mrs. Macdonald, Morag has the newspaper. There was a party of three killed in a motor accident at Muir of Ord. The car was demolished, it was saying. Demolished completely."

"Och, the poor souls," said Mary, with interest.

"Aye. The remains are on view at the Funeral Home at Inverness. But they're no' wanting any flowers."

"Fancy," said Mary.

"Aye," said the old man, beginning to drone again, "Aye. Aye." Jenny and Mary took away the plates and brought in the pudding.

Simon said, "The rats are getting bad, the now, Mary. There was a grand big one in the manger when I put the hay in for the bull."

"Aye, they are that, Simon. Perhaps Mr. Mackay would be seeing to them for us."

She was being cruel, but the old man did not notice.

"Aye, Mrs. Macdonald, I could do that," he said.

That was all. Nothing else was said about the rats. But Jenny, trying to tune in, noticed a feeling of surprise, a certain discomposure, around the table, and realized that something serious and unexpected had *not been said*: a

bargain had been made, that bound them all. The bodach
'ha radan was going to clear the rats from Callum Croichan's byre, using his secret technique, as he had done long
ago. No trap, no poison, no dog could touch those rats
before he did. Inspired, the old man spoke more clearly.

"I was seeing the biast dubh, himself, this morning, before it was light. First it was his tracks I was seeing, by the
Kilduich burn, and then it was Himself."

"Surely not, Mr. Mackay," said Mary.

"Aye, it was," he said.

Simon pretended he knew the Gaelic so Jenny took pity
on him and asked, "What did Mr. Mackay see?"

"The otter," said Mary. "Fancy. The trash. It is cheeky
of it to come that close to the crofts."

"It isn't dangerous, is it?" said Jenny.

"What's an otter?" said Shona, who had not been talking; she had been oddly quiet, watching the tablemats and
arranging them in her mind.

"A sort of big water weasel," said Simon, getting up and
pulling his flapping gumboots on. "However, if Mr. Mackay
will see to the rats, we will not worry about the otters."

"But does it do any damage?" Jenny asks again.

"Och, no," said Mary. "It kills the salmon, and that, so
the gamekeepers drive it away. But it has no business here.
It has left its own place, you see. It's no' right for it to come
that close to where we live." She became sardonic. "It is
Callum's fault, surely," she said. "The wild beasts are coming closer, because they know he is gone."

II

When Simon Johnston was away from his wife, he talked to her constantly, silently, telling her whatever was happening to him, and how he felt about it. He had to have this silent partner in his mind. It made his experiences real and sensible, and he could not remember what he had done before Jenny. That had been one of his troubles, perhaps.

If he had been a writer, or an artist of any kind, he would have kept quiet, even to himself, and recorded things later, in the medium. As it was, each event of his life went into him and was immediately deflected and presented to her—in the past tense, and with a certain amount of shape to it, so perhaps he could have been a writer after all. But Jenny never knew about this. It was so intimate and automatic a process that he took it for granted, and never bothered to mention it to her.

Very little of his mental journalism even came out in speech to her later—he had worn it out in the first round. It would all condense into, "When I walked across the Meadows today, there were seagull feathers all over the grass, something must have given them a hell of a fright," or, "You know that dirty book and contraceptive seller at Tollcross; I like the way he stands in the doorway with his thumbs in his braces, the real prosperous merchant," when either of these had brought on an interior monologue that had taken him halfway across Edinburgh. When they were alone they talked a lot about sex, or swore about the children, and that was all right for every day. At Croichan, of course, that was not enough; and there began to be a space, a hostile blank, between them.

Only once did Simon's recording machine break down. In late November, soon after they got to Croichan, Michael invited Simon away for a weekend. It was a strange trip. For a day, the whole current of his thoughts changed direction, and he did not speak inwardly to Jenny at all.

After that first snow, there was a thaw. The weather turned gray and warm, and it rained. The bracken in the grazing field—a sign of the croft's decay—came out from under the snow wet and heavy, reddish-brown, like partridge feathers.

"Dearie," said Jenny. "This is ridiculous."

"Aye, it is," he said, the seasoned Highlander. "But wait you; winter will be back tomorrow."

That afternoon, the postman drove up in his red van, the golden Royal Mail crown and lettering oddly baroque against the croft buildings. After two cups of tea and a lot of "It is soft today," "Aye, it is," with Mary, he gave Simon a letter postmarked Edinburgh, and drove away, his tires slushing through the mud.

It was too soon for a rent check; it might have been bad news. Simon found himself hoping it was something that would keep them at Croichan; then he was fiercely ashamed of himself, and pretended to be upset. "I can't bear it," he said. "They cancelled my scholarship for next year."

"It won't be that," said Jenny. "It isn't a University envelope."

"It will be from Michael, then. Look, the postmark says *Tollcross*. He's let the flat go on fire."

"Coward," she said, and took it herself. She opened it and read the typed letter halfway down and laughed and said, "No fear, it's only the curtains, and the wallpaper, and a few other little things."

Simon took it and read it all aloud. They were sitting by the fire. Mary was out collecting the few eggs the hens would lay in midwinter. Shona was on the kitchen floor, building a fence of last year's larch cones around a design of sentimental-sadistic tablemats. The first thing Michael said was,

That little gray devil of mine has been naughty.

"I knew it," said Simon. "Those buggering dogs." He could see the salukis curled up in their sheepskin beds, looking at him with their mad, big eyes, benign and capable of anything. Michael told the rest.

I put antifreeze in the car and it sprung a leak. The garage man says that antifreeze will find the weak spots. So it seems. There was a pool of green water in the glove compartment and the windshield was covered with grease and fumes. So I had to leave it to be fixed and the dogs had to stay at home. I usually take them with me and they sleep peacefully in the car while I'm at class. Phoebe was a good girl but Rosiqa didn't like it and threw herself around, chewed the doorknob, tore off some wallpaper, and I guess there isn't much left of the kitchen curtains.

I know I'm lucky that she didn't jump out of the window. I've heard of salukis doing that. I personally knew one who ate the leather upholstery off a Jaguar Mark V. I'll get it all fixed up for you, of course, but I might not be able to match the patterns, so I thought I'd better tell you. You'll be glad to hear she didn't do a thing to the bulbs. The paperwhites will be flowering soon. Should I stake them up? Rosiqa did knock your little tropical houseplant off the windowsill and cracked the pot, but it seems to be all right. My girl, Fran, says it's a cannabis plant. Did you know that? She says, what I'd call marijuana. I was surprised.

But I feel sorry about your apartment and would like to make amends. I'm going to be at the Strathmoy Hotel next weekend. The Sight-hound Club is having its annual Coursing Meet there from Wednesday to Sunday, and I'd like you both to be my guests there for the final day's sport, Saturday, and at the prizegiving and dinner afterwards, which is always a great social occasion with a lot of funny-looking people, I must admit, which should please an observer of human nature like yourself.

"What makes him think I'm a bloody observer of fucking human nature?" said Simon.

The moor can be savage at this time of year, as you know, and there's the killing, so maybe you'd better leave the children at home. If not, maybe one of you could come. I'll be alone too. My girl, Fran, is Anti-Blood-Sport. Let me know and I'll reserve a room for you, single or double, as the case may be. I see on the AA map that Strathmoy is pretty close to where you are now.

Love, Michael

"Love?" said Simon.

"Dearie, don't be such a bastard," said Jenny. "Leave the children, indeed. He obviously has money. With our nanny, I suppose. With our wet nurse."

"Well, I surely won't go," said Simon.

"What, are you Anti-Blood-Sport?"

"I know what kind of occasion it will be," he said. "The

gentry will be there, the huntin'-shootin', the awful toffs. Not for me."

"I think you should go anyhow," she said. "If only to take a bath; it's a three-star hotel, you know."

"What, could you stay here with Mary by yourself, and not go mad thinking of me having a bath in a hot tub, and a pee in a real toilet?"

"I would thoroughly enjoy it. I'm a Scottish wife, after all, and we love martyrdom, even when we're not terribly churchy. No, I want to go, and I can't, so you must. You can just bring me back some bathwater in a vacuum flask."

"And the toilet."

"Don't be childish. Go."

Then Mary came in with three eggs, and the empty hens' bucket, and said that a change would do Simon good.

"Och, aye, you ought to go, Simon," she said. "You would have a good time with the toffs." She lengthened it, malicious, cooing; she meant, go and watch them, and bring back a joke for us to use against them. "Willie-John's nephew, Archie, works at the hotel," she said thoughtfully. "You'll mind on him, Simon, he was a year ahead of you in school. He would be a waiter, now, I think. You will have to say hello to him, for Willie-John, and ask is he getting on all right."

Simon knew if he did not go now it would be rudeness to Willie-John and his nephew, Archie, and that would be serious, a breach of courtesy. So he wrote to Michael, saying *Thank you for the invitation, but I must warn you that I'm a surly bugger in society and am of unstable temperament and liable to get drunk and break up the party.* He was not sure whether that was true or pretense, but he wanted to see what Michael would say. Michael wrote back,

Saturday evening is always a raving drunk and the party usually gets broken up somehow; anyway, maybe you can show us a different way to do it. Also, saluki people know all about unstable temperaments. I've reserved a single room for you for Saturday night. You should be fit to drive home Sunday morning without worrying about this Breathalyser thing. Bring good clothes and warm clothes. See you 9 AM Saturday in front of the hotel.

On Friday night, they got Simon ready for an early start. Mary packed him a breakfast of scones and butter and raspberry jam, and, last of all, she put hot tea into a thermos flask. Jenny set out his rough-weather clothes, put his gumboots neatly together by the scullery door, where he could not possibly miss them in the dark, and hung his suit in the back of the van.

It was his only suit, plain, brown tweed, and it was not exactly unfashionable. He had bought it new, in Edinburgh, in September, to celebrate Alasdair and his University scholarship. It was a solid, unnoticeable suit, and it looked like Edinburgh, not like London. But after he bought the suit, in a different state of mind, he had gone into a Male Boutique and bought a flowered shirt to go underneath. It was not a brilliant flowered shirt; it had small, expensive-looking, drab flowers on a creamy background, and a drab, silk scarf for an Ascot tie at the neck. But Jenny said he had bought it in a what she called his Black Power mood, and he would never be brave enough to wear it.

"That's not funny," he had said to her.

"It is, and it isn't," she said. "But you'll never wear it, dearie; you'll end up giving it to me."

He had not worn it yet, but he felt defensive in advance, and half-savage about the coming Saturday night, and he wanted to be prepared. So he put it on the hanger with the brown suit. He packed his shoes and overnight things and a book, *Recollections of a Highland Boyhood*, in a small duffel bag they usually kept disposable nappy-rolls in.

At that time of year, the sun did not rise till after nine, and it was easy to get up in the dark. Jenny fed the baby at six and put him in bed with them, milky and stinking.

Simon groaned. "It's crapped in its pants," he said.

"Well, I can't change him till I get to the fire, at breakfast time," she said. "It's far too cold in here. Bring back some central heating from Strathmoy, while you're about it, will you."

They put the flashlight on the sideboard, and Simon dressed in the half-dark, Jenny handing him things: two pairs of wool socks and two sweaters and two pairs of trousers, the top pair waterproof. It was exciting, putting on these Army-surplus outdoor clothes. They were made for rescues and struggles and storms and there was a sense of challenge about them, as if he were putting his armor on. The anorak was the best. It was lightweight khaki canvas, with broad shoulders and a pointed drawstring hood. He could never have worn it for farmwork. It was too dramatic. It was made for Scottish-Romantic occasions, to be silhouetted against the skyline, on a mountainside, in horrible weather. It belted in at the waist and buttoned at the wrists and was long enough to button between his legs. It gave Simon claustrophobia and brought out the narcissist in him. It was the anorak that first made him feel wild, that day, and helped him forget Jenny.

He did not forget her right away. In the frozen, half-dark room, she said she was cold and got back into bed and he followed her, wearing everything but his boots. It was exciting to be in bed with the stiff, rugged outdoor clothes between them. They hugged and kissed, avoiding the baby, until Shona woke up and crawled into bed with them. Then Simon started hugging and kissing her, too, and he found her soft little body so delicious, so unconsciously sexy, that he rolled out of bed in a hurry and padded away through the ice-cold house in his socks, saying, "Down, down," to himself.

He could smell cold wood ash, the dead fire, in the kitchen; the room was black dark with the curtains drawn, and he knew he was getting near the scullery by the smell of bottled gas. He stepped into his boots and took the tea and scones. Then he stopped, thought for a moment, put a small pot of water on the stove, finding the matchbox by touch, heated the water, took it to the bathroom, and shaved briefly by the gray reflection of himself in the shadowy mirror. Then he pulled on his sheepskin mittens and got his breakfast again and went out into the inky blue steading yard. There had been a bitter frost. He could see the morning star, oddly big and bright. There was no wind; the air smelled like cucumbers and the whole steading was drawn together in a square of passive, absolute winter silence.

He had backed the car into the dairy shed the night before, and it started with no trouble. As he drove, the road was frosty white, and seemed to rise like a bridge, like a tongue sticking out over nothing, going no place. When the light started to come it was pale gray. The trees along the road were frozen, like gray feathers or puffs of smoke, and the roadside grass and heather was frozen, too, covered with ice. Simon felt eccentric and lonely. Why was he leaving a luscious wife and daughter in a warm bed? Was this adventure or, God help us, pleasure? I should have stayed home, he thought, and fucked my wife.

And my daughter, too? Children spoiled sex. Either they woke and cried and needed you or they got older and woke and watched you. Even if the children weren't watching, some damn thing was. Some stupid trivial problem was always getting into bed with you. Jenny had not wanted sex since they had come to Croichan, and every screwing session had been either martyrdom or rape. Life was going to be chastity from now on, he thought. Chastity and purity and frost.

He drove on, thinking silly thoughts, and horny thoughts, beginning to feel himself detached from Croichan and everything there. At first, this frightened him: he wanted to melt into the croft and never be seen any more, not cut himself off from it again. But as the frozen woods—frozen to an intensity of gray he had never seen before—closed in behind him, he began to feel more daring. Instead of feeling eccentric and lonely, he began to feel eccentric and wild.

It had upset him, writing to Michael, that he had honestly not known whether he really would get drunk and break up the party, or whether that was the image he wished he could fill out, or whether that was a demon he was afraid and ashamed of in himself. Perhaps the day and night were not going to be what he expected. Well, he would not be the expected Simon—whoever that was—either. He would put aside all his masks and preconceptions. He would watch everything hard, and experience it all sharply, for its own sake, not for his, and perhaps his real self would come out of this watching. He had been getting too complicated, lately. He never knew which Simon was going to respond with what obscenity to innocent questions

like, "What side do you dress on, sir?" when he was getting
the trousers altered on his new suit, or, from Michael, "I
don't speak Gaelic. Do you?"

After driving for almost an hour, he followed the road
down into the Moy River valley. The woods got thicker and
richer: he saw a few bare oaks and beeches and a lot of
dark green rhododendron, the long leaves curled up and
stiff with frost. He thought he would stop here for breakfast, before the village, so he pulled off onto the road
shoulder, got out, and wandered down through the trees to
the river. It was running slowly, not frozen, but thickened
somehow with the cold, and the air above it was so stiff
with frost that the water had a tinny, far-away sound. It
was a salmon river and the toffs paid fantastic prices to the
Strathmoy Hotel for room and board and fishing rights.
The crofters and villagers did not use the big hotel, not
even for afternoon tea. As a gesture, Simon urinated into
the salmon river. Then he reminded himself that he was
going to be a tame Simon for that day, and he went back to
his stuffy car for tea and scones.

Then he drove on into Moy village. This was sport and
skiing country and there were more Tourist Homes and
Bed-and-Breakfast places than private houses; but the
Strathmoy Hotel was the biggest. It was hung with AA
signs and Diners' Club badges and RAC placards, and
there was a graveled parking lot at the front. The main
building was Victorian graystone, with a Scottish-style
stepped roof, but there were modern wings, and one two-
story addition was braced out over the river itself.

The village had been frozen, sleeping, but the hotel was
busy. Simon saw a litter of cars—mostly Land Rovers and
stationwagons—nosed in to the front of the hotel, like puppies nuzzling a big bitch. He did not want to join them, and
parked across the road. All the cars were caked with frost

so thick it looked like snow. People were trying to start them, throwing buckets of hot water on the windshields and iced-up door handles, revving up the cold engines, scraping off the ice. Clouds and swirls of steam went up into the gray frost-fog. There was a soft stuttering and roaring of engines and the exhaust fumes made another fog, chalk-white. The whole scene was misty and dim, and quiet, too, with the cold softening the engine noises, and the people moving like shadows.

Then Simon saw the dogs, and they were the strangest of all. He realized he had been waiting to see them, and now he felt strung up, excited, emotional, even, though he did not know why. The hounds were being led back and forth, stalking in and out through the frost-fog and steam, and when they went through the exhaust fumes they sneezed.

He opened the door, to see better, and sat waiting for Michael, and watching the hounds. He wondered why he felt this strung-up sadness; they did not mean anything to him yet. More and more of them were being led out of the hotel, lifting their legs and squirting hot, yellow urine against the porch posts. More steam came up from that, wreathing the entranceway. They came out in pairs and threes. They were not salukis; they were tall gray dogs with bristly fur and deep-set eyes and a medieval look about them. Their masters, sporty types in duffel coats and kilts— toffs, thought Simon ferociously, pseuds, fake, braying, middle-class Scots—but he caught himself and kept his mind pure—their masters were holding them, not on leads, but on ropes: rough ropes like ships' lines, slipped around their necks. Hounds and people dispersed into the fog and more came out of the hotel and the Land Rovers began to fill up with shapes, gray presences, watching and obviously waiting for something to get started.

He saw salukis, too, but they were not so dramatic as the taller dogs. They were muffled up in coats and looked like track grayhounds, but prettier, and they were very sad in the cold. Simon could see their big eyes looking hurt, and their long legs quivering, and their paws lifting and shivering because the road was too cold. Michael came out of the hotel with his two hounds on lead, looked around, saw Simon, waved, and came across the road with Phoebe and Rosiqa trotting alongside. He had on a black and red checked lumberjacket and looked very Northwoods and bright.

"Where is your axe," said Simon, "and your Douglas fir? You look out of work here."

"Don't be funny," said Michael. "I'm too nervous to be funny. I've got a lunch for you. Want to carry mine, too? My pockets aren't big enough and I've got the coursing collars and the first-aid kit and the flask. Want to come in my car? We always go in convoy in case of snow higher up. Oh, my God."

The last was a groan of pure nervous tension.

"A tea flask?" said Simon. "I have an empty one if the kitchen would fill it for me."

"No, no, whiskey. We always bring whiskey. It's good for the dogs. We'll get a big tea when we get back tonight. Here, take these."

Simon put the lunch bags in his chest pocket which zipped horizontally across the front. Full, the pocket looked like breasts, and made him think of Jenny, who was thin and flat except when she was nursing the babies. She would be feeding the new one now, perhaps. He saw her as a picture, more clearly than usual: her sharp face bent down, her breast small and white, with just an edge of purple-brown showing that the baby could not get into his mouth. The breast was surprisingly pretty and soft, because the rest of Jenny was thin and sharp, and she was not a fashionable woman. She had no taste in clothes, and wore scraggy, bright sweaters and skirts that were six inches too long. Her terrible clothes made her unusual, and Simon liked them.

Then he remembered that today he was an observer, alone, without connections, with no wife or family to think about.

Michael gave him a lead to hold, and they took the dogs to the edge of the parking lot, walking them back and forth on the frozen, crunching grass till first Phoebe and then Rosiqa sniffed and squatted and rose, leaving a steaming funnel in the frost, and shook themselves, while Michael watched them with a fond, abstracted face, like a racehorse trainer, or a proud father. Simon held Rosiqa's lead, and he suddenly remembered what she had done to his house.

"They don't seem so nervous, here, as they did when I saw them last," he said.

"No, they won't be nervous here," said Michael. "This is their business. I think she remembers you. Give her a little flattery. Tell her you love her, or something. She'll be all right."

On another day, Simon would have told Michael to stuff his flattery—he wasn't going to say I love you to a bloody stupid dog. But today he was trying to be different. "Rosiqa," he said. "You are beautiful."

The hound turned her narrow head and looked in his direction, wondering what and where he was. At first, she did not see him. Then suddenly, she focused on him with her big, long-sighted eyes; it was like being pinned in sight by a pair of binoculars and the physical impression of being *seen*, of being prey, in fact, was so strong that he shivered. Those were not dog's eyes at all. He knew what dogs' eyes were like; there had always been sheepdogs,

Border Collies, at Croichan, named either Tweedie or Bessie, until the last Tweedie had died of old age three years ago. Dogs' eyes were nearsighted and dim. These were eyes like a hunting hawk's. They were predator's eyes, but at the same time they were not fierce, but soft and rather witless. It was very odd. Simon wondered if all killers had that innocent look in their eyes. Rosiqa saw him; registered him; and did not object to him. They looked into each other's eyes and there was an uncanny moment between them, during which, his heart, like a rabbit's, literally beat faster, in an automatic reaction to those eyes. Then the dog switched off and looked somewhere else, and Simon got a distinct and infuriating impression of being dismissed. She could have wagged her tail at him, at least.

"Look at those deerhounds," said Michael. "I don't know why the hotel puts up with us."

Another gray monster was lifting his leg against the porch. There was long pool of urine now, steaming and trickling down in the road.

"If a beast like that wants to lift his leg, how are you supposed to stop him?" said Simon. "Karate?"

Michael went up to a white Triumph Estate station-wagon, lifted up the tailgate, and the salukis jumped in. Simon decided that Michael's scruffy look came from dogs, not poverty. The Triumph was not a poor man's car.

"Did you get the car fixed all right?" he asked.

"Oh, that," said Michael. "It was just a leak in the radiator."

They spent a few minutes starting the engine and scraping the ice off the windshield and asking the salukis if they were comfortable, though the back of the car was piled with rugs and creamy sheepskins and both dogs looked comfortable to the point of decadence. Now the milling and drifting of hounds and people through the steam was starting to have some direction. Something serious was about to begin. The deerhounds were tall, waist-high, and lanky; some were dark gray and brindled, and some were really massive, with longer, pale gray fur making curly manes and bristling eyebrows and mustaches. They took long steps, heads down, and their shapes passing in the fog reminded Simon of racehorses in the paddock before a race. Again he felt the excitement, the ritual getting-ready, as he had felt it getting himself dressed in the morning.

Dogs were lifted and encouraged to jump into cars. Doors slammed, the fumes began to clear; with some skidding and wheel-spinning, the cars got onto the road one by one, where they formed into line along the shoulder, chugging and waiting.

"We always go in convoy," said Michael, driving into place. "Then if the hill roads are blocked the Land Rovers can break through."

"Where do you go?" said Simon.

"Moy moor. The Laird has all the sheep cleared off for the week, and he lets us use his gamekeeper."

Michael said use his gamekeeper as if the keeper were an extra Land Rover or a shooting blind. Simon remembered that the great landowner who had Moy moor and village also owned Strath-Ard and all its crofts, and that Callum and Mary—and himself, perhaps, some day—were all his tenants; that the Keeper's Cottage above Croichan had once been lived in by one of his under-gamekeepers; that the Hill west of Croichan was a grouse moor, with shooting blinds, and parties of gentlemen, and sporting occasions, just as Moy Moor was. It amused and upset him to think that for one day he was going to walk with the gentlemen, and think like a crofter, and at the same time play no roles at all. He had said, "I'd like to be both, and still remain uncommitted." Possible? He would find out, starting now. The cars were all in line. The leader, a Land Rover with three deerhounds looking out the back, drove west out of the village and took a single-track road towards the hills.

In Michael's car, the salukis folded up in angles, like camels, put their chins on the back of the front seat, and sighed. Michael drove with both hands tight and high on the wheel. All three of them were so self-absorbed, so contained in their nervous tension, that they were untouchable, like holy men. Simon felt that they were going towards some kind of extreme experience, and he wondered what it would be. All he could see were a bunch of toffs going out to chase hares in a most inefficient way. A shotgun would do a better job, though you'd be breaking your teeth on the pellets afterwards, when you tried to eat the creatures. You could snare a rabbit. Could you snare a hare? Snare a hare? Snare a hare?

He grinned and then felt silly. He half-turned to Michael, putting his elbow on the back of the front seat. Rosiqa put her chin onto the elbow, graciously accepting it, and closed her eyes. "What *is* happening?" said Simon.

"Rosiqa is in the semi-finals," said Michael.

"And what do you get if she wins?"

"My God, what difference does that make," said Michael.

"Well, my God," said Simon, "what are you doing it all for, then?"

"I can't explain," said Michael. "Well, there's the running, maybe. It's very beautiful."

"Then why not just let them all lose on the Braid Hills in Edinburgh, and sit back and watch? Why all the formality if there's no reward?"

"Oh, there's a reward, if you win, but that's not the point. There's a stake, and the winner gets a lot of money, but that usually goes for drink. There are some silver challenge cups. Those are nice. The winning saluki takes the Moy Trophy and the winning deerhound gets the Moy Plate. It's an elimination—the winner of each pair goes on to the next. You know. Like the World Series—I think."

"They don't all run together in a pack, then," said Simon, delighting himself with a mental picture of all the hounds, deerhounds, salukis, fifty, sixty, in one tremendous Wagnerian charge across the heather, chasing ten thousand hares off the moor and into the Moray Firth. "I suppose that would be too much like Berserkers," he said.

"Well, it would be a dirty trick on the hares," said Michael. "The Anti-Blood-Sports people would never allow it. Christ, if I have to talk about it, I'll blow up for sure, and then she'll blow up, and then—look, couldn't you just watch for yourself and see what goes on. We'll be there soon." He went on, muttering, "It's a miracle she got this far, she's such a nut I could hardly get her into the slips at all and she had such a bad slip the first time because she was fighting, and went out backwards in fact, then she recovered and passed the other dog going uphill, you should have seen it—"

So Simon gave up and left him to his nerves and the salukis to their mysteries, and looked out of the window. To do this he had to take his elbow away from Rosiqa, who seemed to be satisfied with it; but he decided that he was going to stay sane, whatever, and he eased his arm free. She looked at him with sudden black eyes that made his heart beat faster again, withdrew and curled against Phoebe, who growled and then put her chin down on top of Rosiqa, so they lay twined together like cats, or snakes, in a shared suspended nervous waiting.

Now the sky was a clear, dark blue at the top and white at the horizon, with a copper-colored wash where the sun was going to rise. They drove past ponds, lochans, that were frozen, flat, glowing dull orange. The road was going up a rising terrace of flat moors, each one brown, without snow, each one a step higher. Ahead, on top of a hill, was a Forestry plantation, a sharp green-black in the morning light. The spaces were so wide that the first Land Rover looked too small.

"The Meet starts off past those trees," said Michael. "We always park at the shepherd's cottage and work our way across the moor and back, wherever Fraser takes us."

"Fraser. That would be the gamekeeper. The one the Laird lets you use."

"Mm, he's the head keeper on Moy Moor. He's indispensable to us. Always has been."

"You know," said Simon thoughtfully. "I am not very familiar with hares."

"They look like jackrabbits," said Michael.

"Thank you," said Simon. "I see one of those every day."

"I am losing my sanity," said Michael. "Sorry."

"I've killed one or two on the road," said Simon, "but they were rare and strange at Croichan. If you saw one bouncing away in the distance you had something to talk about. It was rabbits we killed for the pot. That was before the myxomatosis came. Then the rabbits died off and the hares hadn't the competition, you see, so they started to spread. But I had left Croichan by then."

"A rare hare," said Michael.

"Do you do that, too?" said Simon. "I was killing myself with snare hare a minute ago."

"Last year at the end of the Meet we had a spare hare," said Michael. "We auctioned it off. But you'll see hares today. You sure will see them."

They crossed a railway line. Past the railway crossing

gates the road was very rough, a private estate road more like a stream bed or a sheep track. The cars scattered rocks and pebbles; one rut was way below the other. As Michael's car hit the bumps and the rattling pebbles, the salukis, who had been draped quietly over each other, raised their heads—just their heads; and stretched their long necks, reaching to see past Michael. They did not sniff, as dogs would have done. Their ears went up in a fluff around their heads, and they stared hard into the distance. They knew where they were.

At the top of the ridge, a mile past the Forestry plantation, there was a cottage. As the cars arrived, they swung in and parked here and there around the steading. The cottage had a few stone buildings, sheep pens, and a peat stack. Simon was impressed. Croichan was on a country road; Croichan used coal and had not kept a peat stack as long as he could remember—never, perhaps. Croichan had neighbors. Even the Keeper's Cottage was part of Strath-Ard. Here there was no farmland, no garden, not even cabbages or a potato patch. It was higher and harder and more alone than any place in Strath-Ard. When he and Jenny had come to Croichan they had felt they had come a long way; the last part, over the Monadliath, had taken him past all limits, cut him off from things that had bothered him before. They had come over the dark and snow of that pass into the globe of stillness that Croichan had always been to him. He had felt safe. Now, seeing this sheep steading, he was shaken all over again. There was something further-out than Croichan and the Monadliath. There was another step.

Michal swung into place beside a white Cortina full of salukis, who all sat up and stared at them. Phoebe and Rosiqa stood up and began to pace around the back of the car. Michael was dithering so much now that he had to try twice before he could switch the ignition off. Simon thought he would leave Michael and his dog leads and salukis to sort themselves out while he went to have a look at the scene. He got out of the car. The sun was almost up and the sky was a bright, light blue. It was bitter cold, no wind, with snowdrifts on the north side of everything, each snowdrift reflecting blue. There was peat smoke coming out of the cottage chimney, and two black and white collies locked in the hen run, barking and snarling at the big strange hounds stalking by, and some hens keeping themselves out of the way behind the peat stack, but there was no sign of the shepherd or his family.

Simon breathed in the air, smelling snow, and looked around with all the power of his eyes. He saw earth colors: the gray-brown steading, and the mud, and the deerhounds, and Land Rovers; and most of the people, in their kilts and rough-weather clothes, were the somber colors of the hillside. Then there were spots of bright color: a few bright ski jackets, the salukis' blue and yellow coats, a man with yellow vinyl sailing trousers on, and one bright red Ferrari car. There was no room for a dog in it. Some toff, doubtless, come up to watch the sport, thought Simon. Michael came up and said, "Have you got the lunches?"

"Isn't it obvious," said Simon. "I look like a nursing mother."

"Christ, have I got the coursing collars? Look, would you take Phoebe for the day, you'll feel more at home if you have a dog, and she's out of it anyway, but Rosiqa's in the second brace and I'll have my hands full with her, she's such a madwoman."

"What did you do yesterday?" said Simon.

"With Phoebe? Oh, I just gave her to people. Melanie Stevens-James took her for a while but she has three deerhounds to cope with, after all. She'll help you if you get in trouble. Here, take Phoebe. If you can't hold her, fall on her. That's what we always do."

Simon was enchanted. "Fall on who?"

But Michael pushed Phoebe's lead into his hand and wandered away with Rosiqa.

The crowd began to collect around the young man with yellow trousers, who seemed to be a secretary or an organizer of some kind. He was standing with a long list unrolled like a proclamation in both hands, and three saluki leads wrapped around his arm. Simon wondered what would happen if a hare jumped up on the spot and the three shivering salukis exploded in all directions, which they looked ready to do. But no hare came and the man called out, in a London accent, "All right now, will you listen to me, please; *may* I have your attention, please. Fraser says that the hares will be sitting very tight this morning, so will you try to keep a close line, without any conversation, please. We don't want to walk over any hares and let them get up behind the line." He turned to an old man with a patient face, who stood next to him, leaning on a long stick. That would be Fraser; Simon thought he looked like Mary. He had a web-and-canvas game bag slung over his shoulder. His face was not ruddy, but tight and gray, as if he had spent his life outdoors, and the outdoors had given him trouble. He made no move or comment. The young man went on, "Right. Fraser says we'd better start off along the fence and work our way down past the railway line to the ruin. We'll stop for lunch there. Now. Could we have the first brace in slips, please? Salukis first; we'll run off the Losers' Stakes before we come to the finalists. Faisal and Esmail, Faisal in white. Could the first deerhound brace get ready, please? You'll be next: Cabal and Finn, Cabal in white. Then the saluki semi-finalists: Rosiqa and Sandpiper, Rosiqa in white."

"I can't find my white collar," called out Michael from the crowd. Simon could not see him.

"Red, then, if it's all right with Sandpiper. All right, Mrs. Baines?"

"Jolly good," came an extreme South of England voice that made Simon bristle. "But he's welcome to borrow my white if he likes."

"Okay, thanks," said Michael.

"Rosiqa in white, then. All move off, please; we haven't much daylight and there's a long list to run through today."

Simon saw a tall young man in a canvas anorak like his own. The man was holding some kind of harness and straps. Moving slowly, almost dreamily, two men brought two salukis up to him. They all bent briefly over the dogs, the young man straightened up and the owners stepped away carrying dog coats and leads and the two hounds were shining in a brace, each one held by a massive spring-collar and lead. One saluki was a foxy-red color, and the other was sandy, with a grayish cast, like desert rock. The red dog had a white, knitted collar above the slip-lead, and the sand-colored dog wore red. The young man held one trigger of the slip-leads in each hand. He walked forward, and the two hounds lowered their heads and stepped away in front of him.

He went off down the slope east of the cottage, towards the rising sun. Slowly, the other hounds and people formed a ragged line and followed him. It still seemed to move so slowly, as if Simon were seeing it through the glaze of a dream; like a church scene, or a hunting procession carved in stone. That much was clear—they were not just people now, they were hunters. They all left the road and walked down through the heather. Simon saw a thickset man in a red coat walking off at an angle from the line, toward the hill crest. The judge, perhaps. He saw a few loose dogs in the line, too; some whippets trotting free, a terrier, and a big yellow mongrel who moved in a series of hopping lunges forward. Simon looked again, and saw the dog had only one leg in front.

Simon was shivering after the long wait, and his feet were cold as wax. The heather was springy and crunchy but he had to lift his knees high at each step so as not to trip over it. The strain on his cold muscles was so exhausting that all he could do was struggle forward, watching the ground. Phoebe, head and tail down, followed him, her long legs shaking and spindly with the cold. Was she a madwoman, too? Was he going to have to fall on her, or was it Melanie Stevens-James he was going to have to fall on, and if so, why? Or was it, perhaps, an Americanism of some kind?

He was cold, and gasping for breath. He remembered Phoebe's fangs and her crocodile yawn; but, like Rosiqa, she did not mind being held by a stranger. She followed him, bland and golden, muffled in her blue coat, gently picking her way through the heather and jumping over the bog pools. He noticed her paws, sleeked and wet to the bone: she had strange bony knobby toes, long as hands, with big knuckles and arching claws. She did not notice him. He was a thing to her. Or perhaps she was the thing, the hunting machine. She moved like a precious object, aware of her professional worth, going to business. Or perhaps they were both things, and nothing except this hunt had direction and will.

They went dreaming in the line after the slipper-man and his two hounds, stumbling through heather roots and hummocks and chunks of ice and hollows full of bog water. Phoebe was clever-footed and sometimes she jumped, making Simon leap desperately for fear of being dragged down. He could not believe that her spindly legs could have much power, but she was light and fast. After a while he felt more at ease, sure that Phoebe was not going to bolt, or bite him, or wind the lead around his legs. He looked up, sweating and aching, needing a rest.

He saw the line of hunters moving in a slow, ragged line across the great brown heather slope to his left, the end figures tiny in the distance. On his right were only three walkers: a tall girl with three deerhounds and a short man with gray hair and spectacles, wearing a kilt, and wool stockings, and glengarry, the clothes all worn and hill-weathered. He had a camera, but no dog. At the end of the line was the gamekeeper, Fraser, looking straight ahead. He made Simon think of Mary, or a younger bodach 'ha radan. He walked at the far end, thinking about something else. He was of a different class, and the moor meant something else to him. Simon wanted to reach him, and knew it was impossible. If he could speak Gaelic, he might make contact. Fraser was watching a hawk overhead and Simon, watching too, suddenly became aware—as if he had never seen it before—of the enormous, opening sky.

Ahead of them all, the snow-spotted hill sloped down into a vast flat plain, with hills on either side. The plain was dotted with lochans, bright blue; and far away, through a cleft in the furthest circling hills, Simon could see another line of blue, the Moray Firth. He realized that he was going to walk all day across the flat moor, under that sky, in that slow, quiet line of hounds and hunters. Without warning, he was flooded with such excitement he almost sobbed out loud. He could hardly keep quiet. He wanted to yell and run and give himself to that great space; but how could he do it, with his legs tired and dragging through the heather, and his clothes under the waterproof shell already soaking with sweat. He looked at the hounds in the slip, and wondered if they were strong, and how far they could go.

He heard the bell-like bleating of a grouse in the quiet. The hounds in the slip walked ahead, sometimes in step, sometimes breaking rhythm as one trotted to keep up. They paced in the walk like camels. The slipper held the leads watchfully, like reins. Simon kept his eyes on them, wondering and stepped on a clump of sphagnum moss; it sank and he sank into a bog hole and ice water gurgled in over his boot tops. "Bloody hell," he said. He was bored, cold and tired. Just then the sun broke over a cloud at the horizon and light began to spread across the whole moor, unrolling from the east, brightening the great plain as far as the hills. Colors blazed out, the vivid pink and green of moss, and the heather began to glow from underneath with a polished green light. The wire fence on the horizon pinged with light. The lochans shone hot blue.

In the line, a woman screamed, "Hare up! Hare!"

Simon did not see the hare but the line of hounds went mad at the word *hare*, barking and howling, twisting against their leads, standing on their hind legs to see or leaping straight up into the air. A deerhound on his right was making a deep, foghorn moo, like a conch shell, and one saluki in the line was yelling in a high, singing scream. The hunters stood still. Phoebe pulled the lead tight and crouched, shivering, sighting. Then Simon saw one of the snow spots, running, moving. It was a hare, in its gray and white winter coat, running with its ears flat back, down the hill towards the plain. The slipper tried to swing both hounds to face it, but they were struggling with excitement, leaping and trying to break free in different directions. He reined them around as if they were a chariot team. Then they both saw the hare. Simon knew the split second when they fixed on it, sighting it together; he felt it; he knew when their eyes snapped into focus, as he had felt Rosiqa's on him. They saw the white, running spot. Their bodies began to arch against the slips' restraint, but the man did not let them go yet, and they started to run, dragging him.

The slipper gave the hare a head start and did not let the hounds go at first. He ran with them, holding them, faster and faster, his legs getting away from him, across heather and rocks, too fast now, and at last he snapped both hands downwards and the slip-collars flew back open, letting the hounds free. The young man planed down on his face in the snow with a great splashing of bog water. As the two salukis bolted out of their slips the line went quiet, watching, silent, dogs and hunters turning their heads to follow, tight as wires.

"Jolly good slip," said the girl next to Simon. She held her three deerhounds on ropes. Rough ropes seemed to be part of a deerhound mystique.

"Is he supposed to go arse over tip like that?" said Simon.

"Oh, he doesn't have to, but he's supposed to judge the hare, see that it's fit to run, give it a good start, and so on. But that was a jolly good slip. They both came out together."

They watched the three runners, all made in the same shape and moving in the same way, floating across the brown hillside, touching a point of pure speed that denied physical motion. The red and the fawn salukis were running in a pair, and the fringe on their ears and tails looked like fire. They poured down the slope toward the bottomland. The hare was galloping, bobbing up and down, well ahead. They began to close in. They came down onto the flat moor, into the tall heather, and the hounds began to leap over it, lunging at speed, their bodies arching and flattening in terrific strain. Then the hare turned and went up the hill to the right, and on the short dry heather, the red dog began to move past the fawn-colored one. Again Simon wanted to cry, or shout, or follow them. He knew; it was not mechanical superspeed of a sports car or a plane. It was the heartbreaking speed of flesh and blood. He had been gasping and plodding through the bogs and the tough, tangling heather. The hare, with the hounds right after it, disappeared over the hill ridge. The judge, in his red coat, ran laboring to the ridge and stood still at the top, field glasses up, turning, following what the line could no longer see.

Below, the Meet re-formed itself. The slipper shook the leads out straight. Two more dogs were led up to him, deerhounds this time—tall, dark, and scary. He fastened them into the slips. Simon was surprised and a little angry. Was that all? What was the end? He was unsatisfied; it wasn't finished.

"There's the judge," said the deerhound girl. Simon saw the red-coated man turn on the skyline, waving a white scarf. "Well, that was obvious, wasn't it," she said. "White passed red going uphill."

"But the hare," said Simon.

"Hare? Oh, it got away, I expect. I don't think they made a kill, we'd have heard it. Here, they're coming back now. Hope they can catch them. These salukis are so scatty. Never come to hand and interfere with the next course and so on."

Two hunters, the owners who had bought the first salukis to the slips, had left the line and were walking towards the hill crest. Against the mass of brown hillside they looked tiny, and their movements looked hopeless, overcome. The red and the sand-colored saluki came loping along the ridge, trotted halfway down and stopped, panting, uncertain. They made no move towards the hunters, who edged up tactfully, almost creeping towards them, and gently caught, and leashed, and blanketed them, and led them slowly towards the line. The Meet went forward again, moving along a double line of early morning shadows, long and crooked, hounds and hunters, and in front the slipper walked with the two deerhounds: their shadows were enormous. They went down the slope with the sun to their right.

"I thought that was the point," said Simon, walking next to the deerhound girl. "Killing hares."

She looked at him. "Are you one of those Anti-Blood-Sports spies?" she said.

"No," he said.

"That's all right, then. You're Michael's friend, I suppose. Michael said he was bringing somebody new. No, it's all done on points, so much for turning the hare, so much for passing the other hound, etc., etc., etc. Sometimes there's no kill. It doesn't matter. Sometimes the hound that makes the kill doesn't win the course. And so on. End of lecture for the day. Isn't that Phoebe? Pretty little thing. I had her yesterday."

"Are you Melanie Something-Something?" said Simon. "Michael was telling me about you. He said, 'if you can't hold Phoebe, fall on her.' It was you he meant, surely."

She liked that, and gave a crow of upper-class vulgarity. "Ow, did he. He meant Phoebe, most likely."

Simon thought perhaps that was just as well. The girl was as tall as he was and certainly broader. In her fur-lined anorak she looked like a giant Eskimo. She held two deerhound hawsers with her left hand and one in her right, and all four of them went with giant strides, like heroes of Scotland. Simon thought that if he did fall on her, he probably would not be able to bring her down.

They went through a stretch of burnt heather, where

the ground was ash-gray and the stems were bleached white, with sharp black tips, like antlers.

"Tear a hound's feet to pieces, this," said Melanie. She had a South of England accent, but instead of the middle-class BBC voice that Simon expected and loathed, she spoke with the uncouth twang of absolute aristocracy. At Croichan she would be the great enemy. But today he was not from Croichan or anywhere else. He was walking down a hillside, in peace, in the simmering sweet air.

Someone shouted, "Hare up!" and this time Simon did see the hare start up from a crouch almost at his own feet and scuttle, not forward, but back into the line and through, past all the hounds. Both deerhounds in the slips saw it, and the slipper braced back for a few seconds to give the hare a clear run, and then let them go. They came through the line together in huge gray leaps, and the Meet went berserk. Melanie's deerhounds began to charge and pull and she dug in her heels against their strength, left boot furrows in the mud and then sat down backwards, hard, splashing while the dogs whined and barked and tugged against her dragging dead weight. She fought them in silence. Simon laughed, then saw that Phobe was rearing backwards, straight up, like a horse, facing him, biting the lead and twisting, steadily, backing and backing and working the collar off over her head. One ear got free.

"For God's sake," screamed Melanie, "don't let her go."

Simon played the frantic hound as if she were a fish, trying to say quiet things, but she backed and reared until, with a stab of terror for his own skin, he threw himself towards her like a rugger tackle and fell on her. He was sure she would snarl and snap at him, but she only cried, and shivered, and heaved underneath him with a fantastic nervous strength, watching the running deerhounds from under his chest, with her two big eyes.

In a few seconds, the hare was fifty yards past and the line of hounds gave up and relaxed, and half the hunters got up out of the snow and bog, their waterproofs pouring off wet.

"I thought she would bite me," said Simon.

"Why?" said Melanie.

He knew, of course; the hound was a thing and he was a thing, and they were only real in relation to the hunt, so why should there be any personal squabbling between them? They watched the coursing. Simon did not like it. The deerhounds did not flicker with speed like the salukis, running: they arched and lolloped with big, slow jumps after the little struggling hare. The salukis and the hare had been more evenly matched. The deerhounds were too big. Soon they were loping almost on top of the hare and it dodged at a right-angle between them. They were clumsy and it left them behind, but with their power and long strides, they caught up in a few yards. It dodged again, sharper, and again, and each time, its run was shorter. It began to dither from hound to hound. Simon had a moment of sudden, awful horror. The white-collared dog bent its head with a delicate, precise motion and picked up the hare, whose four legs kept on running in empty space. The other hound snatched and grabbed it and they bit and tore the hare between them. The hare screamed. It was a sad, hoarse, cawing cry. To Simon, the cry sounded like his own baby. The judge and the slipper and a few hunters came running, and pushed the hounds away.

"Damn, the hare's spoiled," said Melanie.

"I thought it didn't matter," said Simon.

Again, she looked at him suspiciously. "I have three dogs to feed," she said. "We use them. Don't you know? We always use them. We have to use them. If I didn't feed the hounds I'd cook it up for myself. Jugged hare's jolly nice except you've got to go to the trouble of the wine and all. It's a bit rich for the dogs anyhow. Gives them the shits."

The judge waved a red flag, though it had been the white-collared hound that had touched the hare first. He held up a few bits of hare that looked like knotty string. Fraser came up with his gamebag, lifted the knotted bits on the end of his long stick, and shook his head. The judge dropped the torn pieces into the heather, and the slipper re-coiled his leads for the next brace, and the Meet went on. Simon knew that a part of himself went into the hounds running, but that in the past few minutes he had not been the deerhounds, killing, but had been part of the hare, being trapped and killed. He found himself sweating with claustrophobia and death.

"I think they're grotty, your deerhounds," he said to Melanie. "Hares are too small for them. It's not fair."

The two hare-killers came galloping back, splashing through a bog pool, and he did not like them. They were strange, blackish things, demonic, angular. They reminded him of the blackish, crumbling hills above Croichan. As they cantered above their own reflections at the edge of the bog pool he thought they would do well as Celtic demons of some kind: the Water Horse, or some hill god that comes up out of a wet place, talks in pictures, and bargains for your soul.

"You can't let them chase deer, clot," she said. "There's been such a stink about stag hunting on Exmoor, and now there are hunt saboteurs all over, don't I know. Daddy's MFH at home, and what about all the Anti-Blood-Sport stuff on the telly and in the Sunday papers. Even the coursing people will have to go underground if this Anti bill goes through. Why don't they make a law against fly fishing if they're so sensitive, that's what I say. Michael told me about you," she said with good humor. "He said I was to watch out for you. You're not to insult my dogs. I'll punch you if you do."

There was nothing skittish about her. Or her three dogs. One was standing, lanky, with a lanky shadow, and the other two were sitting, long and observant, like vultures. Simon decided that there were enough deerhounds on Moy moor that day to supply all of medieval Scotland; and if such a time and place had ever really existed, with kings and swords and kilts and noble hounds, which he did not believe for one minute, then it was welcome to guardians like these.

Now Michael brought Rosiqa to the slipper. There was a tall black and tan saluki already in the slips, standing quietly, but Rosiqa began to struggle and back away. Michael whispered to her, and the slipper said cheerful things, and they both laid hands on her like seducers and begged and persuaded her to do it, but she twisted and braced her feet and tried to break away. She was gray, like a spider web, and looked like a pen-and-ink sketch of a dog. She looked too fragile to run on velvet, much less over bog and rock; but Phoebe was no thicker, and Simon had already felt her tough muscles fight back. He knew that the silver-lace look was a trick. He wanted to see the salukis run again.

"Why does she struggle?" he asked Melanie. "Doesn't she want to go?"

"Nerves," said Melanie. "She doesn't want to do anything else. Salukis are all lunatics."

At last Rosiqa agreed to go into the slips, and she walked forward with the other dog; but she jittered, and twisted, and looked behind her for Michael, who walked alongside, talking quietly to her. The line turned in a great sweep and went pacing eastward, into the sun, slowly.

Fraser must be guiding them somehow, he must know where the hares would be lying when the sun was strong in the east, the wind was almost calm from the west, and there were snow patches in each hollow. But he had not spoken yet, or made any move except to lift and dismiss the ripped-up hare with the end of his long stick. He only walked, and carried his stick, not looking at the gentleman, watching something remote in the distance.

They were crossing a stretch of dry, crumbly heather. Here there was no snow or bog, and the heather was short and bouncy to walk on. It was a relief, like stepping out of deep water. There were piles of crumbly rock, and beaten-out hollows full of dry grouse droppings. The sun gave a little warmth now, thin and pale, like melted butter.

As Simon brought his feet crackling through the dry heather, enjoying it, he saw one small, round snowdrift below a tuft of moor grass, and he went out of his path to step on it, for the pleasure of leaving a footprint. As he lifted his boot he saw it was a hare. Its paws were tucked in, its ears set back, and its nose working up and down, but it crouched, round and still, and did not move. He did not know what to do. If he had seen a hare jump up running he would have yelled, "Hare! Hare!" as the hunters were supposed to do; but he could not yell anything if the jolt of excitement was not there.

He squatted down to look closer, and the hare sat like a snow statue. Phoebe did not notice it, perhaps because it kept still, and she squatted down too on her frog haunches, waiting for Simon, and yawned. The smell of sun and fresh air and dry grass, and the sweet catlike smell of the hare's fur, rose around them and Simon yawned, too, feeling sleepy and safe. He could have crouched all day, enclosed in the hillside, like the hare, and let the Meet go off without him.

Melanie and the three deerhounds crunched towards them through the heather and stood over them, looking down. Phoebe growled at the deerhounds. Simon felt like growling at the tall hunter girl.

"What have you got there?" she asked.

She would see it for herself anyhow, so he said, "There's a hare sitting here. I don't know what to do."

"Oh, so there is. Hello, son. Uppies outies." She put her boot toe under the hare's bottom and gently levered it up and prodded it into the cold air. It spread its ears up in a black-tipped V and hopped innocently down towards the line. "That's what you do," she explained. "If it's not a good one he'll let it pass by. It looks fit enough, though. *Hare up.*"

The hare looked around and saw the fifty hounds foaming and yelling at it, and the hunters fighting their dogs in silence, and the slipper with the two salukis diving and plunging around him, and sensibly enough bolted away. It went across the hillside at an angle away from the line, with a long head start, towards the fence.

The slipper started to run with the confused two on the leads, trying to sight them at the hare. Rosiqa braced back and struggled wildly in all directions, first to see the hare, then to get away from the terrifying running man, then to get away from the strange dog at her side, then to find the hare again. At last, she did see the hare and pulled straight forward, and the slipper, in disgust, used that one straight pull to snap the leads down and let the slip-collars go. The jerk on her neck scared her again, and she stopped and swerved and leaped to the side, and finally broke out of the slips ten yards behind the bigger dog. Simon saw Michael standing, watching, almost relaxed, at the spot where the slipper had started his run. The slipper came back, recoiling the leads, shaking his head; Simon could tell he was apologizing, saying sorry, it was a bad slip, and Michael was saying, it's all right, you did your best, a few more Meets and she'll learn how to behave.

This time they went running in a line: the white hare first, then the black and tan dog, then Rosiqa, back in stride and running like a speeded-up old-fashioned film, gray and black, comically fast, so fast the brown hill seemed to stop and flow backwards.

Melanie giggled. "Isn't she super," she said.

"It's too much," said Simon. "I can't bear it. It's too beautiful. I can't look any more."

He would not have spoken to Jenny like that. He went down on his knees and took hold of a deerhound for support. It was watching Rosiqa and did not notice him.

The hare wriggled through the wire fence and darted off towards the sun on the other side. The tall black hound refused the fence, sliding sitting back like a rodeo horse, then stopped and whined and circled, afraid of the wire, until Rosiqa, galloping up behind, took off and jumped: she left the ground without judgment, on springs, yards too far back, and sailed over like a gray fly, absurdly, magnificently too far back and too high over and too far past on the other side. The line of hunters, shading their eyes, saw her flick across the morning sunshine and laughed out loud, in relief and delight—it was extravagant, a moment of pure physical freedom and joy. She seemed to land without any jolt, in full stride, and ran on even faster, closing up on the hare. The black hound dived into the wire and scrambled through below: twang, twang, twang, and he was on the other side and running again, but last.

"He's got more sense," said Melanie. "Only the top strand has got barbs."

A quarter mile past the fence was the dark brown line of a drainage ditch. The hare disappeared down into it and popped up running on the other side. Rosiqa took off and jumped again, misjudged, and hit the far edge. She was going so fast that she pinwheeled over, gray back, silver paws, and tail, and then she rolled side over side into the ditch. The black dog jumped, tripped in the heather on the far side and somersaulted, too, but recovered and ran on after the tiring hare. When the second dog fell Simon stood up, beginning to feel sick. Twenty yards past the ditch, the black hound snapped at the hare and caught: in the shock of the sudden stop both animals swung in a circle and rolled over and then the hound was up, tail wagging, crunching, and the hare was killed. It might have screamed briefly, but nobody heard it, because Rosiqa came scrambling up out of the ditch, crying louder than a dozen hares; but clearly, without the hoarse, braying sound a hare would have made.

"They are babies, these salukis," said Melanie. "They yell if you even look at them the wrong way. Last year one cried and complained and said it was lame, and do you know, Mr. Grandison carried the thing all the way home on his shoulders, six miles the shortest way, and when he put it down at the cottage, away it went, as sound as could be."

But Rosiqa made no move to start back. The black hound was nosing the hare about in the heather, found it boring now, and came loping back towards the line; but Rosiqa held up one front paw and howled on a long, rising, tearing note. Simon was sickened but not surprised to see part of the leg swinging loose.

"No, she means it," he said.

Michael, the judge, the secretary in yellow trousers, and three or four other people—one man with a veterinarian's bag—ran to the fence, tied their dogs to the wire and climbed over and went cautiously towards her, but it was a long way. The day went hard and still as glass. Nobody could move. It was a baying noise, not like a dog's voice or any animal voice. It was more like an electronic sound, something on a twelve-tone electronic scale that splits and tears soft things apart. It had the shrill, stretched-out essence of all terror and pain. Simon felt himself shaking, with real tears running down his face, and they were tears of pure physical sympathy. He looked around and saw that the other hunters, people he did not know and would dislike if he did, had that same heart-stopped look, the same tears. He wanted to kill the dog. He wished he could be closer, to kill her and stop the shattering noise. There was a small dark crowd around Rosiqa now, but the howling still did not stop.

Fraser had not moved. Now he went slowly towards the fence, got over the wire, went past the crowd and came back, carrying the hare. He held all four paws in one hand, so that its back bowed and its head swung down. He did not look at the crowd or the screaming dog. The hare's head and ears swung in a half-circle, back and forth, back and forth. Fraser stopped, felt for the game bag, slung it around to the front and put the hare inside. Then he climbed back over the fence and went towards the line again. He did not seem to be touched by the terrible noise.

The black and tan saluki came wandering up to the line, like a loose horse on a battlefield, and the salukis tied to the wire got upset as he squirmed through and they began circling and whining and knotting themselves into their leads. Simon, desperate to move somehow and break the frozen glass of sound, took Phoebe and went down to them and untied them. They accepted him, as he knew by now they would. The howling stopped, and the silence caught at his breath. He heard the caw of a crow, a small tinny noise, far away unseen on some other hill.

Hounds began to get restless, getting up and sitting

down in the line, eager to move on to more hares. Hunters began to breathe deeply and stamp their feet in the frost and talk. Now they could talk.

A man in a kilt—not the short gray-haired man with spectacles—loosened his deerhound's neckrope and said to Simon! "Damned hard luck—one of those freak accidents; haven't had a thing like this happen in fifteen years. Only had one like it in fact in the whole history of the Meet."

And another man, with two salukis, said, "It was the same thing; I remember a deerhound went into another ditch too fast and hit the far side and just snapped the foreleg. Just snapped it. It was the same sort of thing, exactly. Isn't that right, Mrs. Baines. You were there, weren't you."

And the Englishwoman said, "Quite. Exactly the same. Snapped the foreleg. It's just one of the risks you have to take, you know. A coursing hound could break a leg playing in the garden at home. It's just one of the risks, isn't it, Mr. Grandison."

And a tall old man with a white mustache, wearing a kilt, said, "Quite right. Just one of the risks."

And they all went on quickly in that kind of chorus, all turning to Simon and speaking to him, as if he were blaming them, but he was not. Then they began to say to each other, "Shocking. Shocking. Rotten bad luck. The first time in fifteen years." But Simon found that he could hardly hear them. He was listening to the stopped screaming, and shaking again—now with the sense of sudden crash, of tension unreleased, of speed cut off in midair. It was not finished, not finished, and he felt himself part of that fall. It was a sense of terrible frustration, in one way worse than being killed with the hare.

Michael and the rest began to come back from the ditch, slowly, not together. Their shadows came first. The sun was behind them. Michael was carrying the hound awkwardly, flat in both arms. Her front leg stuck out in a stiff temporary splint, and her muzzle was taped shut. The secretary stepped the fence wire down for Michael to get over but she began to struggle in a horrible sleepy way.

"I can't hold her," said Michael. "Give me some advice, Mr. Hutchinson." His voice was so clear, so calm and practical, that Simon was surprised, and full of respect. Perhaps Michael was not the comedy act he had thought he was at first.

The vet called out, "Fall back and lie still with her. I'll give her a shot."

Michael let himself down backwards on the far side of the fence, first sitting, they lying carefully on his back in the cold heather with Rosiqa clasped flat on his chest. Their shadow disappeared. The vet injected the sedative and Michael lay flat for a long time while the cold morning closed around the Meet.

The hunters were beginning to say, "No reason to stop the coursing." "None at all." "Better to carry on before we all lose our nerve," and the hounds in the line shifted and whimpered with cold. Then Rosiqa collapsed, her head thumping down. Two men lifted her off Michael and put her on a stretcher made of three anoraks, and Michael took off his lumberjacket and covered her, and they went on towards the line.

The secretary came up to Simon and took the three salukis, saying, "Those are mine, thanks," and, "it's a compound fracture, you know, the bone was sticking right out."

Simon followed him back to the group around Rosiqa. There was a quick, practical discussion:

"I'd better stay with the coursing," said the vet. "In case I'm needed again, God forbid."

Mr. Grandison said, "There's a good vet in Inverness. Can we get her there?"

The other kilted man, with one deerhound, said, "I'll walk back and bring the Land Rover across the hill. We'll get her to the cottage and then I'll come along with Michael in his own car and give him a hand."

"Right."

"Right."

"Thanks."

"Jolly good, then. Edward, take Cabal for me, would you, he's got to run again this afternoon."

"Right." Edward, who was the secretary, went off trailing three salukis and a deerhound, saying calmly, "Can we have the next brace in slips, please? Deerhounds. Anne of Perth and Fingal, Anne in white."

"Wait till we get past the fence, Edward," called out Mrs. Baines nervously. "I won't have them running towards the fence." As if the fence had hurt Rosiqa. But it helped, as if it were a real precaution; there was one stillness, and then the whole scene came back into focus, and the two deerhounds were brought up and collared and put into the slips, and the slipper stepped forward, north, parallel to the fence, and everything went on as before.

Leaving Michael, the kilted man was already walking back alone to get the Land Rover. The shepherd's cottage and steading and even the trees around it were out of sight and Simon was frightened for him. He looked too small for the vast distance. The ridges and swells of moor were shifty and impossible to understand. At Croichan, the Hill, the moor, was a place the crofters did not go. In summer, in the few calm days, they had all gone walking west from Croichan, once or twice in Simon's childhood, sedately as far as the Loch Avoch burn and bridge; and then about face, half-afraid, and home. Only Callum, who had cut peats past

Loch Avoch when he was young, ever went west to the Hill by himself.

Michael was sitting cross-legged in the heather, by the wrapped-up, unconscious dog. Phoebe did not notice Rosiqa on the ground. She swung her tail briefly for Michael, and then looked towards the Meet, which was moving and dreaming off into the distance, and pulled to follow it.

"Do you want me to come with you?" asked Simon.

"Oh. Thanks. No," said Michael, a bit slow, in shock, but still cool, as if the worst, happening, had somehow made him feel better. "No, you don't have to miss the fun. She's out cold now and John will be there to help anyway. You take Phoebe. You can let her run a 'friendly' if there's time."

"I hate to just leave you sitting here," said Simon.

"It happens," said Michael. "It's part of the whole thing. Look, you'd better not let the line get out of sight. You don't know Moy and you could get lost."

Simon looked around. The Land Rover man was out of sight. Distances were immense and tricky on the hill; the line already looked small and far away. Phoebe circled him on the lead and gave a singing, whimpering complaint, like syllables.

"See you back at the hotel," said Michael. "I'll save you a seat by the fire. Or you save me some tea if you get back first. Have a good time."

So Simon and Phoebe walked on alone. They went only a small part of the way and Simon looked back and saw that Michael, now, was a tiny shape, sitting by the flat, still shape of the dog; the brown hill swelled in a ridge between them as if it were diminishing him on purpose. The Land Rover showed up over the furthest hill to the south, bumping over no road down the slope. It had a square shadow, like a box. It was a ridiculous, Victorian scene, thought Simon: the faithful horse lying, back broken, in the ditch, a sacrifice to the blood lust of the ruling classes. What now? The merciful pistol to the noble head?

Ahead of him he saw the Meet, still small, still—for that one moment more—something apart from himself. He was joining them now. Another white hare got up and two deerhounds went running.

They walked all morning. By noon, they were down in the flat bottomland, where the lochans were. There the heather was waist-high and grew standing in peat bogs where there was no solid footing at all. They had to jump and splash from one tuft of rushes to another, and the coursing hounds struggled and forced their way through the tall heather and came back sleek and wet as seals. After coursing, they steamed in the cold dry air. Simon saw poison-green fingers of staghorn moss edging the pools, looking as if they were trying to crawl out. Six hares were killed, and Fraser's gamebag was almost full, a puzzle of white and gray and smoky tan fur, with paws sticking out through the netting, and eyes crushed against the web.

Simon was almost too tired to walk. He had never been so worn out and weak and hungry in his life. The few weeks of farm work and tattie-lifting at Croichan had made him fitter than most students, and he had strong muscles to begin with; but for the first time he found himself at an absolute exhausted full stop. He couldn't lift his legs. He was damp all over with sweat and had taken his anorak off long ago.

Melanie drifted up to him in the line and said, "The hotel gave us porridge, juice, bacon, eggs, sausages, grilled tomatoes, toast, rolls, marmalade, and coffee this morning, and oh, yes, there were oatcakes, too, and I had some of everything and now I'm starving again. You need it, don't you?"

They were walking towards an old steading with ruined walls and a broken-down building, on the shore of the biggest lochan. Simon had seen the ruin all morning, from above, far away, and now with the hill-tricks of distance they were suddenly in front of it and it was full-size. There was a rotten rowboat heeled over at the water's edge. Close up, the lochan was the same vivid winter blue. The sun had been warm, rising, but now at midday, it was still low in the southern half of the sky and seemed cold and thin.

The Meet came up to the steading, and the hunters began to tie up their dogs and find sheltered spots to settle down in and have lunch. They took off their packs and got out lunch and spread out coats and waterproofs. Simon climbed the rubbly stone wall into what had once been the steading yard and at the top his knees trembled, and when he jumped into the yard with Phoebe behind him it was a long fall, suddenly dark, on the other side. But he didn't faint after all, and he found a smooth grassy place in the shelter of the wall and sat down with his back to the stones and just sat. He was too tired to unzip his lunch pockets.

Turf instead of heather grew inside the walls. The grass was dried white and curly and the walls caught the sun. The cottage itself was stripped and fallen in, the door frame was gone, and the roof joists showed like bones. It had been a small croft, a two-room butt-and-ben, with a few sheds and a sheep pen. The family had used the boat to get fish from the lochan. Where had the arable land been? He saw a stand of bracken up the hillside to the west, past a railway line. It had been there.

Suddenly, in his exhaustion, he could no longer control his thoughts, and he told himself, in five or ten years, Croichan is going to look like this.

It was not a free day for him after all; no day was.

Croichan was just under the surface. But not like that: to him, Croichan had always been the only place that was alive. Not once, never in all the time he had been away, living outside, living uncertainly, had he ever thought that Croichan could be a ruined steading, with bleached stone walls and fallen plaster and dry dead grass. Why did he see it dying now? Where had that picture come from? And now that Croichan's death was with him, he could not question it, or rub it away.

He felt like the hare, picked up and running in empty space.

Phoebe lay down next to him, stiffly, to show that the ground was too cold. Melanie, broad-faced and bland, came up with her three Celtic demons. There was a broken post next to Simon and she hitched all three hounds up to it with an expert slipknot on the tieropes. Any one hound could have uprooted the post immediately but they crouched or sat down around it in their blackish, brooding way.

"Oh, bugger off," Simon said to her in despair. Phoebe curled up at his feet and put her nose under her tail and looked sour.

"But you're not taking care of Phoebe," she said, and took out a silver hip flask and unscrewed the top. "You can have some, too," she said, "but wait just a minute till the dogs get theirs." She took a small jar of milk out of her pocket and mixed milk and whiskey half-and-half in the flask top, and tipped some down each deerhound's throat in turn. The hounds sat blinking.

"Michael always gives Phoebe a shot, too," she said. "Shall I?" She poured some into Phoebe, who stood up and shook herself and sat down again more comfortably, looking bright, and bird-brained, and gratified. "Poor little girl," said Melanie. "She was coldies, wasn't she. We always see to the dogs first," she explained. "That's part of it."

He wondered if she were to going to mix milk and whiskey and pour a topful into him too, but she gave him the topful straight, and let him drink it himself, and then sat down and took one for herself. It was the best and most expensive whiskey, a rich, single-malt with the taste of peat in it. It stunned Simon and then made him hungry, and he weakly unzipped his breast pocket and took out two lunch bags.

"Christ," he said. "I've got Michael's."

"Oh, good," she said. "We can give it to the dogs."

"We will like hell," he said. "I'm going to eat them both myself."

"I bet you won't. The hotel really does us proud with the box lunches."

In the clear air, and the monotony of coursing, Simon had almost forgotten Rosiqa. "But what about Michael?"

"He'll get something at Inverness. I shouldn't think he'd want to eat much, though."

Simon was surprised that he, or any of them, wanted to eat; but he looked inside his lunch bag and found roast beef sandwiches, cheese sandwiches, pork pies, hard-boiled eggs, tomatoes, apples, and fruitcake, well-wrapped in polythene.

"Nothing to drink," he said.

"Coffee or tea's too bulky to carry on the hill," she said. "We get a super big tea back at the hotel at four-thirty. You're proper dehydrated by then. I always leave a flask of coffee in the car and if I'm really dying when I get there I have it with whiskey. But it's better to torture yourself and wait. Then the tea's really heaven when you get it at last. You can't imagine."

"I've never been so thirsty," said Simon. "I've been sweating all day."

Whiskey flasks were coming out all around the steading. Dogs' and hunters' heads tipped back, swallowing.

Simon and Melanie ate the lunches and the hounds sat by with their unearthly composure, accepting what was left: the pork pies, which were too salty to eat without water, and all the breadcrusts, and some fruitcake, and the hard-boiled eggs, which were too cold, somehow. Melanie, sitting down, had to reach way up to feed the tall deerhounds. She gave them the eggs whole, shells and all. They took them at first gently, exquisitely, between their front fangs, as they had lifted the running hare: then snap, crunch, gulp, swallowing them whole. Phoebe refused the shells.

"Extra calcium," said Melanie. "Don't be so picky."

But the saluki would only eat the yolks, and Simon had to break them up for her. Simon and Melanie sucked the tomatoes for the juice and sat back against the stone wall, and Phoebe leaned against him, and Melanie and the three deerhounds leaned against each other, and they all sat quietly, breathing in the cold sunshine. Simon tucked his hands under Phoebe's coat and hugged her to keep his fingers warm, and her body was hard and sleek, like warm wood.

The group of hunters next to them was talking about apples.

"This apple is disappointing," said a white-haired man in a deerstalker tweed cap and a sheepskin coat. "It's wooly, you know. Soft. These imported apples always are soft."

"I'd rather a Cox," said Mr. Grandison, who was sitting on a stone with his knees spread wide apart and the kilt draped in a curve between them. Simon wondered why kilties always did sit in these exposed, masculine positions, as if they didn't care what happened to their balls. If he were ever corrupt enough to put a kilt on, in some other country, in some other life, he'd damn well keep his legs together. "Give me a nice Cox's Orange Pippin any day," said Mr. Grandison. "A good crisp English apple."

In the center of the steading yard, the slipper and the judge and Edward were passing a whiskey flask and talking about hounds. Edward had one of his salukis on his lap; it was gray, like Rosiqa, but bigger, and his other two, at his feet, were black and white. The gray saluki had its head resting on his shoulder and he was bringing his flask top neatly up past its ears. He clasped the hound exactly as Michael had that first day in Edinburgh, and, seeing him, Simon suddenly missed Michael very much, and felt sad about him, and wondered what was happening to him.

"Really, James," said the judge to the slipper. "You can't raise a deerhound puppy for less than twenty pounds."

"No," said the slipper. "But I can't sell them for more than that. There isn't the demand, you know. I had to sell one of my cars last spring to pay for the last lot. Do you know, I had thirty deerhounds running around at one point. Father said he wouldn't put me through vet school and support thirty deerhounds at the same time. Can't blame him, after all."

The three-legged mongrel and a bristly, brown terrier began to sniff and lift their legs against the cottage wall. A man in tweed plus-fours waved a long stick at them and called them back.

Fraser sat inside the cottage, by himself. Simon could see him through the empty window frame. He was sitting in its square of sun.

The sunlit, cold, brown hills were all around them. The grass was warm. On the hill to the west, across the railway line, a few sheep wandered and baaed, and again, in the quiet, came the rattling call of a grouse. Simon's mood changed. This was one of the sweetest moments he would ever have. Time had stopped. They had all passed a morning of escape and strange peace. They had been the archetypes: hounds running, band of hunters following. It had been thoughtless, anonymous, like dancing or sex or prayer. They had killed hares. Now they were resting in the sun, taking care of the hounds, and time was at an absolute still point.

Sharing food with the dogs was best of all, because in their game, their dream hunt, the hounds had caught meat for them, and fed them in another way, too: with their speed. The hounds had given them the hillside and all the great space that the hunters were too weak to take. In a way, even Rosiqa's disaster had been part of the dream game, too. That was why Michael had been so calm.

They all half-slept and woke up cold and stiff. The sun was in the west, and there was a sudden feeling of hurry. They had to course their way around the lochan and back before night came. The Meet gathered again and began to move off; hounds shook themselves and yawned out loud and waved their tails.

"Could we have the saluki finalists in the slips, please," called Edward. "Hamadi and Sandpiper. Who wants white this time? Hamadi is me, and we all had white before. Hamadi again? All right, Mrs. Baines. Deerhound finalists, you're next; would you get ready, please—"

Not many hares sat in the deep bog next to the lochan and they walked a long time without a course. The hounds got tired and let the slip-leads fall slack. Fraser walked, slashing heather with his stick, to the right, to the left, looking for hares, swinging the stick without anger. At last a hare stood up and the salukis went after it through standing water that glittered in the sun; the line and the course were walking toward the light and all they could see were moving splashes, three flying, shining clouds of spray, one small, two bigger, two catching up, and then the water broken and twisting up into bits of light, and the hare dodged and the salukis danced around with it. They churned up a real rainbow, blue, purple and green, which dissolved as they grabbed the hare and killed it. It screamed for a long time, drowning—Simon heard a hawk, an oboe, a baby, lots of things, and finally, in the end, a hoodie-crow.

All the spray and mud sank down and the salukis were standing there, black and spidery against the sun, their ears and tail fringes dripping, looking for the hare. It was under water. The judge held up a white scarf, for Edward's dog, and the salukis walked splashing back.

After that they started home, and ran what they called "friendlies." The winning deerhound raced the winning saluki, who won, and two deerhound puppies were allowed to have a try, and then the three-legged mongrel was matched against the white whippet. The whippet floundered in the bog, but the three-legged dog ran demonically on its one front paw and followed the hare across the railway line and up the sunny hillside among the sheep. The sheep baaed and scattered but the dog turned and came obediently back. And all the time the line went on up the long hill with the sun in their eyes.

Even Melanie, big as she was, got tired and began to yank the towropes and swear at her dogs.

"Switch?" said Simon and took the three deerhounds, giving her Phoebe. His calf muscles felt like warm water and he hoped the deerhounds would pull him up the hill. Holding the three long, tall beasts on their coarse ropes gave him a mad sense of power and he wanted to yell and crack a whip and drive them on like a war chariot. He reined them back and kept beside her.

Now they had climbed high enough to see the country spread below them in all directions but south, where the moor still went up towards the shepherd's cottage. They could see the Moray Firth again, but the sun had left it and it was gray. West, they could see part of the Black Isle and the pointed hills of the West Highlands behind it, turning pink. "Look over there," Simon told Melanie. "The Ard River runs between those first hills and the Black Isle. Strath-Ard is fifteen miles southeast of that. I live there."

"That's nice," she said. "What do you do for a living? Write?"

"Och, no," he said. "I run the croft. We're tenants of the Laird. He owns Moy as well. We have sixty ewes and half a dozen beasts. And the bull."

"You're not a farmer," she said.

"Aye, I am," he said. "Why not?"

"You're one of Michael's friends," she said. "I thought you were one of those arty types, or something."

He smiled. "I'm a crofter," he said.

"You aren't," she said, upper-class, positive. "Unless you're the kind I saw on the telly. There were three young families who got rights to a fantastic old crofting village on Lewis, or somewhere, you know; they were all teachers or craftsmen and they were going to raise food with their own hands and restore the crofting economy and make things to sell to the tourists. They were gorgeous, all beards and broad shoulders. You must be that kind."

"That's flattering, but no, I'm a real crofter," he said, stubbornly. "My home is in Strath-Ard."

"Balls," she said. That shook Simon. He didn't go on with it, because they had to separate and cross an oozing, bright green river of moss and mud that had cut a sharp bank through the peat hillside. Then a big white bird rose from the lochan, way below, by the steading, and began to fly across the moor toward the railway line. It flew below them, slow, slow wingbeats, as if it were a very big bird, and the hunters wondered what kind it was.

"I didn't notice it when we were eating lunch," said Mrs. Baines. "Edward, did you?"

"Is it a swan?"

"Not enough neck," said Melanie. "We've got swans at home and they often fly, you know."

"James, have you got your field glasses?"

"I gave them to the judge."

"He's gone over the hill."

"It's a heron."

"Herons are gray," said Melanie.

"How about the Great Black-Backed Gull?"

The bird flew so slowly and pleasantly that just watching it made the hunters feel the afternoon was very sweet, and warmer than it really was. But frost had come into the northside hollows where the sun had drawn away. The bird flapped slowly on across the sheep hill, out of sight, and the hunters tried to walk on, so tired.

The last course of the day was a violent one. A hare got up between the slipper, who was holding two deerhounds, and the line. With the sun in its eyes, the hare went wild and whipped around and darted straight into the line. The slipper, so tired, let the hounds go by mistake and they piled in after it among the hysterical leashed dogs. About ten hounds tore free and followed the hare. For a few seconds the hare dodged through the line like the ball carrier in a football mob, and then struck Mr. Grandison, the old man with the white moustache. It scrabbled up his leg into the shelter of his kilt while he beat frantically at it; and then the dozen hounds exploded together on him and the old man went down, shouting, with deerhounds and salukis fighting and snapping in his lap. Simon thought Mr. Grandison would be castrated, if not killed; but only the hare was killed, and torn to bits, and he was helped up and the hounds were caught and calmed and pulled away. The hunters made jokes about it, and left the bits and gut ends in the heather, and went on. In the shadow of the last hill, they found a sheep track leading home, and walked along, the hounds trotting quietly, towards the cottage and the cars.

The frost was blue and hard now, and the darkness in the hill's shadow was cooling to their eyes. The sun still lit up the moor behind them, and made the heather a bright red-gold. Simon saw one hare that they had missed, way in the distance, playing by itself on a smooth gravel patch. It hopped and kicked out and pirouetted, and the sun turned it pink as spun sugar; very pretty. It sat down, hearing the tail end of their voices, perhaps, and raised its long ears up in a V. Then it started playing again.

"Provocative," he said.

"At the dinner last year the Laird told me that the keepers beat the hill for hares at the end of the season. They drive them into nets and shoot them and sell them to butcher shops at Nairn and Inverness," said Melanie.

"So it hardly matters," said Simon.

"The Laird was out with us today," she said. "Did you see him?"

When they got back to the cars the sun was down and the air was a frosty, liquid green. The hunters put the dogs in and then slumped into the front seats, trying to remember how to drive. Melanie had a scruffy green van with straw in the back. The deerhounds climbed in, tired, leg after leg, and lay flat in the straw, but Phoebe sat bolt upright, her eyes black and hard, missing Michael and her soft sheepskins.

Simon got into the front seat with Melanie, and they finished the whiskey. The red Ferrari cut off down the bank and away on the pebbly road before any of the coursing cars were ready to move off.

"That's one of the Laird's cars," said Melanie.

Then she drove back down the terraces of flat moors, and as they went each step lower, night came on in a deeper key of blue and gray. They passed a lochan that had been orange in the sunrise and it was dark gray, with a half-moon curve of shining ice. A heron was standing in the rushes at the water end, curved in and looking like a treble clef in the half-dark.

"You see," said Melanie. "He's gray. Now will you tell Mrs. Baines when we get back that I was right? Herons are gray."

Simon could not answer. His clothes were soaked with sweat, and he was freezing cold, and too tired to get his anorak on. He was, exactly, dehydrated: he felt limp and at the same time brittle, stiff and fragile, like burnt paper. Melanie drove the van firmly down the frosty road. When they got back to the hotel, and swung nose-in to the best parking place, it was quite dark; but Simon could see that Michael's white station wagon was not back yet.

"Leave the dogs in the car," said Melanie. "We always go in and have tea first and see to the dogs when we feel a little better. They're warm and settled and they'll sleep till dinnertime. If we fed them so soon after coursing they'd sick it up anyhow. Come along."

"I'm worried about Michael," said Simon.

"Remember, it's an hour to Inverness. More, if he was coming from the hill, and an hour back, and a compound fracture might take a long time to sort out. Come along, I'm panting for my tea."

Simon felt that Phoebe was his responsibility but she looked peaceful enough, curled tightly into a corner away from the deerhounds, so involved around herself that she seemed to be slowly turning inwards, like a mandala. The deerhounds were sprawled around, snoring, like drunken heroes. He followed Melanie towards the hotel.

As they were going up the porch steps Fraser came out of the cold dark and without speaking or even looking directly at anything, emptied the game bag on the stone floor. The hares fell out stiffly, sliding on top of each other, and he went off into the dark again. The hares had cooled and stiffened into odd shapes as the bag had squeezed them, and in the dark and the yellow light from the lobby they looked like a heap of agony. On some, the fur had peeled back, showing the dark red muscle, which was now meat. One of the kilted hunters going by stopped and said, "Why, those hares look as if they had been torn by dogs! Haw."

"They have," Simon began in surprise, and then, "Oh." But he was too dry and tired to feel silly. Dehydrated, dehydrated. He would go mad without something to drink.

"Jolly good," said Melanie. "I'll go get a sack and bring them round to the kitchen. We have to buy back the hares," she said to Simon, "five bob apiece, even as dog food, and the money goes for tipping Fraser. See you later." She went off around the side of the hotel into the dark.

He went alone into the hotel lobby. It had a deep red carpet, and a fireplace burning wood and coal on the side wall. Radiators lined the other walls and the radiators were hung all over with drying wool socks and dog jackets and waterproof trousers, with pairs and pairs of gumboots and kilt brogans set in front. The rich, thick smell of feet and hounds and woodsmoke made a reek that did not go well with the glittering big rooms—lounges and a dining-room —opening off the lobby. Simon took his boots off and went on shyly in his socks, remembering Willie-John Kilduich and his nephew, Archie.

He heard clicking spoons and cups and the sound of

voices coming from the back of the hotel, so he followed a hallway back and came into a big sitting room, where tea was being served. The room was decorated in the Hotel-Highland-Modern style, with a stone hearth and fake beamed ceilings and lots of plastic tabletops. But there were comfortable chairs set out in groups around white tea tables and by the fire, and some of the hunters were already there, weakly stirring tea and eating scones and stretching out stocking feet to the warm hearth.

A waiter was keeping the main tea table, pouring tea for the gentlemen. He was a pale, short young man with the unmistakable crofter look: not unhealthy, not frail, not exactly ill; it was an unmade look, lost, as if some essential quality, perhaps the ability to pay attention, had gone somewhere else. Simon stood back. For a moment, he found himself caught in a nightmare. He had forgotten his own language. He did not know what to say, or what voice to say it in.

The waiter poured his cup full and said, without looking at Simon's face, "Milk and sugar, sir?"

Simon had a moment of voiceless panic and then tried, "Och, you'll no' do, Archie, you never saw me take sugar in my tea at Croichan, surely."

Archie looked up and touched Simon very lightly on the arm, and giggled, and said softly, "Och, Simon. What are you doing here? Were you motoring past?" He saw the rough sweater and waterproof trousers and stocking feet, and said, "Och, never; are you with *them*, then?"

"Aye," he said. "I was invited; Mary said I was to have a good time with the toffs." He dragged it out, as Mary would, and it worked: the unspoken became quite clear, the secret understanding unfolded between them. It was going to be all right. Besides, Archie had been at the Strath-Ard school, and he respected Simon.

They understood a lot, without speaking, and passed it

back and forth while Archie poured him tea with milk, and found it all very funny.

"Och, well," said Archie. "Sit down. You'll be needing your tea."

"I am needing it," said Simon. "The gentlemen give themselves a hard day on the hill, with their sport. I am dehydrated. I am that." He drew *dehydrated* out too, and Archie liked it. "I was to ask you, for Willie-John, how are you keeping," said Simon.

"Och, I'm getting on all right," said Archie. "I'm no' complaining."

"Good, good, I'm glad to hear that," said Simon, helping himself to a plate full of scones, pancakes, jam tarts, and small iced pretty things.

"And how is it with you, Simon?" said Archie. "I was hearing that you have a wife and child now."

"Two children."

"Och, never."

"Aye; a girl and a boy."

"Och, well," said Archie. "I'm no' married myself, yet."

"Och, it's a good thing, marriage; I'd no' advise anyone against it." He took his cup and plate and turned, looking for a chair.

"Behave yourself, now, Simon," Archie called quietly after him. Simon knew that Archie would be watching him all evening, and he wondered what else there was to come. He almost staggered to a soft chair by the fire and fell back into it, balancing his tea, and stretching out his legs and thought he was going to die of exhaustion. He drank the cup of milky tea and the brittle feeling began to pass away, leaving him limp. A log broke in the fire with a soft collapsing noise and Archie came to take the firetongs and pile on wood and coal, and the fire heat flared out immediately. Simon began to float in bliss.

He heard Mrs. Baines say, "Michael is back."

"Oh, poor fellow," said another woman. "Ask him how it went."

Simon sat up and looked around. Melanie was sitting having tea with Edward and James, the slipper, and some of the other young men, on a square of sofas across the room. So she won't be seen with me indoors, thought Simon. Fuck her, anyway. He also saw Michael and Phoebe, standing in the doorway, surrounded. Simon waved. Michael saw him. He stood politely answering a lot of questions and then went to the tea table and came with his cup and plate and Phoebe to sit next to Simon. Phoebe was swinging her long tail and pushing her long nose up against Michael, who looked tired, but not relaxed, like the hunters; he was pale and green, as if he had been smelling antiseptic in the vet's office all day.

"Hi, how are you," he said. His hand shook a little and the cup chattered on the saucer.

"Knackered," said Simon. "I can't move. What about you? And the dog?"

"Wait 'til I've had some tea," said Michael. "I need it. I used to be a coffee drinker but since I've been here I've gotten to like tea, too. You can't beat it when you're thirsty or feeling sick. Isn't it something, walking in the heather, the way you have to keep lifting your knees to go forward? It almost killed me the first time. Well. How do you like coursing?"

Simon realized he had been waiting for Michael to ask him that, but at the same time, he had no answer ready. He thought, and Michael drank his tea, and after a while, he said slowly. "Well, it's a very deep experience. But I wouldn't want it to be my fault."

"I know," said Michael. "But you can't do it without taking the blame. That's part of it. If you're going to do a thing like coursing you can't try to excuse it. You've got to take the responsibility."

"Do all these people take the blame? I can't believe it."

"In their way, maybe," said Michael. "Maybe not all of them. But I do."

"It's too much guilt for me," said Simon. "It's bad enough that things die; I don't want them to die and blame me for it." He stopped, confused, wondering why such an obvious statement gave him such a stab of misery and pain. He felt that he wanted to get closer to Michael, and explain things he had not thought up yet. "What are you doing here?" he asked. "I mean, in Scotland. Is it the draft?"

"Of course," said Michael. "Also, America—I couldn't stand it any more. I kept hearing it rattle. Everywhere I went, even in the woods, it rattled; it was never quiet. And then it started looking like one of those Op Art designs, you know, that move and move, always out of focus and making you sick to your stomach. Wherever I went, I would turn around and there it would be. Geometrics. Op Art. I got so I couldn't see straight. I never had any peace of mind. But most important, it's absolutely impossible to keep salukis properly in America."

Simon smiled. "A question of priorities."

"Well, that says more than you'd think. A lot more."

"Perhaps," said Simon. "Do you turn on?" he said. "Grass, pot. You know."

"Not much," said Michael.

"There's an ounce or two at the bottom of the oatmeal jar, at the top righthand kitchen cupboard," said Simon. "Help yourself. I always unpack a Players and put it back half-and-half, with the grass in front. I didn't think I'd want it where I am now."

"Salukis do it better for me," said Michael. "But thanks."

"The reason I asked," said Simon, "was that I'm always looking for the still center to things, and I only get it when I'm stoned. I used to feel it on this croft, where I am now. And for a few minutes on the hill today, as a matter of fact."

"When you stopped walking," said Michael.

"That's right." Simon had a sense of great peace and safety with Michael. He could say anything, and Michael would tune in perfectly without really listening at all. So he said, "I came up here, you see, to keep the croft running during a spell of—family illness. But it came to me this afternoon that perhaps I am deluding myself, and the croft is going to ruin, whatever." He noticed with surprise that he was using a Highland voice unconsciously—the same voice that he had lost and panicked over and then found, with Archie, half an hour ago.

"Mm," said Michael. "Of course, I look on the Highlands as a dying culture. It's my business to step in and collect the broken pieces before it disappears entirely. I'm a sort of carrion crow in the Highlands."

"Surely not," said Simon, and then, uneasy, backing away from the subject. "Well. How did you get on with Rosiqa. Where is she now?"

"I left her in the car, asleep," said Michael. "The vet gave her another shot—enough to put her out till tomorrow morning. They treated us as an emergency and rushed us right in past the waiting room. Just as well, she was beginning to struggle again. But the vet put her out and set the leg in a cast. I don't really trust him, though. I think he's more of a farm vet and these cow doctors don't like treating small animals. Do you know him? Harrower and McLean, the sign said."

"There has never been a vet, with us," said Simon. "Custom, or poverty, perhaps."

"Anyway, the leg will hold for the moment, but I think I'll take her to the Dick Vet School when we get to Edinburgh, and let them take a look at it."

"Could she recover, then?"

"Maybe. It depends on how well the leg knits. I personally knew a white saluki who jumped out of an upstairs window by mistake and broke both her forelegs. They healed so well she even goes coursing again. I don't think Rosiqa will go coursing again. The end of the bone was splintered. We'll see. We might save her for a quiet life."

They looked at the fire. It was cooling down to dark red and blue but Archie did not come again, as tea was almost over. The hunters were beginning to groan and get up and go out to their dogs. Phoebe stood between them and the fire, leaning against their knees, and her nose began to run clear drops, out of pleasure, and she curved her head against Michael's knee, and the drops fell onto the carpet. Michael, as they were talking, had given most of his cake and scones to her.

"Take my last pancake?" he said to Simon. "Phoebe's had enough. She won't eat her dinner if I give her any more."

"That's the second time today I've been second to the dogs," said Simon. "No, thanks."

"Do you resent it?" said Michael. "You mustn't get supersensitive. We're all second to the dogs."

"Well, in my case, I'm usually second to the people," said Simon. "Supersensitive is not exactly the point."

"Mm, well," said Michael, not committing himself. They were the last ones in the big room. Archie came in briefly and went to a panel of light switches on the wall. He turned out the main lights, leaving a deep dark with only one red coal, like an eye, in the fireplace. Then he switched on the lights of a small bar annex in the corner. The bar was glittering bright, with high stools and a few tables and a wall of bottles behind. It was the stage corner lighting up as the scenes change

"What we always do now," said Michael, "is go upstairs and feed the dogs in our rooms and have a bath and change and come downstairs for an hour's drinking before dinner. If you want a bath you'd better hurry and get it while the rest of us are feeding the dogs; not every room has a tub and there can be a pile-up later on. Come on and register at the desk. I'll get Rosiqa and show you upstairs."

Simon went to the van for his suit and bag, shocked at the cold black night outside, and went quickly back into the hot bright hotel. Michael followed him through the lobby carrying Rosiqa, leaving a wake of "poor little thing," and "rotten hard luck," and "pretty little bitch." She was drugged, out, with her mouth half-open and the whites of her eyes showing in new-moon shapes. There was a plaster cast covering one leg and shoulder and reaching into a brace below her paw.

Simon signed in and took his key, a small plain key, attached, for security perhaps, to a big wooden egg. Then they went up the wide, red-carpeted stairs. The lobby and stairs were crowded with hounds and hunters: deerhounds tethered by ropes to the carved banister rails, to Victorian sideboards with jugs of chrysanthemums on them, yellow and white, the flowers jumping as the deerhounds got up and sat down. There were salukis tied to door handles in the corridors and deerhounds going upstairs from floor to floor with the effect of many legs. Disheveled hunters went along the corridors carrying bowls and tin plates of steaming dog food. From the rank, gamy smells in the air, Simon guessed that yesterday's hares had been bought and put into a communal stewpot. There were salukis waiting in the rooms. He could see their long necks craning and big eyes shining as the hunters opened the doors and went in. Simon's room was Number 23 on the upper floor.

"See you about seven, in the bar," said Michael.

"No, I'd rather go down with you," said Simon, feeling suddenly childish. "Would you knock on my door on the way down?"

"Sure," said Michael, and went off down the corridor with Phoebe trotting at his side.

Simon's room was a small, featureless hotel room without any Victorian frills, but the bathroom in the hall, when he found it, was sea-green and full of brass fittings and complicated pipes, with curly door bolts and an ENGAGED lock that worked on a little wheel. The room was steamy, with a used, doggy smell, as if another hunter had just come out. The tub was narrow and seven feet long.

He had not felt water on his body for a month. He stripped, fighting off the sweaty clothes, and turned the hot tap on. Cold water came out, and he waited, naked and suffering, for long minutes until at last the angular pipes rattled and began to thump; there was a smell of cooked steam and a thick frill of almost boiling brown water poured into the tub. He was surprised and a little revolted by the clear tobacco-brown water, until he remembered it had been colored by the peat ground it had come through. He filled the tub to the brim, too hot on purpose, and got in, hoping he would have a heart attack and die in ecstasy. His flesh had gone cold and stiff in the dry, dirty weeks. The reversal was shattering now.

He lay back, dissolving, his breath catching, and shut his eyes. Then he looked to admire his body, which he liked and had not seen since Edinburgh. He did like himself. A genetic joke had given him his mother's head-hair and his

father's short-knotted, African bush; he liked that especially and said it proved a basic duality in his sexual nature, which fascinated white women of a certain type. Not
Jenny, unfortunately. She took him in one piece.

What was Jenny doing now? And who was she, with
her ivory-blue body and blue veins showing?

But who was he? He looked and below the waterline he
saw a strange black man, with dark black skin. He was not
that dark. He had changed color. The sight stunned him
with shock and confusion, and for a second, all he could
work out was an odd equation of himself and Croichan—he
had been there and somehow turned blacker: why? Then
he realized that the peat water had set brown against
brown and changed his color, and he laughed; but not very
loud. Then he found that hot water was not what he
needed after all. Swearing at himself, he got out, sloshing
water, feeling dizzy, dried himself and dressed quickly,
saying, "Oh, fuck it all, anyway."

He went to his room and got *A Highland Boyhood* out
of the nappy bag and sat on the bed clutching it and reading hard until Michael came by for him, without Phoebe,
and knocked on the door.

The big room was dark. The one glowing coal was gone.
When Simon and Michael got downstairs, most of the
hunters were sitting or standing in the bright bar corner,
shouting cheerfully at each other. There had been a
change; they were sportsmen now.

Simon had not seen the toffs in full dress before. Some
of them were dressed as the Scottish Aristocracy, antique
and beautiful. The men were wearing kilts, in the rich, dark
reds and browns and blues. They had short, black velvet
jackets above, with foaming lace jabots and cuffs, and thick

stockings with daggers, and silver-buckled shoes below. They had sporrans of tasseled leather or bristly gray badger fur hanging in their laps, where codpieces would have been. The women wore tartan dresses with lace fichus and tartan sashes; the dresses were long-skirted and tight-waisted and beyond all fashion except, perhaps, the Scottish Antiquities look. They were so beautiful. Simon almost wished they were real.

The Englishmen wore London suits—some, like Edward, expensive and swinging, with near bell-bottoms. Some of the Englishwomen were obviously dog fanatics, a little scruffy and strange, like Michael, who looked subtly gauche and American in a narrow dark suit and narrow dark tie.

"What would you like?" said Michael.

"Whiskey, please," said Simon, needing it. "No water."

He saw Melanie sitting at one of the tables with three young Londoners. She had on a black velvet dress that only an English heiress in 1955 could possibly have put on; but he saw that she had soft, big-girl shoulders and breasts. She did not notice him. On purpose, perhaps. Michael came back with Edward, the secretary, who was a slight short man, a bit ferret-faced, half-drunk.

"Edward, let me introduce you to Simon. You probably met on the hill."

"How do you do," said Edward. "You had Phoebe. We three are unattached."

"Edward's fiance and my girl Fran are Anti-Blood-Sport," said Michael. "And Simon's wife couldn't leave the children. So here we are."

"Ah, you're married," said Edward. "Would you tell me something, I thought I might marry Ellen, but I'm having second thoughts. Do you think I'm making a terrible mistake?"

"I think you should carefully consider it," said Michael. "After all."

"Yes," said Edward. "The dogs are so important to me. I spend a good deal of time and money showing and coursing, you know, and one would want one's wife to fit in." He turned to Simon. "You seem to be married. Tell me, out of your experience, how far will a woman follow one? I mean, if one goes off and does something that's so terribly important, and they couldn't care less about it, what do they do? Go off on their own, or come along? I mean, and then what about the children?"

The noise level in the bar had risen with the level of drinks taken. In the moving fragmented scene of black velvet and glasses and silver, in the thick smell of powder and perfume and whiskey and best after-shave, Simon began to feel hot and frantic. That was a tricky question for him, too. Again the picture of the hare, grabbed and running, came back to him.

"What will you both have?" he said, realizing, with relief, that Edward was just past noticing whether he answered the question or not. He had enough money with him to stand a drink or two.

"The same again, thanks, Scotch and water," said Michael.

"Whiskey and ginger, thanks very much," said Edward. "Tell that waiter fellow, will you; syrup, not ginger ale."

"Ugh," said Michael.

"No, you must try it, it's quite nice."

Simon went to Archie, who was behind the bar, and in the fragile Highland way they shared the humor of the gentleman putting ginger syrup in a glass of whiskey, and found that very good, too. Simon had another malt whiskey, double. He saw that Archie made a good bartender. His patient face looked old, though he was younger than

Simon; his white coat was gleaming like a pearl shell but the color of his face was in another key, somehow; it did not blend with the glittering hotel and the beautiful gentlemen. It had a retreating grayish quality, dusty perhaps, thought Simon, like wood ash, like stones. It seemed to turn the bar party inside out: a keyhole to another state of things. But the wall behind the bar had been stocked with everything the guests might want to drink, and Archie prepared it all expertly, dealing out gin and whiskey, all kinds, and Cinzano *bianco* and Dubonnet and Pimm's any number and lemons and cherries and fat, shining glasses. Simon was amazed at his cool.

When he brought back the three drinks, Edward asked him how he liked coursing.

"As I was saying to Michael, it's an interesting experience," said Simon, "but I wouldn't want it to be my fault."

"Your fault? You mean Michael's little bitch? But that was a freak accident. Not typical at all."

"I was thinking about the hares. The screaming put me off."

"Yes, that does put people off," said Edward. "Pity they have to do it. It's giving us a lot of trouble, Parliament, you know, and the Anti-Blood-Sports people, and all that TV coverage."

"But the hare has its own rules," said Michael. "You mustn't think it's screaming because it's hurt or killed."

"I beg your pardon," said Edward.

"Oh, it's being killed, *too*," said Michael.

"Do you mean," said Edward, with the pedantry of a little too much whiskey, "that the scream is the defense mechanism of the hare, and that it makes all the noise to frighten its pursuers, whether it's in mortal danger or not?"

Michael was not drunk yet, and looked vague. "Or something."

Mrs. Baines—without her sheepskin coat, she was a thin, middle-aged woman with fluffy gray hair—and another dog woman joined them. "Good evening, Michael. How is the little bitch."

"Sleeping, thanks. Mrs. Baines, Miss Mitchell, meet Simon Johnston."

"Oh, hello," said Mrs. Baines. "This is the young man who had Phoebe. Michael, you must let me tell you this, before I forget. Last year I had a bitch who was bitten on the lip, and my vet gave her a general anesthetic to sew her up, and do you know, she was still under the effects eighteen hours later; my vet says that these deep-chested breeds absorb the same amount of anesthetic for weight as ordinary breeds but they take twice as long to detoxicate. So remember that if your little bitch takes a long time to detoxicate. Are you going to the Thame Show, Edward? I got the entries last week."

"That depends on who's judging," said Edward. "I thought the judge last month was far too fond of that awful red-grizzle puppy, Mrs. L.'s, you know the one."

"Well, we must have a good turnout in the saluki section," said Mrs. Baines. "I thought that three-legged thing was going to turn on the sheep today. Michael, what did you think?"

Simon, who had been following the shop talk with delight, grinned at the thought of turned-on sheep, but nobody asked him to explain his joke.

"I wasn't there, you know," said Michael. "But I heard about it. Thank God it wasn't a saluki, or it would have been roast mutton for dinner."

"Oh, God, sheep," said Edward. "Don't talk to me about sheep. They *will* chase them."

"Whenever I send a saluki up to Scotland, I always ask, what about sheep," said the other Englishwoman. "They will chase sheep, I say; have you got a place to exercise it where it can't get at any sheep."

"Death to sheep," said Michael, raising his glass. "Baaaa."

"Could we hill farmers keep just the odd one or two?" said Simon. "It's the sheep subsidy that keeps us going over there at Strath-Ard. I'd no be wanting to trouble you too much, however."

They laughed and booed and asked what made him turn bolshie all of a sudden like that."

"Och, well," he said, feeling suddenly articulate and full of good humor, "here you have a country that's been so thoroughly—" he was about to say buggered but held back and said, "raped, by the government, and the landowners, and the English, and every other sod that happens to pass by for the past four hundred years: perhaps you will allow us the few shreds of economy we've got left."

They were all getting hilarious now and applauded Simon. "Jolly good," "say it again," and "we won't go coursing sheep for you, old boy." But one of the kilted men, the short gray-haired one with spectacles, who had walked next to Simon on the hill, turned towards them from another group and said, "Come, come, I can't agree with that."

He had a cheerful, soft voice, and sounded like an Oxford don. "The crofters are the most degenerate and shiftless economic group in Great Britain. I know. What are you drinking?" he said, and waved to Archie, who left the busy bar to take his order. "The landowners keep the crofts alive. The tenant system is totally uneconomic. There's no doubt whatsoever about that."

"The lairds have murdered and plundered the crofters for the past four hundred years," said Simon, "with logic. In cold blood."

"I beg your pardon, young man. I can't allow that." The dog people drifted into another group and went on about the Thame Show. Michael stayed with Simon, listening. "Believe me, I support my crofters hand and foot. I improve my land and charge nominal rents—ridiculous rents by today's standards. I put my own money into improvement schemes—hydroelectric dams and tourist centers and suitable light industry; and what happens? The young people go off to London and the old ones sit on the land collecting their sheep subsidies and old-age pensions. No landlord or Crofters' Commission or Highland Board—and I know the Highland Board, young man, my brother serves on it—is going to bring a corpse to life. The Gaelic peasantry has always been the most degenerate culture group in Europe. I swear I do my best to help them, but they are *simply impossible to revive.*"

Simon was angry and said, as offensively as possible, remembering how Melanie had shaken him, "Balls. The landowners are sucking the government for every penny, too. What about water rights, compensations, marginal land subsidies—? They have power, so they get £100,000 and we get the subsidy for our two dozen bloody sheep."

The other man was angry now, too. "I have spent my whole life improving the lot of my crofters," he said. "And you have the brass neck to tell me that I am responsible for their condition."

"You are responsible," said Simon passionately. "We have always been victims, of the climate and the poor soil and the landowners—the Clearances and the sheep and the '45 and exploitation and terrorism of every kind. Why are we sitting at the top of Strath-Ard without electricity or water and the land going to pieces all around us?" He could see the ruined steading on Moy moor again, and again the hare picked up and running. He had known about that ruin all his life. With a cool corner of his mind, he looked on and wondered why he was making such a rant about the Gaelic peasantry when he was a victim in so many other ways as well.

"Strath-Ard," said the gray-haired man. "I own Strath-Ard." He watched Simon for a long, cold minute. "You are not one of my tenants," he said.

Simon went cold sober, and for once had nothing to say. He took a drink of his third whiskey, the Laird's, which he had not tasted yet.

The Laird watched Simon from behind his spectacles, and after a few minutes identified him. "*We*," he said mildly. "I cannot imagine what makes you claim *we*. You have no rights to the Macdonald's croft, young man."

Michael said, "My logic is pure and simple. I have a dog; the dog chases sheep; therefore, I would like to see all sheep at the bottom of the sea. It's known as the Egocentric Theory of the Economic Universe. Maybe we can thrash out the future of the Highlands another time. Edward and I have to arrange the seating for dinner. Want to come with me, Simon, it'll keep you from starting a fight with *our host here*."

The Laird raised his glass to them and waved them out of the room with utmost good humor and turned to another drinking group. Simon and Michael, both a bit light-headed, went toward the dining room. The red-figured carpet seemed twice as deep now.

"You do pick them," said Michael.

"Did I make trouble for the coursing," said Simon.

"I don't think so," said Michael. "He didn't take you seriously."

"He took me too seriously," said Simon.

"I don't exactly know your situation," said Michael, "but did I get the feeling there might possibly be repercussions?"

"Shit," said Simon. "What have I said. What have I said now."

"Crofting economy's not my field, of course," said Michael. "That socio-economic thing's beyond me. I'm a pure anthropologist. Come on, forget it for the moment; let's find Edward. We've got to arrange the seating together and it's a terrible job."

They went through glass French doors into the dining room. There, long tables were set in a T-shape and covered with stiff, white tablecloths, silver, three glasses at each plate, flowers, napkins highly folded, tall, thin candles down the center row, and trophies for a centerpiece where the T-cross met the stem.

Edward was already there, with a stack of place cards, and he and Michael began a long wrangle: "No, he's stone deaf, you can't put him next to Lady Anne," and "The factor near the head, or he"ll be insulted," and "You drunken sot, you've put all the husbands and wives together."

"But I can't put *him* next to *her*," said Edward. "They ran off together last year and it was April before he got her back, and then *he* is carrying on with Jane, don't you see?"

"Oh?" said Michael, interested. "Who kept the dogs?"

"Him, I think."

Michael said to Simon, "How would you like it if I put you between Mrs. Baines and Melanie? You already know them both, and that should keep you out of trouble, and that way Mrs. Baines will act as a buffer zone between *him* and the other man, who simply has to sit directly across the table. I'll be on the other side of Melanie and Edward can be near the head to butter up the Laird. Safe enough?"

Edward agreed and Simon did not feel like saying anything, so they quickly set out the cards at each place. Archie came in with a box of matches and went down the table, lighting candles, bringing up the firebuds slowly, one by one. Then he opened the French doors and went back into the kitchen.

There was a sudden, heart-stopping, droning noise in the corridor. Simon looked out and quickly turned back in: he had seen, coming towards him, the near-castrato from the hill, in full piper's dress: kilt, leggings, Balmoral cap and plaid, and bagpipes at full blow.

"We always ask Mr. Grandison to pipe us in to dinner," said Michael. "He's very good at it and it makes a nice touch."

Simon had never heard the pipes playing close up, in a confined space, before. It was a squealing, roaring sound that went straight to the guts, more a vibration than a simple noise. The piper and the sound filled the narrow corridor and the howl of the pipes seemed to make the walls bend away. He came marching, stopped at the French doors and stood to one side piping and marking time in place while the guests paraded in couples from the bar. They came with lace and black velvet and tartans and silver and excess of gallantry and no self-consciousness at all, and Simon, who wanted to laugh and cry, put his elbows on a sideboard and his face in his hands, overcome. The piper stopped as the company reached the doors, and in the abrupt, appalling silence there came a faint baying of hounds in the rooms upstairs.

The hounds went back to sleep. The sportsmen broke ranks to find their seats, and the gallantry turned into conversation, half-drunken and cheerful. Archie came from the kitchen in a clean white jacket and turned out the main light switch. In the first second of darkness, the candle flames were enormous, like street lamps, and then they shrank and the room was flickering, gleaming, archaic, full of wine bottles and Celtic silver pins. Simon held the chair for Mrs. Baines, and Michael helped Melanie. When they were all seated, Melanie leaned across Simon, onto his lap.

"So you're there, are you. How very nice. Excuse me, will you, I'm pissed as a newt."

Michael took her by the arm nearest him and gently pulled her upright. "I guess we're all bachelors tonight," he said.

"Is he black?" she asked Michael.

"Of course," said Simon.

"My God," she said.

It was a long dinner, with cold salmon and roast venison and hotel-French desserts, and whenever a wine glass was empty Archie came patiently up behind and filled it again. The candle flames made round globes of light, spreading outwards from a still center, and the tablecloth and the lace jabots shone like panes of frost.

Mrs. Baines told Simon all about the history, origin, birth, physical points, raising, training, natural habitat, coursing, showing, problems, and future of the saluki; and Simon was touched because she trusted him and his interests so openly, as if, with his face and his manners, he could care. She talked so earnestly to him that he wanted to be nice to her. Melanie was quiet, because she was drunk and found eating complicated, and also because they were not talking about deerhounds.

Michael was quiet, too, until Mrs. Baines started talking about the future of the saluki, and the price of puppies. The future of the breed looked good, she said; she had just exported one to Canada, one to Australia, and a potentially brilliant stud dog to Trinidad.

Then Michael said, "No, the saluki has no future at all; they're a total anachronism. I have a Chinese print at home that explains what I mean. Let me describe it. I minored in Oriental Art History, did you know, Mrs. Baines? I published a paper on *The Saluki as Art Object and Hunter in the Ancient World*. It was great doing the research. Anyway, I found this print. The original is on a silk scroll in three colors in ink, done with a wolf's-hair brush. A Tartar painter—I can't pronounce his name—did it nine hundred years ago. He was at the Chinese court, in all the luxury and sophistication, and I think he must have been homesick.

"He drew three horsemen, Mongol hunters with shaved heads and long robes. The sleeves come over their hands. They're riding little ponies with big heads and thick silky tails and manes, and the riders have short stirrups, Tartar style. Each horseman has a saluki riding with him. One has a white saluki crouching behind the saddle. The second has a silver-grey hound, like Rosiqa, and he clasps her with one arm in front on the saddle bow. The third has a grizzled, sand-color saluki clasped in the same way, in front. The hounds and harness and ponies and riders are done in the clearest detail, as if the poor painter was breaking his heart for the desert.

"But that's where they are—in the desert. And they're riding forward into nothing. Because the painter only suggested the desert with a few brush strokes, sandhills and scrub, and the rest fades into the drab silk. They're going nowhere. And the salukis have this attitude of command that we know so well. They are giving the directions into nowhere. They still are today. They're driving us into no future."

"My word, Michael," said Mrs. Baines. Then, "Are you sure they are salukis? I know the Bedouin take them on camelback, but I never heard of one riding behind on a horse."

"Stop in Edinburgh on your way South tomorrow," said Michael, "and I'll show you."

Edward stood up and tapped the table with a spoon.

"Ladies and gentlemen," he said. "Shall we adjourn to the lounge for coffee and liqueurs and the trophy presentation?"

The sportsmen cheered him, and finished their wine, and got up and began to drift in pairs and groups out through the glass doors and down the corridor to the big room at the back. They moved carefully, like loaded balloons. In the lounge, the sofas and chairs had been rearranged into a square, with the open side facing the fireplace wall. There was a trestle table beside the hearth, covered with a white cloth. The fire was burning hard again. Archie brought the trophies in from the dining room on a tea trolley and set them out on the cloth gently, precisely, with a mockery that only Simon could see. Then he went quietly out to bring coffee.

Simon and Michael and Melanie went to look at the trophies. There was a heroic silver cup with two handles; a silver deerhound statue on a wooden block; a silver tray; and two small, joky figures, savage Highlanders, each with a mace and a round, studded leather shield, Tartans up to the nose and red hair covering the face. They were the kind of little doll that Edinburgh tourist shops had for sale as Scottish souvenirs.

"Those are for the Losers' Stakes," said Melanie. "I've got the deerhounds' one."

Last, there was a round silver dish, or shallow bowl, about four inches around and two inches deep, set on a small base, with two square, horizontal handles set flat to the rim.

"I recognize that," said Simon. "Callum used to have one of those. In wood."

"Callum?" said Michael.

Simon could not possibly explain who Callum was, or

what Callum was to him; he could not explain Callum even to himself. So he got out of it, saying, "Callum Macdonald. At Croichan. It was a drinking dish. A *cuach*, he called it."

"Has he still got it?" said Michael. "Maybe he'd let me see it. I'd write a paper on it. Do you think he would?"

"If he still had it, I am not sure he would not care about it any more; but I doubt that you would be brave enough to ask him for it."

"Oh," said Michael. "Is he like that. Still, I'd like to meet him some time. Maybe I could get him on tape. Is he a Gaelic speaker?"

"They use the odd phrase between them now and again," said Simon, amazed that Michael did not know he was trespassing. Archie would have felt it immediately, and stopped.

"That's how it always is; in one generation, Gaelic has gone almost out of reach."

"Aye, well," said Simon, and went to get coffee. Archie, in a third clean white jacket, was pouring coffee as he had dealt out the tea. He had a silver coffee jug in one hand and a silver hot-milk jug in the other and was pouring and deftly filling the tiny white cups. There was Demerara sugar set out in little dishes, and as the guests helped themselves with silver spoons, the brown crystals seemed to creep and move, more lively than Archie, as he poured. Simon took two cups, one for himself and one for Melanie. Archie lit up briefly for Simon and said, "Sugar for the young lady, sir?" and Simon knew that Strath-Ard would hear about that and enjoy it for months, years perhaps. "And were you hearing, Simon Croichan at the big hotel with all the toffs, taking coffee for the English lady and putting the wee spoon of sugar in it for her as well. Och, Simon is a case, surely."

The quiet laughter would not be entirely on his side.

"Dinah won me that funny little Highland man," said Melanie, when he brought her the coffee. "Clever for a fourteen-months' puppy, don't you think."

Michael brought them all Drambuie, fiery syrup, and they sat together on the soft couches, facing the fire, with Melanie in the middle. The room was quiet except for the chink of spoons and the soft crash of a falling burning log. Edward sat down with them.

"Hamadi won, and I can't present the trophy to myself, so Mrs. Baines is going to do the honors," he said. "What are you drinking? Drambuie? Right, I'll start with that. Scotland, after all, you know." He went to the bar for more.

After a long comfortable time, Mrs. Baines got up and stood by the trophy table. The silver was burning and flickering smoothly in the firelight. She presented the cups and plates and there was handshaking and clapping and sometimes a good-natured drunken boo from the back chairs. Edward got the big, two-handled cup, and Mr. Grandison, the piper, took the silver deerhound on the wooden block. When Melanie got up to take her Highland grotesque, Simon saw a new Melanie: not the dog girl, but the Young Lady from the Big House, who opened church fetes and hospital balls and strawberry teas in the garden, with all the same handshake and society smile. Add a curtsy, and present her to the Queen. She came back with her little Highland man and set him in her lap and giggled at him.

Then Mrs. Baines asked if their kind patron, the Laird, would be so kind as to present the Moy Challenge Cup for Deerhounds, known as the Moy Quaich. The Laird stood up and she gave him the little drinking dish to hand on to the winner.

"*Cuach*," said Simon out loud, innocently, surprised.

"Quaich," said the Laird.

"No," said Simon, "*Cuach.*"

"What, you again?" said the Laird. "Quaich, young man, the Deerhound Quaich."

"That's Anglicized," said Simon. "*Cuach.*"

"Ha ha," said the Laird. "Let's not get started again. Quaich." And he began the presentation speech.

"That's interesting," said Michael, writing it down.

After that, things began to fragment. The winning dogs were brought down for photographs and praise, and then, being tired, went to sleep: there were bristly, medieval shadows of hounds under tables and behind chairs, and salukis draped like harem favorites in the best places, with their eyes shut.

"What we always do now," said Michael, "is fill the cups with the best liqueur brandy and pass them around the room."

"Christ," said Simon, looking at the Viking size of the two-handled cup.

"The winners pay," said Edward. "I won £20 in the stake. I'll just about cover my expenses this year. Didn't last year."

"I haven't, yet," said Michael.

Archie came with two dim, crusty, green bottles covered with seals and gilt and cellar dust, and poured each, softly gurgling, into the silver. Edward took the cup and the *cuach* winner took the little dish and they went around the square, Archie following with the bottle because the *cuach* emptied too fast. They offered each cup with both hands to each hunter, who took a swallow and returned the cup with a compliment, sometimes mumbled, sometimes well spoken.

"Don't wipe the edge," said Michael. "The brandy disinfects."

Simon looked at the glowing, volatile brandy, shimmering in the circle of the silver cup. He took a mouthful, getting mostly fumes. So much spirit let loose had a demonic presence, as if it could rise up out of the silver, enlarging into shapes. He tried to pass it back again to Melanie, with vaguely lecherous intentions, but Edward stopped him.

"No, no, never," he said. "Not widdershins. We have to pass it right to left, clockwise. That's part of it. Bad luck otherwise." He took the cup with a graceful gesture, in two hands, and moved on with it. After the cup had gone once around, Edward raised it and finished the brandy himself while the sportsmen cheered and booed and stamped. Then Archie turned off the lights and the deerhound people began to show films.

Simon saw gray deerhounds sitting in front of gray castles, and that was enough for him. He and Michael sat on each side of Melanie, with their heads, like salukis', on her soft bare shoulders. She smelled like fresh brandy and clean underwear and a good dinner. She watched the film with intense interest.

"There's Finn," she said. "That's him winning the Quaich last year. See how snowy it was then."

The room, the couch, the girl; soft and warm. Simon relaxed.

"Do you know what happened once when I was trying to make love to Fran?" said Michael, across Melanie. "Phoebe came and put her paws on my backside."

"A cat did that to me once," said Simon. "It dug its claws in. I threw it across the room. What did you do?"

"I put Phoebe in her own bed," said Michael. "That's the thing with salukis. Discipline. Discipline. She came back pretty soon, though. It was like sleeping with a bag of antlers." Michael put his arms around Melanie. "All I want

is to be followed around through my whole life by salukis,"
he said. "More and more salukis. The rest is incidental."

"Look, Michael," said Melanie. "There's Jock and
Phoebe running a friendly the year before last."

"We'd just got here then," said Michael. "She was just
out of quarantine, and she won."

The projector whirred.

"I don't know what I want," said Simon. "I hardly know
who I am, to want, or what I've got now."

Edward and James, the slipper, and few others were in
the bar corner drinking and singing "The Ball at Kir-
riemuir."

"Where's Mr. Grandison, the piper?" called out Edward.

"He's not here."

"He knows the fourth verse," said Edward. "Where is
he? He's got to come and pipe it for us and teach us the
words."

"He's asleep."

"What?"

"He's gone to bed. He isn't here."

"He can't have gone to bed. Let's wake him up," howled
Edward. "He knows the fourth verse. It's the filthiest of all.
I know how it ends: *his forty-acre cornfield was nearly
fuckit flat.* We've got to learn the rest. Come on."

"Right," said the others. "Let's go wake up Mr. Grandison."

"We're going to wake up Mr. Grandison."

"His room's upstairs."

"Out we go."

They went shouting up the corridor, singing raggedly:
"Balls to your partner, ballocks to the wall," and a few
hounds barked in the distance.

Simon put his arms around Melanie, too. There was
enough of her.

"Time to walk the dogs," she said, getting up, throwing them off to either side. "Time for them to spend a penny. Uppies outies. Michael, come along now, Phoebe will pee the bed."

She strode out the door. Shaken, they got up and followed. The couch was too cold without her and they were not drunk enough to lean against each other. They went shivering after her, through the corridor and up the stairs. The Victorian sideboard and the arrangement of yellow chrysanthemums had been bumped into and stood disturbed on the landing. In the upstairs hallway, Edward and three sportsmen were banging on one of the doors and hooting *Are you there, piper, are you there*, into the keyhole.

It may or may not have been Mr. Grandison's room. The door was locked. There was a sleepy woof from inside, but no answer. Simon and Michael and Melanie left them beating at the door and yelling for the piper, and went to get their coats. When Simon came out of his room, Michael and Phoebe were waiting for him but Melanie was ahead, being pulled by her three scrabbling deerhounds quickly down the stairs.

"She mustn't get away," said Michael, and they ran. They caught up with her in the lobby. Michael took a deerhound, and Simon took Phoebe, and they all burst like cavalry through the porch doors into the cold.

Again, there had been a sharp frost. The road looked like furry silver and the hotel's Ye Olde carriage lamps, above the porch, had shimmering coronas of frost-fog. The night had full power, the intensity of midnight, midwinter. There was a full moon. The patch of grass by the parking lot was like silver steel wool, crunching under their feet. Simon's head was hot and bright inside and his face outside was icy cold. They walked along the frozen grass verge, leaving boiling wet spots as the dogs stopped and squatted or lifted their legs, and went on until they got round to the back of the hotel and saw the river.

The water was black and milk-white, curling up mist. The whole river cleft and the air above it was filled with moonlight and frost-fog. It did something to them. They all began to run wildly along the bank, the dogs fanned out in front, pulling them.

To Simon, in the moonlight, the deerhounds were bleached gray and really ghastly, lolloping along like ancient wolves. Phoebe was more delicate, like tinsel, a warmer color in the moonlight. Melanie and Michael were black shadows. They ran like hunters down the riverbank, tearing through whin bushes, which were spiky silver like the deerhounds, and broom thickets, straight silver, like knitting needles. The icy needles scratched at them as they ran. They stopped, panting and laughing and feeling a little sick, and turned to look back at the hotel.

Its flat annex wall, out over the river, was lit up bone-white by the moon.

"My God," said Melanie. "Look, there's a man."

There was a man, bright black against the white wall. He was letting himself down from the roof onto a windowsill. He knelt on the windowsill and tried to pull the window open from the bottom. Then he reached up and pushed up against the center bar, but the window was locked. The hounds saw him and stiffened, sighting; they wuffed and growled and the deerhounds' neck fur went up in curly bristles.

"It's a burglar," said Simon.

"Shoot the bastard down," said Michael. "Bang."

He didn't have time to aim again. The man stood up straight, said something to the window, stepped firmly backwards and fell, scraping and grabbing for the moonlit wall, ten feet down into the river. The splash came up thick and slow in silver chunks, and settled, and the water ruffled along, taking him with it. He drifted towards them in a sitting position. The river was stony and shallow. He wedged against a rock below them as they stood on the high, frozen bank, and he just sat in the river, trailing his fingers in the fast-running cold.

"He's not killed, he must have fallen in a pool," said Simon.

"It's Edward," said Michael.

"He'll catch cold," said Melanie.

"If somebody would take Phoebe," said Simon, "I'll go and see if he wants to come out."

The bank was steep. He had to claw through a thicket of moonlit broom and whin bushes before he slid onto the rolling wet stones and found that there was no beach. The water ripped over his good shoes and he gasped at the burning cold. Above him on the bank, the others had set-tled down as if it were a picnic, squatting on the frosty grass. Michael had his head tipped back, staring at the moon. Melanie was patting a deerhound. The dogs watched Simon with interest, ears cocked up. With the blue-black sky behind them and the moon overhead, they looked like frost vultures, ice fiends. Only Phoebe, the moonhound, was unhappy, shifting and lifting one front paw and beginning to moan, because it was a cold night and she wanted to be in bed.

Edward waved. Simon waved. Simon walked deeper into the river. The flowing ice knotted his feet into cramps.

"You incredible shithead, will you come out of there," he said.

"Yes, please," said Edward. His hand was colder than a stone, and he was heavier than a stone, with the ice water his clothes had soaked up. Simon, struggling, dragged him out. There was blood, greenish-black in the moonlight, on him here and there. As soon as he was on his feet he had such a spasm of shivering that he doubled up and vomited into the river. Then Simon, feeling heroic and powerful and cold, hauled him up to the top of the bank and he stood there, green and white and shaking and bloody. Michael looked away from the moon.

"What were you doing," said Michael, "falling in the river like that?"

"I was trying to wake up Mr. Grandison," said Edward, shuddering and hiccuping and confusing his words.

"Climbing all over the roof?"

"I was trying to get in at the window."

"Is that his window?" said Melanie.

"I thought it might be," said Edward.

"Oh, God, you are a silly ass," said Melanie. "Well, come along, we'd better get back, it's late and the dogs have had a hard day."

She got up and Michael followed her and the dogs all got up and shook themselves, pleased to be busy again. They all trotted back across the crunching silver grass, steering Edward. By the time they got to the porch, he was rimed with frozen fog, frozen over, like a fancy biscuit. Inside, they left a trail of mud and water and ice chunks across the lobby. There was a dog towel drying on a radiator and they rubbed him a little with that and started him towards the stairs.

As they passed the dining room doors, Simon noticed that Archie, James the slipper, and a few others were sitting around the clear end of the table. Most of the T had been stripped and set for breakfast. They were playing poker. Archie was dealing the cards.

Edward left an icy trail up the red stair carpet. Water kept swelling and rising out of his shoes.

"We'll say that one of the deerhounds jumped in the river," said Melanie.

They put the dogs to bed and started trying to save Edward. First they took him to a bathroom and while Simon and Michael tried to pull his clothes off, Melanie filled the tub with steaming, peaty water. With their cold outer clothes and cold faces and Edward's wet icy things, the room fogged up with a thick mist smelling of brandy and, though they were all put away, of hounds. They could not get his clothes off: they were half-frozen and stuck to the bloody parts, and Edward was so cold he tried to clutch them on tighter, so they were fighting Edward and the wet clothes, too. They took their coats off.

"Could somebody please take my dogs out," said Edward, indistinctly. "So they can settle for the night."

"Sure," said Michael, and put his coat back on. He waited till Edward's clothes were finally all wrestled off and took them away to hang on the hall radiators. Edward sat on the toilet seat, swaying from side to side, naked and dozing. When Simon and Melanie heaved him into the bath he yelped as the hot water touched his sores and then lay back and went instantly, totally, to sleep. The warmth made Simon feel luxurious and high. It was a damp, secret, fragrant steam.

"Isn't he a mess," said Melanie. The wall had scraped raw patches on Edward's forehead and palms and shins. "I've got some super stuff my vet gave me to put on the dogs when they cut their feet," she said. "We could put some on him, couldn't we." As she opened the door, letting in a splinter of cold air, she looked back and giggled. "He's sweet with no clothes on. Isn't he skinny. Like a skinned rabbit."

Simon sat on the edge of the tub to make sure Edward did not sink and drown in the bath. The heat, and the enclosed steam, and the nakedness—man or woman, never mind whose, it was enough—had given him an erection, and when Melanie came back with her plastic medicine squeeze-bottle he wondered if he might fall on her then, at last, right there. But if he turned his back on Edward he would sink under the water. They would have to get rid of him first. So they spread four white hotel towels on the floor and hauled Edward out of the bath and spread him flat on his back on the towels while the water gurgled down the drain. They patted him dry and then, with the squeeze bottle, puffed antiseptic healing powder on the worst of the scraped skin. Edward slept peacefully. Then Melanie started giggling and puffing powder up his armpits and over his crotch.

"That isn't fair," said Simon, and she turned skittish and puffed some at him.

"I'm raving for a good poke," she said. Simon did not understand at first, but then decided it must be an upperclass expression for what he was wanting himself.

"Come on, then," he said. "Let's put him away. Do you know which one would be his room?"

They wrapped the murmuring Edward in towels and supported him down the corridor to what Melanie said was his room. She knew his room so well that Simon was sure the other Coursing Meet nights had ended with her in his bed. They did not meet Michael. The hotel was quiet, but Simon thought he heard a card players' murmur still going on in the dining room downstairs.

Hours ago, a chambermaid had turned down Edward's bedcovers and put two hot water bottles between the sheets. They were cold now but Melanie refilled them at the wash-hand basin tap. She was awkward with them and could not screw the tops in properly and he had to do it for her. The picture of Mary filling and punching and corking hotties, as he had seen her do them so gracefully, for half the nights of his life, came into his mind; it embarrassed him, here, but he could not blank it away. They wrapped

Edward in a blanket with one bottle at his feet and the other in his arms. Then they laid the man-cocoon straight on the bed, covered him well, left the light on in case he had nightmares, and went away.

"Come to my room," she whispered, like a film star.

"Not with your grotty dogs watching every move," he said. "You come to mine."

She fretted at leaving the dogs, but went with him. After the hot bathroom the corridors and his room felt cold, and they shivered, but they did not bother getting into bed. He opened his trousers and she hopped out of her underpants and she got on top of the bedspread and he got on top of her.

"Oh, what a nice big one," she said in her loud English voice. "This'll be good." She came before he did, however, which was a shock; Jenny was very slow, and now, after Alasdair, reached no climax at all.

They cuddled up together, half-hostile, on top of the bedspread and fell briefly asleep. Simon slept, thinking. He put his arms around her from behind, not because he felt tender, but because he was lonely and he liked to sleep with his arms around something. That quick screw had been the natural, inevitable end; it had released the tensions of that sensual day. But the hounds had led all his deeper feelings, somehow. He had brushed by the humans —except, perhaps, for Michael—without contact, with the thinnest mesh of drink and words. He felt perverted, overturned. In fifteen minutes, he woke up grabbing and shouting with terror.

"What's the matter," she said, looking over her shoulder at him, through her brown hair.

"Christ," he said, laughing. "I dreamed you were a deerhound."

And then he dreamed that she smiled and said, "I am,"

and he went falling through space and woke with a horrible jump.

She rolled away from him and got up. "I'm not going to stay all night," she said. "I never do. I've got to see to the dogs in the morning. Foo, mucky," she said, putting her underpants on. Then she left and he finished undressing, filled his hottie, got under the blankets, and went to sleep at last.

Simon woke up with aching eyes, just as the windows of his room were lightening with the morning frost-fog. It was about nine a.m. He thought he might try to eat breakfast. He did not meet anyone in the corridors and the stairs were clean, the chrysanthemums set straight, the red carpet vacuumed. The dining room was cool and plain and half-empty. The glitter and silver of the night before had gone, and the few people drinking coffee and waiting for their eggs were not hunters or sportsmen or anything but plain guests, a little hung over, dressed for traveling. Simon poured himself coffee and milk from the jugs at the center of the table.

Archie came in from the kitchen, wearing the cleanest white jacket, and said to Simon, "What will you be having this morning, sir?"

"Och, anything," said Simon. Nobody was sitting near him so he said, "And how did you get on last night, Archie; I was seeing you at poker, with the gentlemen."

"Och, well," said Archie. "The gentlemen were not sober, you understand, and I was." They enjoyed that, and then he looked worried, and said, "You'd no' be telling Mary that I was playing cards, would you, Simon?"

"Och, no, Archie, why would I do that?"

"And how was it with you," said Archie. "I heard there was somebody went into the river."

"Aye, well," said Simon. "Fun and games; there was not any harm done."

Michael came in, and sat down next to Simon. He looked thin and even more neglected than usual. He said, "A boiled egg, please," to Archie, and Archie said, "Yes, sir," and went away.

"How is Edward?" said Simon.

"I heard him throwing up as I passed his door just now," said Michael, "so he's alive. God, what a night I had. I was up with Rosiqa. She got hysterical as the drug started wearing off."

"Good morning, Michael," called out Mrs. Baines from the far end of the table. "How is the little bitch today?"

"All right now," said Michael. "Thanks."

The Meet was breaking up. After breakfast, Simon saw the lobby piled full of expensive suitcases, dead hares, dog beds, bowls, slip-leads and hound gear of all kinds. Deerhounds and salukis lay sleeping, tied to inappropriate things, chair legs and radiators. Simon packed his few things, took his suit and returned his key on its big wooden egg.

"Mr. Berger has seen to your account," the desk girl said.

Outside he found a faceless winter morning, with the frost-fog thinning and parting overhead. To his surprise, the car started after one or two moans, though it had stood a whole day outside in the cold. He let it run with the choke out for a few minutes, feeling listless and a little bleak. Then he got out and stood, watching people leave, waiting for Michael.

It was so cold, but he did not have the energy to get back in the car. The people were sad; he could feel it. As he watched them, he was hit by a sadness of his own, a sense of breaking bitter loss for the breadth and richness of the hill, even for the coursing, which was not part of his world and never would be: he would never see it again. It was a cold day, and he felt he had nothing to look forward to.

Michael came out, looking like a mother with too many children. He was leading Phoebe, who was cranky and stiff, and carrying Rosiqa in both arms. Rosiqa made a swan neck and put her head on his shoulder. Michael lowered her to a patch of white crusty grass and she squatted and stayed down for a long time.

"Unbelievable bladders these salukis have," he said. "Well, goodbye."

"Aye, well," said Simon. "Thanks."

"Yes," said Michael. "Well. Shall we correspond?"

Simon, startled, said, "What? Write letters, do you mean? Why?"

"You are suave," said Michael. "Why not? The rent checks aren't what you'd call expressive. Well, we'll see how the winter goes." He picked up Rosiqa, who was standing on the three legs and the brace, with her head low and swinging from side to side, rather like Edward on the toilet seat last night.

Simon was too cold and sad to say anything else, so he reached out and shook Rosiqa's good paw—because Michael had her in both his arms and had no hand free, and Simon felt that he wanted to touch them somehow, if only to make sure that they were real. She gave him a mindless, meaningful look and he went back to his car. The last thing he heard as he shut the door was Mrs. Baines to Michael.

"You weren't joking about your saluki print, Michael? Shall I stop off and see it? It sounded most interesting last night."

And Michael in return, "Sure, and stay for lunch; afterwards I'll show you my favorite walk, if you can spare the time. You go over the Braid Hills and down into Mortonhall, there's all kinds of game there—I've seen a fox—

the dogs have a great time but you have to watch out the greenskeeper doesn't catch you."

Their strong, irresponsible, innocent life was going to move on without him.

As he drove away through the Moy valley, the fog came down like a box around his car and he had to put the side lights on. Again, as in the beginning, there was nothing for him but fog and the frosty tongue of road and the trees like gray lace meeting overhead.

Then the road began to climb to go over the hills, and the mist thinned out, and the sun rose behind it. He suddenly drove into a freak band of refracted sunlight where every color and object was bleached into silver and gold. It was all flashing, blinding, gold and silver and he was so shaken with wonder that he stopped the car to get out and stand in the dazzling broken light. But by the time he had braked and pulled over and stepped out, he had passed through the refraction and the air was clear again.

The sky was a wet, vivid blue, the bracken red-brown and the rhododendrons a bright, dark green. It was frightening, too clear and cold. Simon could see more fog where the road went on down into Strath-Ard. Rooks, crows, were cawing. He looked behind and saw the deep mauve logs and rolls of frost-fog he had left.

Enter in glory, he said. He stood by the car, shivering, listening to the crows. They sounded like the screaming hare, but the hare was on the bottom; the crows were on top. The hare was picked up and running nowhere. The crows were waiting for the lamb. When had he said that? He's waiting for the lamb, the bastard. He can sit around and wait all winter. The hare sounded like a lamb. The hare sounded like his own baby.

He knew too much now. He had said too much. He could not possibly live at Croichan any more. He could never face Callum again. He was not sure he would ever love anybody else. He could not keep Callum out of his mind, but strangely, in that moment, he could not remember what he looked like. He was there, massive, but without any shape or face. Simon struggled, and at last heard his voice:

"That time I was at the Edinburgh Zoo, there was a daft thing, a blue-eyed cat, no' in a cage, you understand, Simon; it followed us around, and followed us around, and it would no' leave off following us around. I never saw another one like it." Callum laughed. Then he said, "Fochan was telling me, Simon, he was at Edinburgh for the Highland Show, he was telling me that there are a lot a them foreign students walking about there. He was saying it is a grand sight. Darkies, and all. Is that right, Simon, are there a lot a them darkies in Edinburgh now."

The fog was only in the river valleys. On the high places, on the Monadliath, at Moy, at Croichan, on the high shifty places where realities burned away and left something else, and another kind of fog that did not do Simon any good—up there it was going to be a perfectly beautiful, bright, winter day.

III

Croichan did not move much while Simon was away, and it was very quiet there. Mary milked the cows and fed the hens. The bodach 'ha radan slowly dragged a bale of hay out to the sheep, and more slowly broke it up, taking most of the morning; and after dinner he slushed the cow dung from one side of the byre to the other, and scraped down the drains, while the bull watched him. Jenny took care of the children. At first Shona talked, as usual, but Jenny felt weak and sleepy and did not listen to her. Toward the end of the day Shona noticed, for the first time, that nobody was listening to her, and she began to stop talking. Then there was no sound at all.

Sunday morning was cold and bright. Jenny was surprised to find it Sunday; she had forgotten most of Saturday. Simon got back before noon, and kissed her as soon as he got out of the car, in the steading yard.

"Och, love," he said. "I forgot to bring the bathwater."

"Well, you'd better go back and get it," she said.

"Aye, another time, perhaps."

She put her arms around him, trying to pretend he was someone she knew. The anorak felt stiff and cold. She tried to lean against him, but the canvas was hard as a shell. "Did you enjoy yourself?" she said.

"Aye, I did," he said. "I thoroughly enjoyed myself."

He sounded so miserable that she looked hard at him. "Are you catching flu?"

"No," he said. "Perhaps I enjoyed myself a little bit too much."

They had both felt that way before. "Well, I won't waste time feeling sorry for you, then." But he looked so wretched that she carried the suit and duffel bag towards the house for him. "Did you wear the shirt?" she said.

"Aye, I did. Michael had bad luck," he said. "Do you

remember the grey dog? Rosiqa? It fell and broke its leg. It may recover, though."

"Oh, that is a shame, dearie," she said, not caring very much. Mary came out onto the scullery doorstep. The valley was enormous all around her. Jenny put down the duffel bag, weakened by that feeling of being perched insecurely on top of everything. At Croichan, she felt that way over and over again.

"Were you seeing Archie, Simon," said Mary. "How is he getting on, then."

"Och, he's no' doing so bad," said Simon. "It is a grand big place, and they give him four white coats in the one evening, to keep him clean, every time he was to wait upon the toffs."

There was a dart of amusement between them, but Jenny felt it go thin, and disperse, like the jet trail that was in the sky at the same time. There was an anachronism, she thought. RAF jets from Lossiemouth crossing Strath-Ard. They went into the house, and she put Simon's clothes away, sniffing the rich brew of sweat and tobacco and whiskey and general aristocracy that came out of all the folds. She smiled, trying to imagine the scene. When she got back into the kitchen, Mary was giving them all tea. Dinner was almost ready, but tea was expected, because there had been a Return.

Some days passed—perhaps they were weeks, she was not sure—and Michael's December rent check arrived in the mail. Simon was cleaning the byre when the postie's red van came and went, so Jenny took the envelope and opened it. There was a piece of best writing paper folded around the cheque, and on the paper Michael had typed, in capital letters, a few words only:

CALEDONIA STERN & WILD

It reminded Jenny of one of her own titled comments on the world, and pleased her, as if she had found an ally. Croichan was quirky and obscure, but other things could be so, too. She suddenly wanted to share it with Simon, and got together the pram and all the boots, mittens, blankets, hoods, sleeping bags and covers necessary and dressed the children and took them across to the byre, and showed it to him. He didn't like it.

"He said he wanted to *correspond*," he said. "To write letters."

"Well, this is a letter, dearie," she said. "Write something in return."

"Och, I cannot spend my time creating epithets to please that lunatic, that dog hippie." Forking and turning the straw in the cow stalls, he said, "Look you, the bull has got ringworm. You're not to let Shona go near him."

"No fear," said Jenny. "I wouldn't go within ten yards of him myself. We wave to each other across the midden; that's how *we* correspond."

"Och, Himself is a quiet beastie," said Simon, droning, imitating the bodach 'ha radan. Jenny laughed, willing to follow him into any kind of good humor, and Shona said, "Do it again, Daddy."

"He'll no' ha-arm ye."

"Do it again."

"Not just now."

"Aw, Daddy, will ye no' do it again," she said, with such a perfect mixture of Edinburgh street brat and, now, Highland brat, in her voice that Jenny and Simon looked at each other and laughed again, almost meaning it, with a precarious kind of warmth between them, something Jenny had not felt since he had come back from the coursing at Moy.

"Holy Mother," said Simon, "she's changing."

"Quick, send for the School of Scottish Studies," said Jenny. "Michael would never believe it."

"Would you just bring me my Cultural Anthropologist's tape recorder, and the wee notebook as well," said Simon. "Very good. Now. Would you repeat that, young lady, for the School of Scottish Studies. The linguistic future of Scotland is in the balance."

But Shona knew that they were making fun of her for their own sake, and refused to say anything. Simon went back to his work. The byre was dark and stinking, but warm. The wind rattled outside.

Shaking up the matted straw, Simon told them, "When I was little, I used to spend hours in here."

"No doubt," she said. "Squatting over the drains."

"Away, don't be crude," he said, throwing in a bit of Jenny's East-Fife accent, to continue the safe game. "It's my favorite place. I'm still fonder of it than of the house."

"Surely," she said, "It's warmer."

"It is that. Once Callum had got his boots on in the mornings, Mary would turn him out of the house, so that she could get on with the baking, and he would come out to the byre and sit right down again in the straw. He would say, 'It will be raining soon, surely, and we'll no' be getting to work until it has stopped,' and of course at Croichan it always would be raining soon, off and on, so he was always right. When I was little, when I first came, he used to talk to me a lot. He would tell me all the regimental names and colors—he used to be a Cameron Highlander, in the Great War. He would tell me what the cock said when it was crowing: *'ha mac an righ a' ruarachd.* It means the king's son is digging."

"That's very good," said Jenny. "That's right; it's far better than cock-a-doodle-do, anyhow."

"Do it again, Daddy," said Shona.

" ' *Ha mac an righ a' ruarachd.*"

"Do it again."

"Not just now. He would say, 'who's chief with me?' and I would say, 'I am,' and he would take me onto his lap."

Simon left the cow stalls suddenly. He hurried down the aisle and through the small door at the end of the byre that led into the barn section. Jenny heard him thump the pitchfork onto the rack, against the wall, and she felt pain for him, too; but it was dim, as if they were not close enough. After a while, she and Shona went to look for him.

He was in the barn, yanking the feed sacks around, trying to organize them and pacify himself. The barn, unlike the flat-roofed byre, had a peaked roof with a ridgepole, and rafters, and the ceiling space made it big and cold. It was half-dark in the barn, and the roof and walls were lost in a brownish-black haze. The threshing machine, a big square wooden thing with iron wheels and chains and handles, stood in one corner, and fifty years' threshing had covered every surface with a furry matt of oat dust. The small windows were almost buried under the rich film. There were no edges, no shapes, in the dark. It reminded Jenny of the Room on that first night, when she had been nursing the baby and trying to see the photographs, and the surfaces had swum up at her like dust in the flashlight beam. Every square and bar of light here, too, was alive with floating dust.

She saw dark brown blurs of rubbish, shaggy spider-webs, harness, empty sacks. Surely some of it had been there before Callum. Each year's broken junk and tools had sunk deeper into the threshing dust and had less identity: in the end, no name at all. The walls might have been walls or they might have been dust, thickening and then diffusing out into nothing. What was on the other side? At night, rats went in and out of the nameless dusty heaps. Shona went burrowing into them now. Jenny had a sudden fright that she would be lost, too, and screamed at her.

"There might be something sharp," she explained to Simon.

"Och, don't be stupid," he said. "Every plough and harrow and fork and spade on the place is rusty as hell. Everything I have to use is rusty; I can't seem to keep anything sharp, even when I'm using it, and what would be sharp in there—that's all been thrown away." He dragged the sacks into straight rows, and they fell crooked again. "I was thinking of my dream, my first dream," he said. "You know the one. I couldn't keep it out." As he shifted a sack of hen food, the edge of the strawstack beneath it peeled up, exposing a rat's nest, with pink young ones curling and uncurling like maggots. "Agh, rats."

"Where, Daddy," yelled Shona from some black place behind the thresher.

"I'll stamp on the buggers," he said savagely.

Jenny—and Shona, still out of sight—shrieked, "No!"

"Of course I couldn't stamp on them!" he shouted, and ran out of the barn, and exploded at the bodach 'ha radan, who was forking something feebly from one side of the midden to the other, doing no good, and knowing nothing at all. "There are rats everywhere," said Simon. "They are even into the hens' food now. What can be done about it, Mr. Mackay."

The old man looked vaguely frightened, not so much at the violence as at the direct question, which was not polite.

"I'm just waitin on the right one," he said. "Aye. Aye. I'm needin a dead one for the job. I have to make a tantalizer, you understand. A female would be the best, for the tantalizer. And it cannot be poisoned. I'm needin it freshly killed." He looked at Simon for a moment. Simon was ex-

cited and he was not, and the only way he could express
this difference was to touch the front of his cap, which was
not the front because the earflaps were off-center, and say
"Aye. Aye." again, droning, and limp away with the pitchfork.

"What am I going to do," said Simon. "What."

Jenny had come out behind him and they were both
standing in the wet wind, in the ammonia mud swamp of
the yard. "Poison the lot, in secret," she said, misunder-
standing him on purpose, because there was no answer.

"I don't dare," he said.

Shona came out of the barn, filthy, draped with spider-
webs and blurred with oat dust, as if the barn walls had
really tried to absorb her. She had forgotten about the rats.
"Look, Daddy, I found something funny, what's this?" she
said.

She gave him a wooden tool of some kind. It had a long
handle joined, by a leather thong, to a shorter piece. Where
Shona's hands had rubbed the dirt away, the wood showed
through, shiny gray, probably ash.

"You are a dirty, grotty little thing," said Jenny.

"I don't know what this is," said Simon, turning it both
ways. "Ask Mary."

They took it onto the house. Mary was baking. She
looked at the wooden thing, wouldn't touch it, and said,
"Ask Callum," forgetting he was gone.

"Aye, it is a farm implement of some kind," said Simon.
"Callum would know. He was a good farmer."

Jenny did not see how Callum could possibly have been
a good farmer, but Mary and Simon both nodded, accepting it. Then Mary said, "Och, Simon, take the dirty thing
outside," and he gave it back to Shona who went out swinging and whacking the short piece against the garden posts,
scaring the hens. Jenny had the odd feeling that Mary,

looking at the wooden thing, could have recognized it, but did not want to.

That evening, in the hissing white light of the lamp, Simon spread out paper and an envelope on the oilcloth tabletop and wrote a letter. Jenny was knitting. She had finished Shona's yellow sweater and was working with four needles, making bedsocks for Simon. Mary was just sitting with her big knuckly hands folded in her lap, waiting nervously till it was time to make tea again. Simon finished writing, and was going to lick the envelope, but Jenny said, "Is it to Michael? Couldn't I see it, dearie?" because they always used to read each other's letters, all letters except Simon's to Mary. He gave it to her and sat uneasily while she read it. It did not start with *Dear Michael*. She smiled. It went straight into:

> Thank you for the weekend. I was thinking I might try to learn a bit of the Gaelic; we have the long winter evenings here but I don't feel like going into Inverness, where they have classes. I thought perhaps there would be a book lying about at the School of Scottish Studies, that I could borrow. I am not interested in the complications of the language, but Instant Gaelic, survival if you were wrecked on the shores of the savage Hebrides, if such a thing exists.
>
> Also, Shona has found an implement in the barn, and none of us knows what it is. Perhaps this would be more your sort of thing. I'll draw it.

I have been thinking about Rosiqa, let me know
how she is getting on, poor thing.

Simon

"Is it all right?" he said. She gave it back, and he folded
it and licked the envelope and pasted the flap down.

"Very nice," she said. She put down her knitting. The
fire was dead and cold and her fingers were too stiff to knit
with four needles. Mary got up and went out, probably to
the henhouse corner. "But dearie, I'm not sure I understand
about the Gaelic," she said.

"Why not?" he said. "I mean why not learn a little? It's
becoming fashionable to study it. Gaelic is having a revival.
One of the London Sunday papers had a thing about the
Gaelic Revival, in the Color Supplement, before we left.
Remember."

"But who would you speak it to *here*?" she said.

"Well—Mary," he said. The white light made his skin a
cold color, like slate.

"Mary does not even use it any more."

"Och, well, she used to say things to Callum in Gaelic,
now and again. And he would speak a little. 'The King's son
is digging.' I told you."

"But they have stopped using it entirely now."

They sat looking at each other. She felt betrayed. She
felt no love for him at all. Then Simon said the worst possible thing.

"Och, well," he said casually, "I would teach it to the
children."

She had a moment of quite deadly fright, like an electric shock, and said, meaning it, "In that case, I should
promptly leave you, and take them with me."

He did not ask why, but "Where? To Fife? *Your* half-caste bastards?"

"Edinburgh. I'd work as I did before. If the children were in a day nursery, they'd be better off than here. At least they could play and make noise. Shona has stopped talking here. Have you even noticed that Shona has stopped talking?"

Mary came back into the kitchen and put the black kettle down to boil for tea. She took three scones out of the bread box in the sideboard, split them, buttered them, spread on the raspberry jam, and put them on the oilcloth, one for each.

Jenny dreamed about death, again, in the Room that night. When she woke up, she was crying, and Shona was sitting up watching her. Outside, the cockerel was crowing, *ha mac an righ a' ruarachd*, over and over, and further off the rooks were cawing, a confused racket, as if the flock were flying and settling from field to field around the croft. This time Simon did not turn over to comfort her.

Mary was old-fashioned Free Church, and bicycled down to Strath-Ard for the services every Sunday; and at Croichan they did not celebrate Christmas. As the children were too young to notice, Jenny did not object. There were cards, however. In the fortnight before Christmas, day after day, the postie brought cards for Mary: from Sydney, and Perth, Western Australia, and from Nova Scotia and Alberta and British Columbia. Mary put them up on the mantelpiece, on both sides of the pendulum clock: a bleak row of relatives. At Windygates, Jenny thought, all the relatives will be at the table, around the turkey and pudding. All except me, thank God. Which have more personality, my Lowlands family or these Canadian *Thoughts-*

across-the-sea and *For-those-at-Xmas-far-away* cards for emigrants? She wondered if anyone in the Room photographs had sent any of the cards, or if they were all dead. It was obvious that Mary's family had gone far apart.

She did not think of Callum as having relatives. A family did not suit him, somehow. Mary wrote letters now and then, in the evenings, probably to him, but he did not answer, and they knew nothing about him now.

She and Simon got one card. It was from Michael. It was one of the semi-religious art prints sold as Christmas cards by the Edinburgh University Library: a Veronese with two salukis crouched in one corner.

That was Christmas in the Highlands.

Hogmanay, New Year's, was more important, and Mary started preparing for it weeks in advance. She made another Black Bun, and ordered extra butter and rice flour when the grocer's van came up, and on the last day of December, she built up the kitchen fire until the varnished wood walls began to reflect and shine, like melting syrup, and she made shortbread. She baked the flat, frilled cakes in the old oven above the grate, and they had a grainy, buttery smell, baking, like sweet bread. Then she went into the Room.

Jenny helped her get it ready. They took the childrens' beds out and put them in a small room off the kitchen that was usually kept as a storeroom. Mary took the Christmas cards away from the pendulum clock and rearranged them on the modern tile chimneypiece in the Room. There was a stuffy bedroom smell, so Mary opened the windows and let the bitter cold blow in. They tidied everything away, and then Mary brought in paper and sticks and wood and the coal bucket, and Shona and Jenny knelt with her and

watched her light the fire. First, rolled-up sheets of *The
Northern Scot*, then kindling, then a few bigger logs. There
was a dull, crumpled glare and the smell of burning paper,
and white paper smoke mixed with their frozen breath.
Jenny did not know why it was so exciting just to get the
Room fire ready, but Shona felt it, too. Then the sticks
caught and snapped, and all the smoke came back into the
Room. Up the chimney, a jackdaw's nest loosened and
dropped into the fire, a horrible blackish burr, and the
smoke went freely up the cleared flue. The fire burned.

Mary took the genteel firetongs that stood by that
hearth, never in the kitchen, and put on lumps of coal. Then
she put the firescreen in front, and set out the small tea
tables, and carried in cups and saucers and plates of shortbread and Black Bun, neatly covered with napkins. Last,
Mary shut the window, and they left the Room empty until
the evening.

In the evening, after Simon and Mary had done the
chores, and Jenny had put the children to bed, they all
changed their clothes and left the kettle simmering on the
kitchen grate and took the radio and the paraffin lamp into
the Room. Mary had her Church dress on, navy blue, with
a brooch at the neck and a pink cardigan buttoned over it.
They sat stiffly, with their hands in their laps, looking at
the fire. The Room had only one door and no draughts, and
the fire kept it almost warm. The firelight and the paraffin
light did not go well together; they had different shadows,
going different ways. Jenny could feel the night outside.
There was no wind, and thick slabs of stars came down
against the house, like stone.

The night passed. At eleven, Simon switched on the
radio and they heard a BBC voice soberly describing New
Year's Eve in London. In Fife, there would be large late
dinners, lasting till midnight, and after midnight the First-

Footers would set out. A few people, usually courting couples, would stay in each house to receive callers, and everyone else would put bottles in their coat pockets and go in groups around the village, along the blue-gray streets, past the councilhouse rows and the miners' terraces, into the tiny front yards, into the parlors to eat and drink; the whole town would be on the move until morning, and the groups would sing, and bump into each other, and start fights, and cars would weave down the streets and drive up on the sidewalks. The first guest in each house had to be a tall dark man, carrying a lump of coal, to bring luck for the year. Jenny waited to see what would happen at Croichan.

At midnight, in the kitchen, the pendulum clock struck twelve times. In the Room, Simon switched the radio off. He and Mary and Jenny stood up and shook hands gravely and kissed each other on the cheek. They sat down again, except for Simon, who went out of the Room; Jenny heard him go through the kitchen to the scullery door, out into the steading yard, through the kitchen garden gate and along the gravel path to the other door, the formal front door that she had never seen open. It was at the end of the narrow hallway that divided the kitchen from the Room. To prove it was a front hall, there was a coatrack to one side, and an umbrella stand, full of moldy umbrellas, and a shotgun braced across the coathooks. Simon knocked, and Mary went to the door. Jenny heard him murmur, "Many of them," meaning New Years, and Mary thanked him and formally let him in. There was the first-footer. Then they all sat waiting again. The lamp shadows were flat and still and the fire shadows kept moving against them. Jenny did not know what Mary was thinking about.

They heard footseps on the gravel path, and a knock at the door. Mary got up and let Morag in. Morag left her coat on the rack but wore her flowery hat and her sheep-skin boots into the Room. Jenny had not met her before; she looked rather like Mary, with smaller hands and feet, perhaps, but her voice was the same. Again there was the sober handshaking and the murmured *many of them*, and the two old woman kissed each other quietly on the cheek. Morag sat down in one of the formal chairs and said,

"It was wild, the day. There was a strong wind, earlier."

"Aye, it was that, Morag," said Mary.

"And the man on the wireless was saying, snow is expected again on the high ground."

"Fancy," said Mary.

"I was hearing that the road is blocked again, at Kilburnie. And Jimmie MacLean"—she pronounced it Jeemy—"was driving with a lorryload of cement blocks from Burns' in Inverness, and he had it off the road at Balmacarra. There was nothing he could do, so he left it and went home for Hogmanay."

"Fancy," said Mary again, with a little gasp.

"I am sure he was speeding with it," said Morag, sitting straight, with her hands in her lap.

"Och, well," said Mary. "He would be."

"Aye," said Morag, on the indrawn breath, so that it became another little gasp, like Mary's. "The hydroelectric scheme turned him off for reckless driving. And he'll no' get another driving job from Burns."

"Och, well," said Mary.

"And have you had your first-footer, then, Mary," said Morag.

"Aye, Simon came in just after twelve."

"Good, good," said Morag. "I was no' wanting to come up too soon, and I sent the old man up ahead of me; he was black when he was young, you see, Mary; he had a wee black moustache, quite the thing, and hair; but I'm no seeing him the now; he is lost, surely."

She and Mary laughed quietly, back and forth between them.

Simon said, "I was thinking of hiring myself out in Strath-Ard, Morag, for the next Hogmanay, to go first-footing, as a real black man; I would become a millionaire, with no trouble to myself."

That was very good, too; Morag laughed, and said, "Och, Simon, you are a case," with a sideways look that made Jenny remember all the Cnoc-Muidhe bastards Simon had told her about. Jenny sat without speaking. She knew she was not expected to take part, and she was glad of it.

Mary got up to make tea. When she came back with the teapot, she said, "Aye, the bodach 'ha radan is lost, surely."

"Perhaps he is in the woods," said Simon, and they all listened to him. "He was telling me, there is a thing he needs to bring the rats together: a tantalizer, though I would not be knowing what sort of a thing it is. Perhaps he is away in the woods looking for it now."

"Och, aye, it will be that," said Morag. "A *tantalizer*." She drew that good word out through all its syllables, and let it hang there in the Room.

Mary poured tea and took the cover off the shortbread plate. There were more gravel footsteps and another knock.

"It will be the old man now," said Morag. Jenny wondered why he, only he, was the old man to them. But it was not the bodach 'ha radan. Two other men—old men—came in. Simon introduced them to her, around the handshaking and the *many of them*.

"Jenny, here is Fochan, he takes care of the Laird's sheep; and here is Willie-John."

They were both shy of Jenny, and ignored her. They were dressed-up in old-fashioned tweeds, and they were newly shaved, and looked very clean. Willie-John was small,

with gray hair. Fochan was bald and had big sideways ears.
They all sat down, and Mary poured two more cups of tea.
Jenny, feeling like a daughter of the house, handed round
the shortbread and the Black Bun.

"How are you keeping then, Mary," said Fochan.

"Aye, fine, thank you, Fochan," said Mary, with that
thinnest edge of extra politeness; not enough to push him
away, because he was one of them, and understood, but
enough to remind them all that he was also a servant of the
Laird. There was the chink of good china cups on saucers.

"Was I telling you, Mary, I had a letter from Archie,"
said Willie-John, "Simon had a grand time with the toffs, he
was saying, at the hotel."

"Aye, Simon, will you tell us about that, then," said
Morag, and they waited. Simon smiled, and tried, but after
a few minutes he shook his head.

"Let it be," he said. "I cannot think of anything good
tonight."

An exhaustion came over them all.

"Where is the old man tonight," said Willie-John. "I
thought he would be first-footing you, Mary."

"He is away out, in the woods," said Morag. "Looking
for his *tantalizer*." They all laughed, quietly, and Jenny was
surprised to feel how much power that soft laugh had,
when there were six people in the Room. But they could
not keep it going.

"He'll no' come here, then," said Willie-John, and they
all knew he would not, and there was nothing more to say
about him. Nobody else was going to come. They sat looking at the fire. It was a nervous, active fire, with busy
flames, in contrast to their stillness. Even the shadows flickered on the wall, the photographs moved, but they did
not.

Fochan said slowly, "The winter is hard, this year, do you not think so?"

They nodded and murmured, "Aye, it is," looking into the fire and Morag gave the indrawn *aye* under her breath.

"There has never been such a winter for the wild beasts," said Fochan. "The tracks go everywhere, in the woods."

"And what have you seen, then."

"I was West, with the ewes," he said, "and did I not see a raven; where the rocks are, past Loch Garbh Bhreac."

"Och, no, Fochan," said Mary. "It will have been a crow, surely."

"I shot the thing," said Fochan, "and picked it up, so there is no doubt."

Willie-John said, shyly, "And I have been smelling foxes, by the Kilduich burn."

"It was the old man you were smelling, looking for his *tantalizer*," said Morag, and there was a laugh, but Willie-John said:

"It was not, and I have been seeing them as well, and one was a vixen in whelp."

"That will be bad for the lambs," said Simon, and they all nodded. "I thought the Laird employed a gamekeeper. What is he doing about all this?"

"Och, Sandy lives in one of the Laird's cottages across the river, where there is the *electricity*," said Mary. "And he is that tired, poor mannie, taking the toffs' shooting parties around the hill in September, he'll no' be bothered with a fox or two down here."

Again, the laugh, in the Room.

Then Morag said. "If the hill is snowy, the now, grouse will be coming down onto the stooks," but she said it with half a voice, because she meant poaching; and Fochan did belong to the Laird, and they had to show respect.

"And are you a good man with the shotgun, Simon," said Willie-John.

"The old gun makes that much noise, you can hear it in Inverness," said Fochan, to show he was with them.

Simon went to the coatrack in the hall and brought the big shotgun back into the Room, with the bag of cleaning rods and shells, and set it on the floor between his knees and began to clean it. The others sat watching him, amused.

"Aye, it is a relic," he said. The gun had a crude wooden stock and the barrel was heavy, almost belled, like an old musket. "It is a muzzle-unloading gun. Callum used to say it had been used at Culloden," and that was a good joke, in the Room to comfort them, but it had been a mistake, too: Callum was there, now, in the firelight. They sat silently, one by one realizing he was there.

"Will he be getting his dram, do you think, tonight," said Morag sadly.

Mary shook her head. "He's no' allowed to have spirits. For the diabetes."

They needed him, and they were afraid of him. After a few minutes of flickering quiet, Simon went to the sideboard and got the whiskey bottle and glasses and began to pour six drams. Morag got up, restless, and went to read the Christmas cards on the mantelpiece. "Och, Jessie is a case," she said. "Look, she has drawn a picture of the mealy puddings, and she has made two wee arrows pointing to them, and she has written on it too: 'Mealy puddings.'"

"Aye," said Mary. "She does that every year."

Jenny did not understand, but she felt that the Room was charged now, loaded, overtired. They all took the whiskey straight. The taste—rich, burning, bitter and then flat—translated the way they felt. "Slainte," said Willie-John, and they murmured it after him, with flat voices. Soon after that Fochan and Willie-John stood up and shook hands again, gravely, with Mary, and left by the front door.

Then Morag stood up and shook hands all around, but kissed Simon, making Jenny think once more about the bastards. He laughed and looked surprised and kissed her in return. She left by the front door. Mary and Jenny cleared away the cups and glasses and then Mary took the lamp and went to bed, leaving Jenny and Simon in the empty Room.

With the lamp gone, the firelight made the Room perfect. They stared at each other, stunned by the sudden comfort. They were in the center of something warm, brown, orange and red, like a giant chrysanthemum. It gave perfect protection.

"I am going to take off all my clothes," said Simon.

"In the Room?" said Jenny.

"In our bedroom," he said. "We've been sleeping here for two months. It will be a whole year before the fire's lit again."

Unless somebody dies, she thought. "Will we still be here a year from now?" she asked.

"Who cares," he said. "Live for the moment. Grab it. I'm going to strip off and walk around the room, just for the pleasure of it."

So he walked around, naked, and then undid the bedsettee, straightening it to the floor with a challenging snap. She undressed slowly and went to look at herself in the sideboard mirror. Her breasts were heavy, the nipples enlarged and purple-brown, but her ribs and collarbone stood out.

"Look at me," she said. "Man used to say that once a woman passes twenty-five she either goes to fat or goes to scrag. Like 'neck of mutton, scrag end' at the butcher shop. Lovely, isn't it. I'm going to scrag. Look at the bones."

"I am," he said.

"No, but look. My body is awful."

"You sound like Shona. 'No, but listen to this.' Come help me do the blankets."

They made up the bed together. The fire was hot enough to burn their bare skin. "Don't worry," said Simon. "According to all the sex books you're still approaching your prime. I'm going downhill." He lay down on top of the covers, on his back, and stretched out gorgeously at full length.

"Downhill; no fear," she said. "There's nothing downhill about you, dearie. When am I supposed to be reaching my prime?"

"Och, at thirty-five, or thereabouts."

She sat down on the bed. He curved around her so she sat in the angle of his lap. "Feel that," he said.

"Thirty-five," she said. "I hardly expect to be much of a sexpot ten years from now."

"Sexpot," he said, and moved down a bit and put his arms around her hips, and stroked his cheek against her thigh, and sniffed. "Mm, you do stink," he said happily. He was quiet and thoughtful for a minute, and then he said. "If I grew a beard, a long, tangled beard, would I look like an aborigine? They have straight hair."

She laughed. "Aborigines are circumcized, dearie," she said.

"How do you know that?"

"I read it in a book, while I was nursing Shona."

"God, how can you resist me?" he said.

"How can you be horny, after tonight?" she said, a little angry.

"What happened tonight?"

"You refuse to see anything," she said. He uncurled himself from her and lay straight again.

"Look," he said, "do you want me to fuck you, or not?"

"I don't know," she said. She knew—she didn't; but she was afraid to be so blunt.

"Come to bed, your arse will be getting cold." She knew
he would not be able to excite her, and though the nakedness was some comfort, after so many weeks of cold and
long underwear, she was right. She could not touch; she
could not love; she could not think. Her one vision of death
had been so strong that now loss, and passing, and the
eventual hopelessness of everything was the first reality for
her. It checked every move she tried to make. The only
pleasure she got out of that night was lying in the dark,
with Simon asleep, watching the last chunk of the fire, like
a glowing nest in the black Room. In the morning, they
were strangers to each other again, and remained that
way.

January first and second were days of total immobility
in Scotland, but on the third a small parcel came, from
Michael. Inside was a small, gray, very old paperback:
GAELIC SELF-TAUGHT. *An Introduction to Gaelic for Begin-
ners. With Easy Imitated Phonetic Pronounciation. Third
Edition: Over Ten Thousand Copies Sold.*

"It exists," said Simon. There was a letter, too. Michael
said:

THAT BARRIER WHICH THE CELTIC TONGUE PRE-
SENTS—My colleagues here think that your study
plans are reasonable and praiseworthy. Most of
them also weave their own tweed plus-fours and
bake their own bread.

P.S. It's a *flail*, Mr. Farmer.

P.P.S. Will you travel to the West Coast to say
Good Morning? Who are you going to find in the
Central Highlands to speak to you in Gaelic?
Ghosts? The Celtic dead?

Love,
Michael

The winter months went by, in the helpless tension of waiting, and Jenny was always cold. The children grew, somehow, in the cold. They all waited for the year to change,
and for the bodach 'ha radan to do something about the
rats. By February, the rats were beginning to rustle in and
out of the feed sacks when Simon was with them in the
barn. Everyone did the same dim jobs over and over again.
She took care of the babies. Simon cleaned the byre, fed
the cows and the black bull, ran the threshing machine, cut
wood with the bodach 'ha radan feebly dragging the opposite handle of the bow saw, and dragged out hay and
turnips to the sheep. He looked at the meaningless furry
junk in the barn, the broken ploughs and warped wood and
stiffened leather and rusty blades, and did not touch it. It
had all been there before he was born, and it was beyond
him. Mary did the baking and, with Jenny, the cooking; she
fed the hens until they stopped laying for want of light,
and milked the cows until they went dry in February. Each
night, Jenny heard the wind thudding against the house,
and each morning, she looked out of the Room window and
saw lines and drifts of dim, new snow.

They waited for Callum. They did not talk about him;
they did not hear from him; but he was coming back. In
January, Simon wrote to the Consultant Surgeon in charge,
asking for news of Mr. Macdonald, and his progress and
speed of recovery. Then they waited for a letter in return.

In the middle of February, suddenly, there was a thaw,
the first since Simon had gone to Moy. At Croichan, they
were all sensitive to degrees of cold and light, because the
house was not a shelter; it was a target, a center of wind
and bad weather, and the house was often colder than the
hill, as if it had been turned inside out. So the thaw
stunned and softened them. The sky went a pale sweet

blue, and the hills turned soft brown, like minks. The pale sunlight was hot on the ground. Jenny wrote it out:

EUPHORIA

The midden heap thawed and steamed and stank, and Simon stood knee-deep in it, shovelling loads of dung onto the trailer, and then tractored the loads away to spread on the fields. The bull and cows mooned around, looking gentle, like licorice shapes. Jenny sat on the doorstep, watching.

The peace held for three days. There was a smell of spring mud. The scene ran slowly and then stopped, held in a clear block of sun and blue sky. The baby slept. Shona dug muddy holes in the kitchen garden. The bodach 'ha radan hammered something wooden in the dairy shed. There were rooks floating and cawing high over the house, out of sight, a faint sweet noise. Mary let the hens out and Jenny sat watching them.

There were two dozen hens, creamy brown and red, and one white cockerel, his tail sprouting into arching curves of green and black and gold. The flock came dotting closer to her at the doorstep, making its constant, inquiring noise. The scratch and peck and flap was quick and sharp, but the drift across the steading yard was slow, like the slow drift of a fat honey bee. Jenny had not noticed the hens before, but now they became a focus for her. There it was: that moving ring, that *nothing* wheel with Croichan at the hub; it stopped for a few days and what did you have at the still center? Hens.

The February air became even more luminous, and soft and warm. Shona dug up a worm. It was bright pink, like cheap plastic baby goods, too pink to be living underneath Strath-Ard.

"Throw it over the fence, to the hens," said Jenny.

The worm fell writhing on the gravel mud and the whole flock came sprinting, wings out for balance, strong two-legged pumping strides, and the nearest hen gave a quick look with a side eye, to make sure, and pecked it up. Shona screamed with the delight of feeding something, and dug for more worms. The hens waited. The cockerel stood up and flapped and said it: *ha mac an righ a' ruarachd*. The bull and cows came up to watch, and Jenny thought how pretty they were, head on, faces like big black flowers, orchids or pansies, with almond-shaped petal ears. She laughed at herself. EUPHORIA.

It did not last, but for three nights there was no wind, no grinding and rushing of wind around the house, and no frost; the house was in a kind of free fall, as if Croichan had been disengaged, lifted out of gear. The night sky had the same luminous shine as the day. Simon sat at the kitchen table reading the Gaelic paperback, and felt relaxed enough to talk to Mary about it.

"Look you, Mary," he said, pointing to the Table of Values in the front of the book. *B* is *p*, and *d* is *t*, unless it's *k*; and *s* is *sh* unless it's omitted, which it is often for completely irrational reasons, and *n* is *r* and *t* is *ch*, 'which is spoken in the throat and has no English phonetical representation,' and *bh* and *dh* and *gh* and *mh* and *t* and *rt* are all exchanged for different sounds, unless they are omitted as well, under rules that seem absolutely random to me. There's logic in every language, surely."

Mary giggled and took the *Gaelic Self-Taught*, holding it out with long arms because she was far-sighted. She did not question Simon's studying Gaelic, but seemed amused and mystified that it should be written down at all.

"It's no' a language for reading, you see, Simon," she

said. "Och, well, he's wrong here; fancy; *b* is not *p*; perhaps it is on the West Coast. On the West Coast they say *chust look, will you, surely that is a fine poat out there in the pay*, och, it's comic, surely, the way they talk out there," she said, and went to make the tea.

"There is no knowing at me, Mary, whether the book is at me, or whether it is not," he called after her.

"Och, Simon," she said, bringing in the teapot and a tin of oatcakes. "You are a case."

"That is the construction, look you," he said. " 'I have the book' translates as 'The book is at me.' " She took an oatcake and set it carefully flat on the oilcloth to butter it, because it was crumbly. Then she passed it to him, and buttered one for Jenny. "Mary," he said. "Do you think in Gaelic, or in English?"

She was reaching for the boiling kettle but she stopped and sat down on the fireside chair and shook her head. He had gone too far. Even Jenny could feel it. For the first time, Mary's voice was sad, without the usual faint, wicked twist in it.

"Och, Simon, I'm no' knowing that. You should no' be asking me that."

The sadness frightened him. "Very well," he said. "Where's my tea, Mary, I'm needing my tea, after all this reading."

Later, when she was out, he whispered to Jenny, "Come here, I want to show you something." She felt trusting and peaceful, and went over to the table. "It's more than difficulty of sounds," he said. "It has a daft bloody logic, in its way; look at the spirit of it. When I learn English, I learn the cat is on the mat. But look here."

She read down a table headed FIFTH LESSON IN GRAMMAR: PREPOSITIONS.

Of the mist
To the grave
Under the table
Like the tree
About the part
From the court
Under the fist
To the eye.

"My word, dearie, I see," she said.

"That's grammar. Look at the dictionary section," he said. He held the pages, letting them fall. Adder's-Grass to Adventurer, Captive to Castellated, Grave-Clothes to Growl, Scriptural to Sea-Beaten. Sea-beaten, she noticed, was tonn-bhuailte. "I have been trying for three days now, and all I can do is say *the man who is king in Scotland*, over and over again. I tried hello and goodbye. There's nothing under *g* for goodbye; you have to look under *f*, and there you find it: farewell. I don't know yet where hello might be."

"But you did think to look under *f*, didn't you," she said.

"I have left Croichan again and again," he said, "and I always wondered why Mary never says goodbye. I know now; she can't; it would be nothing less than *blessings go in thy company*, and how could she say that, even to herself? So she says nothing."

So they all say nothing, thought Jenny. How bleak, having a whole language and no world left to make sense of it. And how frustrating. And what happened to all those dead words—did they dry up like husks or did they ferment and make odd tracks, like snail trails, in people's heads? Mary came in and began to fill hotties for them all. Simon stared at her, probably realizing for the first time that he and

Mary were made of different words—or different words had made them: wondering who she was.

On the fourth morning, Simon drove another trailer-load of dung up to the west field, and Mary let the hens out, and Shona started to dig worms again in the kitchen garden, and the bodach 'ha radan began to hammer on his aimless project in the dairy shed. Jenny put the baby down for his nap and went out to sit on the doorstep. Then she noticed that the air was thinner, and harder, and the fragile feeling, the soft shine on everything, had gone. Little needling winds came from all directions, and she shivered. The day went gray and yellow, gray and yellow, as clouds went over the sun. She thought she had better wheel the baby inside, but then a strong square of bright blue sky came overhead, and the yard blossomed with such simmering heat, that she thought the calm would surely last a few hours more, and it would be nice to take Shona for a walk.

So she persuaded Shona away from the worms and they went off toward the west, through the tractor gate where the cattle had gone to graze. The turf was cow-printed and churned into mud. As they turned to face the westerly slope a strong wind hit them, and Jenny saw that the sky was a glittering dark blue. One cloud was coming from the west, blowing a perfect rainbow arch in front of it, and the wind was a solid block fit to lean on. They turned and ran, the cloud galloping after them, then covering them, the wind flapping in all directions and finally hitting them with a black horizontal squall of rain, snow and hail. The air turned gray-green and Shona shrieked with the stinging hail on her face. They ran for the house, which was so distorted by the storm cloud that it looked like static. Shona screamed. In the pram, the hood folded back and hail full on his face, the baby yelled. As they ran across the steading yard Jenny realized that the ground was rising and falling in waves. As each gust of wind hit the larch tree, the tug of its roots lifted that corner of the yard and let it sink down again. She reached the baby and grabbed him out of the pram and they stood in the doorway with burning faces and streaming tears. The cloud passed on towards the east. The steading yard bloomed out blue and sunny again, and the hens came out, croaking and singing. The white crust of hail immediately began to melt. But Jenny could see more clouds blowing towards the croft from the west, and took the children inside. On the twelve-noon news and weather program, the BBC voice told them, "Seasonable temperatures: sunny periods and showers, possible wintry showers with snow in the North."

After that the snow came down again, and stayed. On the first of March, the wind changed and came from the east, and that was the worst of all. It came with a savage, terrifying green light and swept the fields bare, piling up ten-foot snowdrifts against the stone dikes. The pregnant ewes were in danger of being frozen or buried, and the bodach 'ha radan brought Morag's sheepdog up for Simon to use. It was a scabby black and white collie, its coat diseased because it was fed only porridge, but it was wise about sheep and Simon followed it while it gathered the ewes and drove them into the steading yard, in front of the house. Then it went home.

Shivering in the bitter cold, Simon wired up a makeshift pen in the shelter of the house wall, to keep the ewes safe while the east wind lasted. They milled around, churning up chunks of frozen mud like brown glass. He did not let the cattle out that day, and the cows groaned and complained, and the bull rattled and stamped in his stall. Mary went out and scattered turnips for the sheep, and came in out of the screaming wind and snow wiping her nose and saying, "In the Gaelic this is *gaoth le casan nam marbh*, the wind with the feet of the dead."

Then Jenny could see the real, greenish presence of death on the croft, concrete and vivid, sitting in their own chairs and stepping, with feet, in their footprints. When she sat reading to Shona at bedtime, the house trembled steadily in the wind, and with every gust something went crash in the steading.

Now all the sheep and lambs are sleeping soundly,
But they bleat softly when the Tomten peeps in at the door.
All my sheep, all my lambs,
The night is cold, but your wool is warm,
And you have aspen leaves to eat.

The gale went on through the night. Shona woke crying and crept into their bed saying that the house was going to blow down.

"I agree with you," said Simon. They lay listening to every whine crash and snarl crash of the wind until the uproar, and the air pressure, scared them too much and they all got out of bed at three in the morning and got dressed and went into the kitchen. Mary was there, too. They lit the fire, which blazed up bright yellow and roared with the draft, and made tea. There was a groaning and a wild flapping sound outside. Nobody knew what it was.

"It's a wild night, is it not," said Mary, with composure. "I'd no be surprised if we had a chimneypot come down. And some slates, as well. You'll mind on the time the chimneypot came down at Kilduich, Simon?"

"Och, aye," said Simon, although he did not.

Shona fell asleep by the fire, and the rest of them watched the gray-green light come at seven. They looked out the kitchen windows and saw that the larch tree was across the stone wall with a vast rosette of earth and roots turned flat to the east. It had ripped a great cellar hole up out of the yard. Then they saw that six slates had come off the roof in the night. The wind had whipped them down like meat cleavers into the steading yard, among the sheep. One slate had split diagonally into razor-edged triangles with spear points, and these were standing on end, shaking in the gale, between two ewes. No sheep had been killed, and only one was cut—there were drops of frozen blood around the yard. The ewes lay calm as cats, folded into squares, in the mud. Jenny remembered the blackface ewe on the Cairngorm road, and wondered if the hoodie-crow was still waiting for her lamb. The Croichan cheviots lay blinking and looking at the spearheads and cleavers with their yellow eyes.

A sleet shower came hissing down into the dung and snow and mud. Jenny could not see anything but the whipping sleet, and the sheep: the only color in the steading was their yellow eyes. The storm seemed to be coming right through the house.

Simon said, "As soon as this passes over a bit, I'll get up on the roof with a ladder and see how much damage was done. We can't have slates off for long in weather like this."

Mary answered, but Jenny could not hear what she said. The wind was down a little, but there was a kind of static reaction inside the house, as if the battering all night had scrambled and exhausted all the indoor noises, cutting off what communication they did have. She thought Mary said something about old slates in the barn.

"Callum put the leftover slates away to use later. They will be in grand shape still, Simon."

"And nails? Have we got roofing nails?"

"Och, aye, there will be, somewhere."

The cloud blew over, the sleet shower stopped, the air lightened to a clearer gray-green. The east wind rumbled in the chimney. "Now," said Simon. He pulled his canvas anorak over his head and fastened all the drawstrings, tied a scarf on as well and put his gumboots on. "Would you come and hold the ladder for me, love," he said.

Jenny persuaded Shona, who woke crying, to stay in the house and have breakfast and watch through the window, and got her own coat and boots and gloves and scarf on and followed Simon out among the sheep. The green wind snapped at her, as a dog would. Simon got the extension ladder out of the dairy shed but as soon as the wind touched the ladder it blew him staggering in a full circle, fighting to control it. Jenny ran and caught one end. Everything was in full flight, moving, except the sheep.

"Look at the buggers," shouted Simon. "The shitheads, they just lie there, chewing. Who do they think they are."

"But dearie, their wool is probably so wet and heavy they can't stand up. Perhaps they're frozen to the ground."

"But chewing. And I'm risking my bloody life." The ladder fought them like a live thing, on end, turning in the wind. They carried it through the sheep; one or two ewes gave low digestive bleats that stank of turnips. They got it into the kitchen garden and struggled till they got it flat against the house wall. Then Simon quickly stepped three rungs up and his weight held it down. He had the tools stuck into the belt of his anorak. Jenny, bracing the ladder against the ground, felt it vibrate and shudder in the wind. Simon went right up to the top and leaned against the roof, examining the slates. The wind undid Simon's scarf and sent it lashing like a live snake through the air, over the house roof, gone.

"Look at the crows," he said.

Jenny heard them first, and then saw the flock of black birds, hundreds, pouring from the northeast like a funnel of smoke, across the valley towards the croft. They came closer, and she saw that they were jackdaws, playing with the wind, floating into the updrafts and letting the gusts wrench and spin them like black rags, then falling and tumbling into another updraft. The flock, slowly, but with interior motion, came over Croichan, and the steading was full of their creaking, cawing noise. Then the birds took control and flew deliberately against the wind, down into Callum's lower field, the Muir. They made a racket in the bare larches and willows there.

Simon stepped a rung higher to the top of the ladder, and leaned out along the roof. Then Jenny saw the cattle coming out of the byre. The black bull humped down his head and shook it and trotted a few steps, because he had been shut in, but the pregnant cows strolled quietly out. Simon, looking down, saw them.

"Who let the fuckers out of there?" he yelled, and Jenny knew he was scared, high up, battered by the wind. She saw the bodach 'ha radan wavering in the doorway, with a pitchfork, weakly pretending, at this hour and weather, to clean out the stalls.

"Mr. Mackay is here," she called up to Simon.

"Oh, Christ, no."

The cattle thought Simon was interesting and came stepping across the sheep, through the open garden gate, and stood in a ring around the ladder, snorting, licking their noses, plopping down cow dung. The bull came closer. He had no horns, but he was a massive beast with an enormous, muscled neck. His black coat was gray and patchy with ringworm. He put out a long blue tongue and licked the ladder. Then he began to rub and butt it with his head.

"Hold steady," called Simon, busy with the slates.

"It's the bull, dearie; he's playing with the ladder."

"Well, get rid of the bugger," he said.

"No, you," she said faintly; Simon backed halfway down the ladder and leaned out and shouted, "Fuck off; get out of it!" and swung viciously at the bull with the hammer. The bull stared at him, and lowered his head and shook it and backed off a few steps; but then he bucked heavily, like a burly horse, and trotted away towards the fallen larch tree. The cows followed him, more slowly. Simon ran up to the top of the ladder and waved his arms wildly in the gale and sang.

"I'm the king of the castle, and you're the dirty rascal."

He got his knees up onto the gutter and lay flat against the slates, reaching and testing them as far as he could. To Jenny, the roof looked as gray and wet and slippery as fish scales. She heard him say:

"All the nails are rusty, I can pull any slate right off if I try; the whole thing needs reroofing. Here's where they went last night, look; Christ, what's this, then."

"What is it?" she called.

"Och, another damn thing." He scrambled back to the ladder and came shakily down. "Will you help me bring the ladder into the house now, love. I want to take a look at the roof from the inside."

"Did you find anything wrong?" she said.

"Wait, and I'll tell you," he said. They could have brought the ladder in through the front door, as the trapdoor to the roof space was right above the coatrack in the hall; but that would have insulted Mary, so they had to fight the ladder out through the garden gate, in the scullery door, through all the angles of the kitchen and hallway and finally up into the black square of the loft. Simon took the flashlight, went up the ladder, grabbed the edge of the black square and pulled himself up into it. Shona and Mary came to watch. Shona said, "Daddy, I'm coming too," but he called back, "Not just now; there's no floor between the joists and you'd put your foot through the kitchen ceiling."

Jenny held onto the little girl and watched the black and yellow moving shapes as he moved the flashlight beam across the loft.

"Och, it's horrible up here," he said, echoing. "And hot: here's where all your heat goes, Mary; and flies. They heard the steaming, buzzing noise of a thousand waking flies. Simon and the light beam moved away down the loft. Suddenly, there was a soft splintering noise and a thump on the kitchen ceiling.

"Och, Simon: has he stepped between the joists," said Mary.

"I didn't," said Shona.

There was no sound, except movement and creaking above their heads. Soon the flashlight shapes came back, and then Simon. He came down smudged with black spiderwebs, like Shona in the barn.

"What is it?" said Jenny.

"There is a wee bittie woodworm in your roof joists, Mary," he said.

"Aye, well, Simon, but it'll no' be very bad."

"I would say it has been going on there quite a while."

"Aye, but Callum got Norwegian pine, you see, Simon, to make the roof joists of," she said. "And he was sure the woodworms would no' go for the Norwegian pine. He was always saying that Norwegian pine was a kind of wood they'd no' eat."

"Perhaps we'd better have a wee look around the house," he said gently, puzzled, and they went from room to room, with the east wind thumping and blowing outside. Shona thought it was a game. Once she had seen the first cluster of tiny holes in the kitchen door frame—the round, neat, pleasant-looking holes—she went looking for more, and found them in the varnished wood walls by the fireplace, and on the underside of the kitchen table, where Mary did the baking, and in the armchair by the fire, where Jenny sat knitting in the evenings, and in the bodach 'ha radan's window chair.

She found them in the storeroom off the kitchen, where Simon had dreamed Callum would be lying.

She found them in the wooden drainboard of the scullery sink, and on the china shelves above the stove, and she found them in the wooden brace that held the warm-water tank over the bathtub. She peeled back the oilcloth on the pantry shelves and saw that the wood underneath was riddled and eaten away, and that heaps of fresh sawdust were stuck and smeared to the underside of the cloth.

She found woodworm holes in Mary's clean, cold bedroom—along the base board above the flowered linoleum, on the windowsill and on the bedstead, where the wood met the flowered chenille spread.

At last, she found them by the photographs, on the mantelpiece of the Room.

Then Simon told her to stop looking, and not to mention them to Mary. The bodach 'ha radan came in stinking of cow dung, and Mary gave them midmorning tea. The old man sat in the window chair and Jenny knew that it probably would not collapse under him. He was too frail.

"Aye, it is wild out today," he said, loud and slow. "There was a man on the Scheme drowned in the Ard River yesterday, Mrs. Macdonald. Morag was hearing it on the wireless."

"Fancy," said Mary, indrawn, backwards, as Morag said *aye.*

"Did you see me up on the roof, Mr. Mackay?" said Simon.

"Aye. Aye. Aye," said the old man, droning, shaking his head at the hardness of all things.

"We had a few slates come down in the gale, the night," said Simon, "and there is the odd rusty nail in the roof, and a bit of woodworm here and there, and we are needing some new pantry shelves; I was thinking I had better go into Inverness today, if the weather does not get any worse. Could you bring the hay out to the sheep, perhaps, and see that the beasts are *well shut in,* while I am away."

"Surely," said the bodach 'ha radan, drawing the word out into a long melancholy sound, like a woodwind. Jenny saw Mary record it for future amusement.

"I was seeing the wee tins of woodworm killer at the ironmonger's in Inverness, Simon," said Mary. "With the wee spout you put into each hole where the sawdust is fresh."

Simon looked at her, but kept quiet. After tea, he took Jenny into the Room, alone, and told her.

"I put my foot through the main roof beam, and one of the supporting joists crumbled to bits in my hand. I didn't dare touch the others—I had to leave something to hold up the roof. Callum was wrong. The house is not safe any more. How could Callum have been so wrong? It won't come down tomorrow, or next week, or this summer— perhaps—but it's past saving. There is nothing, not any- thing, that I can do to stop it."

"There are companies that clear up woodworm infesta- tions," she said, automatically practical. "You know: they show a picture of a 'Magnificent Elizabethan Structure' that they've saved, and they give you a certificate to say you're safe for twenty years."

Simon smiled for a minute, and they both smiled to think of what Mary would say about a woodworm certifi- cate.

"We couldn't pay for that," he said. "And it's riddled. It's past saving."

Jenny had imagined that the walls were no shelter, but now it was true. The structure had no more substance than the language. The east wind was blowing sawdust through a million little tunnels they could not even see. There was nothing Simon could do except hide the ruin from Mary, and hope that the house would last longer than she did.

Simon put a box of gravel and a spade in the back of the car and left for Inverness. Jenny stood on the bank watching him drive down the road. Wherever there had been no shelter from the east, the track was drifted with snow like beach sand, ripples and long sharp curves, so deep that the stone walls were buried. The car skidded through and went out of sight in the deep woods. The wind was still strong: black chunks of cloud were blowing toward the west, and the taller trees were whisking back and forth like horsetails.

The baby woke up from his nap in a cheerful mood that afternoon, and Jenny made a conscious effort to play with him. Her voice felt rusty and slow and her mouth too stiff to smile, but she knew it would be bad for him if she did not. While they were playing claphands Shona came into the kitchen and said,

"Mummay, there's an awful big mouse in the Room, and a funny smell."

"Did you see it?" said Jenny, wondering how a rat could have come into the house. Had Simon disturbed something in the attic, perhaps?

"Aye, I did," said Shona, imitating the bodach 'ha radan. "It ran behind that thing you and Daddy sleep on. It made a smell."

"A rat, perhaps," said Jenny. Mary came in from the scullery and got the poker from the grate.

"The trash," she said. "In the house." They went across the hall together, leaving Alasdair strapped in his little seat, content for the moment with the placemat pictures to chew on.

The Room door was shut. They opened it and looked in. The air was dim and stuffy, moving a little with the east wind outside. There was a piercing reek, a stink of something very wild, in the Room.

"I didn't think rats smelled like that," said Jenny. "The barn doesn't smell like that. It's more like tomcats."

"Perhaps the poor wee boy with the three legs got in, looking for shelter," said Mary.

Jenny thought it was unlikely: no sane cat would go into the riddled house when he had the solid byre to curl up in. She did not say that to Mary. The smell was stronger than tomcats. It made their eyes burn.

"What's all that on the floor," said Jenny. There were slimy drops in a trail leading to the bed-settee. "You saw it go that way, Shona?"

"Aye, I did; it went wriggling underneath."

Wriggling. They all had a few seconds of faint, puzzled fear, and didn't move, and then Mary went and put her hand on the back of the bed-settee—which was made up and folded for the day—to move it from the wall. At the first touch, a small animal whipped out from behind with a twittering scream of rage and attacked them, snapping at their ankles. They jumped back in shock and Shona gave a wholehearted, unrestrained screech of terror and ran out of the Room.

The little thing scuttled back under the couch again. In the kitchen, the baby began to cry. Jenny and Mary stood shaking. Their minds had not registered what kind of animal it was, but it had been alive with anger, glowing and zapping like a fuse with self-confident rage. It had been so furious, and Shona's yell so out of control, that the deadly peace of the Room was shattered, smoking, gone.

Mary reached for the sofa again, as if the first explosion could not possibly have been real; and the animal bolted out at her again, ecstatic, snapping, screaming. Jenny found herself reacting like Simon did in extreme situations; "Shit," she whispered, and then it all became hopelessly funny. Ha, life's a bugger, isn't it. The little beast was not frightened, not defending itself. It had taken possession of the Room and it was foaming mad at anything that dared to come in. It was about ten inches long, red-brown on top and white underneath, and supple, like a snake. It had small paws and a small head and a cold, chattering voice; it was the voice that drove them out of the Room, far too big for the tiny body. The yelling had the volume, the fright potential, of some huge, spiky, dangerous bird of prey. The thing came screaming and blasting at them and pure instinct put them both outside, in the hall, with the Room door shut.

"It's a weasel," said Jenny. She watched Mary's face; understanding. A wild beast from the woods had, impossibly, against everything that was right, gotten into the Room and taken possession of it. Of the Room.

"Och, the trash," said Mary, equally furious, quieter; she took up the poker and went into the Room again. This time as soon as she opened the door the weasel darted out and went for her, weaving and dancing and chattering out that clear, ferocious scream. Mary said, *"You trash, you brute,"* and slammed the poker down, but she was stiff, and the weasel was quick, and she missed it. Jenny had a strange, set-apart feeling, as if the fight was not her business; *how odd*, she thought, detached, *that it's not white; you'd expect a weasel to be white this time of year.* Mary struck again. The weasel jumped for the poker and held on to it with such a horrible scrabbling and biting and screaming that Mary threw the poker down and ran out into the hall. "The dirty thing, he'll no' keep me out of there," she said, but then she stood there helpless, looking at the door.

Jenny heard the baby yelling in the kitchen, and thought of Shona, who was silent, hiding somewhere, terrified, and realized that she could not let the weasel and the children live in the same house. "If we could throw something over it, and trap it," she said. She ran to the scullery and got the broom, and one of the bath towels that hung, always damp, never used, on the back of the bathroom door, and came back and went carefully into the Room. Again, the weasel ran furiously at her, and this time, feeling like a bullfighter, she dropped the towel on top of it and twisted the heavy cloth around and over until it kept still, pulsating with malice, but still.

Mary picked up the poker, but there was too much anger trapped in the bundle; she was too old to kill it that way.

"Could you open the door, please, and I'll sweep it through," said Jenny.

"Put it out the scullery door," said Mary.

"It's too far; it might unroll," said Jenny, and Mary had to open the formal front door, into the stinging wind, and Jenny pushed the towel out onto the front doorstep, and left it there.

Without speaking, Mary went immediately to the kitchen, to make tea.

Jenny picked up the baby, and calmed him down, and took him to the window. They saw the brown and white head peer out of the towel folds, a pretty S-curve. The weasel looked both ways and then slipped free and went off in quick leaps, its long back arching, across the garden. For a moment, Jenny wondered if it might not try to get right back into the Room again, but the old three-legged cat saw it from a fencepost and, with no time to sneak up on it, bolted after it in a cat's sudden, savage way, and grabbed it at the wire. The weasel stood on end and exploded at the cat, which was five times its size, and even through the rattling windowpane Jenny could hear the weasel screaming, and the snarling hiss from the old cat. Then the cat drew back, shaking its ears, and the weasel squirmed through the mesh and slipped into the cover of a flowering currant bush by the fence corner. It did not show itself again.

Jenny thought of Shona, and went searching, and found her under Mary's bed, against the wall.

"Don't tell Daddy about that big mouse," said Jenny, after she had carried Shona through the house to prove that it was gone. She would not tell Simon about the weasel, and Simon would not tell Mary about the woodworm. For the same reason.

The children were asleep when Simon got back, the headlight beams alive with blowing sleet and rain. He came into the kitchen carrying parcels, and put them on the table: a six-piece jigsaw puzzle for Shona, a bag of Pan Drop Mints for Mary, a women's glossy magazine for Jenny, a sack of roofing nails, some woodworm killer, and two letters. There was another parcel, heavy for its size. It clinked, and was wrapped in gray paper. Simon did not open it yet.

"I met postie," said Simon. "He was trying to get the Strath-Ard post delivered; he was riding on the back of a tractor, poor wee soul. He said he'd no mind being spared the journey up to Croichan, the road was that bad."

He struggled out of his anorak and sweater, both soaked through. Jenny hung them on the door of the drying oven, where she knew they would not dry. "Did you have trouble, dearie?" she asked. "Were you in the ditch?"

"Och, no," he said, "but I met the priest from Inverness, with his wee Volkswagen thing off the road, and I got my shoulder to it behind and heaved it out for him, but he kept revving the motor up in my face and nearly gassed me to death."

Mary giggled. "They've no' got any sense, the R.C.'s," she said.

"And then I met the snowplow, clearing the bus route, and I thought I would follow it as far as the phone box corner; it was a grand big machine, throwing up eight-foot walls of snow right and left, quite the thing. And there was a gritting truck as well. The truck went first, with a wee mannie standing up in it behind, shoveling the grits onto the road; and then the plow followed, you see, with its blades set just high enough to scoop up all the grits and throw them into the ditch. I followed them to the corner, having a grand time, thinking all was well, and then I saw what was going to happen; I leaned out of the window and flashed my lights and shook my fist at them, and they all waved and smiled, the daft loons, and went ahead and plowed an eight-foot wall of snow across the Strath-Ard road at the phone box corner.

"And then I had to dig my way through. And I'm late getting back, you see."

Mary went a suppressed pink in the face, and said, "Och, Simon," as the full beauty and intricacy of the story came to her, and they all sat quietly over it till the bodach 'ha radan came in from the byre, and sat in his window chair, expecting tea. The gray parcel was still on the table, unopened.

"What's in that one, dearie," said Jenny.

"Och, well; Mary, would you open it. It occurred to me—I was on the High Street, you see, and I passed a shop where this sort of thing is sold—it occurred to me that

Callum might need a wee bittie extra help, perhaps, when he comes back, and that this might be useful."

Mary took the heavy, clinking, small parcel and unwrapped it slowly. She held up a long chrome handle and a packet of screws. The white light ran along one side, the firelight down the other.

"It is to help him get up out of bed," said Simon, looking away from it. "It screws into the wall beside the bed, you see, and he can use it to support himself."

Mary turned it all ways, watching it. The bodach 'ha radan was fascinated, and came hobbling to the table and examined it minutely, as if it were a complicated piece of machinery, nodding and droning eagerly at it.

"I thought I would put it up in the little room, off," said Simon. "And then see about getting some sort of bed. Perhaps we could get proper hospital equipment under the National Health."

He read the instruction paper that came with the handle, from The Surgical Supply House, Edinburgh, and drilled holes and screwed it onto the wall at the correct angle, where the bed would be. The bodach 'ha radan followed him around, saying, "Aye. Aye. My cousin Rory, he was in the Veterans' Hospital after the Great War; they had the handles, and the equipment, and it was all for the walking, and the sitting, and the getting out of the bath; och, it was all grand."

When the handle was up, Mary went into the small room and drew the curtains, and left the door open, accepting it as part of the kitchen, from now on.

Then they sat quietly, heavily. "Did you read the letters?" Simon asked Jenny.

"No," she said. "I forgot." He picked up the first, said, "Michael," read it, put the check in his pocket and passed the letter on to her. "Notes from a happier life," he said.

I have lost Rosiqa. When the cast came off the
leg just went to pieces again. I think too much disinfectant kept it from healing.

"The dog died? That's not happy," she said.
"It is, somehow," he said. "I can't explain."
She did not understand. Michael said a lot more. He
was communicating in full this time.

You at the Arctic Circle will never believe it,
but it's spring in Edinburgh. The filthy lilac tree in
the next door yard has leaves and buds. It's snow-
ing, too, big chunks of gray snow, but never mind.
It makes the factories look a little better.

Last Sunday I took Phoebe on one of our favorite walks in East Lothian. Fran came, too. There's a
footpath along the River Tyne from East Linton to
Hailes Castle. It looks more like Japan than Scotland. There are weeping willows and little bridges
and swans and things. Sunday the hillside was
covered with masses of wild daffodils. I've never
seen such blazing yellow.

Jenny laughed, almost tearfully, shaking her head.
"There's a daffodil in the kitchen garden, I think, but it's
not even in bud yet," she said.
"We stood the ladder on top of it this morning," said
Simon.

At one place the river goes through a field; you
have to go over a stile. Phoebe goes under. We feel
safe there, because there are usually hares, and no
livestock.

But on Sunday we were climbing the stile, and

Phoebe went running on ahead of us, and suddenly we saw that the field was full of ewes and baby lambs. I have beaten Phoebe time and again about sheep, and she will not learn, Fran said "You and your bloody dogs," or something like that. I think we've about had it. Anyway, Phoebe went trotting towards the sheep in a thoughtful way, and they started to shift and baa and mill around, the way they do, the damn things. That got her excited, and she gave a sort of playful lunge at them, and the whole flock bunched up and started to run.

She started to lope after them—not really chasing yet. Then, as it says in melodramas, I found my voice, and gave one last despairing yell, not hoping for very much, "*Phoebe! No, no, NO!*" And she stopped. She did stop, and came back, looking silly, the way a dog does when it's apologizing. I put her on the leash and we all had to sit down for a minute. She must have been just inside the edge of obedience. But if the field had been more open, or if the sheep had been running a little faster, it would have been mutton chops—and a Court Order to Destroy the Dog—for supper.

One of my colleagues gave me this one: MO MHOLLACHD AIG NA CAORAICH MHOR. You look it up. I had to.

Love,
Michael

"Always *love*, you see," said Simon. "He is a hippie."

The second letter affected them all. Simon read it, and Jenny, and Mary, and the bodach 'ha radan absorbed, somehow, what was in it; and they all sat around the kitchen, without speaking, letting the night pass. Simon spent a few minutes with Michael's letter and the Gaelic handbook, translating, and passed it to Jenny: *my curses on the big sheep*. That made her smile, but there was another presence in the kitchen, circling them like the rim of a wheel, and it was stronger.

> Dear Mr. Johnston,
> Thank you for your inquiry of 15 February.
> Mr. Macdonald is progressing quite well, considering his age. The therapist reports that he is strong and has mastered the practice short legs in a remarkably short time. Last week he was measured for a pair of jointed permanent legs and once he has learned to balance on these, there is no reason why he should not be allowed home.
> His diabetic condition has been stabilized; however, he will have to keep to a strict diet, with daily insulin injections, which will be supervised by your local District Nurse. Suitable invalid equipment, including a bed and a wheelchair, will be available to you under National Health auspices.
> We shall inform you of the date of discharge nearer the time. Early May would be a reasonable estimate.
>
> Yours faithfully,
>
> A. G. Wood
> Consultant Surgeon

Jenny was sitting up in bed at six one morning, nursing the baby. He was almost weaned now, and was a person, not the curling little embryo shape that he had been at first, and it was almost embarrassing to have him at her breast. But he still woke early, and it was easier to feed him on the spot than get up in the deadly cold of the Room and the kitchen and make him baby cereal.

The window was open, and as she sat there, sleepy, she suddenly felt the wind blow across her, swinging the curtains. It was blowing from the west. Something was different. It was as if she were waking up in a strange place, confused. The windowpanes were pale gray instead of black. There was light and noise outside.

"Oh," she said, as if someone had spelled it out to her at last.

There was a racket of birdsong, like a crowd deliriously smashing up wine glasses. The west wind brought the call of some moor bird, a curlew perhaps; four painfully sweet whistles and then a long bubbling cry, over and over. There was a faint stitching of rooks' caws over the whole croft, like a canopy. And she even heard—faintly, from the Muir to the north—the spoken words; cuckoo, cuckoo: the final statement.

The light had probably been growing since January, but she had never noticed it before.

Spring did not mean warm weather at Croichan; the February thaw had been warmer than the next two months. It meant daylight, the return of light. In winter it had never been light, and in spring there was a reversal; it was never dark. They got up early and went to bed late, but they could not find the night any more. It was bright at five in the morning, with the hens frantic to get out, blackbirds singing, swallows dive bombing the barn cats. Mary did not light the lamp until eight, nine, ten; they all sat in the kitchen by the chilly fire, the room getting dimmer and softer, the curtains open and the pale cloudy evening outside. Jenny was annoyed, because she could not knit properly, and Simon found it a good excuse to stop reading Gaelic; but the bodach 'ha radan and Mary seemed more content to sit in the half-dark, in the vague twilight that defined nothing, isolating them completely, than they had ever been in the glaring paraffin light.

In the first few weeks of spring, the whole character of the croft changed. In winter, Croichan had been part of the moor. It had belonged to the ice and rocks and the battering winds, exposed on the topmost jagged edge of Strath-Ard. Now Jenny was sure she felt it settle towards the bogs and willow woods in the north and east; it was protected and surrounded by the forest. Very strange. The flowering currant bush at the house corner bloomed, lumpy sprays of pink and red with a tomcat smell that made Jenny think of the weasel. Perhaps he was still in there.

There were days and days of rain, until the whole steading was filled with a soft fine spray. One afternoon, the rain slowed down into a pale yellow drizzle, with a flat circle of sun like tissue paper. Jenny had not been out of the house much since February. Now she took Shona and they went across the road and through the gate, down into the Muir. The woods were almost tropical. The opening leaves made a green fog, and clouds of midges went floating in the air, under the trees. There was a smell of cinnamon—the wet willow bark; and sweet medicine, which was bog myrtle, growing up out of the swamp. It was hot. The air was too rich, like an overripe melon. The whole Muir was hung with Victorian curves of wet larch trees and spiderwebs, beaded and swinging.

They found a rocky streambed running downhill with a set of whinstone steps cut beside it like a heavy necklace thrown down, and followed that down and down until the forest became hardwood, with young oaks and beeches.

They could hear sheep bleating in the valley, and crows way overhead. It was hot. It was too much. They struggled back uphill, coughing on midges, and got back to Croichan exhausted, dripping sweat, and Shona fell asleep and missed high tea. In Fife, the seasons were cold and bare, but sensible. Croichan seemed to go by moods; the seasons were complicated and shifty. There was no easy answer.

Still, everything began to move. Both cows calved at the same time, black bull calves, minute curly things with slimy noses. Mary put them into the calf pen, in a corner of the byre, and fed them out of a bucket. The dairy filled up with pans and pans of milk, set out to rise for cream and butter. Simon objected. "It's bad management. We've been drinking that Carnation stuff all winter, Mary, and now we have gallons too much. You don't sell butter any more. Why not get rid of that scabby bull, and get the A.I. instead. Then you could space the calves properly."

"Och, aye, Simon, but you sound like the BBC. 'Crofters are advised to contract the Ministry of Agriculture for details of the breeding program.' Callum would no' have it. He called it The Bull with the Bowler Hat."

Jenny agreed with Mary; she liked the dairying, the fresh-sour smells of too much milk. Each morning, they all got lumps of warm cream on their porridge. They passed the hand churn around whenever they were all in for tea, each taking a turn, and made pale waxy lumps of butter, and Mary let the skim milk set and made crowdie, curd cheese, for evening tea.

"My mother would be salting butter and storing it in crocks now, for the winter," said Mary. "There will be the cheese press about somewhere, still. We would wrap up the cheese, you see, and bury it in the kitchen garden, till it was wanted."

"We could find the cheese press, perhaps, and use it

again," said Simon, but Mary looked vague and tired, suddenly; and Jenny knew that no one would make winter cheese for Croichan any more.

"Och, well," Simon said to Jenny later. "It would be arty-crafty, no doubt. We might as well spin and dye and weave our own wool, if we're going to have a Celtic Revival. And I distrust that."

"I thought we were having one, dearie," she said.

The first lamb was born. Simon and Jenny went out to inspect the sheep one evening after the children were in bed, and found the ewe, her hind wool matted and wet, in a far corner of the croft, below the stand of birch and whin that divided Croichan from the Keeper's Cottage and the open moor. The sky was lavender and the lamb was equally lavender, almost transparent in the evening light. The ewe trotted away and the lamb staggered after her, trailing the umbilical cord. She gave a deep belching bleat and it answered three octaves up. The next morning Simon found the lamb dead, half-eaten by a fox. The hoodie-crows were taking what was left.

In the next two weeks, a dozen lambs were born and half of them were killed by foxes. At last, Simon went down for Morag's collie again, and each night he persuaded the dog, who was surly and overworked now with Morag's own sheep, to drive the ewes and lambs into the steading yard and he penned them there, letting them out to find grass in the morning, and for a while they were safe. But the substance of the croft seemed to be willfully leaking in spite of all he could do, because then the lambs began to die of something else.

One morning near the first of May, Jenny and Shona left the baby asleep in his pram by the sunny house wall, and went for a walk to see the lambs. The hens were all out, purring and wandering around in the sunny calm, the way they had done in the February thaw, long ago, and as before, they made a kind of traveling still point, utter peace. There were a few primulas blooming at the top of the kitchen garden, and the flat, bright flowers reminded Jenny of coloring-book flowers she had crayoned purple, yellow, red, when she was little. The cockerel flew up to the pram and flapped and crowed on the rim for a second and the baby did not even wake; so Jenny and Shona went on across the fields, thinking that he was safe.

The ewes, hunting the new thin grass between the bracken stalks, had wandered far to the east and were grazing against the dark green wall of trees at the edge of the Forestry Plantation. Jenny saw the surviving lambs, skipping like fleas, some white, some brownish-black, in and out of the flock. She heard them bleating. Their high, reedy baa was so like the yell of a newborn baby that she stopped in a sudden fright and turned back, with a shock of anxiety about her own child. She had heard the lambs before, but not when the baby had been out of her sight. She looked back—Alasdair was safe asleep, the hens had not tipped the pram over, and the bull was far away, and the baby was past the newborn baaing stage anyhow. Jenny laughed at the mother-animal in herself, but it had been a real shock, enough to make her heart beat hard, and her back go sweaty and cold. Shona ran on ahead. Jenny was still struggling out of her mother-human-ewe confusion when she saw the bodach 'ha radan limping in slow motion toward them, coming from the flock. He was swinging something heavy, too heavy for him, in his left hand. She saw that it was another dead lamb.

He held its four feet together, so that its back bowed and its head swung down. Jenny knew she had to help the old man, so she went to meet him and took the hind legs, shuddering at the touch of the cool, small bones. It was so unlike a sheep, with its plush fur and waxy, yellow, unused hooves. The umbilical cord was bloody at the navel and the hoodie-crows had been pecking at its eyes, but it had not been torn up. Foxes had not killed it.

"Och, Daddy'll fix it," said Shona.

Simon was away on the tractor so they brought the lamb to Mary.

"Och, it just died," she said. The bodach 'ha radan nodded. "They do that. Perhaps the ewe's milk was no' good for it. Poor wee boy."

She threw it on the midden. When Simon came back he took it off and examined it, without learning anything, and buried it, in case it was infectious. Then he went looking for the ewe, thinking that if she had milk he might persuade her to adopt an orphan or a twin; but he found her collapsed and paralyzed, half-hidden in last year's dry bracken. Heavy and stinking as she was, he put her across his shoulders like a furpiece and carried her back to the house and put her in a small side paddock just under Callum's window.

Shona was pleased, because the healthy sheep were wild and ran away from her. She brought out chopped turnips on a plate, and stroked the ewe's face and horns, but the ewe would not eat. Her head was alive, with its yellow eyes and curved Cheviot nose, but her body was empty and limp. The wind beat at her all day as if it were beating a flat sheepskin rug. Next morning, the ewe was dead.

Simon buried her, which amused Mary, who would have left her for the crows. Then another lamb and ewe died. They could not afford vet bills. Morag's mother had been a white witch, able to cure strains and sick sheep by the power of the Trinity, but she was dead. Fochan was too busy with the Laird's hill ewes to come to Croichan and advise them, and the bodach 'ha radan knew nothing about sheep.

"It might be a calcium deficiency," said Simon. "Do sheep get eclampsia? Or liver fluke? Or God knows what. They've always grazed over the same pasture, and I don't think Callum ever gave the sheep any supplements."

He went to Inverness and brought back a crate of bright blue mineral squares. He set them in the field and the sheep and cattle crowded around the licks, but it was too late for the lambing ewes—if it was the right answer at all; many collapsed, and lay like damp rugs, and there was a crop of dead and orphaned lambs.

But Simon could not pay full attention to the sheep then, because the autumn plowing had been neglected, and it was time to prepare the arable land. Croichan had three plowed fields; two east of the steading, set in level grassland, and one west, on the steep, stony hillside at the southwest corner of the croft. The Laird's deer fence formed its western boundary, so it was up against the high moor—higher even than the Keeper's Cottage. It sloped south, toward the Kilduich burn, and in winter, the blackish southern hills kept it in full shadow, and it seemed a mad place to put crops. But in summer, the sun got above the hills and made it the brightest place on the croft. The three fields grew oats and barley, turnips, potatoes and hay, in rotation, most to support the livestock, some for sale. Simon had spread the dung in February but now he had to work fourteen hours on the tractor day after day.

From the Room windows, Jenny could see the red tractor crawl down and dangerously up the hillside—tractors could pitch over backward if the grade was too steep. After dark, the headlights, yellow eyes, kept moving along the black slope, and long after Mary had lit the paraffin lamp he drove into the yard, the wheels churning up great dragon tracks of mud. He did not bother to put the tractor away in its shed. It would barely cool off by morning.

While he was plowing, he drove down to the house for dinner and left the tractor standing in the dooryard, chugging and stuttering and scaring the hens into the branches of the fallen tree. But when he started sowing, he had to stay on the spot, especially at the west field, until the soil was harrowed and the seeds covered up: rabbits and birds, he said, were waiting for the minute he turned his back. So the first planting day, when he put the barley into the west field, Jenny and Mary packed morning tea for them all and carried it up to the hill.

Mary put buttered scones and jam, cups and the flask of tea into a basket, and Jenny picked up the baby, and Shona followed them through the field gate and up the stony, sunken track to the west, trying to avoid the tractor ruts. The bull and cows watched them, but did not follow. They went along the edge of the hill to the highest part of the croft, and chose a rock, as big as a man, to sit down by, and settled there. Jenny let the baby crawl free on the grass, which was cold, but dry, and they unpacked the tea things. Simon came up the hill towards them, finishing the row.

He had the seedbag hung on a strap over his shoulder and he walked and reached into the sack and threw the grain broadcast, perfectly in tune—and aware of it—with the lovely, swirling motion. Jenny silently congratulated him. He had recreated himself at last: HIGHLAND PEASANT, SON OF THE SOIL.

"The rats have got into the seed-corn, now," he said, sitting down with them. His boots were so clotted with sticky mud that he could hardly lift them, and he tried to scrape off some of the mud with a flat stone. "There must have been heavy rain, west," he said. "The burn is in spate and the field is flooded at the bottom. I must bring a spade tomorrow and ditch and drain it or the tractor will bog down at the harrowing, and who will help me get it free? Mr. Mackay?"

Jenny thought of the empty kitchen and said, "Will the old man get his tea all right?"

"Och, the mannie; aye," said Mary. "I poured him out his cuppie and put the sugar in and stirred it for him and left it on the table with a piece next to it and a wee saucer on top," and they laughed. Alasdair laughed and squeezed scone and jam in his fist till it came out in grayish-pink worms between his fingers, and Shona, who was jealous and did stupid things on purpose, copied him.

"Stinkpot," whispered Simon to her, unclenching her fists and trying to scrub them on the grass, and he and Shona began an exchange of insults, in whispers so that Mary would not hear: Smelly Bum, Crappy Nappy, and so on, which Shona loved.

Mary said, "I'll bring you up the spade at dinnertime, Simon, but Willie-John would bring his tractor, if ours got stuck. He used to do the plowing for Callum, and he is a contractor all around Strath-Ard."

Simon nodded, and went back to whispering with Shona, but Jenny had noticed that: do they need Simon, then, she thought; are they helpless, or are they still farmers, a community—does Croichan need him? Through all the bitterness, she had never doubted that the croft would immediately die without him.

Does Croichan need Simon, or is it entirely the other way around?

She looked at Simon, and wondered what he knew.

It was a blue and white day with the wind from the west, off the moor. Beinn à Bha-ach Ard was still glazy white with snow and seemed to float in the moving air. They sat in the strong cold sun. To the south, level with them, were the blackish, crumbling hills, marked with dull green squares of Forestry planting; she saw bits of yellow-green birch and jade-green larch growing among the pine. At the foot of the hills was the Kilduich burn, and then the field, sloping up towards them.

Between those hills and the Ard River valley, a broad ridge of land ran east-west, rising from thick woods in the east to the edge of the moor, where they were sitting now, pouring out second cups of tea. It was a ridge of land like a whale's back, swimming toward the west. That was Strath-Ard, the crofting community, though she knew that *strath* really meant a valley, in this case the river bottom. Along the ridge, at random, was a pattern of stone walls and gray croft cottages. At each steading she saw a bright red dot of flowering currant. Otherwise the ridge was a drab gray-green, with the brown of last year's bracken. Some black and white birds flew down Strath-Ard and their calls bounced off the hills to the north and swung, like a pendant, across the deep space to the Beinn in the south: plink—plink; a thin high note.

The baby crawled away and tried to stand up against the big rock, and Shona climbed up, yelling *I'm the king of the castle, and you're the dirty rascal, see me, Daddy, SEE ME*, and as a rule her voice would have shredded peace and quiet; but up here, the deep air blotted her out, and Jenny looked down across the ridge as if they were in total silence. They were all looking that way, to the east.

They could see a dozen steadings, but only three smoking chimneys: Morag's, and Willie-John's, and Croichan itself. Even in the distance they could see doors, roofs, windows—black and broken in. The Laird's Blackface sheep, the hill breed, were grazing across Strath-Ard as if it were open moor. There were a few pastures, with the cottony white Cheviots quietly standing, and a few black cattle, but the goatlike hill sheep were walking in and out of the cottage doors. The crofts were all overgrown, some with bracken and rushes, like Croichan; some, in the older empty steading yards, with sapling birch and willow.

"The Laird doesn't want to pay rates on those abandoned crofts," said Simon, "even when he owns them again; so when he gets repossession of the crofting rights he knocks a hole in the roof and declares it uninhabitable. Then he patches it up and stores hay inside. *What do you mean, feudalism?* he says. *That's husbandry.*"

Jenny started to cry. Mary, embarrassed, switched off and looked somewhere else. Simon stared as if he did not know what to do with her—ignore her, perhaps—he put his hand briefly on the back of her neck and said, "Och, love," and then got up and swung the barley sack over his shoulder and started down the row again. Mary repacked the tea things. Jenny sat by herself until Shona noticed and came down from the rock, saying in her shrillest voice, *Mummy, what are you doing, Mummy, what are you laughing for in that funny way,* until Jenny found the voice so maddening that she stopped crying, just to stop the noise. But she was not finished. As she and the children followed Mary back through the mud and stones to the gate, they passed the cattle standing by the larch tree, chewing on the roots, and their black shapes were blurry against the hill.

Fits of sobbing took her by surprise all day. They wrenched her and made her feel sick. By afternoon she was frantic, and she had begun to see the crying fits as little bodies, with personal lives apart from herself: small, gray-green, phlegmy frogs waiting, between the blankets of Alasdair's crib when she straightened them after his nap, in the baby food jar that she warmed up for his dinner, on the pump handle when she refilled the tank after giving the

children a washtub bath. Mary did the milking and shut
the hens up for the evening and never looked at her. At last
relief came. The baby was asleep and Shona, ready for
bed, was trailing after her, sucking her thumb, when Jenny
looked out the scullery window. She saw the three-legged
cat sitting on the gatepost like a messenger, a spindly thing
against the great mass of Beinn à Bha-ach Ard. There was a
big rat in its mouth, hanging down, with a limp tail,
dead.

She remembered the bodach 'ha radan. Her mood spun
and changed. She ran and got the milk jug from the larder
shelf, poured half into a porridge bowl, forestalled tan-
trums by lifting Shona to the drainboard so that she could
see out of the window, took an old newspaper from under
the sink, carried the milk outside and set it down tactfully,
not too near the cat. It was a wild barn cat, but it had
learned to take milk sometimes from Mary. Then she hid
behind the house corner to watch. When the cat jumped
down, set the rat beside the bowl and started to lap, she
scared it hobbling away and grabbed the rat with a piece
of *The Northern Scot*. She left the milk down as a reward
and took the rat into the house. It was a soft, heavy rat. She
was sure, somehow, that it was a female. Shona was crying
with tiredness and bad temper, but she cheered up and
helped Jenny fold *The Northern Scot* into a neat parcel
around the body, and they left it on the scullery sink.

"A present for Mr. Mackay," explained Jenny when
Mary came in, and Mary giggled. "Och, he will be pleased."

Shona wanted to stay up until the bodach 'ha radan
came in, so Jenny held her on her lap and read a story, and
when the old man came in for his tea they told him. He
finished his cup and the scone and jam, and then he got up
and limped into the scullery to judge the rat. Shona wriggled down and followed him, and Jenny wondered if he

would chase her back; but he did not. He made no sound in the scullery, and he was there a long time. Jenny and Mary drank their tea politely. Mary was pink in the face. Jenny felt hilarious and wild, and wondered if laughing fits were going to take her now the way the crying fits had, and if so, what they would look like. Outside, the wind rattled against the house from the west, bringing the noise of Simon's tractor. He was using the harrow. They could hear it jingling, dragging behind the tractor, covering the seeds.

Shona came back. "Mr. Mackay looked in between the rat's back legs," she said. "He's cut it up into wee bits. He's got a knife in his pocket, but it's no' very sharp. He's put the head and all that into the bucket, and something else in his pocket.

"Mercy," said Mary.

The bodach 'ha radan limped back into the kitchen and sat down in his window chair. The evening light was turning blue and pale and made him look blue and white and faintly shining. He sat without speaking.

"Will it do, then, Mr. Mackay," said Mary.

"Aye," he said. "Aye. Aye. It'll be the one. I'll be staying out there all night, Mrs. Macdonald."

So they all sat and waited through the long light evening. Shona fell asleep at ten and Jenny carried her to bed in the Room. They sat watching the small flicks and triangles of fire in the grate, while outside the light got bluer and bluer until the steading dissolved into infinite blue, luminous and suffocating. At ten-thirty Jenny went out to the henhouse corner and heard some late wood pigeons going to roost in the Muir, hooting and echoing, coo-coo, coo-coo-coo. When she got back to the house it was dark night somehow, though she had only been out a few minutes. A small black thing flew in circles above the steading yard. It was not a bat; it made an odd croaking, purring noise, as if it had a motor. A nightbird of some kind. Callum would know. In the woods, she heard an owl mew. Inside, the house seemed warm and close, though it was not. Mary began to light the lamp.

She put the match to the basket wick first and it flared up, dirty orange, lurid purple, and then it caught and hissed bright greenish-white. The windowpanes went black in contrast and the bodach 'ha radan, ill at ease in the sudden light, blinking, got up to go out.

"Will you have the torch, Mr. Mackay," said Mary.

"Och, no; no," he said. "I'll no be needin that, Mrs. Macdonald."

He left the flashlight, but took the flask of tea she made up for him, and went heavily out through the mud to the byre. They heard the squawk of unsettled hens and then the steading was very quiet, until the wind blew the monotonous grind and jingle of the tractor to them again.

He had left the rat's head, tail, paws, and, as far as they could tell, most of its cut-up body in the hens' bucket under the sink.

"The old man's no' got any sense," said Mary. "The hens would no' like that. They would take fright at the rat smell, you see." She picked up the bits in her big fingers, and took them out to the midden. Then they settled down again, to wait for Simon.

Simon finished the harrowing late—past eleven, in the black dark. He drove the tractor down through the gate and into the yard, so tired that the lurch and sweep of the headlights made him dizzy. His brain was thick with the monotony of the field rows. He was half-asleep on the high seat, exhausted, and he decided not to leave the tractor out that night: he would put it away in the shed. The west field was done. He was fed up. Bloody farm work.

He was going to take a holiday; things were not going well. He remembered the day of coursing at Moy as something very sweet and clear, and wondered why he never felt that way at Croichan, when it was the same country, the same kind of moor, the same language—besides, at Moy he had been an observer, and here he was family; and yet, here he had begun to feel defeated and old. If he could take Jenny and the children west tomorrow, just go out onto the hill and walk around a little, perhaps things would be better.

He was so tired that he had to concentrate bitterly to steer the tractor through the yard into the narrow shed, and forgot how low the doorsill was, and ducked just in time. The sudden yellow glare of the headlights trapped between the tractor and the shed wall shocked him awake. Every splintery board zigzagged into bright relief, like lightning. So he woke up. He switched the engine off, and it gave a few thumps and everything was quiet, and dark, and he almost fell asleep again. He slid down, feeling the ground rise and turn under his feet.

When he was tired he became a plodding, methodical person, and made lists, and tried to do things by rule. He knew that it was not proper to put a tool away, at Croichan, if there was any possibility of it being used again tomorrow, or next week, or in this lifetime, or any other; but he felt a flare of disgust at such slovenly farming and decided that he would 1) unhook the harrow, 2) carry it into the barn next door, 3) carry it to the proper place inside the barn, and 4) put it squarely, neatly down. Following the list—each item took a separate lurch and fastening of the will—he got the harrow off, his wheel-stiff hands feeling like clumps. It was heavy. He half-dragged it jin-

gling to the barn door. It belonged inside. It was supposed
to lean against the wall that divided the barn space from
the byre. The barn was thick black and smelled oaty and
warm. He left the barn door open behind him.

He knew he was an excitable man, but not a timid one;
he did not scare easily. He had never been afraid of the
dark. But as he bent forward in that thick dark to set the
harrow down against the wall, in its own place, the place it
had belonged in ever since he had known Croichan—the
harrow fell forward, through the dark, through no wall,
and he went off balance and almost fell with it. He caught
himself and scrambled upright just before the harrow, and
his hands, touched—what ground? He did not hear the
metal fall. He straightened up, terrified, and he was lost.
He did not know where he was, or which way he had
turned. He could not hear the cows. He was choking in
dust. The dust came spinning around him like a cocoon,
winding him up. He touched something, dry, slippery:
what? He felt it desperately. It made no sense. He didn't
recognize it: the threshing machine. But that was in the
corner behind him, and he had not moved. He saw a dark
blue rectangle upright in front of him, and he did not know
what it was. He tried to touch it, but his hand went
through. After a moment of panic, his brain made sense of
that: the open barn door. He must have turned full around,
and gone floundering across to the far wall. In horror, he
ran through the door, hitting his shoulder on the hard
frame, and the ammonia reek of the byre drain outside
woke him, like smelling salts. Shivering, he went into the
house.

He took off his boots in the scullery, and blinked in the
kitchen light.

"How is the old man getting on, dearie?" said Jenny.

"Old man?" he said, confused. "Which, me?"

She laughed. "Mr. Mackay," she said. "We heard you bring the harrow in, and we thought you must be talking to him. Has he got any yet?"

"The mannie is away out, Simon," said Mary. "Seeing to the rats."

"But you were in the barn," said Jenny. "Do you mean you didn't know he was there as well?"

"What, in the barn?" said Simon. "There wasn't a sound —and it was very dark."

"Och, Simon, you are a case," said Mary. She and Jenny laughed at him. "Aye, well," she said, "perhaps he was on the other side with the cows."

"Aye, surely," he said. She gave him tea. He did not want it, but he drank it, because it was expected. Even now, after the long months, he and Jenny usually went into the bathroom together and brushed their teeth by the flashlight beam, teasing and jostling each other and trying to spit froth on each other's fingers under the tap. But tonight he went alone, and locked the door, and sat down on the side of the tub. He felt his face twist, like a child about to cry. There had been a reversal—savage, unfair. The barn had always been his favorite place. The barn had always been the safest place. Now there was no safe place left for him anywhere.

When Jenny woke the next morning, after no dreams, she was alone in the Room. Simon had gotten up early and dressed the children and taken them into the kitchen without her. She found him reading to Shona, waiting for breakfast. Mary had been milking and was stirring the porridge.

"I couldn't sleep; I have a headache," he said. "Too much bloody tractoring. Have we got any aspirin?"

"Hasn't Mary?" she said.

"I finished all of hers in the night," he said. Jenny found a bottle of baby aspirin, made adjustments for his size, and put ten of the little orange pills in water for him. He sat watching them fizz up.

"Do something else today, dearie," she said. "Take a holiday. Perhaps we could all go on a picnic or something."

Mary came in. "The bodachan has left us a grand pile of rats," she said. "Och, it looks like Culloden. It'll no' be me taking them away."

"And what am I supposed to do with them?" said Simon, and to Shona, "I can't read any more just now, love. It makes me feel sick." He drank the baby aspirin, and looked sicker.

"Och, put them in a sack, Simon, and take them west the road."

"I'll throw them into one of the Laird's shooting blinds."

She giggled. "Aye, that would do fine."

Shona began, "Let me see. I want to see the rats. Daddy, let me *see*."

"I'll throw them into a peat hag after breakfast," he said.

"Is your head still bad, then," said Mary. "Aye, the fresh air would do you good."

"Daddy, can I come," said Shona. "I want to see the rats."

"Shut her up, love," he said to Jenny, "I can't stand the noise."

"We'll all go," she told Shona. "Where is Mr. Mackay?"

"Och, Himself went home," said Mary. "Sitting up the night—he is too old for that. Morag will look in at him."

"I'll take the trailer and bring back some firewood, while we're up there," said Simon.

After breakfast, they went across to the barn. Simon took Jenny's hand, and Shona's on the other side.

"Where are they, dearie?"

"Somewhere," he said.

"I want to see the rats," said Shona. "Daddy, let go." It was a clear day outside and the chinks and squares of sky showing through the barn windows, the door, the join of the roof, were hard and bright, like bluestone chips. The cattle moved slowly past the barn door. "Where?" said Shona. "Daddy, let *go*."

"They will be in the byre, perhaps," said Simon. "Not in here."

"Why?" said Shona.

"I don't know where Mr. Mackay was sitting last night," he said.

"You weren't joking, then? You really were in here with him, and didn't know it?"

He didn't answer, but she noticed, with surprise, that he was still holding her hand, and Shona's. They were not a hand-holding family. They went through the low-framed door into the byre. It was not a windy day, but the tin roof was never really still. The stone floor and drains were copper-colored, seasoned by generations of cows. There were two calves alone in the pen, sucking on the wooden bars, which had been gnawed and slimed over before, by other calves. Blue and yellow stripes of sun lay across the cowstalls. Jenny took a good look at Simon and said, "Why, my dear love, did anything happen last night?"

"No," he said. "I don't want to talk about it."

Shona said frantically, "Daddy, *let go*," and he did.

"Very well," she said, because she had to. Shona, set free, started looking into all the stalls and corners and at last she screamed out,

"Look, Daddy, rats," giving it the full Highland treatment: *rrrots*.

Then Simon let go of Jenny's hand and went for a shovel and a feed sack to put them in. Shona bent over the heap. "Och, Daddy, can I keep *one*," she said softly.

"Would you two hold the sack open for me," he said. Jenny took one edge and Shona the other, holding them apart. Until Simon began to put the shovel in, the rat pile was pretty. It reminded Jenny of a stack of dead moles she had seen once on the golf course at Windygates. The moles had been blackish-brown velvet, and these were gray velvet. The dusty light and shadow of the barn seemed to coalesce around the heap, giving it blurred edges and a dusty shine, a few details of round rumps and pink feet. But when Simon got the shovel under the pile and started to move it, it became horrible. The dead rats squirmed and oozed and the plop into the sack made Jenny's shoulder skin creep.

"For God's sake, get them in," she said, hopping and shivering with disgust. He threatened her with a shovelful. "I would go stone mad, do you hear," she said, and again she felt that same odd hilarity as last night, the reversal of crying, as if things were changing, faster and faster, and looking at Simon she knew he felt it now, too. He smiled, and scraped the wet shovel on the edge of the stall, and tied up the sack with a bit of rope.

"I thought perhaps I would put them on the trailer with you and the children, and we could all ride up West together."

She looked at the damp sack of rats. "Certainly not," she said. "Put them on the tractor seat with you."

"I'm bloody well not going to drive a tractor up that road with a sodding bundle of dead rats on my lap," he said. She laughed.

"Very well, then. They're charming. They can ride with me."

He took her hand again and they went into the tractor shed, where at last he let her go, because he needed both hands to attach the trailer. She went to get the baby. He backed the tractor and trailer into the yard, and slung the rat sack on with a multiple thud, and lifted the pram body out of the wheelbase with the baby in it and put that on the trailer, too. Jenny and Shona climbed on. Mary came out of the house and gave them a flask of tea and a bag of scones and jam. Simon got an axe and saw for the firewood and then climbed onto the high tractor seat and drove not though the field gate this time, but out the front gate, down the bank to the road and west, where the dirt road became a stony track leading towards the Keeper's Cottage and the open hill. Jenny had not been west on the road before.

Past Croichan the road was used only by the Laird, for shooting parties after August 12—when the grouse season opened—and it was no more than two deep ruts, scattered with round white stones, and a strip of grass and heather down the middle. The tractor roared, and the trailer tipped and bounced and Jenny held on to both children at once. The huge wheels turned ahead of them. The rat sack shifted, from inside, but kept its place and did not slide towards them. Birch and juniper scraped the wheels. The track got steeper, rougher.

They passed the driveway and gate to the Keeper's Cottage, on the left. On the right was the Muir, but Jenny could see, ahead, the deer-fence where the forest stopped and the hill went on. They drove higher until they were exposed to the whole valley—the dun-colored hillsides all sloping down, somehow, never up; the stream of mountains across the Ard River; clouds and cloud shadows. Wide and fresh, cold, frightening.

They stopped at the deer fence, which was seven feet high, well built of wire and slatted wood. Jenny thought that Simon would open the gate and they would drive through onto the moor, but he suddenly began to turn the tractor, about face, lurching and almost tipping it, up the bank and down, ramming the trailer into the Muir fence. Jenny heard the wire twanging and scraping against the trailer and screamed above the noise, "What are you doing?"

"Turning the bugger," he called back. When he had the tractor pointing down towards Croichan he set the brake, got down, took the rat sack off the trailer and carried it to the deer fence. Then he untied the rope and climbed up the wire, holding the sack as if it were wet and heavy, got to the top and heaved the sack over, open, letting the rats slither out and plump down one by one into the heather on the moor side of the fence. They lay in a scattered pile. He threw the sack after them and climbed down.

"The heather will be too wet this time of year," he said to her. "If we go any further in we won't be able to turn."

She accepted that, and looked on through the gate. The track went on over the brown slopes, out of sight. It looked no different than the moor summit they had crossed in November. More sky, perhaps, but that said *nothing* as well. A small bunch of Blackface sheep rose up out of the heather like grouse and galloped away towards the valley. Shona was talking. The turning had frightened her.

"Where does the road go, love," said Jenny, because Simon did not move to go back, but stood looking at the heather as if he would like to walk on it; and she wanted to show interest.

"Nowhere," he said. Then he got angry, and shouted at her, "There's a burn and a bridge. I've never been further than that. I wanted to go, and now I never will. How could

I, *me*, how could I do such an uncomplicated bloody thing
as that?"

He stepped back over the wheel to the seat, put the
tractor in gear and started forward. The roaring of the
engine filled the roadbed, between the high banks. The axe
and saw slid dangerously from side to side. He swung up
the drive to the Keeper's Cottage, and stopped to open the
gate. They heard the crash of dry bracken in the Muir
below them and saw three big stags leaping almost out of
sight into the woods.

"Those are red deer," said Simon quietly. "The bastards
aren't supposed to be in there; the fence must be down.
We'll get wood here."

He drove through the gate and stopped and switched
the tractor off, and in the quiet Jenny saw the steading was
very green. Grass had grown up where the Croichan yard
was mud and footprints, and sheep had wandered there
and grazed it short, and the whole place had the smooth-
cut green look of a graveyard, or a ruined abbey, an ancient
monument of some kind. All the buildings were sinking
into the short green grass. No sound.

Simon took the axe and saw and went to the birch
thicket, the border of the Croichan land. Jenny lifted the
pram body down to a sheltered bit of grass and left the
baby with a toy to chew, and went with Shona to explore
the steading. The buildings were older than Croichan,
made of grey whinstone. There was a well, covered with
rotten boards, a henhouse, tangles of fallen fence wire, and
a two-room cottage. The usual flowering currant bush, but
no barn or byre: just gloomy, velvet, green grass. They
looked in a window and saw a rusty grate, drab linoleum,
gray-brown flowered wallpaper, damp and peeling down;
but there was no light showing through the roof and the

window glass was not broken. The doors, they found, were locked.

They went back to Simon and Jenny asked him why the doors were locked. "When the sheep were walking in and out of the other crofts down there."

"Ah, you miss the nuances," he said. "This has always belonged to the Laird. His servants, his gamekeepers, used to live here—it's tied to the job. He still lets it out now and then. There was a writer with six children here once when I was little." He had his sweater and shirt off and was already waist-deep in fallen trees. She smelled cut wood and wet bark and sweat, and the crushed new leaves. All she could think of was how nice he looked with his shirt off, swinging an axe. He immediately knew what she was thinking and grinned at her and said, "Shona, go away; go back and see Mary."

Shona, of course, said, "I want to stay here."

"You can help me, then," he said. He attacked another tree and it swished down and collapsed, screening him one higher with the transparent green. "Go get handfuls of dirt and rub it on the cut ends; the bright stumps, you see, so that no one will notice them at a distance. The standing timber belongs to the Laird," he said to Jenny. "We always take birch for the kitchen fire, but it doesn't do to advertise."

He held the axe near the head and started lopping off branches, each with a single chop down, stroke after stroke. Jenny could feel the sun at Midsummer strength in the cold air, lying on each surface like gold leaf, not sinking in: on the rocks, the tree trunks, Simon's back. She pushed through the branches and bent over behind him as he stopped with the axe, and kissed his back. She licked him, and the smell of his skin made her mouth water, so she bit him. He said, "Why, love," and turned around and they gave each other a long, rich, movie kiss; she hugged his bare chest, shivering. Shona dropped her handful of dirt and climbed up them as they stood kissing. She clawed at Simon's belt, dragging at his trousers, so they had to pick her up and hug her, too, and it became a family exchange, baby-love, and then back to work, Simon with a hard-on, which Shona did not see.

Jenny went to see the baby, and remembered the tea flask, which she had put in the pram. "Tea cools you off, dearie, would you like some?" she said.

He thought and said, "I don't, somehow; we've been drinking too much of it."

"Yes, I know. I feel corroded. Think what our kidneys must be looking like."

"Well, we don't have to drink it."

She realized that was true, and laughed. "No; we would, at the house; but up here we don't have to drink it." She felt that not drinking tea was terribly important, a breakthrough of some kind.

They stayed at the Keeper's Cottage all morning and came back feeling peaceful, with a pile of silvery-brown logs. Simon took the wood on the trailer and Jenny walked behind, carrying the baby on her hip, seeing that Shona kept out from under the wheels. YOUNG MOTHER GETS CURVATURE OF SPINE FROM CARRYING FAT BABY; THIS IS A VERY SAD CASE, SAID THE PROCURATOR FISCAL, said Jenny to herself, trying to remember when the last Procurator Fiscal had been. She felt wide awake, aware of all the trees and plants along the road, but in a different way: she felt objective, intelligent. She wanted to be scientific and learn names. What do you call it? *Sub-Arctic. Alpine Heath. Mountain Vegetation.* Names were very satisfying. Moss, willow, heather, windflowers, blueberries, moss. She followed the tractor up the bank, through the gate, and into

the steading yard by the woodpile, before she noticed that
the space in front of the house was crowded with strange
cars.

Shona began to suck her thumb. They saw a tractor,
and a Land Rover with two collies in the back, and a blue
Mini-car, and a long Inverness County Council ambulance.
The cows and hens were out of sight, but the bull was
there, licking the Mini, shifting it in spite of the hand-
brake. The house stood silently, telling them nothing.

Simon switched the tractor off and Jenny came up
alongside and said, "How can it be? How can everybody
know about it, and not us?"

He didn't answer.

"But dearie, what did we miss? I've been paying attention. I've been trying to listen. Perhaps Mary didn't know.
Is that possible?"

"*Were you hearing, Callum Croichan is back the day.*"
For the first time, he put on the Highland voice with anger,
with a sharp edge to it.

"The doctor said he would inform us." Still he didn't
answer. "Mary will be giving them all tea," she said. "Shall
I go in and help?"

"Wait you," he said. "It wouldn't do to rush right in."

So they unloaded the birch logs and stacked them, and
everything was peaceful. The bull left the Mini and went
dreamily to the Land Rover, and backed away when the
collies growled at him, and went somewhere else. Jenny let
Alasdair crawl around the fallen larch branches, hoping he
would stay away from the root hole, and that he would not
eat larch cones and choke. Shona climbed the logpile like a
squirrel, and then got bored and started making a house for
herself inside the old Ford on the midden: she put the
spade and an old churn and the flail and some feed sacks
and chains inside, for furniture.

Then Simon unhooked the trailer and rolled it away, and drove the tractor in beside it and put that away; and then they left Shona to play outside, and Jenny picked up the baby, and he took her hand as he had done earlier, in the barn, and they went into the house.

The door to the small room was shut. The kitchen was crowded. Morag and two ambulance men were sitting at the table, drinking tea. The district nurse, a pink-faced woman in a blue coat and cap, was drinking tea and trying to explain the works of a hypodermic needle and syringe to Mary, who was making more tea and not listening.

The ambulance men, who were not from Strath-Ard, stared at Simon. He stared back.

Jenny realized that for the past six months their worries had all been understated, oblique: they were out of practice for head-on collisions. She decided to become a pair of hands in the background. She took a plate of scones that Mary had set out, and began to split and butter them, one by one, and put on the jam. Morag was in a cheerful mood.

"How are you keeping, Simon," she said. "And yourself, Jenny."

Jenny murmured the proper politeness and Simon said, "Och, well, not so bad, and yourself."

The ambulance men looked at each other, and laughed, at his Highland voice, perhaps.

Simon said, "All right, and what's so bloody funny here?"

He sounded so arrogant and ferocious that Jenny was sure there would be a fight. The baby, crawling on the floor, found a hole in the nurse's black stocking, above her knee, and put his finger on the white skin, with a long yell of amusement. The nurse blushed and pulled her skirt down. Simon waited. But the ambulance men were too well trained to start a punchup in a medical situation, and one of them said:

"Nothing. No offense," and they both got up to leave, with, "Cheerio, then, Mrs. Macdonald," and "Thank you very much for the tea, it was grand," and, "I'm sure the bed is at the proper angle now; remember, it's adjustable." But the window was half-open, and outside in the yard one of them said to the other:

"Did you see that, she's white."

Simon jerked the window wide and leaned out and made the V up-your-arse sign at them, shouting, "And I'm black, you Mothers."

The ambulance doors shut and the motor started and the square, blue van drove away, around the house corner to the road. Morag laughed.

"Och, Simon, you are a case," she said. "They're no' mothers."

From behind the closed door, they heard voices, and laughing. Mary poured a cup of tea for Simon. They were using saucers.

The nurse said, "The insulin must be kept cool, Mrs. Macdonald, have you got a cool place to keep it in?"

Jenny smiled at the thought of anything getting too warm at Croichan, but Mary looked terrified and said, "Mercy; I don't know; och, I'll put it in the dairy."

"Himself is in good form, Simon," said Morag. "Are you no' going in."

"Och, well," said Simon, "I thought I would have to queue up to pay my respects," and they laughed. He put down his tea and went to the door and opened it. Jenny could see past him. Callum was holding court. The room was so narrow that Simon had to edge in sideways. Fochan had the bedside chair, because he was the Laird's shepherd, and Willie-John stood leaning against the wall. Next to Fochan was a big wheelchair, and next to Willie-John, leaning unsupported, was a pair of legs: big legs in brown tweed trousers, with harness straps where suspenders would usually be.

Behind the legs was the window, looking southwest, and Beinn à Bha-ach Ard seemed to be coming into the room, too, overcrowding it. Jenny had the illusion of the hill actually inside the room, superimposed, double exposure. Callum was on the bed. Jenny saw that Simon was not at ease with the legs, and the others were; that set him apart a little at the beginning. But he came forward and shook hands as warmly as he could, and said, "How are you keeping, then."

Callum laughed and went pink in the face and said, "Och, I'm no' mindin." He had a high tenor voice with an odd quizzical note in it. Then Simon took his place beside Willie-John, and for a few minutes there was the correct, tactful silence, admitting Simon to the circle and waiting while he tuned in to it. Callum sat quite still, but Fochan and Willie-John sighed now and then and shook their heads and said *aye* on the indrawn breath, because dead silence would have been rude. At last Callum said—to Willie-John; it would have been too abrupt to start with Simon, and too obvious to begin with the Laird's shepherd—"Were you telling me, they found that man from Loch Carran who went missing in September."

"Aye," said Willie-John. "He had gone mental, lost his memory; they found him dead by that lochan on Beinn à Bha-ach Ard."

"Fancy," said Callum.

Morag called from the kitchen, "There is a new priest at Inverness, Callum. Will he be coming up here, to give you the word."

Jenny saw that was an old joke of some kind. Callum

said, with serene distaste, "Och, no; no, he'll no' be coming around *me*," and the rest of them laughed. Another car drove into the steading yard, and stopped. Mary would have gone to the door, but the nurse was trying to explain the insulin again. Callum had not changed: Jenny remembered his big arms and shoulders, his long, rather stupid face, his white thin hair and little blue eyes; above all, his high voice with that quizzical, overcasual note always in it. It made Callum seem shifty, as if he were talking sideways, meaning more than he said.

The only new thing about him was a pair of startling false teeth. They made a mask of his face. And the legs, of course. The blankets were pulled up over his lap and his body was so massive that it looked topheavy, hard to balance. He braced one elbow against the wall and held on tight to the chrome handle. Half of him was on the bed and almost another half was across the room, standing by the wheelchair. The legs seemed to compete with Callum for possession of the room. The legs were more upright, but Callum won; even trapped on the bed, he had power. Jenny could not understand what it was—that heavy, inexplicable presence; there was something more than himself.

She wanted to ask him why the weasel had not been white in February. She almost did, then caught herself in time. It was not correct for her to speak just then. In fact, if she did, they would all pretend she had not. So she kept quiet, and broke off bits of scone to distract Alasdair and keep him away from the nurse's black stocking. Callum said, in that hesitant, half-puzzled voice, as if it did not matter:

"I was saying to Fochan, Simon, our lambs are no' so big as they ought to be this time of year; they've no' come on awful good; what would you say?"

Simon folded his arms, looking nowhere, and shook his

head slowly and said, "Aye," and Jenny shivered for him, and the others shook their heads and said, "Och, aye," as if they were all studying to be the bodach 'ha radan.

"It was a dreadful spring for them," said Simon. "We had a loss of sixteen lambs and nine ewes in April."

It was brave, but not quite proper, for him to be so blunt. There was a slight current of shock in the room. Callum said, still casual, "Aye; that's bad. What would you think it could have been that went wrong?"

Fochan said, in his deep voice, "the foxes were a bother this lambing. I lost a few, west, like that."

"Aye, that," said Simon. "But after that they took sick, you see. They took a wasting sickness. It was the ewes died of that as well."

"Aye; that's strange," said Callum. "I don't know. Fochan."

Fochan probably did know, but by good manners he was not allowed to say, and he did not want to insult Simon; so he neatly expressed all that by, "Och, I don't know. I'd have opened one and looked at the liver; but the foxes were that bad. I never got off the hill throughout the lambing. I left a young dog at home with my wife, and I was away that long, when I got back it would no' recognize me." He imitated the dog barking in horror at the strange man and not letting him in at the door, and the others quietly laughed, but nothing was obscured.

There was a brief, soft knock at the scullery door and a man came in. He was short, with gray hair and spectacles, and was holding Shona's hand. Jenny had not seen him before, but she knew he must be important, an estate official, the factor himself perhaps: he was wearing a kilt and stockings and a tired, expensive, tweed jacket that marked him down immediately as the enemy. As he came into the room, every soul in it switched off in shock. He created a great blank. They were struck dumb, and he was at ease. He let go of Shona's hand and said, in a friendly way, "How are you, Mrs. Macdonald. I heard your husband was getting back today. I know it's a private moment for you, and I'm terribly sorry to intrude, but there are a few important things that can't wait—in fact, I thought this would be the best possible time. You don't mind if I come in."

Mary couldn't speak. She did not even offer him tea. He went through the kitchen to the small room and Fochan stood up out of the bedside chair. "I'm delighted to see you back, Mr. Macdonald," he said, and sat down. Callum went bright red in the face. He might have been embarrassed—or angry; Jenny did not know. The man turned to Simon with extreme good humor. "Aha, the young man with the quaich." He laughed, as if they shared a friendly secret, but Simon looked stunned and did not smile. "How are you? How are you getting along up here? I've often thought about you over the winter, you seemed so unsuited to the place. Is that your little girl I met outside?"

She damn well couldn't be anyone else's, thought Jenny. With her color.

"She seems very clever for her age. Very articulate. My youngest is eight and one can't understand a word he says. She was telling me a long story about the rats in the barn. I was fascinated."

Jenny was fascinated. She had been able to talk like that once, smoothly, at length. She had been able to hear Oxbridge in a voice, and feel contempt for it, perhaps, but not panic. She had changed. She was watching from the Croichan side of the fence. The man spread his knees under the kilt and got down to business.

"Well, Mr. Macdonald, I see the effects of your absence."

No sound.

"Did you suffer much storm damage, Mr. Macdonald? I see the old larch tree has come down. That's a pity. It was an unusual shape for a larch. My shooting parties always used it as a landmark from the moor."

My shooting-parties, thought Jenny. Good God.

"I did repairs," said Simon, "when they were necessary."

"Of course. And what sort of lambing season did you have?"

"Och, not the best," said Callum, recovering some of his casual voice, but Simon leaned forward, speaking out of turn, and said, precisely:

"The lambing was a total disaster." Then he stood back, as if he had made a decision, and was waiting to see the damage. There was some damage. Fochan tried to protect him.

"Och, well, it was a bad year."

"MacLeod is my head shepherd, of course," said the Laird, "and I respect his opinion."

Jenny and Simon looked at each other through the small room door, and shared that: *MacLeod*. The Laird looked thoughtful. "Have you made any arrangements for the future of your croft, Mr. Macdonald?"

"Och, no," said Callum. "Why?"

"Well, let's discuss it," said the Laird. "Strath-Ard is important to me just now. I'd employ the factor, as a rule, but I think your future is a special case, and I want to deal with it myself. Very well. The Cnoc-na-coille rights belong to Mrs. Macdonald." Mary nodded. "Remember, according to the Crofter's Commission, a croft can only be held as such if it's properly worked. Right. The letting arrangements for Cnoc-na-Coille are satisfactory for the moment, we'll let them alone." He looked at Morag. "But you understand, Mrs. Fraser, that your children have nothing to do with the rights. They don't inherit. Mrs. Macdonald and her blood relatives are the only ones involved."

Morag breathed in, "Aye."

"Now: Croichan. It must be worked. You *are* disabled, Mr. Macdonald. The croft must be kept up. Who is going to continue to run Croichan?"

He obviously thought Callum was stupid, and gave him a long silence to understand it in. Callum took the silence, and then said, in the quizzical voice, "Och, well; I kind a thought that Simon would be here, and see to things. I could tell him what to do."

Jenny saw it, too—Callum sitting in the center of Croichan for the rest of his life, in perfect power, giving orders.

"Mmhmm, yes," said the Laird. "But what a dead-end street for you, Mr. Johnston. With your children. Take the immediate future—well, forty acres can't support two families, not even with full subsidies and the old-age pensions coming in." He suddenly exchanged a look of anger, ferocity in fact, with Simon, and Jenny wondered what she did not know. "Economically, it just isn't on. And in the far future, what must happen to Croichan is this. My father let Mr. Macdonald reclaim the rights to the croft, which was derelict, on the basis of family history, and because of wartime, and so on. When Mr. Macdonald passes on, his wife will claim the rights, unless she wants to sell them back to me. That's what usually happens.

"All right? And when Mrs. Macdonald passes on, Croichan will go to her sister in—British Columbia?" Mary nodded again. "Or to her sister's family. They'll have no use for them. I'll be frank; after all, you're the longest-standing tenants, beyond memory, in fact—I *would* like to consolidate my holdings in Strath-Ard. I won't resell any crofts for holiday homes and the like, you can be reassured about that. I do refuse, Mr. Johnston," he said delicately, "to sell or let the croft to you."

"I don't want to stay here," said Simon. "I never meant to stay here. I only came to help in the emergency. We have our flat waiting in Edinburgh."

"Och, Simon," said Callum, and looked away, out the window, tears rolling down his face. Jenny knew that she was the only person in the house who was cruel enough not to believe him. "But what will become of me, then," he said. "I don't want to go into a Home."

"But I can't stay here," said Simon.

"Yes, yes, this is terrible, it always is," said the Laird. "All I meant was that Mr. Johnston should not stay on as unskilled farm labor—it's not economically sound. But don't you think, Mr. Macdonald, that with a little outside help, contracting and the like, cutting down a bit on the stock perhaps, and so forth, that Croichan could go on as before? Under your supervision, of course. You could run it from a wheelchair." The Laird and Jenny, without doubt, saw the same headline at that moment: DISABLED CROFTER CARRIES ON. RUNS HILL FARM FROM WHEELCHAIR. *"The old ways should be preserved,"* SAYS LANDOWNER *"I have my crofters' welfare at heart."* It would be in *The Northern Scot*, next week. The Laird smiled at it.

"Aye," said Callum. "Willie-John could do the tractoring. I could tell him what to do."

"Aye," said Willie-John. "I always did that, anyhow."

"McLeod will be here to help with the sheep-dipping," said the Laird. "And the factor will keep an eye on things as well. Good. Cheerio, then." He stood up. On his way out he said to Simon, "I looked it up, you know; it is quaich." He said good-bye to Shona, and left. As soon as they heard the sports car start up and drive away, Morag laughed.

"Och, he is a case, what does he mean with his quaich."

"He means *cuach*," said Simon, and Morag laughed again.

"The nurse said, "I'll look in on you Thursday, Mrs. Macdonald. You'll be all right till then."

"Och, aye," said Mary vaguely, but the nurse looked hard at her and around the kitchen, and said:

"Very well, then, it had better be tomorrow. Cheerio." She left, and Fochan, and Willie-John. Simon sat down in the bedside chair as if his headache had come back, and he and Callum said nothing to each other. Mary made tea again, for Jenny, and Morag, and Simon, and one with saccharine for Callum. She was awkward with her big fingers on the tiny white pills, and Jenny sorted them out for her. At last, a cup for herself. The baby threw his rattle chain on the floor and dragged it toward himself. It made a dry, plastic noise. Shona brought Jenny a book and Jenny read quietly to her, not knowing what book it was. Outside in the yard, the hens began to croon and wander about, now that the cars were gone. One cow gave a long, vibrating moo, answered by a penned calf in its tenor voice and the bull in deepest bass. The wind was changing, bringing the noise of the sheep, grazing to the east. All this time, Callum and Simon just sat without looking at each other.

At last Simon called into the kitchen, "Mary, what does *fochan* mean? I never knew he had another name."

"Och, *fochan* is the mole, you see, Simon," said Mary. "We called him Fochan because he always had a bald head, even when he was young."

"I thought a mole was a furry animal," said Simon, sounding as if he might cry himself.

"Och, well," said Mary, "In the Gaelic—" she did not finish. Jenny saw the Gaelic handbook on the sideboard, within reach, and decided she would find out, she would learn this one fact beyond question, and slipped the little book in behind Shona's book, and turned to f in the Gaelic-

to-English division. *Fochann,* she read, "corn in the blade."
That was all. She never would know.

"Callum," said Morag. "I was forgetting, with Himself,
and the excitement. I was telling Mary; the bodach 'ha
radan has died. He was dead in his wee room this morning."

"Och, no," said Callum. "The poor old man."

"Aye," said Morag. "We have just had a funeral with us;
will this one be with you?"

Celtic Twilight

*I*n Edinburgh, the all-night factories and the new vapor streetlights made the sky orange and gave the slum neighborhoods a restless, smoky shine. Simon had always thought Edinburgh was a cold gray city, but he was surprised now to find it close and thick and warm. The suburbs seemed rich and leafy, and the spring was far advanced, compared to the place they had left. Every front yard had wallflowers and tulips in it, and there was a smell of growing plants even on his own street off Tollcross.

How lucky Michael had been, after Moy, to go back to this sweet city life, with his salukis, and his School of Scottish Studies, while Simon had stayed in the North.

"Well, love," he said, parking around the corner from their house. "The tropical lowlands."

They had phoned Michael from the Forth Bridge rest stop, and he was expecting them. He made coffee while they put their overtired, miserable children to bed at last. They told him no, they did not want to drink tea, but Simon found he did not want coffee, either; he just wanted to sit and look at the fire, and hold his hands around the warm cup. He still felt numb, which was probably just as well. The window curtains were drawn. He saw with amusement that the cannabis plant on the windowsill had survived Rosiqa. Michael had repotted it, and it was blooming.

Michael saw him looking at it and grinned. "Fran—we broke up, did I tell you?—Fran said that if it was a cooking herb you'd have to pick it just as it was coming into bloom and dry it in a slow oven. I don't know what you do with that stuff."

"Reap it in any condition and roll it up and smoke it greedily," said Simon. He looked at Jenny and saw she was asleep, curled in the armchair, the coffee cup balancing by her hand. Michael took the cup away. She looked old and scraggy, asleep, with lines in her face and her cheeks sunken in; and Simon wondered if it was her nature to always look older than he did, or if perhaps she was older, and never told him, or—most likely—if he looked that way himself. The room blurred in his eyes, in the firelight.

"You know something I don't know," said Michael. "You look like you've had a hard time."

"Laddie, I know a hell of a lot of things you never even thought of," said Simon. Phoebe, the saluki, was curled in her bed, in a warm corner of the room. On the wall above the bed, Michael had drawn a row of tiny ink figures, like the tally rows on a fighter plane. They were little hare shapes. Simon, so tired, found himself counting the hares. Thirty-two. He counted them again: thirty-one. He started counting them again. "What's that scribbled thing? Not a hare?"

"That one was a pheasant," said Michael. "I don't want to talk about that one. You two have a refugee air."

"I'm sure we do," said Simon, closing his eyes. "It was a bad scene. The worst. I couldn't put up with it."

"The poverty, the old age, do you mean?" said Michael. "It could get you if you were emotionally involved with it."

"That, yes; but there were personalities as well." Simon felt almost as he had when Rosiqa had screamed, long ago: overstretched, overwrought. He could not keep quite still, and sat tapping his hand on his knee. He knew that Michael, like Mary, like salukis, was obtuse, impenetrable—in his way, safe. So he said, "He cried; he did cry. And yet, at the same time, while he cried, I was sure he didn't want me."

"Hm," said Michael, letting most of it go by.

"And so I've left them, and I know how the future will

go—they'll die soon, Mary first, perhaps, she's worked harder. And then Callum probably will go into a Home, for a little while. I have no guilt about it, none whatsoever."

"Are you all right?" said Michael.

"Obviously not," said Simon. "But if I can just hold on, I suppose it will pass. Things do." After a while, he said, "You must miss Rosiqa. Are you going to replace her?"

"Oh, that little gray devil, yes," said Michael. "But I have a year of field work coming up in the Highlands, and I won't get another saluki till I get back. I know some people on Lewis, and I'll be there most of the autumn and winter. Even the Pakistani storekeepers in the Hebrides speak Gaelic, culturally it must be a healthy place. Then I want to go Inverness-shire, there's been more East-Coast influence in the Central Highlands. Do you know any place I could stay? Cheap or free?"

"Write to the factor of the Laird's estate," said Simon.

"Of course; I won't have to write," said Michael. "I'll see him at the Meet in November, and we'll talk it over then."

"Do they have a coursing Meet every year?" said Simon.

"Every year," said Michael. "Would you like to come again?"

Simon shook his head.

"Before I forget," said Michael. "The little Gaelic book, have you still got it? The librarian said she wouldn't mind getting it back."

"No," said Simon. "I left it at Croichan."

Michael spent two weeks with the Johnstons, sleeping by the fire. Then a farmer moved sheep onto his favorite walk beyond the Braid Hills, so he left Edinburgh and rented a summer cottage alone in East Lothian. He had been sorry to break up with Fran, and they had both cried about it; but now he knew he was happiest by himself. "People are all right," was the last thing he said to Jenny Johnston, "but salukis are a kind of Holy Communion. Good-bye."

All through the midsummer, he and Phoebe got up at dawn and spent two hours in the Aberlady Bay Bird Sanctuary, where they were not supposed to be. Sometimes, Michael lay down on the mattresses of wild flowers, thyme and yellow vetch and sea pinks, watching the skylarks twittering way up, and listening to the moronic coo of eider drakes in the sea below the cliffs. Phoebe poked around the grassy dunes, too lazy to run. Sometimes, when he wasn't lying flat in luxury, Michael wandered, and watched the swans nesting in the yellow iris ponds, and tried to eat the wild strawberries, but they were too sour in Scotland. They had been sweet in Pennsylvania, but this country was sweeter than America had ever been. Often he had to avoid Boy Scouts, or lovers, or nudists camping in the sand hollows. He and Phoebe sat on the sand hills and looked across the blue Firth to the coast of Fife, and watched the ships come up from Norway to the Edinburgh docks at Leith. Then he drove in to Edinburgh half-drunk and sneezing with pollen and the smell of hot moss, and spent all his research hours with a headache.

By autumn he was fed up with the dreamy soft countryside, and Phoebe was too fat. His supervisor accepted his thesis topic: "A Comparison of Superstitions on the Island of Lewis and the Central Highlands, with Reference to One Family in Each Location." They went to Lewis, but they were unhappy there; the island was covered with sheep, and he had to keep Phoebe on the leash.

In November, they went coursing at Moy, and had bad luck again. Phoebe tripped over a heather root and dislocated a toe, and limped, and couldn't run. Then there was a blizzard on Friday, and even the Land Rovers got stuck trying to open the road on Saturday, and the Meet was called off undecided. The dinner was dreary, and the guests were frustrated; but Michael did speak to the Laird's factor, who offered him the use of the derelict Keeper's Cottage at the head of Strath-Ard, for the months of April, May and June. So, in April, they left Lewis, with its gales, and its luminous drizzle, and its pervasive Gaelic fog, and went to Strath-Ard.

The winter had passed, and Michael was older, and full of doubt. His project on paper was "A Comparison of Superstitions," but his real purpose in Strath-Ard was to find some wild and hopeless country, to let the saluki run loose in it, and to get some peace for himself out of that running. That was all he had ever wanted. But now, there was a question. He wondered if it was right to let Phoebe kill things any more.

When Simon had first told him, "It's a very deep experience, but I wouldn't want it to be my fault," Michael had been too distracted by Rosiqa to pay much attention. He did not pay attention to people anyhow. But now that he was alone again, and Phoebe was on the leash, he kept hearing it:

"Well, it's a very deep experience, but I wouldn't want it to be my fault."

Phoebe's toe had drawn back into place and healed, and she wanted to run. Michael wanted to watch her run. He knew her ancient and complicated habits of mind. He had never been able to teach her anything except hunting, which she knew already, better than he did. It would be hard on them both. At last he decided to let her run, but only in an empty place; he was going to give up killing, for his own good.

It might not be possible. Michael and Phoebe had been killers, and hunters in wild places, for a long time. Rosiqa had been a latecomer, but Phoebe had been with him since California, since she had been a thin-haired, peanut-shaped puppy. Michael had done undergraduate work at Berkeley, but had left because he did not like warfare. He had trained and toughened the young hound by letting her gallop on the rocky sand beaches—Half Moon Bay, Bodega Bay. Michael would wander and turn over stones, looking for meaningful ones, while Phoebe would chase, and keep up with, the circling sea gulls. He learned that the saluki had great physical powers, electric nerves, a certain primitive slyness but not an ounce of common sense, and he managed to keep her alive through all the dangers that make trouble for a young animal like that: cars, wire fences, cows and horses, and sudden loud noises. Then, when she was old enough, they went for long trips into the hills, to run down jackrabbits in the yellow, monotonous grass.

When they first got to Strath-Ard, Michael did not think about hunting. He found it hard enough just keeping awake. Strath-Ard was forgetful, jellied in old age. It gave him the pale blueness in the head that comes in high places. At first, he thought about Simon, and understood how Simon must have been impatient there. But soon, in that obliterating high country, Simon began to fade, and he was alone with Phoebe and the old people at Croichan.

Had they been Simon's people once? That seemed odd to him, and soon he forgot.

Two points only let Michael fix himself in space, in Strath-Ard. At night, in the battering wind, he could see the red lights of a broadcasting tower: that was Inverness.

In daylight, he could look north down to the valley of the Ard River and across it to the hill the survey map called Beinn a' Bha-ach Ard. So he knew where he was. He could have forgotten. To the end, he was always a little dizzy, a little sleepy.

The Keeper's Cottage was rough, and smelled of old wallpaper, but the roof did not seem to leak. He set up his camp bed and Phoebe's bed by the grate in the main room, and the first morning he left Phoebe sleeping in the cottage and walked down to Croichan by himself. He had learned in class that the most important thing was to get the confidence of the natives, and Phoebe was too strange; she did not inspire confidence. He went up the road bank and through the rusty gate. There was a black bull and two cows grazing between the gorse bushes by the driveway, and they lowered their heads and looked at him, and followed him into the yard. He met the old woman carrying milk pails toward the dairy shed. Her name, he knew, was Mary Macdonald.

"Hello, there," he said to her.

"Good morning," she said, as if she were not surprised to see him, or to see anyone; but something made him think she was afraid of him, and he said:

"I'm up here for the Easter vacation, staying at the Keeper's Cottage—you know, the old place up the road from you. I thought I'd do some hill walking, but it's too cold today. Is there anything I could do for you? I'm bored by myself up there." He looked around and saw a patch of earth, in front of the house, that had once been a vegetable garden. The chicken-wire fence was down, and hens were pecking at the dead potato stalks and the sprouting cabbage plants that were still there. "Could I dig up your garden and plant it for you?" he asked.

"Och, we'll no' bother about it this year," she said. She

had obviously carried milk pails for so long that she had become just a shape, a kind of rack, for carrying milk pails —big hands, broad feet, and a bent, hollow back. Her nose was red and running, and she had a brown wool kerchief tied around her head.

"Oh, come on, let me," he said.

"Och, well," said Mary, and went away. Michael took that for yes, but he couldn't find the spade. He looked carefully in the barn, the cowshed, the dairy, the henhouse. At last he found a wild three-legged cat, part of a dead hen, and the spade, in an old Ford that was rotting down into the midden. He scared the hens out of the garden ground and repaired the fence, straightening the posts and re-stretching the chicken wire. At midmorning, Mary came out of the house, gave him something without looking at him, and went back inside. He examined it: a scone, split, with butter and jam between the halves.

Michael took the scone over to a big fallen larch tree that lay across the corner of the yard, and sat on the trunk, eating. The tree had torn up an eight-foot circle of grass with the chunk of roots below, and Michael leaned back against the grass, which was upright at the end of the trunk, like a wall. It was very odd to be leaning against vertical grass, oddly peaceful; grass was always underfoot, and full of life. Was anything going on under this turf? He put his ear against the dry grass, listening, enjoying himself until suddenly he felt that something was buried just under that grass, something important. He got off the trunk and looked hard at the clump of empty roots and dirt. He decided he had been sleepy, and went back to work.

He barrowed three loads of dung across from the midden, and dug, and raked, and then drove into Inverness, where he had lunch and bought carrot and turnip seeds, cabbage and Brussels sprouts and kale plants, and went back to Croichan and put them in while the April wind made his nose run and then blew the drops away before he could get to his handkerchief. At four o'clock, Mary called him into the house for what he knew was the politeness cup of tea; and he saw Callum, sitting by the fire, for the first time—a big man, in a wheelchair, who would not look at him at all.

Michael knew he had disturbed the webby feeling of peace in that house, so he kept his mouth shut and sat in a window chair, away from the fire, letting the peace rebuild. After tea, he finished the garden and went back to the Keeper's Cottage. The cold, gray wind pushed him up the hill.

He spent the next morning writing notes and making plans. In the afternoon he put the book and the stone in his pocket, put Phoebe on the leash and went down to Croichan, where the branches of the fallen tree were hissing in the wind. The few roots left in the ground had fed the tree and there were green needles on the lowest branch, but the rest of the crown was dead. They met Mary dragging a bale of hay out to the sheep, the ragged Cheviots that wandered around the croft and steading yard. Michael noticed that many of the sheep walked limping, and wondered if it were some disease. He took the bale for her while she stared at the dog. Phoebe was shivering, too wretched, in this strange windy place, to notice the moving sheep.

"Och, goodness," said Mary, amused. "Would it be a greyhound."

"More or less," said Michael. "Not exactly." He remembered that Simon had been living with her when he had come to Moy, and wondered if he had told her about the coursing. But she did not seem to recognize him.

"Mercy," she said. "Show her to Callum."

Mary stayed out to break up the bale, and Michael went into the house. He went through the scullery door. A Highland croft was supposed to smell of burning peat, but, like the ones he knew on Lewis, Croichan smelled of the leaking stove, the propane gas, a smell of rotten onions. He went into the kitchen.

Callum was sitting in his wheelchair by the kitchen fire. He looked straight at Michael for the first time. His eyes were blue, but sore, inflamed at the edges, old eyes. For the first time, he spoke. His voice had a quizzical, hesitant manner, as if he were trying to solve some interesting little puzzle. Michael thought it sounded false: talking sideways, pretending not to really pay attention.

"What kind a dog's that, then?"

For no good reason, Michael felt, suddenly, a little nervous.

"A—a saluki," he said.

"A saluki. What's that, then."

"A running dog. Like a greyhound." Michael spoke carefully, afraid of scaring the old man with too much information. In class, he had learned not to be pedantic. "They hunt by sight. They're not supposed to put their noses to the ground."

"Are they not," said Callum.

Michael felt more nervous, shaken. Was Callum making fun of him? He seemed vague, almost stupid, but there was something else: a glitter in his soft voice, a consciousness of power that had nothing to do with his words. Was it just the self-obsession of the invalid? Or something else? Michael felt tension begin to creep around the room—why? Callum decided to communicate. "There was this wee tinker fella," he said. "He was away camping down the road there, by Cnoc-na-Coille, och, nine years ago now it would be; he had a greyhound, an awful pretty one, black.

But it was bad for chasing the sheep. It killed one Blackface lamb. It did that."

Callum shook his head, thoughtfully. Michael kept
quiet. It was no use with Phoebe. There had been salukis
and hunters long before there had been sheep and shep-
herds. Her mind was Oriental, conservative. It wouldn't
change.

"It dragged the lamb away down by the barn," said
Callum. "Fochan caught it sorta chewing on its head."
Michael found his accent very thick and hard to under-
stand. "So he shot it. The tinker was no' pleased, but
Fochan had the right to shoot it."

Callum watched Phoebe, who watched him—with her
eyes; she did not sniff at him as a dog would have done,
and this amused him. She was sitting on her long tail for
safety, and the tip came out between her long front legs,
under her chin. She looked at Michael with her brownstone
eyes, and the tip moved. Callum's face was long, too, but
sick and bluish; his legs were long, but not his. The big,
loose body in the chair did not match the stillness and
precision of the legs below.

"She'll be fast," said Callum.

"Yes, not so fast as a racing greyhound, but tougher,"
said Michael. "I used to hunt jackrabbits with her in California, like hares, you know, only bigger—"

Callum switched off. He swung his chair around, turning his broad back towards Michael, who stood with his
mouth innocently open in the middle of a word. Callum sat
withdrawn into a massive self-confidence that tuned out
Michael, Phoebe, the kitchen, the flickering fire, the slam-
ming of the wind against the house. Michael sat down in
the window chair, embarrassed, trying not to be angry at
the rudeness of a senile old man. But he was angry, and

even more: fascinated. He had learned in class that primitive people were unpredictable, but usually polite.

They sat in silence till Mary came in. The wind whipped the door shut behind her. She began to make tea, without taking off any of her three cardigans, or the wool scarf about her head. Michael noticed that the kitchen was cold. His fingers were cold. Mary set the square table with scones, oatcakes, raspberry jam, and a lump of pale butter in a glass dish.

"Cheekie is milking the now," she said. "Her calf was no' good, its hind legs would no' bend, you see, so we sent it away. I was churning and churning, the night, the milk's no' good yet, for the butter, there's no' grazing yet, but I got a bittie. You'll have it for your tea."

"Yes, thanks," said Michael. She took a scone, split it, buttered it, put on the jam, and gave it to him with his steaming teacup. He felt somehow off balance. Either they would not look at him, at Croichan, or they chattered to him, and still he felt he was missing something else, though he did not know what it could be. "What do you do for milk in the winter?"

"Och, well," she said, "we get the Carnation, in the tins." She put a plate down on the oilcloth table and Callum, ignoring them both, wheeled himself up. He got a square of cheese and an apple. Mary tried to get two tiny saccharine pills out of a bottle from the sideboard, but her hands were too big.

"Let me," said Michael, and shook them out for her. She dropped them into the cup and stirred it and put it next to his plate.

"Himself has the diabetes," she said, and patted him absent-mindedly on the shoulder. "And he has a wee bittie boil on the back of his neck."

Callum ate stolidly, as if she were not there. She looked

amused. The fire on the hearth snapped, flickered up a bit, and began to warm Phoebe, who had been lying in her formal, heraldic, greyhound position, like a hound on tapestry. Now she unfolded and became pure saluki. She was a dog who had fits of obscure amusement, as if she heard jokes broadcast on a private, hound, radio set. She rolled on her back, yawning a crocodile yawn, making a sound half-yodel, half-groan, wrapping her forelegs around her head so all the Macdonalds could see was one gleaming, lunatic eye. Then, joke over, she clattered to her feet and shook herself and slid her long head against Michael's thigh.

"Hello, snake face," he said. "You're not getting any. She wants my scone," he said to Mary. "If she wanted petting, her eyes would be soft and brown, and her nose would run. It always runs when she's sentimental. But it's food this time; her eyes are hard and black and round, like two buttons. Look."

"Aye," said Mary, on a curious indrawn breath, like a nervous gasp, "Fancy, they are that. How docs she do it. Och, are you wanting a wee piecie." She took a whole scone, split it, buttered it, even put on the raspberry jam, and reached it out to Phoebe, who took it with the utmost gentility, and chewed it up. Mary tried to pat her head but her big, coarse hand could not manage to stroke such a silky skull, and the pat turned out to be a clunk instead. Phoebe blinked.

Callum finished his tea, sucked and shifted his false teeth, snapped them into place, and said, in his casual voice:

"Fochan was telling me, there are plenty hares up west the road. There did not use to be any, but now they're all over. It would be a fine thing, now, to see her after one a them."

Without thinking, Michael said, "That would be great. As long as there are no sheep up on the hill."

"Is she bad with them, then," said Callum.

"Well, I wouldn't really trust her," said Michael. Mary looked frightened, and he saw he had made a mistake.

"She must *no'* be chasing the sheep," said Mary, quite sharp, and he said soothingly:

"I won't let her."

"Fochan will shoot her," said Mary.

"Wait you," said Callum. "Across the road there is a Muir, with a fence. There are no sheep in there. You can let her loose in that field, the now, perhaps the hares have come down to it. There used to be only rabbits, and that. Fochan will be here soon; he is the Laird's shepherd, but he sees to our lambs as well. When he comes, I'll ask him are there sheep west the road. I think the ewes will be there waiting to lamb, but perhaps he has penned them up. Wait you."

So Michael finished his tea in the silence of the disturbed room and left, to let Mary calm down, and to take a look at Callum's field.

Below the road to the space north was the Muir. It was boggy, half-wooded, tumbling down to thick forest in the river valley. The fence wire was slack, and swung, belling out slowly in the wind. The gate was too rotten to open, so he lifted Phoebe and dropped her into the Muir and climbed down into it himself.

The wind dropped, leaving an abrupt and spooky silence. It was evening, with a new moon, and a pale light coming out of the ground. Not darkness yet: transparency. Michael was a little scared. As a child, he had always been too much aware of Things, and he had felt that Things were too much aware of him. The whole world had been awake to him then, in a way other people did not feel; every stone had an intense presence, had a complicated, ritual life of its own, unfriendly to him, and he would never dare turn his back on a tree. The salukis had calmed him down: hunting, they involved him deeper in this world of live Things—the scary pleasure of danger on purpose—but at the same time they were a weapon, an interpreter. Phoebe mediated for him with stones and Things; she was at ease with them.

Now in the Muir, he felt it again. In Strath-Ard he was drugged, sleepy with height, confused about solid things like east and west; but on another level, he was tuned in more than ever, wide awake, bristling, receiving. He did not know why the Muir was so intensely awake. He argued with himself, the way he used to:

You're having hallucinations.

No. There are demons. If there are no demons, why does a cold wind blow when the sun goes behind a cloud, even if that cloud is thirty miles away? It's a personal reaction between you and the grass you're standing in.

They went downhill a little way and came to a belt of scrub willow that ran east-west across the upper third of the Muir. The pen-and-ink branches were scribbled with new green leaves. Phoebe was sand-colored, silvery at the edges. The trees became older, thicker; then they came out into a flat open valley with three small hills in it, like half heads stuck in the ground. One hill grew grass, the next, bracken—last year's dry orange bracken—and the last, heather and three young larches. A deer jumped out of the bracken and went crashing towards the deep woods along the river.

Phoebe took two great leaps in the air to get the deer in her sights, fixed on it, and settled into her arching, coursing run. Coursing, she left even herself behind: she was ancient, the archetype, all hounds running. Ten yards behind the deer, she vanished into the trees.

Michael knew that she was too small to kill a deer, that

she would lose it quickly in the woods—she could hardly follow the freshest scent—and that she herself would never get lost. It was her business not to. Her ancestors had been Arabian hounds, and had known how to orient themselves around the most temporary campsites, and find their way all over the deserts. The deer might kick, if she got too close, and slash or kill her, but that was her business, too. She was not his lapdog or his child. They were two grownup creatures, and their relationship was far more complicated. As with Rosiqa, chance was part of the game. The trouble was, he was frightened without her.

However, he went on alone down towards the valley bottom, wondering how long his nerves would hold. He found a rocky channel that had once been a streambed and followed it down. Someone had cut whinstone steps beside the stream, but the stones were shaggy now and smelled like moss. Maybe this had been a busy track from the bottom of Strath-Ard to the hill crofts. Who had used it? Who had used it last—ten, twenty years ago? It was dark. He could not see much, but he could hear the hillside, alive with the rustle and flick of rabbits, and other Things. Where was Phoebe? The air above the rocky bed was soft and cold. He heard owls.

It was not the owls that turned him at last, but something else; once turned he found it hard to keep from running in a blind panic, but he kept his dignity and forced himself to walk. The uphill was too steep to run anyhow, and he had to use his hands, going uphill at the steepest parts with his nails in the leaf mold. The skin at the back of his neck was crawling in pure terror. He thought about the moor, and Phoebe running, and calmed himself. West, he was sure he would find the peaceful unity that comes with open spaces. He would go there soon. If only there were no sheep.

Phoebe, panting and cheerful, met him at the gate. She did not try to go under it, or through, but waited for him to lift her and set her gently down on the other side.

He found that he wanted to see Callum again, and he remembered his book and stone, so he stopped at Croichan again on the way back. The book and stone had been useful at Lewis, and he wanted to try them on the Macdonalds. The book was a thin, brown *Prophecies of the Brahan Seer*, in English, about Kenneth McKenzie, the seventeenth-century Gaelic-speaking prophet. The stone was a Seeing Stone. It was probably real.

Michael had found the Stone four years ago, walking Phoebe on the beach at Half Moon Bay—a smooth, oval, blue stone with a smooth, round hole through one end. Even then, he had known what it was. He had taken classes in Comparative Religion, and had read the Brahan Seer, and other works on Second Sight, in which the different Seeing Stones and Crystals were described. He had picked up the Stone and, without thinking, looked into it. The seascape in the small hole had sharpened, gone pearly and then, definitely and faster, begun to revolve. He became aware of two certainties at the same time: one, that there was a warrant out for his arrest as a draft dodger, and that he would have to leave America at once, and, two, stronger, that there was something creeping up behind him. He had turned around fast, seeing nothing, and he and Phoebe had taken the next across-the-Pole flight to London. He had not looked in the Stone again, but he had kept it for his researches.

The scullery door was ajar, and the kitchen door was open. Michael went quietly in, and felt they were expecting him. Mary was at the table in the white, hissing light of the kerosene lamp, filling in government forms. Callum was sitting placidly at one side of the fireplace and Michael took the opposite fireside chair. Phoebe stretched out between them. Nobody spoke till Mary got up and reached across the dog and pushed the sooty kettle onto the bar, over the flames, to boil for tea. "Was it a nice walkie, then," she said.

"Fine, thanks," said Michael. "We saw a deer."

Callum heard that and came back—out of his enormous thoughts, or maybe out of vacancy. "Did you."

"Down by those three little hills."

"It would be a roe deer, then. The red deer stay west the road, the other side of the Laird's fence."

"I can see that fence when I go to the well, up there," said Michael. "Can the red deer jump so high? It must be eight feet, at least."

"Och, aye," said Callum. "Them stags is awful big, you know; if they got into the corn they'd no' be much left of it. Did she get it, then."

"Phoebe? The Laird didn't like me bringing her at all. I should hope not—I don't want to land in jail for poaching. And out of season, too."

Callum chuckled, picking his teeth with a long, filthy fingernail. "Och, aye, he'd have you sent up, surely."

The bright new teeth were obviously a National Health prescription, gruesome and elegant in his sunken face. He had probably been given them while he was in hospital for his legs. Michael wondered why he wore the legs; he never seemed to get out of the chair. Maybe they were a decoration, like the teeth.

"It seems to me that there are more deer about now than there used to be," said Callum, in his quizzical voice. "Deer, and rabbits, and that."

He seemed to be offering that to Michael, waiting to see what he would say, almost a challenge—but why? Michael decided to answer seriously, and he said, choosing simple words.

"Well, it usually happens, that when the people start to leave a neighborhood, the wildlife starts to come back. I mean, there are not so many families here as there were when you were young, are there? I saw a lot of empty crofts when I drove up the glen."

"Och, leaving," said Callum. "They're gone; I mind when every croft on this road had a family. Mind you, even then the children was mostly foster-children, Glasgow orphans; we took one. We had no children, you see. Now there is only Morag, and Willie-John Kilduich, and Fochan, and us. The orphans are away."

"Mm," said Michael. "Do you speak the Gaelic much anymore?"

"Och, well," said Mary.

"A wordie now and again," said Callum.

"We have the Gaelic, of course," said Mary. "But it's no' in me to use it very much."

"I guess you'd have to go to the Islands to hear it now. I was at Lewis, not long ago; the language is full of life there, even the Pakistani shopkeepers speak the Gaelic there."

Callum was fascinated. "Aye," he said. "Is that true. Them darkies, and all. Och, never." The white light of the lamp made his face look silvery, cleaner than it really was. "I'd like fine to see them wee West Coast crofties," he said. "They go *effrywhere py poat*." He mimicked the extreme accent of the Hebrides and Mary giggled. Then he said, pathetically, "But I guess I never will, now."

Michael did not know what to answer, and kept quiet. He did not really trust the pathos. The postman had come to the Keeper's Cottage that morning to give him an *Occupant 2d Voucher* for Omo Detergent, and to see who and what he was, and had stayed an hour telling him about "Callum Croichan," how he had been feeling quite himself for a year, but did he go to the doctor? No—and then it

was too late, and Himself with the thrombosis and gangrene in both feet. And now there was Callum's brother
over in Glen Affric, a crofter as well, having symptoms, and
would he go and get his water tested? He would not.

Michael suspected that Callum's immobility involved
more than just the loss of his legs.

The fire, having boiled the kettle, gave up and went
cool, dark. Phoebe was still lying in her warm-room position, flat on her side like a dead horse. Soon she would curl
up into her cold-room snail position.

"I have this little book here," said Michael. He took out
The Prophecies of the Brahan Seer. Mary, pouring tea,
giggled.

"The Brahan Seer? Och, aye, Coinneach Odhar, the
daft loon."

"But his prophecies came true," said Michael. "Hundreds of years later."

"Och, well," said Mary, and giggled again.

"But look," said Michael, "he predicted the Battle of
Culloden, and the building of the Caledonian Canal."

"Aye," said Callum gravely, "so he did."

"A ghost gave it to him, his Seeing Stone, I mean, to
read the future in. Do you believe in Seeing Stones? I've
got one here. Look." He took out the smooth, oval blue
stone, and held it to the lamp. The lamplight grew and
glittered in the hole.

"And would it be a ghostie giving it to you," said
Mary.

"No, I just found it. I haven't seen the future in it yet—
not much, anyhow. Will you?" He gave it to Callum.

The old man put it to one inflamed eye, then to the
other.

"He is a long time," said Mary. "He is seeing the future,
surely. Or perhaps he is asleep."

"I'm seeing your dog, down by the fire," said Callum slowly. "Herself is a comic great beastie. And I'm seeing the fire at the back of her. Now that is awful pretty, in the wee hole." He put the Stone aside and yawned. "I'm wanting my tea," he said.

Walking home in the dark with Phoebe on leash, stalking and blurry at his heels, Michael thought it would be nice, one more time, if Phoebe did catch a hare, and he could show it to Callum. The old man obviously knew a lot about wildlife, and it must be hard on him, being a shut-in.

No. More. Callum was dangerous. More; he was seductive, if such a word could possibly be used about a dirty, inarticulate old man. He had not said or done very much, but in one way he was articulate enough—something about him was drawing, pulling at Michael, frightening him, a kind of religious fear. Michael felt dizzy. He was on the road that ran west from Croichan to the Keeper's Cottage and then the moor, the bare hill. All the road seemed to be on a deep black plate, slowly revolving, sliding him away from the red-lit tower at Inverness, turning him towards the hill.

In the Keeper's Cottage, with the economy of a long-time camper, Michael lit the lamp, lit the Camping gas stove, warmed up a can of beans for himself and a can of Kenno-Meat for Phoebe, refilled Phoebe's water bowl, and put the kettle on, for instant coffee and hot water bottles. Living as he had done for years now, in furnished rooms, with a cold, bony dog and wilful, inconsistent girl friends— now gone, yes—he had learned more than most Americans need to know about hot water bottles. If you overfill them, for example, they explode.

Phoebe got one bottle in her bed, he got two. She lay watching him get ready for bed, the lamplight touching her in strange ways so that she looked, sometimes, like a demon

in the darkish room, with flat, glowing eyeholes and a long
bird's neck. Then she blinked, and became his dog, and
went to sleep. Michael did not go to sleep. He lay in the
dark, in his sleeping bag, on his camp bed, listening to the
wind. He could smell Phoebe, and the lamp wick, and himself. He could not stop thinking about Callum. If he could
imagine Callum as a guru or a Buddha of some kind, that
would be fashionable, at least. But Callum could never be
plump, gold, and smooth, though he certainly was serene.
He was livid and grizzly, like the hill country. Michael was
in for a different kind of god, here. He was in for trouble.

The next morning Michael and Phoebe went up to inspect
the deer fence. It was a gray bitter day and they looked
through onto the moor, shivering. The eight-foot wire was
more than a fence to keep the stags off the croft lands and
on the moor, where the gamekeeper could stalk and shoot
them: it was a formal barrier between places where people
did and did not live. Or ever had lived. At Moy, the coursing parties had found old roads, the ruined shieling and
boat; the shepherd's cottage was there, occupied, and once
they had even found the ruins of an inn, a drovers' wayside
rest. But here, through the fence, he could see no house,
not even a fallen chimney or a scattered stone wall. No one
had ever, ever lived here.

Heather: nothing else. A sour, twiggy growth, not
brown, not green or purple, but a livid combination of all
three. Last year's dry flower bells hissed in the wind. There
was ling heather and bell heather, all dead. It covered the
hillside like a cold fur, rising on the left to crags of blackish
rock, falling, to the right, to the north, down into the valley
of the Ard River. The deer fence formed the western

boundary of the Muir, and the timber stopped short all the way down the hill. Ahead, the road—changing to a cart track beyond the high gate, ran on through the heather to hills, beyond hills, beyond hills. That, sooner or later, was where Michael and Phoebe were going. Michael wanted that calm and space with all his soul, but they were not ready yet. They were shivering, and they had to find out about the sheep. They couldn't go west with Phoebe on the leash.

They turned and walked down to Croichan. Callum was out, wrapped in a heavy coat and a scruffy tartan rug, sitting in his chair at the edge of the roadbank. He was watching the valley through a pair of old field glasses. He said,

"Look; Mackay, across the river, has got two new lambs in his field."

He gave Michael the glasses. Adjusting them, Michael realized that Callum could see all of the Muir below him, the farms and grazing across the river—the river itself, and Strath-Ard, was hidden by the timber at the foot of the Muir—and most of the south face of Beinn a' Bha-ach Ard, still webbed with snow. If he turned the glasses to the west, he could see the deer fence and a good part of the open moor.

"Are you seeing? Across the river, by them two trees. They'd be earlier than us, down there, with the lambs. Ours have no' started yet."

"I can't see any sheep west of the fence," said Michael. "Maybe I could run the dog there after all."

"They kinda get down into the hollows," said Callum. "Wait you for Fochan."

"Do you sit here every day?" said Michael.

"Och, aye," said Callum, indifferently. "When it's no' raining. Will you be going to the house?"

"I'll give her a run in the Muir first. If we raise a hare we'll chase it your way so you can see the fun."

Callum grinned. "Aye, I'd like fine to see that."

They went over the gate. Michael unsnapped the leash and Phoebe trotted away. Michael looked back and saw Callum fix the glasses on them and so follow them down the hill, and he was not surprised when a hare bolted out of a clump of grass, right at his feet, on cue, with a sound like ripping silk.

Michael knew a lot about hares—jackrabbits, brown, lowland hares, and this one, a Scottish blue hare, a stocky, bouncing animal, still half in its winter white fur. It was the same kind of hare they had coursed at Moy. He knew that the mountain hares were not so fast as the brown hares and that Phoebe would probably catch it, unless the brush got too thick. He forgot all his nonviolence and yelled, *Phoebe!* with a squawk of excitement in his voice, *"Hare! Hare!"* and the dog, not ready for coursing so soon, came back like a girl running for a bus, dropping packages, pulling herself together. Then she saw the black-tipped ears, still upright and confident, cruising away through a patch of bog myrtle. Her eyes went hard and black and she started to run. The hare saw what was after it, not a yapping terrier or a civilized sheepdog—and its ears went gently flat down, like a black-edged shawl across its back. Without seeming to move more violently, it accelerated and skimmed away into the first willows, Phoebe right behind, all before Michael could start to unglue his feet from the ground. The sky was gray, but as the two animals went through the trees, a slit of sun turned the branches yellow behind them.

Michael swore at himself, but it was too late. He could feel his heart beating with excitement. He was involved again, irrevocably, though he had no more part in what was happening. He had set it moving, and now he was out of it. He couldn't save the hare, or stop the dog. But the hare was in its own territory, he thought, as he ran after them; it would know where shelter was. It would probably head for the bracken on that little hill. If it tired too soon, it could dodge and twist, confusing the hound and maybe breaking her legs if she tripped doubling back. It could go down a rabbit hole, though that would be a last resort and in bad taste for a hare. It could lead Phoebe to a fresh hare and so start a relay race that would go on till the hound dropped dead. But if she touched it, however lightly, it would scream, and give up, and keep on screaming till she broke its neck.

Those were the rules. It was a ritual, part of a general agreement made and held by all Things. He remembered trying to explain that to Edward, and Simon was there too, once, but they had all been a little drunk and he had not made himself clear. And now he had committed himself and Phoebe to the game again.

Michael panted down into the valley and up the grass-covered hill. He could see the two poised at full speed below him, as if they were hanging still and the valley unrolling alongside. Phoebe gained; the landscape stood still. The hare disappeared. The dog fell—Michael had a split-second of horror: Rosiqa—scrabbled up, leaped into the air looking left and right and uncoiled again as she saw the grass dividing, subtly, ten feet to her left. Then, with awe, Michael saw how well she knew her business. She was no longer following the hare. She knew, as he did, that it was heading for the bracken, and angled to intercept it. For about thirty seconds, Michael saw his dog working the hare exactly as a rodeo cutting horse works a calf. They seemed to dance, side to side, facing each other. Then the hare panicked and tried to break past. The hound twisted, snapped, and fell. The screaming started. It was a hoarse, bleating *an-an-an.* Hares were provocative, running, but when they were grabbed they made the most of their own death. Well, why not, thought Michael, I would. There was such a jerking and yelling in the long grass that he wondered who was killing whom. Then quiet, and the slow curve of Phoebe's tail above the grass.

He walked over, resigned. No blood; she had broken its neck, in the proper way. He had to praise her, or she would worry about it, so he stroked her and praised her formally, sorrowfully, calling her *hound hare-hunter.* He could hear a faint scraping sound in her lungs, and she coughed. It was a sign of overstrain, a small ruptured blood vessel in the lung, one of the things that sometimes happened when a hound was not coursing fit. It was not serious, and would go away in a day or two. As for the hare, it could have been any runner, dead—horse, deer, Phoebe herself—they were all alike, these running creatures: angular, economical. The dog had lost interest. It was not her business any more.

It was Michael's business now, eight pounds of it, three feet long. Callum had seen the chase and was grinning, his face pink and almost healthy-looking, as Michael came up the hill with Phoebe panting and wavering, tired out, behind him. Michael raised the hare in the hunter's way, by the hind legs, thinking for the moment that he was not in Strath-Ard for the School of Scottish Studies, or for his own personal serenity, but just for this: to kill something, using Phoebe, and to present it to Callum Macdonald.

Callum took the hare, pleased, and put it across his lap. He did not thank Michael for it. Urine from the dead hare ran down one of his artificial thighs, and its eyes, open but crusted with dirt, looked at the other.

Mary roasted it for dinner that day, with bacon. While it was roasting Michael read the Brahan Seer to them in the warm, meat-smelling room, while Phoebe coughed by the fire and Callum, eyes half-shut, thought and simmered about something in his own world. Michael offered Phoebe the hare's heart, and as usual she looked insulted until he cut it up small for her. Then she accepted it, out of a bowl. Mary made soup out of the hare's head and blood, and as it was too rich for a diabetic, Michael had to eat most of it. The flesh was like turkey, lean and dry, but rank.

After dinner, Mary wiped the oilcloth tablecloth and set out flour, eggs, milk, syrup, and spoons for baking. She had been about to bake in the morning, when Michael and Callum had come in with the hare. She still had her brown wool kerchief on.

"It will be hare pie tomorrow," she said. "We will be weeks eating it all."

"It's a little strong for me," said Michael.

"It was the hunting I could see again," said Callum. "That was a fine sight, the hunting."

"We'll catch you another. Phoebe's not really fit, though," said Michael, turning the pages of the thin brown book.

"Och, well, the hares are not so common, even now," said Callum. "You may not be seeing another."

"Coinneach Odhar foretold the coming back of the wildlife, though," said Michael, finding the prophecy he had been looking for. "He knew what was going to happen here, listen: *There will come a time when the jawbone of the Big Sheep will put the plough on the rafters.* Here is Big Sheep in Gaelic. How do you pronounce it?"

Mary looked, and giggled, and said, "*Caoraich mhor,*" and it did not sound like anything Michael had expected.

"He meant the Clearances," said Michael.

"Aye, so he did," said Mary.

> When sheep shall become no numerous that the bleating of one shall be heard by the other from Conchra in Loch-Alsh to Bun-da-Loch in Kintail they shall be at their height in price, and henceforth will go back and deteriorate, until they disappear altogether.

"Aye, well," said Mary, "true; it is all tourists and shooting and skiing these days, and even the Laird does poorly with the sheep. Fochan was saying that the great thing now is to raise the stags for meat instead."

"Aye," said Callum, "and they have reindeer at Aviemore, have they not, and a wee Laplander fella to look after them." He and Mary looked at each other and smiled, gently.

> The ancient proprietors of the soil shall give place to strange merchant proprietors, and the whole Highlands will become one deer forest; the whole country will be so utterly desolated and depopulated that the crow of a cock will not be heard north of Druim-Uachdair; the people will emigrate to Islands now unknown, but which shall yet be discovered in the boundless oceans, after which the deer and other wild animals in the huge wilderness shall be exterminated and drowned by horrid black rains.

The room was quiet. Mary slapped a round of dough onto the griddle, quartered it, sprinkled on the flour, and put it down to bake. It swelled and steamed, with a rich, warm smell.

"My sister is in British Columbia," she said. "But I'm no' understanding that last bittie, about the rains."

"It was the end of us all he was seeing, in some way," said Callum.

"I think it was the end," said Michael.

Then Phoebe looked up, her ears in a fluff for listening, and Callum said, "It is a car."

"It is the Land Rover," said Mary. "Fochan is that bad a driver; he had the gate off, last time, and he nearly killed the bull."

Fochan came in. They did not greet him, or introduce Michael, but Callum wheeled aside to give Fochan room in the fireside chair, and Mary gave him tea. Michael was sure that Strath-Ard had been talking about him and that Fochan already knew who he was. Perhaps the Laird had told him. A black and white collie came in with him and sat under his chair, growling at Phoebe, who growled back, her long muzzle wrinkled and quivering and her eyeteeth showing horribly: her canines were twice the length of the sheepdog's, though her skull was more delicate. The two dogs had been bred for thousands of years, one to kill and the other to keep, and they took themselves seriously, enemies. Michael was amused. He took Phoebe's muzzle as if it were a handle and shook it, to stop her, and Fochan said, "Och, you trash," and kicked backwards at his dog under the chair, without spilling a drop of his tea.

Then the dogs were quiet, and there was just the sound of Mary baking, the crow of the cockerel outside, the vague hushing sound of moving cattle and, further away, trees. Then Callum surprised them all by speaking in Gaelic to the shepherd: *"Bheil caoraich air a' mhonadh an drasd?"*

Michael smiled at the lovely, useless words. Fochan's dog peered out and sniffed the air, as if Gaelic smelled new to him, though an older collie would have slept through English and Gaelic alike. Fochan stared. Mary giggled.

"Michael has been reading to us out of Coinneach Odhar," she said, "and Himself will be in a moodie."

So Fochan smiled, humoring him, and said, "*Tha; tha dha' na thri thall air taobh an iar a' Loch Garbh Bhreac.*" But then it took hold of them and the three of them spoke for a while, seriously, but always with that undertone he had noticed of wry self-amusement, as when they spoke English. It might have been the counterpoint Gaelic gives to the voice, or it might have been the way they felt about their lives. Michael could not tell. He wished he could take notes. Fochan drank three cups of tea and left to see about the sheep.

"Och, we were leaving you out," said Mary to Michael. "But we got onto the last time we heard the Gaelic spoken. It was Callum's Old Aunt Maggie, her that died ten years ago; it has been that long. They put her into a Home, you see—she was daft, she was no' able to look after herself— and we were all so afraid of her that we'd no' go to see her in the Home, not even Morag would go. And when Callum went at last, she was wild with him, and she gave him such a talking-to in the Gaelic—so that the nurses would no' understand, you see—and she kept him at it all the afternoon. And Himself just sitting by the bed, quiet as a mousie, imagine Himself so scared: '*tha, tha*,' that was all he could say, while she was ranting, the cailleach: '*tha, tha.*' Och, and Fochan was saying there was foot rot among the sheep, and Himself was asking were there sheep up west the road the now."

She made scones as fast as she spoke. Michael could not follow the knead and slap of her hands, nor the soft patter, like birds' feet, of her voice. He caught up with her at last and said. "The sheep? Are they? Tell me."

"No," said Callum.

They had not expected him to speak for a long time yet

and even Mary was startled. She dropped a scone as she was lifting it off the griddle, and there was a reek of burned flour in the kitchen. Phoebe sneezed.

"No," said Callum, in his quizzical soft voice. "The sheep are no' there after all. He has penned them for the lambing."

Michael had to spend the next day studying again and writing up notes. He was too excited to work well, and spent more of the day looking out of the window. Once he looked out and saw Mary, and thought she was coming to see him. She was standing in the birch trees to the east of the Keeper's Cottage, and to Michael she looked very small and far away, though the trees were not far from the house; small, and old. As he watched, he felt that fear of Things again, the awareness, the oppression, the crowding, and he suddenly realized that it was not trees and stones this time, but words. Simon's flail came into his mind. The croft, the Keeper's Cottage, Strath-Ard, had all been so polished by that dead language that they were as well-shaped, meaningful, and as useless, as the handle of the wooden flail. He had been walking, and touching, and seeing, and every object he had walked past or touched or seen had been noticed, intensely, by someone before him, and they had spoken about it in Gaelic.

The words had all risen around him and clung to him like rags, or shreds, or ashes, and he felt them now, seeing Mary. It was as if she was passing them on to him. Why him? He would never deserve or use them. He could never scrape or wash the words away. He shuddered. He looked again, and Mary was gone. She had probably lost her nerve. Just as well; he had only one tin cup, and no tea to give her.

Then, he found he did not want to go out, and he stayed in the Keeper's Cottage until Phoebe woke up, late afternoon, and yawned with her yarroo-noise and stretched and began to walk around the room. She could walk silently when she wanted to, but now she went clickety-clickety-clickety like a centipede with claws, to show Michael she was restless. So he put her on the leash and they went out, walking west.

Callum was sitting on the roadbank, in the wheelchair. He watched them, waving, till the road curved uphill towards the deer fence and the juniper and scrub willow cut him out of sight.

Michael and Phoebe came to the deer fence and went through the gate and he shut it carefully behind him. He unsnapped the leash, and immediately she went sniffing up on the heather bank to the left, nosing at something at the foot of the fence. Michael went and saw it was a pile of small white bones, with a few shreds of fur. They had been scattered, by crows, maybe. They looked like rodent bones; he could see the gnawing teeth. He pushed Phoebe away and they walked further onto the moor.

It was black, hideous country, but there was nothing in it. It was not complicated and scary like the Muir or the crofts. It was passive, almost vacant. When Callum withdrew into his stupid—or enormous—silence, it was a place like this he must approach. They went along the cart track, going west. Another grey day. Below Michael, but still in the sky, over the valley, was one hawk. Somewhere—in the thick forest of Callum's field, maybe, rooks were quarrelling, cawing.

Phoebe trotted off, limbering up. She was still coughing, from the coursing strain, but a short walk would do her good. There was the bell-cackle of a grouse and Michael jumped, thinking it might be a bleat, a sheep. Phoebe chased birds casually, for amusement; she slithered into them, nose down, as if she were rooting them out of the heather. Two grouse thundered up and planed off, squawking, down towards the river. She watched them go. They were not her business.

In a fold of the hill, below, Michael saw a small loch, like a drop of lead under the sky. The survey map called it Loch Garbh Bhreac, but he did not know how that would be pronounced. Ahead on the track he would soon see Loch Avoch, where the crofters had once cut peats. Tomorrow he would go there, and tell Callum—who had probably cut peats himself there, fifty years ago—how it looked now. The next day, they would go past Loch Avoch, to the hill where there was no road.

There was a flat wooden bridge, in good repair, set into the track, and below the bridge ran a stream, feeding Loch Garbh Bhreac. In the shelter of the deep stream banks, a jungle of elder bushes, in full leaf, and willow, and soft green grass, had grown up. The streambed was so deep that the trees could not be seen from the open moor. Michael sat on the bridge, smelling the leaves and water, thinking what a good private world it was down there. Then he realized it was getting late, time to go back.

He stood up, sleepy, and started walking east, Phoebe loping in smooth circles around him. Up here, darkness started from the ground, as if the heather was exhaling something cold and he was walking into it. He watched Phoebe, trying to invest himself in her running, trying to get some of the peace he had been hoping for, the serenity that she knew about. And he did begin to feel her freedom, her galloping across the dun-colored, slowly spinning hill. The great sweep of space began to accept him, and became a comfort. He began to lose track of the edges of himself. It was a brief tilt of experience, a spillover of sleep, but for that second he was at the still center; he was free of Things, words, hunting. He was cut loose.

As he approached the deer fence, he heard a voice— part of him, the dispassionate, watching part—say:

"There is, of course, a flock of blackface sheep at the bottom of the hill, and Phoebe is chasing them."

"Yes; of course there is," he answered, and looked, and was not surprised to see the little, moving bunch of sheep and dog far away, and started to run down the steep hillside, over bogs and heather roots, but—as in a nightmare— the sheep and dog did not get any closer. There were eight sheep, dirty white, pregnant, with mottled black legs and heads. They were tripping over their overgrown winter wool. There was his running, sand-colored dog. She grabbed the leg of the slowest and most pregnant sheep, and, like the hare, it gave up the minute it felt her teeth. It could easily have kicked her away. It had horns. If it had even turned to face her, she would have backed down. But this killing and being killed was a formal game, played by rules. The sheep, unlike the hare, was silent. It folded up and went to its knees, yellow eyes looking somewhere else, in a perfect passive resistance.

Michael was sobbing, for breath, in frustration. He was running, couldn't reach them. "Stupid," he said to everything. *It's a very deep experience, but I wouldn't want it to be my fault.* "Simon, you are stupid too," he said. "It's everybody's fault."

Except, perhaps, the dog. He couldn't reach them, and the saluki could not hear him, or obey if she did. Now she backed off, tugging like a puppy with a sock, and white wool unraveled against the blackish ground. He saw blood. There was no sound of struggle; the heather was too soft. Suddenly, he was there. He grabbed at the dog, but that, of course, was a violation of the rules. Blind and deaf, Phoebe thought the sheep was fighting back. In terror, she twisted free and bolted up the hill.

"You stupid bitch, you're the worst of all," he shouted. He watched her run; there was nothing else he could do. She was coughing badly now. The air was cold, smelling of mud. Up on the bank, far away, but still within sight—where Callum, of course, was—the air would be fresher, even warm. Phoebe had chased the sheep a long way down into the shadow of the hill. At this distance, looking up, Michael could just see the glitter of last light on the wheelchair spokes, and on the rims and bands of the field glasses. But he knew now why Callum had been watching, and how eagerly.

My dear Simon,

Thank you for your card at Christmas. It was nice to hear that the children are getting taller, give them my love. I hope you are all well, it has been a very wet summer with us, the Corn is all down and sprouting in the field, Willie-John does not think he will be able to lift it this Year, it has been that wet. He will be coming with the Machine on Tuesday. Callum is getting on fine, he has the wee coldie now and then. We had a Folk-Lore man with us in Spring, he did not do very well. Willie-John's cousin Alec died, we all went to the Funeral. Morag came up and stayed with Callum for the day. Archie was

there and he asks to be remembered to you, he will
be Head Waiter at Moy next year. I am to go into
Hospital at Inverness tomorrow, for X-rays and the
doctor says perhaps there will be an Operation,
nothing to do worry about, he says. Morag will see
to Callum and Willie-John will do the milking,
while I am gone. The wee boy with the three legs
must be away at last, I have not seen him around
the barn since June. Do you mind on the bodach 'ha
radan.

Best Wishes and Love to All

Mary

A Note on the Type

*The text of this book was set on the Linotype in Janson,
a recutting made direct from type cast from matrices
long thought to have been made by the Dutchman
Anton Janson, who was a practicing type founder in
Leipzig during the years 1668–87. However, it has been
conclusively demonstrated that these types are actually
the work of Nicholas Kis (1650–1702), a Hungarian, who
most probably learned his trade from the master Dutch
type founder Dirk Voskens. The type is an excellent
example of the influential and sturdy Dutch types that
prevailed in England up to the time William Caslon
developed his own incomparable designs from these
Dutch faces.*

*This book was composed, printed, and bound by The
Haddon Craftsmen, Inc., Scranton, Pennsylvania. Cal-
ligraphy by Gun Larson. Design by Betty Anderson.*